B48 713 ___ KT-489-792

THE SOLDIER'S FAREWELL

As the Irish War of Independence comes to a head, Republican leader Éamon de Valera is arrested but quickly released in order to facilitate peace talks with the British. Stephen Ryan, an Irishman who fought for the British in the trenches, is sent to London. He leaves behind his brother, Joe, who has been jailed for his actions in the IRA. There are those on both sides who would see the Treaty fail; Stephen soon finds himself beset by problems – a legal dispute, a blackmail attempt, even a plot to assassinate Winston Churchill. When his fiancée Lillian is threatened by a man who is violent, ruthless and has a grudge against him, matters become not urgent, but personal.

THE SOLDIER'S FAREWELL

by

Alan Monaghan

Magna Large Print Books
Long Preston, North Yorkshire,
BD23 4ND, England.

British Library Cataloguing in Publication Data.

Monaghan, Alan
    The soldier's farewell.

    A catalogue record of this book is
    available from the British Library

    ISBN   978-0-7505-3774-2

ROTHERHAM LIBRARY &
INFORMATION SERVICES

F

B4871382b7

First published in Great Britain in 2012 by Macmillan
an imprint of Pan Macmillan,
a division of Macmillan Publishers Limited

Copyright © Alan Monaghan 2012

Cover illustration © Collaboration JS by arrangement with
Arcangel Images

The right of Alan Monaghan to be identified as the author of this work
has been asserted by him in accordance with the Copyright, Designs
and Patents Act, 1988

Published in Large Print 2013 by arrangement with
Pan Macmillan Publishers Limited

All Rights reserved. No part of this publication may be reproduced,
stored in a retrieval system, or transmitted in any form or by any
means, electronic, mechanical, photocopying, recording or otherwise
without the prior permission of the Copyright owner.

Magna Large Print is an imprint of Library Magna Books Ltd.

Printed and bound in Great Britain by
T.J. (International) Ltd., Cornwall, PL28 8RW

Ireland is the old sow that eats her farrow.
James Joyce

Part One

LONDON

I

'I appeal to all Irishmen to pause, to stretch out the hand of forbearance and conciliation, to forgive and forget, and to join in making for the land they love a new era of peace, contentment and goodwill.'
KING GEORGE V, 24 JUNE 1921

A horse lay dying in the yellow mud beside the corded path. The other men trudged past unheeding, but he saw it move. The back leg twitched, kicking feebly at the drizzling rain, and then the horse gave a painful snort and blew a cloud of steam up into the dismal sky. He stopped and stared at it. A shell had disembowelled the animal and the grey and purple ropes of its intestines had slithered out between the back legs. But even with its guts lying in a quivering pile in the mud, the horse clung to life. It snorted again, and its barrel chest shook and shuddered as it tried to lift its head.

Stephen knew he had no business stopping there. The mud was yellow from mustard gas and he half expected to hear the earsplitting shriek of another salvo at any moment. Nevertheless, he picked his way off the road, stepping on broken bricks and splintered furniture to stay out of the mud. The horse heard him coming and again tried to raise its head, but its strength was nearly

9

gone and even the leg was starting to sag. As near dead as made no difference, he thought, but still he opened the flap of his holster and drew his service pistol. The lanyard was stiff, caked with mud, and the gun was wet and slimy after so long in the rain. The horse snorted as he stepped closer, but lay its head down and put its ears back. He felt like he should say something, some words of comfort, but he couldn't think of anything. The pistol suddenly felt heavy and awkward in his hand and he held it down against his leg, perhaps hoping that the horse would die first. But the animal was looking at him and he could see his own reflection in its large brown eye. It was a strangely feminine eye, with long eyelashes, and it watched him steadily, unblinking.

Gritting his teeth, he cocked the pistol and lifted his arm until the barrel touched the horse's head just below the ear. It didn't flinch or make a sound, it just kept staring at him. But the eye didn't just see, it also reflected. He was looking at the image of himself standing in the rain, trying to work up the courage to pull the trigger...

He woke with his hand clenching a gun that wasn't there. No mud, no rain. He was in bed; the sheets thrashed half-off. He sat up, feeling sweat cooling on his chest. The room was dark, but it was high summer and the little window threw a faint grey glow over the familiar shapes in the room. It was his own bed in his own flat. As if to make sure, he slid his hand across the mattress to feel the place where Lillian had lain.

10

She was gone; he'd walked her home hours ago, but her scent still lingered. He breathed it in for a few moments, then threw the sheets off and turned and sat on the edge of the bed.

Three times he'd had that dream now. Three times in the last week, and it was the same every time. Was it even a dream? It was so regular, so calm. There was nothing outlandish about it, no feeling of flying or falling or fear. No horror – only sadness. But if it was a memory, he couldn't place it – and he couldn't think why it was bothering him now. It was nearly three years since the war had ended and he'd had his fair share of nightmares about it, but not one like this, and not in a long time.

When he looked down he found his hand had moved to his knee. Almost without thinking, he ran his fingers along the smooth ridge of scar tissue that wound up from the calf and across the kneecap. Another reminder of the bloody war, he thought. He couldn't even see it in this light, but he knew it was there. Maybe that was how it was with the dreams. Maybe they were always there, too, only sometimes he couldn't see them.

Dream or memory, he knew he wouldn't get back to sleep now. He stood up and pulled his dressing gown from the chair near the bed, then padded barefoot into the living room of his basement flat. This room was darker with the curtains drawn but he knew his way to the desk and sat down before he turned on the lamp. The desk was bare except for a single piece of paper that lay full in the beam of the lamp. It had a single equation written neatly near the top:

$$\sum_{n=1}^{\infty} \frac{1}{n^s}, \quad \Re(s) > 1.$$

The Riemann Zeta Function. This was his life now, mathematics, not war. Stephen had written that equation down two weeks ago, and since then he had done nothing but stare at it, often for hours at a time. Sometimes he felt like he didn't know what he was looking at; the figures and letters seemed to go out of focus, becoming mere marks on the page and losing all their meaning. Sometimes he thought it spoke to him – it whispered something in his ear that set him running, scribbling furiously for a page, or maybe two. But he never got anywhere, always ending up in a hole, a dead end, tearing up and starting again. It bothered him because he knew there was something there. Deep inside his own mind there was a meaning, a connection – he just couldn't see it clearly.

A faint bump overhead made him look up at the ceiling. He heard footsteps come softly down the stairs and then turn along the hallway directly above his head. Dunbar was on the move. Stephen listened, holding his breath, and when he heard the sitting-room door click shut, he glanced at his wristwatch: two in the morning – it looked like neither of them could sleep. Stifling a yawn, he looked down again at the page, but he knew it was no good. He felt distracted, his head too full to focus. His brother was in trouble again and his friend and mentor Professor Barrett was very sick. If Lillian were here she would take his mind off it, but she was gone home, out of reach ... and now

12

the dream had rattled him as well. If he could just relax for a minute then maybe his mind would clear – he might even get some sleep. But he knew he was fooling himself. He was more awake now than he had been during the day and his head was throbbing with Barrett and his brother, his brother and Barrett. One in prison and the other in hospital. And the horse; the poor bloody horse in the mud with its guts hanging out ... it was all too much. The sheer weight of it was stretching his nerves, making him tense and edgy. He could feel the roughness of the paper through his fingertips, the cool air against his skin. He knew that if he went back to bed now he would just lie there, open-eyed, waiting for the sun to show at the window.

He switched out the lamp and walked around to the narrow stairs that led up to the ground floor. If neither of them could sleep, then at least they could keep each other company. Ten steep steps and he emerged into the main hallway. This was Dunbar's part of the house and as his eyes grew accustomed to the dark, Stephen could see the gleam of the lacquered floorboards stretching back to the sitting room and the dark patch to his right where the door to the surgery stood ajar, the faint tang of ether drifting out to him on the still air. Straight ahead, there was a bar of light under the sitting-room door and noises were coming from beyond it. Scraping, thumping, the clang of something metallic. What the hell was Dunbar doing? Stephen went forward and put one hand on the handle and the other flat against the door. But then he stopped. He felt like an intruder,

13

creeping around in the dark. This was Dunbar's house, after all, and he could rattle around in it as he saw fit. But then a louder thump and a string of muffled curses made up his mind for him. He twisted the handle and went into the sitting room.

Dunbar was kneeling at the fireplace, peering intently up the chimney. He was wearing a quilted dressing gown and blue pyjamas and was so engrossed in his task that he only looked around when he heard the door close behind Stephen.

'Come here and give me a hand,' he said peremptorily.

'What on earth are you doing?'

'The damper's stuck. I can't get the bloody thing open.' Dunbar jiggled the brass knob on the flue above the fireplace, and Stephen was struck by how bony his hand looked – the skin translucent, with a yellow tinge. He stopped short and frowned.

'What do you want to open the damper for?'

'So I can light a bloody fire, of course.'

'But it's the middle of the summer.'

'Well, when you get to my age you'll ... oh, bugger it!' With a final angry tug at the knob, Dunbar pushed himself painfully to his feet, pulled his dressing gown tighter, and plumped down in the Chesterfield armchair by the fireplace. Even though he was barely fifty, he looked very much older, and he tried to hide a painful grimace as he settled himself in the chair. 'Not to worry,' he sighed and shook his head. 'Sorry, I must have woken you up with all my banging.'

'Not really. I was up anyway – couldn't sleep. I thought I might steal some of your port, see if

14

that helps.'

'Steal away.' Dunbar waved at the sideboard. 'Although, as a doctor, I should warn you that there's no medical evidence that port will help you sleep.'

'Do you want one?'

'Oh, no, thank you.' Dunbar picked up a glass full of white liquid from a side table. 'I've got my nightcap.'

'What's that?' Stephen poured himself a glass of port and sat in the other armchair, facing Dunbar across the fireplace.

'Baking soda and milk – for my stomach.'

'Good grief.' Stephen swirled the port in his glass but studied Dunbar out of the corner of his eye. His face had the same translucent yellowish tinge as his hand and he looked drawn, uneasy and ill. 'You know, you don't look well. Perhaps *you* should see a doctor.'

'Very fucking droll,' Dunbar muttered, taking a hefty swig from his glass and making a face. 'I'd sooner operate on myself than let one of those bastards poke and prod and roll their eyes at me.'

'All the same–' Stephen began, but when he saw Dunbar glaring at him he shrugged and took a sip of port.

'And what's your excuse?' Dunbar asked, his eyes narrowing. 'My innards might be at me, but what has you up at this hour? Is it the nightmares again?'

Very perceptive, Stephen thought, looking into the bottom of his glass for a moment. He was conscious that it was in this very room, in these very chairs, that he had unburdened himself before.

15

That was less than a year after he'd come home from France and he'd been in a right old state – nightmares, hallucinations, the whole bloody lot. Worst of all was the feeling that the war had broken him; that he was beyond repair, not worth saving. But Dunbar had saved him. He was a doctor, yes, but also a soldier, and he knew what war was like, what it could do to a man. After all the things they'd talked about here, Stephen wondered if this wasn't trivial, wasn't somehow insignificant. He hardly wanted to bother him with it.

'It's only a dream,' he said after a few moments. 'At least, I think it's a dream.'

'What do you mean?' Dunbar asked. He looked at his glass as if he was about to take another drink from it, but then set it down on the side table and stretched out his legs, looking at Stephen expectantly.

'Well, it's just that it's so realistic I'm not sure if it's a dream or a memory. Only it can't be a memory because, when I'm awake, I can't remember it ever happening. When I'm asleep it feels like a memory, but when I'm awake it feels like a dream.'

'Tell me about it,' Dunbar said, and Stephen told him about the horse and the gun and his own reflection in that dying eye. It wasn't long in the telling, but he felt like it poured out of him – so much so that he stumbled over the sudden ending, looked down into his glass again and took another sip of port.

'Where do you think it could have been?' Dunbar asked, after they had both listened to the steady ticking of the long-case clock for more than a minute.

16

'The mud makes me think it's Ypres, but, really, it could have been anywhere.'

'You must have seen your share of wounded horses. Did you ever have to do it – shoot one, I mean? Put it out of its misery.'

Stephen closed his eyes and thought of horses. He'd seen them, all right. He'd seen them whole and in pieces. He'd seen them drowned, mutilated and sometimes just dead of fright.

'No, never. Not as far as I remember, anyway.'

'Hmmm. You're not making this very easy, are you? Perhaps we should look at the physical factors. How's your head?'

Stephen's eyes opened in surprise. Why hadn't he thought of that? It was a month since it had happened, but there was still a tender spot above his right ear to remind him where the rifle butt had caught him. A reminder, too, of his friend dying in his arms, of hot blood on his hands and the stink of smoke in his nostrils. It could have been worse; with all the shooting that had been going on around the Custom House he could easily have caught a bullet, but all he'd got was a bang on the head and even that was fading. Now it only troubled him if he touched it.

'It's fine,' he said.

'Are you sure? That was quite a crack you got. No headaches, no blurred vision?'

'No. Nothing like that.'

'Then we must look to the psychological factors,' Dunbar said, his voice trailing off. Stephen let the clock tick another few seconds before he took the bait.

'What do you mean?'

'You don't think the fact that your brother is to be tried by court martial in the morning might be keeping you awake?'

Stephen allowed him a smile as he shook his head.

'We've talked about my brother before. He's big enough to look after himself. Besides, he's been tried before and worse – he's been shot, twice. Not to sound heartless, but it never kept me awake before.'

'But you're still going to the trial in the morning, aren't you?'

'He's still my brother.' Stephen shrugged. 'And I don't see what he has to do with horses.'

'Probably nothing,' Dunbar admitted. 'But what can I say? You had a dream about the war. Some of them take a while to catch up with you and sometimes it takes years to realise where they came from. I had one like that once, after I came back from South Africa. This bloody ... well, I'm not sure how to describe it exactly. This bloody voice, I suppose. I kept hearing the same words over and over again – you know, in the middle of conversations and so on; a sort of arrangement of sounds, like an echo of sorts.'

'What did it say?'

'It said: "Put out the light." Only it wasn't the words themselves as much as the tone. Anyway, it took me months to figure out where it came from.' Dunbar paused, leaned over and picked up his glass, then set it down again with a disgusted look. He snuggled himself deeper into his dressing gown and gave Stephen a weary smile. 'I can tell from the quality of silence that I have you

18

hooked. Do you want me to finish the story?'

'Of course, please go on.'

'Well,' Dunbar frowned, as if trying to remember the details, 'it turns out it was to do with this boy who was one of my first patients after we got to South Africa. We were fresh off the boat – hadn't even clapped eyes on a Boer – and they put us into this camp near Cape Town which, apart from being hotter than hell, was overrun with snakes. Being from Ireland, our lads had never seen snakes before but it didn't take them long to start teasing them, chasing them and generally acting the maggot. Needless to say, we had quite a few cases of snakebite in the first week, but this lad was by far the worst. He spotted this snake sleeping in the shade of a tree and took it into his head to poke it with a stick. Unfortunately, the snake was a cobra – and one of the sort that can spit. It gave him a full blast of venom right in the eyes and poleaxed the poor devil.'

Dunbar paused, drew a breath and frowned at Stephen, whose eyelids were starting to droop.

'I'm not boring you, am I?'

'Not at all.' Stephen opened his eyes wide, swirled his glass and threw back another mouthful of port. 'Carry on.'

'Well, I did what I could for the blighter with cold compresses and so forth. By a stroke of pure luck, I managed to save his life, but I couldn't save his eyes – the poor boy was completely blind. But the strange thing was, he kept thinking he could see a bright light. I suppose it was nerve damage because there was no question that his eyes were buggered. I even brought in a specialist to make sure, but he wouldn't believe it. "Put out the light," he used to say, and he'd be crying because the light was so strong he thought it was hurting his eyes. Every damn day he was being blinded all over again – and that's where it came from, that's what stuck with me; put out the light, put out the light.'

'*That's* what bothered you?' Stephen asked drowsily. 'After everything else?' He knew Dunbar had been badly wounded in South Africa; shot several times by Boer snipers as he went out to help wounded men.

'Believe it or not, yes – eventually. Years later, after all the other wounds healed, all I was left with was this nagging voice that I could only half hear. Sometimes weeks and months would pass without my hearing it, and sometimes it was like an extra voice in the conversation over dinner. For a while I thought I was going around the bend, I can tell you. I simply didn't know what it meant, or where it was coming from.'

'So how did you make the connection?'

'It happened here, in this very room. We put on a magic lantern show for the nieces and nephews. We were just about to begin when one of the children turned to me and said, "Put out the light." He only wanted me to darken the room, of course, but the way he said it, and with those exact words, it suddenly came clear to me and I remembered everything. Blubbed like a baby, too, I must admit. But after that, I never heard the voice again.'

'Hmm,' Stephen said sleepily. His eyes had closed again and his head was nodding. He wanted to say more but he could hardly find the

20

strength to keep his head up.

'I do believe I can add a cure for insomnia to my other medical achievements,' Dunbar said with a smile. 'Go on, off to bed with you before it wears off!'

Stephen managed to rouse himself enough to set down his glass and push himself out of the armchair. He stood swaying on his feet, yawning deeply.

'What about you?'

'I think I'll stay here for the time being,' Dunbar said, settling himself lower in the armchair and stretching out his legs. 'I quite like it in here, at night.'

'All right. Goodnight, then – and thank you,' Stephen said, and shuffled towards the door, feeling his head lolling and a delicious need for sleep spreading all through him.

'Stephen,' Dunbar called after him, just as he reached the door.

'Yes?'

'Put out the light, there's a good chap.'

Everything echoed under the dome of the rotunda. Every cough, every footfall. A soldier came in with a jug of water and Billy Standing watched him work his way down the long baize-covered table, filling each glass with a gurgling splash, his boot nails ringing and scratching on the tiled floor as he moved from one to the next.

When he was gone, a tense silence returned. Billy was aware of the solicitor sitting behind him, but he kept an uneasy eye on the small door at the back of the hall. Another soldier stood there, as stiff and straight as the granite pillar that rose up beside him, his rifle at a perfect slope. Beyond that door was a gloomy passage that led into the upper yard of Dublin Castle. That was where Billy had come into the hall, and that was where Mercer had ambushed him earlier.

He might have known something would happen. He'd worked in the castle for over a year so he could hardly have expected to go unrecognized. One of the sentries at the gate had given him a knowing wink as he showed his pass, and he'd felt many more eyes on him as he walked up the yard, under the sandbagged windows and wire coils strung out along the roof. But he had hoped to avoid Mercer. Mercer had hired him to investigate the finances of Sinn Fein and the IRA, and if he had never suspected treachery in the year that Billy had worked for him, he surely did now. Billy had seen it the moment he saw Mercer. Not in his eyes, but in the hunch of his back, in the way he stood in his rumpled suit with a surly look on his face, waiting by the door.

'Well, well, Billy,' Mercer had said, straightening his gangling bulk and clasping his hands behind his back to preclude even the hint of a handshake. 'You're playing for the other team, I hear.'

There was a bitter twist in his voice, and Billy had suddenly felt very shabby, though he was dressed in his best suit and shrouded in his black barrister's gown. And why wouldn't he be bitter? Mercer was paying the price for his failure to starve Sinn Fein of funds. Shipped off to England, to some dead-end post in Customs and Excise.

'Good morning, Frank,' Billy had answered

brightly, trying to shrug off his dismay. Mercer had been no paladin himself, and if he was bitter it was only because he had lost at his own grubby little game. 'And congratulations. I hear you got a posting in London.'

It was a dirty little compliment, and Mercer's eyes had narrowed. On the face of it, a posting to London was a step up from provincial Dublin, but not for Mercer. Over here, he was a big fish in a small pond but in London he would be a minnow. Unless he managed to pull off some spectacular coup he would end his career there in anonymous despair.

'And I hear you're defending a Fenian murderer,' Mercer had shot back, thin-lipped and pale. 'How did that come about? I was going to ask why you changed sides, but I don't think you ever did, did you?'

The bitterness of this – not to mention the accuracy – took some of the wind out of Billy's sails.

'Everybody is entitled to a defence,' he'd said guiltily. 'And if you must know, I went to college with his brother. I'm doing a favour for an old friend.'

This last part was very nearly true, but he'd still felt cheap for mentioning it.

'And everybody's entitled to a fair trial,' Mercer had sneered, stepping past Billy and turning as he went. 'At least, in principle. Let's see how *you* like having to fight with one hand tied behind your back.'

This parting shot had troubled Billy ever since. What the devil did he mean, with one hand tied behind his back? This may have been a court martial, but it was still a court of law and still subject to the law of the land. To reinforce this fact, the door opened and two men came in. Barristers, judging by their robes, but looking rumpled and distracted, as if their dignity had taken a knock. The gentlemen for the prosecution, Billy realized. Noyk, the solicitor, had told him that they would come fresh from England for this trial. Delivered to the North Wall by a Royal Navy destroyer and then driven up here in an armoured car. Which would explain why one of them was worrying at a spot on his sleeve with his handkerchief. Oil, no doubt. Those cars were always filthy, and noisy to boot. But wasn't the other...?

'Is that...?' Billy began, half turning in his seat.

'Travers Humphreys,' Noyk whispered very low, careful of the echo.

'Bloody hell,' Billy muttered to himself. Humphreys had helped prosecute some of the most notorious cases in English law: Oscar Wilde, Dr Crippen, Seddon the poisoner and Roger Casement, to name only the most famous ones. And here was he, still wet behind the ears, with hardly a case taken in the last two years, and then mostly torts and land disputes ... Christ, it didn't bear thinking about. He quailed as Humphreys and his junior passed by in a swish of silk. Formal nods, very polite, but faces set, eyes like sharks.

Billy's nerves only got worse as the hall started to fill up. The men who trickled in through the door were mostly soldiers or police, and those who weren't in uniform had the tough, wary look of intelligence men. It was a relief at last to see a couple of familiar faces; Stephen Ryan and his fiancée Lillian Bryce, walking arm in arm. They both smiled and waved at him, shaking him some way out of his funk, and he was able to compose himself a little. With a grave nod in reply, he turned and opened his brief so as to have everything ready. Out of the corner of his eye he saw Humphreys do the same, then set a pair of half-moon spectacles on the bridge of his nose. As if this were a signal, another small door opened and six soldiers trooped in. All senior officers, all with their caps tucked under their arms and their leatherwork creaking, spurs jingling. Lining up behind the baize-covered table, they put down their caps, opened their holsters and set down their service pistols beside the caps. Then they sat.

Very impressive, I'm sure, Billy thought to himself. He had never seen a court martial before, but Noyk had briefed him on the protocol. He knew that the old duffer at the end – the one with red collar tabs and grey whiskers – was the judge advocate. He was clearly in charge, for while the others fidgeted, shifted, or loosened their Sam Brownes, he surveyed the hall, knitting his eyebrows and peering at the barristers and solicitors, officers and onlookers. Only when he was satisfied that the court martial was properly assembled did he turn his head to nod at the sentry.

There wasn't much shouting, just a curt 'Bring in the prisoner!' and the door was opened to the sound of nailed boots stamping up the passageway. Chests out, heads back, two soldiers came out in a burst of immaculate khaki and blanco. Between them walked Joe Ryan in a shabby blue suit, handcuffs clinking on his wrists. He was shorter and stouter than his brother, darker, too, but there was no mistaking the resemblance. He looked tired and dishevelled, but he had shaved, combed his hair and walked with his head high, his eyes coldly sweeping the whole echoing chamber.

Billy smiled and nodded to him as he sat down, but neither of them spoke. Silence was restored as the prisoner's escort retreated, and for just a few moments Billy thought he detected an air of uncertainty. His eyes darted from the court martial officers to Travers Humphreys and back again. It was as if they were all aware of the incongruity of civilians in a military court and neither quite trusted the other. Well, that's something, he thought, though he didn't think those officers made a very sympathetic jury. They all sat stiff and rigid in their chairs, faces blank, arms folded, until a clerk stood up from a small table, opened a folder, and started to read from it without raising his eyes.

CHARGE SHEET No. 1

The accused JOSEPH RYAN, of 22 Gardiner Street, Dublin, a civilian, is charged with:-

Committing a crime within the meaning of regulation 67 of the Restoration of Order in Ireland Regulations, that is to say, arson, in that he, in Dublin, Ireland, on 25th May 1921, feloniously caused a fire to be started within His Majesty's Customs House.

CHARGE SHEET No. 2

The accused JOSEPH RYAN, of 22 Gardiner Street, Dublin, a civilian, is charged with:-

Committing a crime within the meaning of regulation 67 of the Restoration of Order in Ireland Regulations, that is to say, attempted murder, in that he, in Dublin, Ireland, on 13th April 1920, feloniously, wilfully and of malice aforethought, did attempt to murder Viscount General Sir John French, Lord Lieutenant General of Ireland.

Stephen had never seen Billy move so fast. He was on his feet before the clerk had even finished reading the second charge, turning to shoot a questioning look at the solicitor, who shrugged.

'Sir ... your honour, I must object to the second charge.'

The judge advocate looked up sharply, frowned at what he first took to be impertinence, but then smiled indulgently.

'Well, of course you must, young man. That's what you're here for.'

Muted laughter echoed around the hall, but Billy stood his ground.

'No, sir. I must object to the second charge being read before this court on the grounds that neither my client nor myself has been notified of any such charge. We are here today to plead against the charge of arson only.'

There was proper consternation on the bench this time. The judge advocate whispered something to the major sitting beside him before he glared at Billy.

'Are you sure, Mr Standing?'

Billy had already turned to the solicitor, who was holding up a sheaf of pages and shaking his head.

'Quite certain, your honour. This is the first we've heard of it.'

More whispering and heads shaking along the bench before the judge advocate cleared his throat and said in a louder voice:

'The court martial officer should be able to shed some light on this. Is Captain Martin here? Captain Martin?'

Captain Martin was not there, so the judge fell to conferring once more with his fellow officers. At length, he addressed Billy again.

'Very well, Mr Standing, the second charge is withdrawn for the time being. We will proceed only with the charge of arson at this time. Mr Humphreys, do you have any objection?'

The prosecution barrister rose to his feet and spoke in a slow, measured voice.

'No, sir. The Crown does not object to proceeding with the charge of arson.'

'That means they weren't notified, either,' Lillian whispered to Stephen. 'What on earth do you think is going on?'

'I have no idea,' Stephen answered, though he knew enough of the army to suspect that there was nothing sinister about it at all. This looked like the sort of simple bureaucratic cock-up he'd seen many times before. At any event, the judge advocate seemed keen to move past it, and set about his business with a renewed air of efficiency.

'Very well. Mr Standing, how does your client

28

plead to the charge of arson?'

'Not guilty, your honour.'

'Corporal, take a note of that. The defendant pleads not guilty to the charge of arson. Mr Humphreys, please state the case for the Crown.'

'Sir, we intend to prove not only that the defendant was inside the Custom House on the day in question, but also that he was in possession of a petrol can and that he threatened certain members of staff in order to force them to leave the building before the fire was started,' Humphreys said, and paused to let his words sink in. 'To that end, we wish to call our first witness, Captain A, of the Royal Irish Constabulary Auxiliary Division.'

Joe Ryan recognized Captain A the moment he stood up before the court. He knew his real name was Norton and that he was an Auxie – and a right hard bastard at that. Last time Joe had seen Norton had been at a checkpoint in Beresford Place. The air was thick with ash and smoke and some of Norton's men were still taking pot shots at shadows in the upper windows of the Customs House. Joe knew they were wasting their time. The roof had fallen in by then, and the floors wouldn't last much longer if the orange flames gushing and roaring from most of the windows were anything to go by. He'd held on as long as he could inside, but eventually the heat and the smoke had forced him outside, hands up, playing the civilian. He might have got away with it, too, only Norton had the civil service supervisor with him, vouching for those who were Customs House staff and giving the lie to those who weren't.

Joe had tried to feed him a line about being in

there on an errand, but Norton hadn't swallowed any of it. A sneer and a smack and they started dragging him off to one of the lorries. He tried to make a run for it but a sharp crack with a rifle butt brought him down and then they all laid in with their boots. He'd rode it out as best he could, curling up in a ball to protect himself, but by the time they got tired of it his back was a mass of bruises and he could taste blood in his mouth.

Apart from the beating, Norton's account was more or less accurate as far as Joe could tell. Nevertheless, Billy wasn't long in setting about him. He was on his feet even before the prosecution counsel had returned to his chair.

'Captain A, you say that you noticed a strong smell of petrol from my client's clothes. Is that correct?'

'Yes.'

'I see. And how do you know it came from him?'

'Well,' Norton shifted his feet and frowned sullenly at Billy, 'the smell of petrol was very strong when he stood near me.'

'But you said in your statement that you were standing near the Customs House at the time. Is that not so?'

'Yes, I was at a checkpoint in Beresford–'

'Well, captain, I must congratulate you on a very acute sense of smell. For were you not standing near a burning building which, according to the police reports, had been liberally doused with petrol? Did you not say yourself that the smoke and fumes coming from the fire were very thick and strong? And was it not the case that everybody who came out of the Customs House smelled of

30

petrol to some extent, having been kept inside for some time by the men who set the fire? So, please, captain, will you tell the court how you were able to discern that the smell of petrol came solely from my client and why it warranted his arrest?'

'Well,' Captain A stammered, and his eyes roamed around the room for a few moments. 'It was especially strong off him. And he tried to run as well.'

'Oh. He tried to run, did he? And it never occurred to you to mention this fact before now?'

'Billy's rather good at this, isn't he?' Lillian whispered to Stephen a few minutes later. Having disposed of Captain A, Billy was picking holes in the statement of Mr B, the civil servant who had been with him at the checkpoint. He was a rather pompous little man, much given to standing upon his honour. Only, in this case, he was having trouble keeping his footing under Billy's onslaught, which was neither furious nor concentrated in any one direction, but which ranged around him, nipping and pushing from every side. After a few minutes of this, the witness was perspiring heavily, and becoming visibly unsure of himself.

'He was born to it,' Stephen agreed, but he was afraid that Billy would have his work cut out if he was trying for an acquittal. He'd been studying the court martial officers and had concluded that he didn't like the look of two of them. The others seemed like regular army officers of the better sort – keen-eyed, sharp and attentive – but the two dourest-looking ones were also the most senior. He had once had to sit on a court martial himself and he knew how hard it was to break the hierarchy of rank. Those two old buggers looked like they had made up their minds long before they ever sat down and he doubted the others would have the nerve to gainsay them.

Then again, he was beginning to think that it might not come to that, since the judge advocate was starting to look restless. He had already glanced at his watch twice while Mr B was being cross-examined and Stephen was sure that the business about the second charge had been preying on his mind. He sensed an adjournment at least and, sure enough, when Constable C was called to give evidence but failed to appear, his face hardened.

'I believe we've heard enough for one day,' he said abruptly, nodding to the clerk. 'This court is adjourned. The defendant will be remanded in custody for one week, when we will reconvene.'

They came out blinking after the gloom of the courtroom through the narrow passage and into the upper yard of Dublin Castle, where the noonday sun shone out of a cloudless sky and the cobbles glistened and shimmered in the heat. With birds twittering under the eaves and the sun glinting on the upper windows the yard felt like a calm oasis, cut off from the bustling city outside the walls. But as Stephen turned and surveyed the scene, he saw a sentry standing on the roof, his rifle at high port, and he was reminded of the night he had come here during the Easter Rising. Lillian had been here, too, but that was the only good thing he remembered about that night. The whole atmosphere had been different. Half the city had been burning, and the pair of them had made a night-time dash up from Trinity College to look for her sister, who had been stranded here when the fighting broke out. And just as bloody well, too, Stephen reflected, for if it hadn't been for Lillian's sister, Joe would probably have died that night. His blood had run out over these very cobbles and Stephen didn't have to turn far to see the gate where Joe had been brought in, carried by the army patrol that had shot him as he tried to escape across the river after his post was overrun by troops from the castle.

Stephen thought his brother had done well to stay out of jail since then. Joe's experience in the Rebellion had only strengthened his republican beliefs and he'd spent the last five years fighting against British rule. Perhaps because he had long since given up believing in any cause, Stephen couldn't help but admire his brother's devotion. He had dedicated himself body and soul to something he believed in and had walked a very dangerous path for those five years – although it looked like he'd come to the end of it now. The police had caught up with him at the Customs House and it didn't look like they would be letting him go. That second charge, of attempting to murder the Lord Lieutenant, had been no mere accident, and Stephen knew very well how much truth there was in it. It was their second shot, he thought glumly. Even if Billy managed to get him off on the arson charge, they'd have something else to make sure he didn't get away.

As if reading his thoughts, Lillian put her arm through his and gave it an encouraging squeeze.

'Have faith, Stephen,' she whispered. 'Joe will be fine. The way Billy is going, he'll be a free man in no time.'

'I wouldn't be so sure of that,' Stephen answered distractedly. His attention was focussed on a figure moving slowly through the shadows of the colonnade on the far side of the yard. The figure stopped, turned and stepped out into the sunlight, revealing himself to be a small, elegant-looking man in a grey suit. He stood still for a few moments, as if he was simply basking in the heat, but then slowly raised his hat and inclined his head in Stephen's direction.

'Will you wait here a minute, sweetheart?' Stephen asked. 'I need to talk to that man.'

'Of course,' Lillian answered. She had seen that man before but she did not know his name, or what he wanted with her fiancé. She trusted Stephen to tell her when the time was right, though already she had suspicions as to what they were talking about. These were more or less confirmed when Billy came out of the passageway carrying his wig and gown in a bag slung over his shoulder, and his briefcase in his other hand.

'Well, well,' he said, squinting in the sun. 'What a beautiful day. But where's Stephen going?'

Stephen was halfway across the yard by now and Billy had to lean a little to one side in order to see where he was headed. He recognized Andy Cope from his time at the castle, though he had never actually met him. A most mysterious man; officially Cope was only an Assistant Under-secretary, but unofficially he outranked even the Chief Secretary, and was rumoured to be con-

34

nected to the Prime Minister. Well, at least that explained how Stephen had managed to finagle passes to such a secure court martial.

'Ah, I see. I shall say no more. Hush hush, and all that.'

'Congratulations, Billy,' Lillian said, planting a kiss on his cheek. 'You were wonderful. The way you picked those witnesses apart, I daresay you'll have him out at the next bout.'

'Well, I suppose we'll see about that,' Billy said doubtfully. He had just spoken to the solicitor, who suspected that they would receive notice of the second charge before the week's adjournment was up. 'Still, I did do rather well, if I say so myself. It could have been worse – it could have been very much worse.'

By now, Stephen had reached Andy Cope, who shaded his eyes with one hand as he held out the other.

'Good day to you, Mr Ryan. I trust I find you well? And how do things stand for your brother?'

Stephen gave him a succinct appraisal of the trial, including the mysterious second charge and the sudden adjournment.

'Well,' Cope remarked, having considered a moment. 'That could have been worse – though he's not out of the woods yet, I'm afraid. In any event, I'm glad I caught you. Some things are happening that may come to concern you and I.' Cope took him lightly by the arm and walked him a little way towards the centre of the yard – away from the open windows above. 'You heard about the King's speech yesterday, I take it?'

'Of course.' Stephen nodded. The King himself

pleading for peace in Ireland was not something that happened every day. 'It was all over the newspapers.'

'Yes, well, what wasn't in all the newspapers was that we managed to arrest Mr de Valera last night.'

'Bloody hell,' Stephen said under his breath. Eamon de Valera was president of Dáil Eireann and the de facto president of the Irish Republic. He was the leader of the movement to overthrow British rule in Ireland and, next to Michael Collins, probably the most wanted man in the country.

'That's exactly what I said,' Cope admitted drily. 'It was a complete bloody accident, of course. Some soldiers nabbed him when they raided a house and never even knew who they had. He gave a false name and nobody was any the wiser until they dragged him in here. Fortunately, I was able to have him released before word got out – though I'm afraid I might have put a few noses out of joint on the military side of things.'

Stephen frowned. 'You had him *released*? Why?'

'Because we can't make peace with a man when we've got him locked in jail.' Cope allowed himself a little smile at the surprised jerk of Stephen's head. 'Yes. Peace, Stephen. His Majesty's speech has breathed life into what we all thought was dead. The King has spoken and suddenly a negotiated peace with the republicans is not as abhorrent as it was before. The hawks in the Cabinet have had their wings clipped – for the time being, at least – and I am instructed to explore every option as a matter of urgency. Now is the time,

36

Stephen. We must strike while the iron is hot!'

'All right,' Stephen said cautiously. This wasn't the first time that Cope had tried to broker peace with the republicans and Stephen had helped him before by carrying messages, via his brother, to Michael Collins. It wasn't that he doubted Cope's sincerity, but he had seen how futile it was. Twice he had thought they were making progress, and twice their efforts had been reduced to nothing.

'You sound doubtful,' Cope observed.

'Well, not to be obtuse, but I don't see how I can be of any help to you now.'

'How do you mean?' Cope asked.

'My main – my only – point of contact with the IRA was my brother, and he's just been remanded back to prison.'

'Yes, well, that was unfortunate, but necessary. Still, it's probably the best place for him, for the moment.'

'Necessary?' Stephen stopped in mid-stride and turned on Cope. 'Wait a minute. Are you saying you *had* him remanded?'

'Certainly not.' Cope looked directly at him, his face blank but his eyes alive. 'Though I imagine it was an unfortunate consequence of what I did do, which was to perform a little sleight of hand with the court martials clerk to make sure that the second charge didn't get out of the starting gate. Not that they even needed to remand him, anyway. Under the powers of the Restoration of Order in Ireland Act they could intern your brother from now until doomsday and there's not a damned thing your legal friend over there could do about it.'

'Then why did you have the charge suppressed? For that matter, if they can just lock him up anyway, why was it even brought in the first place?'

'Because that charge wasn't aimed at your brother, it was aimed at *you* and, by implication, at me.' Cope held up his hand to stop Stephen from interrupting him. 'Before you say anything, let me tell you what we know about that evening. We know your brother was wounded during the ambush on the Lord Lieutenant. We know he escaped from the scene and went to you for help, and we know that you and your doctor chum fixed him up and sent him on his way before the army came looking for him. We know all of these things and we can't prove any of them – but that's not the point. The point is to put *you* on the stand to explain yourself. Then it looks like I'm consorting with a man who aided and abetted in the attempted assassination of the Lord Lieutenant. Do you see where this is going, Stephen?'

Stephen had opened his mouth to answer, but no words came out. His head was spinning. For all he thought he knew about Cope, the man was still full of surprises, and clearly playing a much deeper game than he had ever imagined. Cope gave a little laugh and then set off walking again, slowly tapping the tip of his cane on the cobbles as they progressed to the middle of the yard, far from the watching windows.

'Look, I apologize if I spoke out of turn,' he said, stopping again and placing both hands on the top of his cane. 'I don't mean to impugn you or your friends – far from it. But I need you to understand how finely balanced everything is. I have the support of the Prime Minister, but even he has enemies, and very powerful enemies in this matter. For the moment, the wind is at our backs. Cardinal Logue is still with us, and General Smuts is keen to help, too. Between us, I believe we might be able to put a stop to this interminable bloody fighting and murder. But the wind can change at any moment, Stephen. Time is of the essence, and I need your help.'

'And you are welcome to whatever help I can give,' Stephen told him. 'It's just that I don't see what I can do. My brother is in jail and there isn't anybody else I can talk to.'

'Well, if you think that being in jail puts him out of touch with the IRA command, you are sorely mistaken, but I think you do yourself a disservice in any case. You are an Irishman but also a decorated British officer with a good war record. Furthermore, your brother is in jail for his republican beliefs. That means you enjoy a certain amount of trust on both sides, and I believe doors will be opened to you that would never be opened to me, no matter how hard I try. So, I need you, Stephen. It will be hard work and no mistake, but I really think that this time we might be able to pull it off.' Cope was holding out his hand again as he nodded down the yard to where Billy and Lillian stood waiting under the eyes of a stiff-standing guard. 'Now, I've kept you long enough. Your friends will be getting impatient.'

Stephen shook his hand. 'I'll wait to hear from you, then.'

'It may be sooner than you think.' Cope smiled. 'Remember, time is of the essence.'

II

The cell door closed with a clang that reverberated off the narrow walls. Joe Ryan turned with his blankets in his arms and looked at it for a few moments. Scratched green paint and the peephole in the middle. As blank as the one he used to stare at in Kilmainham, only newer. And different. He never thought he'd miss his cell in Kilmainham, but here he was, only five minutes in Mountjoy and already wishing he was back there.

He dropped the blankets on the narrow bunk and sat down beside them. At first glance, it looked like he hadn't been moved at all. Here was the same thin, lumpy mattress rolled up on the bunk, there was the rickety table and chair and the bucket. The window was the same; small and barred and high up the wall, and the gas jet sounded just like the one in Kilmainham, burring and farting and flickering as the long evening drew down to night.

But it wasn't the same. The atmosphere was different, and the sounds. The squeal and clang of the gate on the landing, the echo, the muffled shouts of screws making the evening rounds. They all sounded foreign to him and he felt isolated in this strange cell that looked so familiar. He didn't know anybody here, didn't have any friends.

But there was no use crying about it. He kicked off his boots and rolled on to the bunk, resting his head on the mattress and breathing in the strong smell of carbolic soap. He had been washed, scrubbed and deloused when they brought him in and his skin still tingled from it. He lay and listened, trying to get a feel for the place. He could hear footsteps out on the landing. Now and then they grew closer, stopped, and then there was the whisper of a scrape on the far side of the door before they were off again, squeaking away into the distance. He knew they were watching him through the peephole. They always watched the new ones.

After a while, he got up, pulled the chair out and stood up near the open window. It was mid-summer and the night sky still held a faintly luminous blue tint, with the stars floating in it like little silver flecks. He could hear the hum of the city out there; even see the glow of light from the hospital across the road. He didn't have a watch, but he knew it was getting late. The noises of the prison were growing fainter and the place seemed to be settling down to sleep.

He was startled by a hoarse whisper that seemed to come out of the air just beyond the window.

'Hello! Are you there?'

'Hello?' Joe answered cautiously. 'Who's that?'

'My name is Pat. Pat Whelan. I'm next door. I heard them putting you in.'

Joe didn't answer. This could easily be a trap – a plant to get him to talk. He wouldn't put it past the Auxies. They'd had a man in Kilmainham for a while who had caught out a few fellas with his bedtime patter. They knew that the night time was the loneliest. You'd talk to anybody in the

41

dark, but then you'd be dragged off for interrogation in the morning and your new friend would be nowhere to be seen.

'You can talk, they won't hear us,' came the voice again.

'What are you in for, Pat?' Joe asked.

'Murder. They got me for shooting an intelligence man back in November.' Whelan's voice trailed off for a few moments. 'I'm innocent.'

Joe smiled to himself. They were all innocent in here, just like in Kilmainham.

'My name's Joe. Joe Ryan.'

'What are you in for, Joe?' Whelan asked.

'Nothing yet. They keep remanding me. I'm on trial for arson, but they're trying to stick me with attempted murder as well. To tell the truth, I don't think they know what to do with me. They had me over in Kilmainham for a few weeks, but now they're after moving me here.'

'Arson?' Whelan asked. 'Was that for the Customs House?'

'Yeah.'

He heard a wicked cackle of laughter.

'By Jesus, boy, good on you so. I was sorry I missed that. We could see the smoke from here, and smell it, too. The screws got in a right panic over it.'

Joe smiled to himself. 'I bet they did.'

Silence stretched out between them. Joe stayed where he was, but spread his elbows on the sill and rested his head on his forearms. He felt like he could almost touch the outside from here. The breeze blew cool on his face and the sound of the city was muffled and soft, like a heartbeat. A motor car rumbled past, close under the walls, and boots crunched slowly across the yard. His neighbour might have gone to sleep, but he didn't mind. He was used to these long, broken night-time talks. They were just the same as any other conversation, only more spread out. Because they killed the time better that way.

'Are you married, Joe?' Whelan asked eventually, and Joe started, raising his head up off his arms. He wasn't sure if he'd slept.

'What?'

'I said, are you married?'

'No.'

'Got a girl?'

Silence again as Joe thought for a moment. Poor Maggie. Even now she gave him a pang – though it made him smile to think how she would have bristled if he'd called her his girl.

'No. Not any more. What about you?'

'I'm engaged to a girl. May is her name. May Brennan.'

Joe wasn't sure what to say so he said nothing. More time passed. Maggie was in his head now and he could hear her voice, her laugh. He rested his head on his arms again and let his eyes close so that he could picture her. Just her and him. He didn't want to talk any more, but he didn't want to lie down either. It was nice just to stand here, alone with her. The silence was growing, filling the cell, spilling out the window, but he didn't mind. The morning would be noisy. He would wake to a clanging bell and after that there would be doors crashing open and feet thumping along the landings and screams and shouts and the

43

rattle of tin plates and tin mugs. He would have to learn faces and names, which were the good screws and which bad. He would have to find his place in here and learn to endure. But all that was in the morning. For now it was all right to stand here and rest, just him and Maggie.

'Hey, Joe, are you asleep?' Whelan's whisper was very low. Almost as if he didn't want to be heard.

'Nearly,' Joe mumbled, without opening his eyes.

'Well, good night, so. And welcome to the Joy.'

They got back to Dawson Street just after six o'clock in the evening. The sun was still shining and the air was so warm that Stephen was in his shirtsleeves, his jacket slung over one shoulder, while Lillian carried her cardigan folded over her arm. They were on their way home from visiting Professor Barrett at the nursing home where he'd been sent to recover after his stroke.

'I thought he seemed quite cheerful,' Lillian said as they walked along Stephen's Green.

'Yes, he did – all things considered,' Stephen agreed, though he suspected Barrett had been putting on a brave face for them. The stroke had paralysed his right side, leaving him unable to write and badly slurring his speech. He was unlikely to teach mathematics ever again.

'I do wish the college hadn't been so quick to re-place him, though. The poor man's only been sick a few weeks and already they're shoving him out the door. I think it's very unseemly, don't you?'

'I do. But, then again, he was retiring next year, anyway – and you know he's never been the most popular man with the college board. I'm sorry to say it, but they probably couldn't wait to see the back of him.'

'Well, I suppose that's true,' Lillian agreed glumly. She knew very well that Barrett had long been a thorn in the side of the college board – not least on her account. She was one of the few female academics in Trinity College and she was there solely thanks to Professor Barrett, whose belief that ability should trump all other considerations had won him few friends amongst the Fellows of the College.

'What about this man Keach?' Stephen asked. 'Have you ever heard of him?'

Mr J. G. Keach was the man the college was bringing in to replace Barrett as the head of the mathematics department. According to Barrett he was a specialist in mathematical physics, which was outside Stephen's area of expertise. Lillian, on the other hand, worked in that very field, and was using her summer vacation to finish a paper that explored the mathematical theories behind Einstein's theory of relativity.

'No, I can't say I have,' Lillian admitted, though she was planning to look him up in the mathematical journals. It was a small enough world they all worked in and his published work would give her at least some sense of the man. However, the sight that greeted them as they turned the corner into Dawson Street pushed all thought of Keach from her mind. 'Oh my Lord!' she exclaimed. 'Look at this!'

The crowd of onlookers had more than doubled since they'd been there that morning. They lined the pavement and spilled out into the roadway –

although no cars troubled them because the police had blocked off the street at both ends. Some had settled down to wait in the shade of the plane trees; some had even brought food with them and made a picnic on the kerb. Nobody seemed to know what might happen next but it was a fine, sunny day and an excited buzz filled the air. There was a palpable sense of anticipation, a feeling that something momentous was about to happen.

The street was so crowded that they couldn't get very far down it. But since they were both quite tall, they had no problem seeing as far as the Mansion House, where a few anxious-looking men in dark suits stood glancing at their watches from time to time.

'Well, at least it looks like we haven't missed him,' Lillian remarked, and Stephen grimaced.

'That's assuming he's going to show up, of course.'

'Oh, hush now, misery guts – it's about time you had a little faith,' Lillian said with a grin and a nudge. Stephen didn't answer. After all the work he'd done, all the time spent in meetings in hotel rooms and in corridors, all those miles in taxicabs and walking back and forth across the city – after all that, he still didn't know how this was going to turn out. What he did know was that it went far beyond Dawson Street. The man everybody was waiting for was himself waiting. He was sitting in his barracks waiting for the telegram from London that would tell him what to do next. To sign or not to sign, that was the question…

'If he is coming, I wish he'd hurry up,' he said, looking at his watch.

'Patience, sweetheart.' Lillian patted his hand. He had been like a cat on hot bricks these last few days, which was so out of character for him as to be almost amusing. He was usually so calm and imperturbable that it was strange to see him so agitated – but pleasantly so. Although he had been deliberately vague about what he was doing, she'd been sharp enough to put the pieces together and conclude that he was involved in some way with these peace talks that had been taking place. She was proud of him. Even if he had only played a minor role, he was in some way responsible for bringing all these people out to throng Dawson Street, hoping to see an end to three years of war. Small wonder he was so nervous.

'Here we are, here we are,' he said, excitement in his voice. Lillian held on to his arm for balance and stood up on tiptoe so that she could see what was happening at the bottom of the street. There was a ripple of applause, and then he saw a policeman run into the road and shoo some onlookers away as a motor car turned in and nosed slowly up towards them. It was a big car, an open tourer, and there were two men sitting in the back. As it came closer, Lillian was able to make out that the two men were soldiers, and that they both had a lot of red and gold braid around their hats.

'That's him, all right,' Stephen whispered. 'General Macready.'

'Who's that with him?'

'Colonel Briand, his aide-de-camp.'

The crowd was cheering now, and when the car pulled up outside the Mansion House, people from this side of the street surged into the roadway

47

so as to get a better view. Stephen smiled at Lillian and then shook his head. It wasn't every day that the Commander-in-Chief of British forces in Ireland got such a rapturous reception from the citizens of Dublin.

A man came down the steps to greet the two soldiers as they climbed out of the car.

'That's the Lord Mayor,' Lillian remarked as the three men paused to smile and wave at the cheering crowd.

'So it is,' Stephen agreed, though he keenly noted that the general had come unarmed. His service revolver, which should have hung from his gleaming Sam Browne belt, was missing. He wondered if anybody else in the crowd would notice, but he had learned for himself how important these little things, these symbols and signs, could be. As they climbed the steps and went inside, to where de Valera and Arthur Griffith from the republican side, and Lord Midleton the unionist leader were waiting, he knew there would be a little pantomime of precedence, of who would stand and who would sit and who would shake hands. For all the brutality of the things they hoped to put an end to, the niceties were suddenly more important than anything.

'Well, that's that, then,' he said, after the door had been firmly closed and the cheering had died down. Some parts of the crowd had started to drift and break up, even though there had been no agreement yet, no announcement. It had been a long day with plenty of comings and goings, and he had the feeling that people were growing tired. For all the goodwill in the air, he had no

sense of how things stood. They could as easily
have come here to sign or to break, and either
one could take minutes or hours.

'I suppose we'd better be going,' Stephen suggested. 'They could be in there all night.'

'Oh, I doubt it,' said a voice from behind him. A
familiar voice, but not one he had expected to
hear. He turned and saw Andy Cope standing a
few feet away, leaning on his cane. He was smiling
at them and Stephen was pleased to see that he
looked more like his old elegant self. They had
both worked hard on the negotiations that had
brought General Macready to the Mansion House
and in those weeks Stephen had noticed the long
hours and late nights taking their toll on Cope's
appearance. The last time they had met, Cope had
just returned from his third trip to London within
a week and he had been red-eyed and unshaven,
wearing a rumpled suit with his shirt open at the
collar. Then, the strain had been visible on him
like a rash, but now he stood watching them
calmly, cutting his usual dash in a light grey suit
and waistcoat, shoes and spats and a carnation in
his buttonhole.

'I'm reliably informed that the gentlemen won't
be long,' Cope went on. 'A matter of minutes, in
fact. It may be worth our while to wait.'

Stephen was so surprised to see him here that
he was momentarily at a loss as to what to do. He
had never introduced Cope to Lillian – partly
because their relationship was so secretive, but
also because he knew that it contained an element
of risk. The people they were dealing with were
violent men for the most part, and it had seemed

safest to keep her as far away from them as possible. Cope himself had been complicit in this. He had never imposed himself, never intruded or put himself in a position where he might meet her directly – until now. Clearly he felt that things had reached such a point that it was safe to do so.

'Lillian,' Stephen said, 'Allow me to introduce my friend, Sir Alfred Cope. Sir Alfred, my fiancée, Lillian Bryce.'

'Sir Alfred?' Cope grinned, putting a notable cockney twang in his voice. It was the first time he had ever heard Stephen use his title. 'Please, my dear, call me Andy. All my friends call me Andy. It's a pleasure to meet you.'

'How do you do?' Lillian murmured as she shook his hand.

'Very well, thank you. Though I believe I will do much better when all this palaver is over and done with. Would you mind waiting with me for a few minutes? After all our hard work, I really feel we should stay until the bitter end.'

'Well, if you say it won't take long then we shall wait,' Lillian said, and they stood in silence together and looked expectantly at the Mansion House.

Stephen had already concluded that Cope's presence was a good sign, but the longer they stood there, the more he began to doubt himself. He gave Cope a sidelong look and thought he detected an air of nervous expectation. Outwardly he looked calm, almost serene, but Stephen sensed a tension that emanated from him like energy from a coiled spring. As the minutes passed, he was surprised to feel the knot in his stomach start to tighten, and a nervy, slightly nauseous sensation creeping over him. After all these weeks, surely it was in the bag? There could hardly be a problem that would arise when the pen was in General Macready's hand. No, there couldn't be. And yet he wasn't the only one. He suddenly realized that a stony silence had fallen over the street. All these people and yet there was hardly a sound save the ticking of the car engine.

Time passed. The warm breeze sighed through the trees and birds sang overhead. Nobody spoke, but Stephen felt Lillian squeeze his hand reassuringly, and he gently squeezed back. Then, without any warning, the door opened and the general and his aide reappeared on the steps, ushered out by the Lord Mayor. The crowd gave a collective gasp, but General Macready hardly acknowledged them as he put on his cap and marched straight to the waiting car. The door was opened; the two soldiers climbed in, and then the car moved slowly up the street, passing within yards of where Stephen, Lillian and Cope were standing. Still nobody seemed quite sure what had happened, until there was a burst of applause from near the doors of the Mansion House as more men appeared on the steps, handing out printed sheets to reporters who were all dashing off to try and make the morning editions. Slowly, the applause stared to ripple along the street, augmented by some uncertain cheering.

'*Sic transit gloria mundi*,' Cope remarked, watching as the car turned on to Stephen's Green and disappeared from view. The moment it had gone, the tension seemed to flow out of him and he became altogether less formal. He clapped Stephen on the arm and shook his hand. 'Thank God that's done,' he exclaimed. 'After all that's gone on, I shouldn't have put it past the old beggar not to turn up. Still, he did it in the end and I'm in a mood to celebrate. Will the pair of you allow me to treat you to afternoon tea?' He pulled out a silver pocket watch and frowned at it. 'Or perhaps even some dinner? It's the least I can do after all the hard work.'

Stephen looked uncertainly at Lillian, but she smiled and took Cope by the arm that he offered her.

'That's very kind of you, Andy. We'd be delighted,' she shot Stephen a knowing look, 'and at least it will give you a chance to explain why I've seen so little of my fiancé these last few weeks.'

Cope laughed. 'Well, my dear, I'm sorry to have to tell you that I'm not finished with him yet. What we've just seen is General Macready signing a truce – a ceasefire, you might say – with the republican forces.' He stopped as they came to the top of Dawson Street. 'Would the Shelbourne Hotel be to your liking? Stephen? Yes? Good, the Shelbourne it is, then. Well now, this truce is only temporary – it answers no questions of itself, but it does give everybody the chance to sit down and hammer out something a bit more permanent. In that event, I believe Stephen and I will have a bit more work to do before we are finished. That's assuming the truce holds up, of course.'

'You don't sound very hopeful.'

'As a matter of fact, I think it will, but I'm pretty much alone in that respect. Some of my colleagues up in the castle have already opened a sweepstake on how long the truce will last, and the most optimistic date they've picked is this day fortnight.'

'Well, I hope it lasts longer than that,' Lillian said, and looked to Stephen, thinking he seemed distracted and not as pleased with himself as he should have been. 'And what do you think, dear?'

Stephen had been thinking of his brother and wondering if he might benefit from the truce. There had been mention of an amnesty for prisoners but with Joe's trial still ongoing, there wasn't much chance that he would be set free. Still, the truce was a start and it gave him reason to be hopeful.

'I think the first days will be the hardest. If it lasts a fortnight it will last a month, and if it lasts a month then there's no reason to think it can't be made permanent.'

'Well said,' Cope agreed. 'Of course, you know whose job it is to make it last a fortnight, don't you?' He nudged Lillian's arm. 'You must make the most of this dinner, my dear. Because I'm afraid you'll be seeing precious little of your fiancé for the next week or two.'

OGLAIG NA HEIREANN

ARD-OIFIG AT CLIATH
General Headquarters, Dublin
9th July 1921

To:
Officers Commanding All Units
In view of conversations now being entered into by

*our Government with the Government of Great
Britain and in pursuance of mutual understandings
to suspend hostilities during these conversations,
active operations by our troops will be suspended as
from Monday July Eleventh.*

RISTEÁRD UA MAOLCHATHA
Chief of Staff

III

Billy Standing came out of the Four Courts feeling rather pleased with himself. The Michaelmas term had just started and already he had a couple of juicy little cases lined up. Nothing quite as dramatic as defending an IRA man in a court martial, mind you, but much more lucrative. Not a bad day's work at all, he thought, especially since he'd been off the circuit for more than a year.

He paused on the steps to button his jacket and thought briefly of Joe Ryan. It was weeks since he'd seen him, though he kept in regular contact with Noyk, the solicitor. Joe was still languishing up in Mountjoy, apparently, and there he would stay for the foreseeable future. Many of the smaller fish had been released as a goodwill gesture after the truce was signed, but not poor Joe. His trial had been postponed pending the outcome of peace negotiations, but he was still being held on remand – a useful sort of limbo for the authorities. He would just have to wait until a more permanent agreement could be reached – which was still on the cards if the newspaper reports were true. De Valera had already been to see Lloyd George in person and, while they hadn't been able to come to an agreement on that occasion, they were still corresponding by letter. There were rumours of more formal peace talks to come and in the meantime the truce was holding up better than expected. The country was quiet and people could go about their lives in peace at last.

Billy set off down the steps, taking little notice of the motor car parked by the kerb until the back door opened and a young man stepped out. His face looked familiar, though Billy couldn't quite place it.

'Mr Standing?'

'Yes?' Billy stopped, his grip tightening on his briefcase as he glanced over his shoulder to the safety of the courts.

'My name is Ned Kelliher,' the young man held out his hand, 'I'm a friend of Joe Ryan.'

'Ah yes, of course you are.' The penny dropped and Billy slackened his grip a little. He'd seen Kelliher once or twice outside Dublin Castle on court days, and had once passed him by at the solicitor's office. He shook his hand. 'What can I do for you, Mr Kelliher?'

'Mr Collins has sent me to ask you if you have a few minutes to come and see him.'

'Mr Collins?'

'Michael Collins.'

'Why does he want to see me?'

Kelliher grinned amiably. 'He says he has a job

for you.' He gestured at the back seat of the car. 'We can take you to see him now if you like. Or if it's not convenient, he's asked me to arrange an appointment for you to see him another time.'

Billy looked uncertainly in the door. There was a time when an invitation to see Michael Collins might end with a bullet in the back of the head. But things had changed since the truce was signed. He had heard Collins was operating more or less openly from an office in the Gresham Hotel.

'All right,' Billy said. 'I suppose now is as good a time as any.'

Kelliher rode up in the front seat and didn't seem minded to talk. They drove down the quays, following the river for a while, and then turned into Sackville Street. Billy's suspicions were confirmed when they pulled up outside the Gresham and a uniformed porter opened the door for him. Kelliher led the way across the lobby and into the lift. Only when the two of them were securely locked inside the cage, with the motor whirring high above them, did Billy work up the courage to lean across and ask the question that was still bothering him.

'This job he wants me to do. Any idea what it's about?'

'I think he wants you to go to London with him,' was all Kelliher said, before the lift stopped with a jolt and a ping and the doors swished open on a long carpeted corridor. London? Billy thought, as they walked down the corridor to the end door, which Kelliher held open for him. What on earth could take Michael Collins to London?

56

He was so lost in thought as he walked in that it took him a moment to notice that he had entered a large suite and that this area had been laid out as a comfortable anteroom. There were two sofas and an armchair and a typewriter set up on a table by the window. A tall man stood solemnly by the connecting door, his hands clasped in front and the butt of a revolver sticking out from under his jacket, but he wasn't the one who caught Billy's attention. Rising up from one of the sofas and looking every bit as surprised as he must have himself, was Stephen Ryan.

'Billy? What on earth are you doing here?'

'Well,' Billy stammered, caught unawares. He didn't know how much Stephen knew, or how much he should give away. 'He wants to see me for something,' he got out, jerking his head towards the connecting door. 'But what about you? What are *you* doing here?'

'I'm not sure. Same as you, I'd imagine. He sent a man up to fetch me out of college.'

'Well,' Billy sat down on the sofa beside him and dropped his voice to a whisper. 'My man mentioned something about going with him to London.'

'London?' Stephen looked puzzled. 'I'd have thought that was the last place Collins would want to go to. There's still a price on his head.'

My thoughts exactly, Billy said to himself, but before he could say it aloud, the connecting door opened and a young man came striding out. They all look so young, Billy thought, and yet this one was perhaps his own age or a little older. He was rather slight, well groomed, and had a distinctly

57

military air about him. He reminded Billy of Stephen, only not so tall.

'Mr Ryan?' he said, stopping in front of Stephen and giving a barely perceptible bow. 'My name is Dalton, Emmet Dalton. My apologies for keeping you waiting so long. If you please? Mr Collins will see you now.'

Stephen looked for a moment as if he might ask straight out what the hell was going on, but he kept his mouth shut and pushed himself to his feet.

'Good luck, Stephen,' Billy said in a low voice, and then they went into the other room and the door closed behind him.

Stephen was the last one in the library that evening. A porter had come across him as he went around to lock up, and he had started up from his work, all apologies.

'Sorry, I was miles away,' he said, gathering up his papers. He was surprised at how far he had got. There were pages and pages of equations, of scribbles and hypotheses, of little questions to himself. On top of it all was still that equation, the zeta function, the one that had been bothering him for weeks. But it no longer had a page to itself. Finally he had cracked it open and managed to tease out some of the intricate threads it contained. Some did not lead anywhere, just looped around on themselves, but some were bound to take him places. His head was still full of them when he walked out of the library and found Andy Cope waiting for him outside.

'Oh.' Stephen stopped sharp as Cope pushed

himself up from the bench where he had been sitting. It was early October, and quite dark at this hour. He might not have seen Cope were it not for the oblique band of yellow light that spilled out from the door of the library. 'Hello, Andy. Have you been here long?'

'Not as long as you might think,' Cope answered. 'It seems both of us are working late tonight. I have a motor car outside. Can I offer you a lift?'

'By all means,' Stephen said, and they set off together towards Front Square. As they walked through the darkness he glanced sideways at Cope, who seemed preoccupied. It was several weeks since he had seen him. As predicted, they had both been kept busy in the fortnight after the truce was declared, but as time went by, their meetings became less and less frequent before finally they stopped altogether. The new academic year began and Stephen had gone back to his work and his research, thinking no more of the matter until he had been summoned to see Michael Collins the week before. Even that had not given him much pause for thought. Collins had seemed an affable and friendly man – much more easygoing than he had been led to expect by the newspaper reports – but he had spoken only of possibilities, of 'perhaps's and 'maybes'. He thought he might have to go to London, and if he did, then he might need somebody...

'I've just come from a meeting with a very learned gentleman,' Cope began, apropos of nothing. 'Dr Bernard, the Provost of this college. He is a man with some very fine sherry.'

'So I've heard.' Stephen smiled. He had met Dr Bernard a few times in the normal course of college life, at receptions and prize-givings and the like. Otherwise their paths might never have crossed, since Dr Bernard's field was divinity; he was an expert on theology, philosophy and the history of the church. The Provost was also, as Stephen had quickly gathered, a staunch unionist and very tight with his sherry. 'He must have taken a right old shine to you if he poured it out.'

'Well, of course he did. I'm such a likeable fellow, you know.' Cope grinned so that his teeth gleamed as they passed under a hissing gaslight on the corner of Front Square. 'Though I don't think he took as much of a shine to me as did the other fellow who was at our meeting. Professor Keach. He's your gaffer, if I'm not mistaken.'

'He is,' Stephen said slowly, beginning to get the picture. Whatever else it might have concerned, Cope's meeting had clearly concerned him. 'But he's not a professor. Not yet, at any rate.'

And just as bloody well, he thought to himself. He had not seen much of Keach, but what he had seen, he did not like. At the reception to welcome him to the college, Keach had arrived late, had feigned surprise and claimed to be flattered, even though this was common courtesy. He was in his late thirties, smooth and distinguished-looking. Quite the ladies man, Stephen thought, noting the lingering kisses and rather tactile embraces as he was introduced to various wives and sweethearts. His instinctive reaction had been polite hostility, which took on a jealous edge when Lillian said she liked him, that she thought he was nice. And

Stephen had to admit he *seemed* nice. He was attentive, charming, self-deprecating. But there was something false about him, and Stephen was sure it wasn't just jealousy colouring his opinion. He found Keach superficial, thought he had no depth, no bottom, and this business of him calling himself *professor* did not surprise him. He was still only acting head of the mathematics department and had not yet been appointed to the chair. A minor enough point, but one that seemed to greatly bother Keach, who struck him as rather vain.

'Oh?' Cope asked. 'I didn't know that. I wondered why Bernard gave him such a queer look when he introduced himself.'

'So, what was your meeting about?' Stephen asked, although he already knew full well what the answer would be.

'I think you know very well that it concerned *you*,' Cope said, smiling, and in the pause that followed, their footsteps rang together over the cobbles for a few paces. Then he suddenly seemed to change the subject. 'I understand you finally met Mr Collins.'

'I did.'

'I'm yet to have the pleasure, myself. What is he like?'

Stephen didn't answer for another few paces. He wasn't sure if he could adequately describe Michael Collins. A bear of a man, but agile. Quick with a handshake, firm, and looks you in the eye. Other than that, he was bland, ordinary – not the sort that would stand out in a crowd. And yet there was something about him, something behind those blue eyes. He was complicated, yes, many

61

things to many people. That was it; he was a man anybody could follow.

'I think you'd like him,' Stephen said.

'I'm sure I will. I dare say I'll finally have the pleasure when he comes over to London.'

Three more paces. The porter had heard them coming. Stephen could see the light as the wicket gate creaked open.

'So he's going over, then. For the Treaty talks.'

'I understand he asked you to go with him.'

Stephen couldn't help but smile at the recollection. Collins stretched out with his feet on the desk and his arms behind his head. Almost talking to the ceiling. If it comes to pass, then I may have a need...

'Not in so many words. It was more like the intimation of a possibility – a very distant possibility. He sounded reluctant, almost as if he didn't want to go himself.'

'If you were him, would you want to go?' Cope laughed. 'I mean, talk about putting your head in the lion's mouth. Well, in any case, the possibility is now a reality. He's going, and so are you.'

'If I remember rightly, I was even more reluctant about it than he was. In fact, I believe I said no.'

Cope gave him a sly look. 'I believe you said you wouldn't be able to get the time off work, a situation that has now been resolved, thanks to the good offices of Dr Bernard. And a letter from the Prime Minister.'

Stephen stopped walking. They were still thirty yards from the gate, just out of earshot of the porter who stood waiting with a lantern in his hand.

'Work wasn't the only reason,' he said.

'Oh? Well, it was the only one given to me. I was asked to see if I could smooth your path and, well, here we are. Path smoothed. The provost has granted you a leave of absence for the duration of the talks. You are free to go.'

'That's hardly the bloody point,' Stephen protested. 'I don't even know why he wants me to go. I'm not a diplomat, or a lawyer.'

'If I'm not mistaken, they already have plenty of diplomats and lawyers,' Cope said quietly. 'As a matter of fact, it's turning into quite the flaming circus. Trust me, I'm the one who has to arrange safe-conduct passes for all the beggars. There's the official delegation itself, with all its attendant lawyers and whatnot, and then there is Mr Collins's personal cohort of advisors and, dare I say, bodyguards. It's this last you will be attached to, as will your friend, Mr Standing.'

'Well, at least Billy is a lawyer.'

'Indeed he is. But he's not the one who's been working with me for the past year. And since I will be there myself, in a more or less unofficial capacity, of course...' Cope's voice trailed off and he shrugged.

Stephen wanted to be angry but he'd had a feeling it would come to this from the moment he'd seen Cope waiting for him. In fact, he'd suspected it ever since he'd met Collins. There was an inevitability about it. For all his hemming and hawing, Collins wouldn't have sent for him if he wasn't certain he would be going himself.

And then there was Cope. How much of a hand he'd had in arranging this *fait accompli,* Stephen would never know, but he didn't blame him. His job would be to work behind the scenes, to try and keep the negotiations from going off the rails. Given what was at stake, and the enormous gulf between the two parties, that would be no mean feat – and not one he could accomplish alone. He would need a contact, a liaison on the other side, and that was where Stephen came in.

'How long do you think it will take?' he asked, turning again and walking towards the wicket gate and the waiting porter.

'God only knows,' Cope admitted. 'We could be there until Christmas, or you could be home in a fortnight. Why do you ask?'

'Well, I actually *do* have work to think of. Research work – things going on in my head that might not wait that long.'

Cope glanced at him as they ducked out through the gate on to College Green. A reluctant patriot, if ever he saw one.

'G'night, gentlemen,' the porter said, closing the door behind them.

'Bring it with you, then,' Cope suggested. 'I'm sure you can guess the sort of pattern our work will take. I imagine it'll be much like what you had in the trenches; days of waiting followed by five minutes' panic. Bring your work if it will keep you from getting bored. You never know, the change of scene might even do you some good.'

The iron triangle rang out loud through the stillness of the wing, the jarring noise echoing up through the landings and penetrating even the heavy doors of the cells.

'Come on you bastards, let's be having you!' the

64

screws bawled. 'Come on now, rise and shine!'

Joe sat on his bunk, already washed and dressed and with his mug and plate in his lap. Three months in and he had fitted himself to the rhythm of the place. He waited until the bolt clanked and the door squealed and then he stood up and walked out on to the empty landing. After the truce had cleared space in the other wings, they had moved most of the men off this one. Only Whelan had to stay behind, and they'd left Joe there so that he'd have a companion. Joe preferred it that way. It was quieter and Whelan had a few privileges that he could share, like the spirit stove he was kneeling over when Joe walked into his cell.

'Morning, Joe. A cold one last night!'

Joe grunted and sat on the edge of the bunk. Cold enough to put a glaze of frost on the wall of his cell and keep him curled under his blankets so that he woke up cramped and bent and still feeling it in his bones. Winter was coming and no mistake.

'A cup of tea will do you good after a night like that.' Whelan grinned and hopped up from the boiling pot to fetch the tea and sugar and the open tin of condensed milk. There was a touch of the bird about Whelan. Something in the quick way he moved, the way he turned his head, the trill of his laugh. And yet he was also remarkably tidy. His cell was spotless, with a near military neatness in the way everything was so carefully folded and placed. Blankets drum-tight on the bunk and all his tins and books in an orderly row on the table. But it was not the barracks that Whelan had been in, it was the seminary, and even though he'd never been ordained, Joe could

65

tell the place had left its mark on him. There was the well-thumbed bible on the pillow and the plain wooden cross on the wall.

The tea was sweetened with sugar and even sweeter from the condensed milk. As Joe sipped and blew, sipped and blew, he heard distant shouting and drumming as the men from the other wings were mustered for the morning count. That was another one of Whelan's privileges. With only the two of them here they didn't have to muster in the mornings, though the screws checked their cells every hour through the night.

'You're very quiet this morning, Joe,' Whelan said, pulling out his chair and perching on the edge of it. He was a small, wiry man, probably not much older than Joe was, though he looked and acted as though he were.

'I'm grand, Pat,' Joe answered. 'Bit tired, is all.'

'Well, if you ever want to talk about anything...'

Joe stopped in the middle of blowing on his tea and rolled his eyes at Whelan.

'You mean you'll hear my confession.'

'Only if you want me to, Joe.' Whelan grinned sadly. 'And only if you want to.'

But it wasn't Whelan he wanted to hear his confession. After breakfast he went down to the circle, which was already ringing with the echo of a thousand little taps and clinks. Men were keeping themselves busy with work; hammering and scraping at coins and tins and marrowbones to make rings and pendants and tools, something to show for the long days in here. In the midst of all this clamour, some men sat reading with wisps of cotton waste sticking out of their ears. Some tried

66

to write, and some made a ceremony out of rolling cigarettes. Joe passed through it all and into the relative silence of B Wing. He was looking for Jimmy O'Dowd and found a man standing outside his cell, his arms folded and one foot back against the wall. Joe didn't have to say a word. Stony eyes followed him as he came closer, and then a jerk of the head motioned him inside.

'What can I do for you, Joe?' O'Dowd was sitting on his bunk, his feet crossed at the ankles. He was a small, round-headed man with a pot belly and a trim moustache. Like Joe, he'd been arrested at the Customs House but his case had been more clear-cut. The Auxies had found a single round of ammunition that had slipped through the lining of his pocket and that was that. A good hiding and three years for unlawful possession of firearms, and now he was in command here, the senior IRA officer in Mountjoy.

'I want to talk to you about Pat Whelan,' said Joe, and O'Dowd gestured for him to sit on the chair.

'What's wrong with him?' O'Dowd sat up and swung his legs off the bunk so that they could lean close and talk in whispers. If Joe had managed to get the idea of a confession out of his head, it was back now with a vengeance.

'There's nothing wrong with him. As a matter of fact, he's in good form. It's just that... Well, you know he's on a death sentence.'

'I know. That's why he's on D Wing, and why they let him have somebody to keep him company.'

'But he's innocent.'

O'Dowd's face split into a broad grin. 'Sure

aren't we all?'

'No, I mean it. They convicted him for the murder of Captain Bagely on Mount Street, but that's wrong. He didn't do it.'

'Bagely's wife would tell you different. She picked Whelan out. She identified him, Joe. That's what did for him. She testified against him; said she saw him shoot her husband with her own eyes.'

'No, no.' Joe put his head in his hands. 'He didn't do it, I'm telling you.' He looked up, looked O'Dowd straight in the eye. 'I killed Bagely.'

O'Dowd wasn't grinning now. Joe wasn't surprised that he didn't know. Including Bagely, fourteen men had been killed that Sunday morning and even Joe didn't know who all the other shooters had been. It was safer that way.

'Jesus, Joe, are you sure?'

Joe stared at him, thinking of that morning in the boarding house on Mount Street. The terrified woman curled up in the bed, screaming as the shots echoed around the room. He'd pointed the gun at her and told her to shut up, and she'd looked at his face, staring right at him through the tears. She must have seen him clear as day. 'Of course I'm sure. Ned Kelliher was with me. You can check with headquarters, if you want.'

'No, no, Joe. It's all right. But what do you want to do? Do you want me to see if you can be moved to another wing?'

'No, not that.'

There must have been something in the way he spoke, or maybe it was the look on his face. In any case, the penny suddenly dropped for O'Dowd.

'Ah Jesus, Joe, you're not going to say something!'

'But they're going to hang him for what I did.'

'And if you open your gob they'll just hang the pair of you for it.' O'Dowd leaned even closer, his eyes darting towards the door. 'It's a done thing, Joe. He's been tried and convicted and he's even lost an appeal. Do you think they'll just let him off if you say you did it? Think about it. It'll do neither of you any good.'

'It might do one of us some good,' Joe said, standing up suddenly. O'Dowd followed him, bringing himself up with his pot belly sticking out, his moustache bristling.

'Well, I'm ordering you to keep your mouth shut, Joe. At least until I can get word through to headquarters.' O'Dowd had his hand on Joe's arm, a strong, angry grip. But then he softened a little. 'They're not going to do anything for a while anyway. There's a stay on all executions while these Treaty talks are going on in London. Keep quiet, Joe. That's the best thing you can do for the time being.'

'All right. For the time being,' Joe said sullenly, and he walked out of the cell, more angry with himself than anything else. This wasn't what he'd wanted, but what had he expected? What sort of answer was he looking for? The truth was, he didn't even know himself. The moment he'd learned the truth of Whelan's case, he'd known there was nothing he could do about it. But he'd thought, if only he could say something, if only somebody would tell him what to do. Well, they had told him what to do. He just didn't like it.

Whelan was standing on the first-floor landing of D Wing, looking out over the circle. He waved when he saw Joe, but Joe didn't have the heart to respond. Nevertheless, he went up the stairs, hands in pockets, and came back around to the end of the landing, where he leaned on the rail beside Whelan.

'Look at them,' Whelan said, nodding out into the din of whittling and tapping. It looked to Joe as if every man had a marrowbone or a silver sixpence and was trying to beat or scratch some sort of meaning out of it. 'They're like ants, aren't they? Busy, busy, busy. Sure if they weren't in here half of them would still be in bed at this hour.'

'At least ants can get out if they want to,' Joe observed, and Whelan laughed.

They stood together for a while, watching the patterns. The disturbances as the screws circled past, the pauses when a tin of cigarettes was opened and shared. After a while, the din diminished. There was more smoke, more pipes, more mugs of tea. The first rush was passing and they were settling down to spin out the day more slowly.

'What did O'Dowd say to you?' Whelan asked.

'Nothing.'

'Did he tell you not to tell me about what you done?'

Joe felt his mouth go dry. He wanted to look at Whelan, but he couldn't.

'Not exactly, no.'

'There's no point in tormenting yourself over it. I know all about it.'

Joe managed to turn his head. Whelan was hanging his head down, as if he was studying something on the floor below. Was he embarrassed because he hadn't said anything before?

'How long have you known?'

'Since before I was sentenced. Paddy Daly got word in to me during my trial – he said I ought to know.' Whelan raised his head and smiled wryly. 'Maybe he was right, but I don't think it made much difference myself.'

'Why didn't you say something in court?'

'How long do you think I'd last if I gave up one of our own lads to save myself?' Whelan shrugged. 'Not that I would, anyway. Besides, they probably wouldn't have believed me. Mrs Bagely said I was the one who shot her husband and that was all they wanted to hear.'

'I spoke to her that morning,' Joe said. 'She looked me right in the face. I don't know how the hell she picked you out of a line-up.'

Another shrug. 'The poor woman saw her husband shot in front of her and then she had the police and the army whispering in her ear that I was the one that did it. If I'd had two heads she probably would have still picked me out.'

They fell silent again. A minute passed, then another. One of the screws looked up at them, then cupped his hands to light a cigarette.

'It's not fair,' Joe said. 'That's what bothers me.'

'Not fair?' Whelan shook his head. 'No, it's fair all right. You see, you know what you done that morning, but you don't know what I done. You don't know that while you were in Mount Street shooting Bagely, I was over in the Gresham shooting Captain Wilde. That's what I done, and that's what I'm going to pay for. Whether it's fair or not fair, it's God's will, and there's nothing you or I can do about it.' Whelan smiled and clapped him on the shoulder. 'We all pay eventually, Joe,' he said, and walked back down the landing.

TO ALL TO WHOM THESE PRESENTS COME, GREETING:
In virtue of the authority vested in me by DÁIL EIREANN, I hereby appoint

<u>Arthur Griffith</u>, T.D., Minister for Foreign Affairs, Chair
<u>Michael Collins</u>, T.D, Minister of Finance,
<u>Robert C. Barton</u>, T.D, Minister for Economic Affairs,
<u>Edmund J. Duggan</u>, T.D,
<u>George Gavan Duffy</u>, T.D,
as Envoys Plenipotentiary from the Elected Government of the REPUBLIC OF IRELAND to negotiate and conclude on behalf of Ireland with the representatives of his Britannic Majesty, GEORGE V., a Treaty or Treaties of Settlement, Association and Accommodation between Ireland and and the community of nations known as the British Commonwealth.
IN WITNESS WHEREOF I hereunto subscribe my name as President.

Done in the City of Dublin this 7th day of October in the year of our Lord 1921 in five identical originals.

Eamon de Valera

Autumn leaves littered the ground, yellow and amber, damp, decaying. The wheels of Professor Barrett's chair skidded and squeaked in them as

72

Lillian pushed him along the path by the ornamental lake. They were in the Botanic Gardens, near the professor's house in Glasnevin, but it was clear that the crisp air and company had not lifted the professor's mood. Quite the opposite, in fact.

'So, he has really gone, then?' he asked in an unhappy voice, twisting around in the chair. Lillian gave him an indulgent smile. At least he was well enough to be unhappy. He still couldn't walk unaided, but his speech was much clearer and he seemed to have recovered a little of the strength in his upper body.

'I saw him to the boat myself,' she answered. 'He'll be in London in the morning.'

They came to a little iron bridge that arched across a neck in the lake and Lillian pushed him across and then positioned the chair beside a bench on the other side. She sat down. This was the professor's favourite spot, close by the stillness of the water and sheltered by the drooping branches of a weeping willow.

'I really do wish he hadn't gone away.' He wriggled uneasily underneath his travelling blanket. 'It really is most unfortunate that he should go now – not what I had hoped for at all!'

'It was his duty to go,' Lillian said, thinking she had seen Stephen off to far worse places and with far less hope of seeing him come home again. 'You know how he is about that sort of thing.'

In fact, she knew that Stephen hadn't been at all keen to go at first, but as the date came closer the idea had grown on both of them and they had made plans around it. In three weeks' time – assuming the talks lasted that long, of course –

she would go over to join him for a few days. She had been invited to read a paper at the London Mathematical Society and they planned to make a weekend of it.

'I know, I know,' Barrett said in a more conciliatory tone. 'It's just that the timing is so very bad. I shall find it very hard to forgive him for leaving you all alone like this.'

'Bless you, Professor,' Lillian laughed, patting his hand. 'But I believe I can look after myself.'

A stray gust of wind ruffled the surface of the lake and set the willow nodding and sighing. Professor Barrett turned his face a little to meet the breeze and let it soothe him. At least he could feel it now, and even burning pain would have been better than the paralysing numbness he had known. He could feel Lillian's hand resting on his and he wished he hadn't spoken so sharply to her. He simply didn't have the patience to be sick; he knew he was getting better but he was still confined to this damn chair, and it was this that irritated him more than Stephen's inconvenient absence.

'Do you have your paper with you?' he asked in a softer tone, and Lillian opened her bag and produced half a dozen neatly handwritten sheets, handing them to him without a word. This was the paper she was to read at the London Mathematical Society and she watched him carefully as he worked his way through it. He went slowly, but not because of any infirmity. Lillian's work dealt with the Lorentz transformations as they applied to Einstein's theory of relativity and it was very, very advanced. Eventually, he reached the last page and then sat for a few moments watching the shifting colours on the surface of the lake and feeling the pages rustle and flap in the fitful breeze. Even for a man who had spent so much of his life working with abstractions this was on the very edge of understanding, but it was good – it was very good. He would have to study it further to be certain, but he believed there were real insights there, remarkable leaps and intuitive connections.

'Did you show this to Mr Keach?'

'I did,' Lillian answered, a little shame-faced. She knew Barrett had a low opinion of Keach and if she told him what had happened this would certainly be reinforced. The first time she asked for it back, Keach claimed he had misplaced it. Then he had left it at home, then his servant had tidied it up. Since he was in the process of moving his wife and his household from London to Dublin, this had sounded plausible enough at the start, but three times Lillian had asked him to return her paper and three times he had come up empty-handed. The paper Professor Barrett held in his hand was, in fact, a second attempt, worked up from memory and from the notes she had kept in her daybook.

'What did he have to say about it?' Barrett asked.

'Nothing yet,' Lillian answered, looking away. 'I don't think he's had time to look at it.'

Barrett grunted in disdain. He'd been prepared to dislike Keach before he'd even met him, and he felt like he'd been proved right. But now dislike was growing into grave mistrust, and outrage at the fact that Keach was poised to gain everything at Lillian's expense. It was all so grossly unfair.

This paper he held in his hands was world-class. Had a man written it, he would practically be guaranteed a fellowship. Instead, it was Keach who would get the fellowship while Lillian would be left with ... well, it didn't bear thinking of.

'More fool him, because this is excellent work, my dear,' he said, handing back the paper with an admiring nod. 'I'm sure you will be the toast of the Society.'

'Thank you, professor,' she answered gracefully and slipped the paper back into her bag.

'Have you given any thought to the offer from the college?'

'A little,' Lillian answered in a tone that suggested it had been the source of some disagreement. Barrett was not surprised at this. The moment he had heard they had offered her a lectureship, he had known what they were up to. Ostensibly, a lectureship was a step up, but really it was just a sop. It was what they were prepared to give her instead of a fellowship.

'What does Stephen think?'

'He thinks I should accept. He says they're bound to allow women fellows eventually and if I'm still on the staff then I'll have more chance of being elected.'

Professor Barrett nodded slowly. That was the sensible answer and he had expected no less from Stephen. But then, it was not a decision Stephen would ever have to make for himself. There was not a shadow of a doubt that he would be made a fellow at the end of his studentship – provided, of course, he didn't commit some gross offence. But this would not be because he was a better

76

mathematician than Lillian. Rather, it would be because he was a man and she was not.

'But you don't agree?'

'Part of me thinks I should tell them to stuff their job,' Lillian said in a low voice, but with an angry stab in the last three words. 'I mean – a lectureship! It's practically the same job I have now, and I shall probably lose that when I get married.'

Barrett nodded again. This was a very shabby swansong for him. He had hoped for so much more and if he'd only lasted another year he might have had at least some of it. But this bloody stroke had put paid to all that. He was being pushed into retirement and they were putting Keach in his place. The offer of a lectureship for Lillian was a sop to him, but he knew it wasn't what she deserved. *They* knew it wasn't what she deserved, which is why they were offering it. And even if it meant giving them what they wanted, part of him wished she *would* tell them to stuff it, just to spite them. But he would never say that. He would be a poor teacher if he did.

'Well, my dear,' He said, patting her hand. 'You have time enough to think about it, and it's probably best not to be too rash. You never know, Stephen may prove to be right in the end.'

Lillian smiled and her face brightened as if she had decided to put all these gloomy thoughts from her mind. She leaned across and kissed Professor Barrett on the cheek.

'He usually does, doesn't he?'

IV

The fog was so thick that he hardly noticed it getting dark. Up here, high in the house, it was easy to lose track of time. This was the first day Stephen had had to himself since he came to London and he'd revelled in the peace and quiet of the empty house. Now and then he heard the thump of a door closing, footsteps on the stairs, but nobody disturbed him, nobody called him, and he had worked until he felt his concentration going. As his mind wandered he found he kept staring into the swirling fog just outside the window, listening to the constant burring of the lamp. Enough. He capped his pen, then yawned and stretched and shook out the cramp in his hand.

Suddenly the room seemed very small. When he stood up to stretch his back he found his head almost scraped the ceiling. He was in the attic, in the room he shared with Billy, although he hadn't seen him all day and had no idea when he might appear. All there was to show of him was his laundry, washed and starched and folded neatly on the second bed. Billy worked very long hours and spent most of his time either in the main delegation house in Hans Place or else in Downing Street itself. Stephen, by contrast, did his official work only in fits and starts. He had met with Cope a couple of times and had gathered from him that the talks were going well so far –

too well for their services to be required. Yesterday he had carried some documents up to Hans Place and today he had been left to his own devices. He had done some good work, he thought, skimming through the pages that had accumulated. Perhaps Cope had been right; maybe the change of scene had done him some good.

For all that, he was restless. He had been at his desk all day and he longed to get out. He went downstairs and took his overcoat from the hook in the hall. The fog would be thick, but it would be good to escape, to lose himself in it for a while.

He heard a step and then Emmet Dalton came into view in the sitting room. Dalton was in charge of Collins's bodyguard and wore a pistol in a holster slung across his chest, but he was no ordinary gunman. He was a slim man, softly spoken and with the unmistakeable stamp of a British army officer. Stephen had already gathered that they had both served in the same regiment during the war, though they had never met until Collins had summoned him to the Gresham Hotel.

'Oh, it's you,' Dalton said. 'I thought I had the place to myself. Are you going out?'

'Officer's patrol,' Stephen answered, and he caught Dalton's smile as he recognized the phrase. 'I've been sitting at a desk all day. Thought I'd stretch my legs.'

Dalton grinned. 'Good idea. Mind if I tag along? I could do with a breath of fresh air.'

'Not at all,' Stephen said although, despite Dalton's friendly demeanour, he knew he wasn't just coming along for the walk. In the few days he'd been here, Stephen had felt eyes on him, had noticed the way conversations tailed off when he walked into a room. Just because Collins had personally invited him to come to London didn't mean the others had to trust him. Still, it didn't bother him. He knew he was an outsider and he must expect to be watched for a while.

He buttoned his overcoat and waited for Dalton to do the same. When they were both ready he opened the door to admit a shock of damp air and a few tendrils of fog.

'Christ almighty,' Dalton muttered, peering out into the grey murk. 'I've seen gas attacks that weren't as bad as that.'

'So much for your breath of fresh air,' Stephen said and plunged down the steps to the pavement. It was like jumping into water, and he could sense the fog enveloping him, feel it rubbing against his skin and smell the grime and carbon that it carried. When Dalton joined him a few moments later, he was so wrapped up and indistinct that Stephen's sense of isolation was only heightened.

'Which way?' he asked, his voice muffled by the scarf he had pulled up over his nose and mouth. Stephen looked up the street and then down. Then he shrugged. They might as well have been wrapped in cotton wool.

'Does it make any difference?'

'I suppose not,' Dalton agreed, and they set off together, walking in silence to the end of the street and then turning and passing along the railings of a small park. Trees loomed over them and Stephen could feel the emptiness in the fog and smell the damp grass and leaves. He stayed resolutely silent, having made up his mind not to let Dalton off the hook too easily. If he insisted on following him about then he could damn well make some conversation. Dalton seemed to enjoy the silence, however, and they had almost reached the end of the park before he finally spoke up.

'I understand we've got something in common, you and I,' he said. '*Spectamur Agendo,* and all that.'

The old motto made Stephen smile. He agreed that they did indeed have something in common and after a few minutes' talk it became clear that they had quite a lot in common. They had both been Royal Dublin Fusiliers and if their paths had never crossed they had very nearly been the reverse of each other. While Stephen had been in Turkey for the early part of the war and then had been transferred to the Western Front, Dalton had been in France early on, before being sent to Palestine. Both had won the Military Cross – Dalton at Ginchy, during the battle of the Somme, and Stephen at Ypres – and both had qualified as expert marksmen.

Once they had got this much out of the way the silence returned, although it was a much more companionable silence. Stephen felt he knew Dalton now, although one thing still niggled at him.

'So how come you got involved ... you know, how come you're...'

'Batting for the other side?' Dalton chuckled under his scarf. 'Don't worry; I'm sure every single one of the lads I messed with would say the same. But that's not really how I see it. I was in the Irish Volunteers before I ever joined the British Army – I was one of Redmond's boys and joined up to fight for Home Rule for Ireland. But when I was demobbed it was fairly obvious *that* was never going to happen, so my brother got me back in with the old crowd; only this time it was more fighting, less Home Rule.'

'Your brother?' Stephen asked. Another similarity.

'Yes, little Charlie. He knows *your* brother, as a matter of fact – as do I. So perhaps I should turn the question around and ask why Joe never managed to get you involved?'

'Well, it wasn't for want of trying,' Stephen admitted. 'But the fact is, my brother and I are chalk and cheese. He was always the one for politics, for fighting. All I ever wanted to do was maths.'

It was hard to tell under the scarf, but he thought Dalton was grinning at him.

'Did you do much maths at Ypres, then?'

'Well, that was–' he began, but then jerked his head around at the sound of a footfall behind them. Not even a footfall, half a footfall, the scrape of a shoe. He could see nothing through the fog, but the sound had been clear and close. Dalton had heard it too, and had looked around, one hand sliding inside his overcoat.

'Keep walking,' he murmured, and Stephen could tell by the movement of his head that he was already looking for cover. They had reached Cadogan Square by now, and were walking along another iron railing with bushes looming over the other side. Stephen remembered another park; this area was littered with them. If they could get in there, they might be able to see who was following them.

'Too obvious,' Dalton whispered, seeing where

he was looking, and Stephen caught the thrill in his voice. He was enjoying this.

'Special Branch?' Stephen whispered, out of the corner of his mouth.

'Or the Intelligence Service,' Dalton answered. Two more steps and they came to a gate, which Dalton pushed open so it squealed loudly in the fog. Then he grabbed Stephen's arm and pulled him out into the roadway, crossing diagonally to the other pavement. Their shoes rang out loudly on the cobbles, but Stephen knew how hard it was to pinpoint sound in fog. Another few yards and they found steps leading down into a front base-ment. Down they went, stepping as softly as they could, and then they crouched and listened. A faint glow fell from the window above and Stephen saw the dark gleam of a Webley revolver as Dalton pulled it out from under his overcoat. A service pistol – he had one just like it. They waited, both of them holding their breath, and Stephen could feel his heart thumping inside his chest. Then they heard the footfalls again, but louder now as they hurried. As they came across the street, Stephen frowned. There was something odd about them – a very uneven, lurching tread. But then they stopped with a scuff and the flap of an overcoat, followed by an exasperated whisper.

'Bollocks!'

Dalton had pulled the scarf down and his teeth gleamed as he grinned. The footsteps receded, again with the uneven tread, like a limp, and Stephen glanced at Dalton as they straightened up. Maybe he wasn't watching him as much as watching out for him.

'So, they're watching us,' he whispered.

'Of course they are.' Dalton shrugged as he holstered his pistol and they climbed back up into the foggy Street. 'You don't think they'd let a bunch of Irish terrorists run around London without keeping an eye on them, do you?'

PROCEEDINGS OF
THE LONDON MATHEMATICAL SOCIETY

SOME PROBLEMS ON THE DERIVATION OF HOMOLOGOUS LORENTZ TRANSFORMATIONS FROM THE THEORY OF SPECIAL RELATIVITY

By J. G. KEACH,
Trinity College,
DUBLIN

15 Cadogan Gardens,
London W

17 October 1921

My dearest Lillie,

I can't believe it! I absolutely cannot believe the man has such a barefaced cheek! A whole day has passed since I got your letter and I'm still fuming about it. I'm not the least bit surprised that he is skulking over here and keeping well out of your way. It is probably as well that I don't have his London address as I would be around there like a shot and you would probably end up reading about it in the newspapers! But it is no matter. With any luck he will be at the Mathematical Society on Friday, and we can both tell him what we think of his tricks!

I'm sure that you will have already spoken to the Provost by the time you get this – although I think you did right to speak to Professor Barrett first. He may be retired, but I know he will do everything he can to help. For my own part, I went over to Burlington House this afternoon to see if there was somebody I could speak to about it. There wasn't, as it happened, but I dashed off a note explaining the situation and left it for the attention of the President of the Society. Then, as I was on my way out, I happened to bump into Jacobson, whom you will remember from the seminar we gave at Cambridge last year. He was shocked when I showed him the paper in the Proceedings – your paper, even if it has Keach's name on it – but said he wasn't especially surprised. It turns out he was up at Cambridge with Keach and has a rather low opinion of him. Unfortunately, Jacobson was in a hurry, so I couldn't get as much out of him as I would have liked, but he has invited me to dine at his club tomorrow evening and I hope to learn more then.

As to you cancelling your trip, please put that thought far from your mind. Even if the Mathematical Society had burned to the ground you should still come because I have been looking forward to it for so long and I doubt I could last another week without seeing you. Arrangements have already been made, my dear! Besides, I know you wouldn't like to leave me in the *lurch. A lot of the other men are going away for the weekend and, while Billy is excellent company, I fear that after four weeks sharing the same small room he and I are running out of things to say to each other.*

To tell the truth, I think a weekend off would be a good idea for everybody because things are very tense at the moment. It's not that any new problem has arisen – it's the same old problem or, rather, two of them: Ulster and the Crown. I'm afraid that the negotiations only seemed to go well at the start because there were lots of little problems to be solved. Since these were all easily sorted out it looked like we were making progress and everybody was happy. Unfortunately, all we were doing was clearing the sand and pebbles away from those two great rocks. Everybody agrees an independent Ireland is a fine idea, but what about the Ulstermen who don't want to break the union with Britain, and how independent can Ireland be if the English insist we must swear allegiance to their King?

To avoid these thorny questions, everybody seems to be clinging to the last few simple ones – or inventing new questions to keep us all talking. Collins's questions are all to do with submarines. God knows why, but the man is obsessed with them. Last night even yours truly was called in to give his opinion of the military value of submarines – despite the fact that I've never actually seen one! Poor Billy, who has proved himself a very able negotiator and who, even as I write, is trying to work out an acceptable oath of allegiance, is being driven around the bend by all this talk of submarines.

Of course, if Collins really wants to know about submarines, he only needs to ask Erskine Childers, whose expertise in naval matters you can probably appreciate better than I. Unfortunately, that will never happen since there is a split in the delegation that grows worse as we come closer and closer to those two questions. On one side there is Collins, Griffith and Eamon Duggan. On the other stands Barton and Gavan-Duffy, as well as Childers and Chartres, the two secretaries. Exactly what is the difference between them is harder to define. My sense of it is that the Collins and Griffith camp are more conciliatory and more willing to compromise while the others always stick to the hard line.

But for the time being they at least remain civil to each other. They are all good men who are devoted to their cause and I only wish I was able to do more to help them. They are immensely likeable, too. Collins can be a real hoot when the humour takes him, and even Childers, who appears very frosty at first glance, is really charming when you get to know him. Perhaps you will meet him when you come over, as I understand he is one of the skeleton crew staying on for the weekend.

Well, I must be going now. Billy has just gone to bed and asks me to send his warmest regards. No doubt he will dream about his oath of allegiance (and possibly submarines!), but I know what I will be dreaming about. I can hardly wait until I see you on Friday and, until then, I remain,

Yours truly,

Stephen

The gas jet flared and flickered and set shadows leaning and bending against the whitewashed walls. Joe stared into the light, anticipating the darkness that would come when they turned off

87

the gas. Any moment now, he thought, and with one final surge the flame blazed brighter and then died with a gentle pop.

Bathed in darkness, he lay on his bunk with his hands clasped behind his head. He didn't mind it. The darkness was bigger than the four walls it filled. It stretched out through the window and across the city. It slid under the door and down the landing, falling through the gratings and oozing down the spiral stairs. But it held no dread for him now. He was armoured, he felt light inside himself. When he closed his eyes he saw the light and he smiled to himself in the darkness.

His lips moved as he recited to himself some of the words of the Mass. Latin from his childhood. He was surprised that he had remembered so much, that it had seemed so familiar to him. He hadn't even wanted to go; had slouched into the chapel, reluctant, wanting to sit at the back, out of sight. But Whelan had coaxed him. It had been Whelan's idea and he had wanted him up there, beside him. There were a few other men in the prison chapel, but they kept to themselves. Whelan had led Joe up to the front seat and Joe had sat while Whelan knelt and prayed. Joe wasn't sure what to do. He couldn't think of any prayers.

After a while, his mind had started to drift. There was something soothing about the chapel, the light of the candles, the smell of incense. Outside was the prison, with its lattice of landings and bars and wires but in here was calm and quiet. Even the figure on the cross looked serene in his suffering. Then the priest appeared and Joe frowned. In his robe and stole he looked out of place, too gaudy for the simplicity of chapel. But when he intoned *'Dominus vobiscum'*, the sonorous words seemed to fill the air and seal the chapel from the world outside. As the rest of the Mass followed, Joe felt himself drawn backwards to his childhood, to the time before all this. He felt like he could touch the peace and happiness and feel the heat of those endless summer days. He grew quite detached, letting the Latin wash over him, but not stirring from his seat. As Whelan and the others knelt and stood and went through all the motions, he stayed slumped on the pew, watching everything from a great distance.

When the Mass was over, he hardly wanted to leave, but he found everything was different outside. The long halls and landings looked less gloomy, the rattling keys and clanging gates didn't jar so much. Even the screws seemed harmless, almost friendly. Even the black door to the execution chamber, the thing that wrenched at Joe's heart every time he passed it by, was just another door.

He remembered Whelan looking worried as they walked back to their cells.

'Are you all right, Joe?' he asked as they parted.

'I'm fine, Pat.' Joe smiled and nodded goodnight before he stepped into his cell...

'Are you all right Joe?'

The voice started Joe awake. The darkness had faded and he could make out the familiar walls, the corner of the table, the dim glow of the window. Had he been asleep? Had he been dreaming? He remembered the comfort, the warmth he had felt. It couldn't have been a dream, could it?

'Are you praying, Joe?' Whelan's voice came again in a harsh whisper, but he sounded apologetic, afraid he had interrupted.

'No,' Joe answered quickly. Praying? How could he know?

'I heard you. I heard the words in Latin.'

Joe blushed in the darkness. 'I was only trying to remember the bits of the Mass, that's all.'

Silence. This time Joe felt it weighing on him. He could feel that Whelan wanted to talk but wouldn't disturb him if he thought he was praying.

'It was good, wasn't it, Pat?'

'Aye, it was good,' Whelan answered and Joe smiled to himself. The tone of the silence had changed. They were happy now, comfortable again. A few minutes later he heard a scraping sound and then the thump of something heavy being set on Whelan's table. He heard the scratch of a match and knew that Whelan was lighting a candle.

'Do you want to hear some music, Joe? Classical music. I got a new record today, a Beethoven sonata. I'll play it for you.'

Joe frowned. He knew Whelan had a portable gramophone player in there – a friendly screw had got it in for him. But they wouldn't like him playing it at night, not after lights out. They could take it off him for that.

'Ah Jesus, Pat. What do I know about classical music?'

'You'll like it, I'm telling you.'

'Yeah, but the screws won't.'

'Ah, don't mind the screws. Sure don't they say

90

that music soothes the savage beast?'

Joe didn't answer, but he listened. He heard the clicks and taps as Whelan set up the gramophone, then the whirring as he wound the handle. He heard the first scrape of the needle and almost held his breath as he waited for the music to start. When it came it was so low that he wasn't sure if he heard it at first. The sound of the piano barely filtered through the crackling, but it grew stronger. Deep notes came slow and seemed to sway back and forward through the darkness. Then top notes, clearer, tracing out a tune that was slow and sad and yet so sweet it warmed the air.

Joe closed his eyes and let himself drift back to the chapel. The light and the smells and the peaceful air. He still had a little part of it with him and he thought he always would. He could feel it in the music that connected him to Whelan and he wrapped himself in it and started to dream. In his mind he floated down the wing, past the empty cells, past the execution chamber. And the music was flowing with him, the notes trickling through the air. He imagined it was filling the prison, touching every man in his cell, and instead of the loneliness welling up through the darkness he felt hope, and he saw faces turned up to the stars floating in the free sky.

And then he slept.

V

They had taken a room for the weekend in the Regent Palace hotel on Piccadilly Circus. Wrapped in a dressing gown, her hair still damp from the bath, Lillian lay across the bed and studied the newspaper, kicking her bare legs up behind her. Stephen had taken his turn in the bath and she could see his head and shoulders shrouded in steam through the open door of the bathroom.

'So he didn't want to see you?' he said, laying his head back against the edge of the bath and wallowing in the heat.

'The Provost is a very busy man,' Lillian answered drily.

'But he did see you eventually.'

'Eventually, yes. Though I practically had to picket his office. You know, Stephen, I may be flattering myself, but I think that man is a little bit afraid of me.'

'He's not the only one,' Stephen muttered.

'What was that, dear?' Lillian asked, grinning behind the newspaper.

'I said I think I'm almost done.'

Lillian reached across and picked up Stephen's watch from the bedside locker.

'Well, don't stay in there all night, sweetheart. If we're going to confront the man, it would probably be best to be there before him.'

The water splashed and slopped as Stephen hauled himself up out of the bath and out of sight. A few minutes later he appeared again in the doorway with a towel wrapped around his waist.

'You know, we don't have to go if you don't want to.'

Lillian looked at him over the top of her spectacles, wondering if he knew how tempted she was. When she first saw her paper with Keach's name over it, her instinct had been to shy away. Fuss and bother, confrontation; the dread of it had overwhelmed her anger. That was when she had written to Stephen, suggesting that she cancel her trip. But that letter had hardly been sent before her anger reasserted itself. Her righteous anger. How dare he steal her work! And that's what it was – theft, pure and simple! Indignation had carried her all the way from Dublin, but now that she was here, now that the hour was almost upon her, the old fears were crowding back in. There was no certainty that Keach would even be there, but, deep down, she knew he would, and she knew there would be a row. Fuss and bother. That was how it was bound to end, and she wanted none of it.

She shook her head. 'I've come this far, Stephen. I might as well see it through to the bitter end.'

'You don't sound very convinced.' Stephen walked out of the bathroom and sat beside her on the bed. He put his hand on her shoulder, feeling the warmth of her skin through the silk of the dressing gown. 'Are you sure you want to go through with it?'

'I've got to, sweetheart,' she said, and laid her

head against his arm. She had always been shy and she dreaded the mere thought of a public confrontation, but she knew she had no choice. 'If I don't show up to read my own paper then everybody will assume it's really his. But it's my paper and I *shall* read it, and let the heavens fall if they will.'

'That's my girl.' Stephen leaned down and kissed her forehead. 'You'd better get dressed, so.'

'And you'd better have a shave,' she warned, pushing herself up off the bed and giving him a shove back towards the bathroom. She started to dress slowly, watching with one eye as Stephen lathered his face and then started to shave in the mirror over the sink. She loved these little intimate things: the twist of his chin and the quick, sure motion of the razor.

'So what did he say?' Stephen asked, pausing to rinse the razor, one side of his neck now scraped clean.

'Who?'

'The Provost – when you finally got in to see him.'

'He said it was a very serious allegation, and one that was best not repeated until Mr Keach was in a position to defend himself.'

'In a position to defend himself?' Stephen asked incredulously. 'He was the one who bloody ran away!'

'I don't expect I'll get much support from Dr Bernard,' Lillian said, pausing in fastening a stocking. 'I don't expect I'll get much support from anybody except you and Professor Barrett. It's depressing, really.' She sat down on the stool at the

94

dressing table and folded her hands in her lap. She felt weary just at the thought of it. All this fighting, all this pushing, and for what? After ten years, all she'd managed to do was make them accept her. That was all. They still didn't *want* her there; she hadn't won them over. 'You know, sometimes I think it's not worth it. Sometimes I'm tempted just to give in.'

'Maybe you should,' Stephen suggested, though he was grinning at her in the mirror. 'At least then we could get married.'

'Oh, Stephen, please. Not this again.'

'Well, it's true.' He came out of the bathroom again, wiping off the last few traces of shaving soap with a small towel. 'Everything would be much simpler. There would be no need for Mr and Mrs Birkin, for one thing.'

Lillian held up her hand. 'I'll not hear a word against Mr and Mrs Birkin, Stephen. They've been perfectly good to us.'

'Well, you know what I mean.' Stephen sat down on the edge of the bed again. Although the Birkins were a real couple, and Mr Birkin was in fact a junior fellow of Emmanuel College in Cambridge, they were also a useful fiction. As far as Lillian's mother and aunt were concerned she was staying with the Birkins at their London flat. As far as Billy and all the others in Cadogan Gardens were concerned, it was Stephen who was staying with them, while Lillian stayed with her aunt in Holland Park. Meanwhile, they had signed the hotel register as Mr and Mrs Bryce, newlyweds from Dublin. It was all horribly complicated. 'Everything *would* be much simpler if we were married.'

'*Some* things would be much simpler,' she corrected, standing up and smoothing her chemise. 'I know it's a slim chance anyway, but they'll never make me a fellow if I'm a married woman.'

'And what if they find us out?' he asked, stretching an arm around her waist and pulling her down on to his knee. 'You might as well get married then, because they'll never make you one if they find out you're *pretending* to be a married woman.'

'Who's pretending?' She kissed him and felt his arms closing around her. Her lips brushed his cheek as she leaned and whispered in his ear, 'And who's going to tell them? There'll be no fellowship for *you* if they find out you've been fornicating.'

'Fornicating?' His breath blew hot against her shoulder as he chuckled. Then he kissed her in the hollow of her neck, her throat, moving higher and higher as he lay back on the bed, pulling her down with him. 'Now that's a very strange word coming from a genteel young lady. But, you know, I might confess anyway – just so we can be legal.'

'You'd do that for me, would you? You'd give it all up?'

'I could be tempted.'

'Well, then,' she whispered, kissing him, feeling his hands on her back, her waist, sliding the chemise up over her ribs. 'I wonder what it will take to keep you quiet?'

Billy sat at the bar and looked at the lights reflected in his glass. Now and again he raised his head and looked at himself reflected in the mirror behind the bar. He thought he looked about as

96

bored as he felt, sitting slumped over his third brandy, wondering if he should have a fourth or just go back to Cadogan Gardens for an early night. London was a fine city, but it was no place to be on your own.

'Got a light?'

Billy started to pat his pockets almost before he looked at the young man who had stepped up beside him. The cigarette caught his attention first; it was expensive-looking, with a gold band around the end. The speaker held it lightly between long, well-manicured fingers. Billy didn't smoke very often, but he'd had a cigar after dinner and the matchbox rattled in his trouser pocket. He had to slide half off his stool to get it out and he looked the young man up and down as he did so. Tall, slim, rather thin in the wrists but with a strong face. He had blue eyes and a blond moustache with strands of ginger sprinkled through it.

'Thanks very much,' he said as Billy handed him the matches. He put the cigarette between his lips, slipped out a match and rasped it into life, all in one smooth movement. Lighting the cigarette inside his cupped hands, he shook out the match, dropped it in an ashtray and twirled the box through his fingers, handing it back to Billy with something like a magician's flourish.

'Would you like one?' he asked, nodding to the cigarette as he held it vertically over the bar and exhaled twin streams of smoke through his nostrils.

'Oh, no thanks,' Billy shook his head, but he left the matchbox lying on top of the bar, 'I'm not really a cigarette man.'

A quick dip in his pocket and a silver cigarette case appeared and sprung open in his palm.

'Go on, try one. They're good. Turkish, you know.'

Billy had already gathered as much from the pungent aroma of the smoke. The smell was so sweet and exotic that he'd started to regret his initial refusal. He wasn't going to do it again.

'Don't mind if I do.' He got the cigarette to his lips and started to reach for the matches, but they were gone in a flash. Another scratch and a flare and the young man was lighting his cigarette, smiling at him around his own. A faint aroma of cologne drifted up from his cuffs.

'The name's Lionel, by the way. Lionel Manning.'

Billy introduced himself and they shook hands. Manning eased his weight on to the next stool and nodded to the barman.

'Get you a drink?' he asked and, before Billy could refuse, he nodded to the barman. 'Two brandies, please. Keep the cold out, eh?'

Billy's eyes narrowed and he cocked his head a little to one side. His new companion had an English accent, but Billy thought he could detect a touch of Irish brogue underneath. This was confirmed when the brandies arrived.

'You're Irish, aren't you?' Manning asked, handing him the glass. 'Me too – well, sort of. My mum was from Galway.'

'Really?' Billy asked, shifting his seat a little so that he could face Manning and rest his elbow on the bar. 'I'm from Galway. Well, originally anyway. Between boarding school and working in Dublin I haven't spent much time there since I was a boy.'

'Dublin, eh?' Manning's eyes narrowed as he exhaled another stream of aromatic smoke. 'So what brings you to dreary old London, then?'

Billy had anticipated this question – if not from Manning then from somebody else – and he had prepared an answer that he thought was simpler and safer than the truth.

'Business. I'm in the law, you see, and I've taken on a case in Dublin for the Prudential. So, I'm here to gather documents, statements, that sort of thing.' A pause before he leaned closer to Manning and sealed it with a wink. 'It's all terribly boring, to be honest.'

'I'll bet it is.' Manning hooked his elbow on the bar and twisted himself nearer to Billy, dropping his voice closer to a whisper. 'So you've got nothing to do with these Treaty negotiations that are going on at the moment, have you?'

'Oh God, no. Politics? You must be joking! Two things I never have anything to do with: politics and women. Nothing but trouble, the pair of them.'

Manning threw his head back and gave a laugh that rattled the bottles behind the bar. Billy took a slow drag on his cigarette and savoured the sweet smoke, grinning and feeling rather pleased with himself. When he quietened down, Manning's face was red and merry, his blue eyes shining.

'You're a man after my own heart, Billy.' He raised his glass. 'Here's to us, eh?'

'Yes, here's to us.'

By the time they left the pub, Billy's mouth was

numb from brandy and cigarettes. His head felt light and his face glowed in the cold air outside. He wasn't sure of the time, but it was late. The streets were empty and a cold breeze was blowing down the Tottenham Court Road. Manning led the way. He said he had a flat just off Greek Street and Billy followed him quietly, only dimly aware that they were walking off the map of the London that he knew.

They came to a small square and skirted around the edge. Billy was aware of damp alleyways and dustbins, of the smell of greasy food, but he felt as if he was floating through them all. He knew he was drunk but he didn't mind. It was good, relaxing, and Manning was very nice. He wanted to take his hand, put his arm around him. He wanted to dance, to sing. He was tittering to himself, humming the bars of a tune.

'Here we are, my dear,' Manning said, opening a small green door with a key that he kept on his watch chain. Inside was a flight of steep, narrow stairs, barely seen in the meagre light that fell in from the street. Billy walked in and stumbled over the first step, feeling Manning's strong hand on his arm, steadying him.

'Careful,' Manning whispered, without letting go of his arm, and he pushed the door closed so that they were plunged into complete darkness. 'You'll wake the neighbours.'

This seemed like the funniest thing Billy had ever heard. He started to laugh and only laughed harder when he tried to stifle it. Soon Manning was at it too and the two of them laughed together in the dark until finally Billy had to pause for breath and he felt Manning's hands on his chest, pushing him back against the wall. Then he smelled his cologne and his hot breath, and the faint musty scent of Turkish cigarettes. Then the brush of his moustache and the wet of his lips searching in the dark until Billy opened his mouth and met them.

They hurried down Piccadilly with only five minutes to spare. Under the imposing arch of Burlington House and across the courtyard, hand in hand. They were leaving their coats just as a uniformed steward went around the lobby, ringing a tiny silver bell and asking the gentlemen to please make their way to the auditorium.

Lillian had regained some of her nerve on the short walk from the hotel but felt it deserting her when she recognized some of the eminent men moving in a slow procession up the broad staircase. That tall, imposing figure was Professor Littlewood, whom she knew – and the smaller man with him was surely his friend, Professor Hardy. And the older man coming up behind them – was that Professor Whitehead? The stars were certainly out tonight.

She took a deep breath and straightened her dress.

'How do I look?' she asked Stephen.

'Perfect. You're the most beautiful woman here.'

'Stephen, I'm the *only* woman here.'

'That doesn't make you any less beautiful.' He planted a kiss on her cheek as he handed her the folder that held her paper. 'Now stop fretting. Take my arm and let's go in and show them what

101

you're made of.'

'Hello! Excuse me!'

They both looked around at a small man who was hurrying down the stairs, dodging and wriggling against the steady stream going up. He wore glasses and a rather formal black suit and he looked very agitated.

'Excuse me, I do beg your pardon.' He broke clear of the last knot of men at the bottom of the stairs and came across to where Stephen and Lillian stood. 'Miss Bryce, I presume? And you must be Mr Ryan.' He hurriedly shook their hands. 'How do you do? My name is Herbert Richmond. I'm the President of the Society.'

Lillian and Stephen both bade him a good evening and said they were pleased to meet him. There then followed an uncomfortable silence, during which it became obvious that Mr Richmond had something he wanted very badly to say, but didn't quite know how to say it.

'I'm terribly sorry, Miss Bryce,' he got out eventually. 'I truly am, but I'm afraid we won't be able to hear you read your paper to the Society tonight.'

Lillian's answer was calm but cold. She tightened her grip on the folder and glanced in Stephen's direction before she spoke.

'Why ever not, Mr Richmond? I've come all the way from Dublin to read this paper. You could at least have given me some notice.'

'Well, I was away,' Richmond said defensively. 'I was not aware of the problem until I saw Mr Ryan's note this afternoon, and by then–'

'Well, well, well,' a voice said from the bottom

of the stairs. It was Keach. The sound made
Richmond jump several inches in the air, before
he turned around sharply, clearly annoyed.

'I told you I would deal with this matter, Mr
Keach.'

'Let me be the judge of what you will and will
not deal with, Richmond.' Keach came over,
insouciant, one hand in his pocket. He looked
like a man who has just had a very good idea.
'You see, I've been reading Mr Ryan's note and
I've decided I find it rather offensive. In fact, I'm
sure it's downright libellous.'

'Now, now,' Richmond's voice almost squeaked
in his agitation. Stephen's eyes narrowed as he
remembered what Jacobson had told him about
Keach; how he had been involved in a scandal
when he was an undergraduate at Cambridge.
There had been whispers of a remarkable
similarity between his work and that of a fellow
student, allegations of cheating by one or other of
them. Keach had brought to bear the full weight
of his family's wealth and connections, had even
threatened legal action, and the other man, the
son of a not very prosperous dentist, had gone
down in disgrace. But, according to Jacobson, the
other man had been the brilliant one, whereas
Keach had always been a mediocre student.

'I believe I told the truth,' he said, feeling his
colour rising as Keach stopped in front of him.

'Did you, now?' Keach asked. 'Well, I trust you
have proof, because, if I'm not mistaken, your
note accuses me of stealing another person's
work. And that's a very serious charge, Mr Ryan
– particularly when you haven't got the slightest

shred of proof.'

'Here's your proof,' Lillian's eyes blazed as she brandished her folder. 'I have my original paper here.'

'Really? Is that your original paper, Miss Bryce, or did you copy my paper, which was printed for all to see in the last issue of the *Proceedings* of this society? What proof do *you* have, Miss Bryce, that yours is original? We are all mathematicians here.' He looked from Stephen to Richmond. 'I'm sure we all appreciate the importance of proof.'

Richmond's face darkened, but neither of them said anything. Stephen's mind was racing and it was dawning on him that Keach was right in what he said; they had no proof. The paper Lillian held in her hand was the only copy she had. It was handwritten and undated – and even if it had been dated, there was no way to prove that it had been written before Keach's paper had appeared in the Proceedings. Of course, both Stephen and Professor Barrett could vouch for her; they had read it, they knew it was her work. But Stephen was her fiancé and Barrett, eminent though he was, might be shown to have reason to resent Keach. Neither of them would be worth much if it came to court. Christ almighty!

Court. How he wished Billy Standing were here now.

He looked at Lillian, whose face was pale with fury.

'Mr Keach,' she began, but Stephen cut her off.

'Be quiet, Lillian.'

Keach's eyes flashed and he grinned wolfishly. He knew he had them on the back foot.

'Well said, Mr Ryan. You would do well to keep her on a short leash – unless you want to add her slander to your libel.'

Stephen's hands curled into fists. He had the urge to do violence, to grab Keach by the throat and punch him as hard as he could. But then he felt Lillian's hand on his arm, gently pushing it down. He glared at Keach, giving him a look of pure hatred.

'You should watch your mouth, Keach.'

'Me? I'm not the one who's committed a gross libel.'

'Now, now,' Richmond cut in at last, as if he had suddenly woken up. 'Surely *libel* is a very strong word to be bandying about. Perhaps we can view the issue as more of a misunderstanding. Is there not some way that we can reach an agreement, some solution that can be found? Surely there is no need for all this acrimony.'

'Very well, I'll settle for an apology,' Keach said quickly, drawing himself up and making it sound as though he were making a sacrifice. 'An apology here and now, in front of the meeting tonight, or else printed in the proceedings. I don't mind which.'

Of course you bloody don't, Stephen thought, because they were both equally damning. The auditorium had just filled up with half the eminent mathematicians in the country and the half that wasn't there would hear about it as soon as they got back to their universities and institutions. To stand in front of them and apologize for calling another mathematician a cheat would be just as bad as printing the damn thing in the proceedings.

Still, he was tempted. An apology here and now would be less durable; it would pass into memory along with all the other spats and disagreements that the society had seen. It would be embarrassing, but it would spare him a court case and it would free him to sort Keach out on his own terms. And he *would* sort him out, because he knew what he was now, he knew him for a cheat and a bully. He knew Keach was enjoying this; he could see the simpering smile and the amused look in his eyes.

'All right,' Stephen said. 'I'll do it here.'

'Over my dead body,' Lillian said, giving him a furious look. 'You are not going to apologize for telling the truth, Stephen, and I don't care whose blushes you are trying to save. You have done no wrong and I'll not let you make a liar of yourself on my behalf.'

'Well, well.' Keach's smile broke into a grin, which faded as Lillian rounded on him.

'And as for you, Mr Keach, I trust what I said was clear enough for you, but if it wasn't, let me put it more plainly. You are a cheat and a liar and I will see you exposed as both. If you think that's a slanderous statement, then please feel free to sue me alongside my fiancé. I'd sooner stand with him in the dock than watch him apologize to a snivelling charlatan like you.' She nodded to Richmond, who flinched. 'Now, I believe we'll bid you goodnight, gentlemen.'

Stephen sat with his face turned up to the watery sun but he could get no warmth from it. His eyes were closed but they still felt gritty and tired. He

106

had not slept well and the morning had been a dismal drag. In the end, they had drifted into Hyde Park and fetched up against the water. Neither of them wanted to be here, but neither of them knew where else they wanted to be. Last night still hung over them; anger and irritability. This was not what either of them had planned. This was not it at all.

Even with his eyes closed, he was acutely aware of his surroundings. He could smell the weedy water and hear the biting breeze blowing through the bare branches of the trees. He knew Lillian was standing a few yards away, looking out over the lake, and he was aware of the distance between them. They had gone straight back to the hotel last night and sat in frosty silence for a good twenty minutes before Stephen stood up and said they should go out somewhere, it was still early and anything was better than just sitting here, moping. But Lillian said no. She didn't want to go out, she couldn't. He sat down again. More silence. Then he stood up and said he was going out anyway and she said fine, so he went downstairs and sat in the bar for two hours, hardly touching his drink.

By the time he got back to the room, Lillian had gone to bed. He undressed quietly in the dark and climbed in beside her. She was asleep, or pretending to be, and he lay for a while in the dark wanting so badly to touch her but afraid of ... of what? Of rejection? Of a row? A grey glow filtered up from Piccadilly Circus, bringing with it the distant rumble of motor cars and the honking of horns. In the dim light he could see her back turned to him, stiff and unyielding. Her head bowed on the pillow and her shoulder turned as she held her arms to herself. She looked wounded. He thought then of Keach and how much he hated him. He had killed men for less.

Sleep was slow in coming, but it felt like the dream started instantly. Ypres again, the mud and the rain. The horse lay dying as it had before, but this time he was afraid to go near it. It radiated dread and anger and when it lifted its head to look at him it had a human face, dreadfully disfigured and half shot away. Then it rose up, pushing itself on to splayed legs and rocking forward, then back, until it stood dripping mud and blood and staring at him. An old warhorse so badly broken it shouldn't have been able to stand. Its guts lay on the ground between its feet, still steaming and tied to the beast by the translucent grey tube of an intestine, and skin hung from its bones in gory strips. The wounded face gaped obscenely – he could see teeth and bone and brains – but still it snorted yellow breath like mustard gas. Then it started to come towards him. Walk, trot, canter, gallop. Each followed the other in a smooth acceleration, until the beast was bearing down on him with unstoppable force, its iron-shod hooves drumming the muddy earth and he could feel its weight on him, its breath–

He woke and sat up in the same movement. He must have shouted because Lillian was up, too, holding him, hushing him, pressing him back against the pillows. As he subsided, he managed to catch his breath and felt the fear flowing out of him under the soothing warmth of her touch. She snuggled beside him, resting her head on his shoulder, and he pushed his face into her hair, breathing in the scent, feeling the safety.

He'd slept then, but lightly, uneasily, still fearful. The nightmare faded, but it was still there, still lurking in some dark corner of his mind. In the morning they went out, unsure of themselves, suddenly feeling alien and alone in the city. They walked to the National Gallery, up the broad steps and through the chain of high, airy rooms. Suddenly he found himself looking at Whistlejacket, Stubbs's prancing horse. Life-size and lifelike, he thought he could see the muscles and sinews under the chestnut flank, the white gleam of ribs inside the barrel chest. Even the white of the eye, staring at him... It put the willies right up him and he stood rooted before the picture, feeling his guts dropping inside him and his legs going weak. The whole room went dark and he felt like he was falling through it. His balance went, and he would have fallen too, only Lillian had caught his arm and helped him outside. By the time they reached the fresh air his hands were shaking and he was in a muck sweat.

It was a while since he'd had a turn as bad as that. He could still feel it on him, but the cold air was blowing it away. He heard footsteps approaching but he didn't open his eyes. The grind and squeak of a perambulator and the footsteps passed, and then he felt Lillian sitting down beside him, shaking his arm.

'Stephen, did you see who that was?'

'Who?' He blinked as he opened his eyes.

'The nanny. She just walked past.'

The woman with the perambulator was still just

in view. Even from behind, Stephen could tell she was a nanny with her uniform coat and brown hat. He followed her around the curve of the lake for a few moments, but shook his head.

'It's Mary D'Arcy,' Lillian said, barely containing a giggle.

'It is not,' he said, but he looked again. The nanny was about the right size, but with her long coat and hat it was impossible to tell her age or what she looked like. Her hair was tied up in the regulation bun and she walked with a slow and steady gait dictated by the heavy perambulator. 'It can't be.'

'It is so, I'm telling you. She looked right at me – and she recognized me. She looked like she'd seen a ghost.'

'Good grief.' Stephen couldn't resist another look. The Mary D'Arcy he remembered had been beautiful and very well off. Her father had been one of the richest men in Dublin and she had been engaged to Alfred Devereux, whose family were wealthy landowners. But then Devereux had gone off to the war and had been badly wounded – now *there* was a night Stephen would never forget – and Mary had dropped him for another man, an older officer with an unsavoury reputation.

'I heard her father lost everything after the war,' Lillian observed.

'He must have.' Stephen gave her a knowing smile. 'Did you ever think you'd see Mary D'Arcy working for a living?'

They sat together and watched as the nanny climbed slowly up towards the terrace of the

110

Italian Gardens. Stephen hoped she would cross the terrace and turn down the other side of the narrow lake – so he at least might see her face.

'I wonder what ever happened to poor old Devereux?' he asked, thinking out loud. Even though they had once served together, he hadn't seen him in years. Devereux's wound had been bad; a shell splinter to the head. It had left him unable to walk, talk or even feed himself.

'He lives in the country. They have a big house somewhere,' Lillian said and when Stephen gave her a quizzical look, she explained, 'I met his sister last year. She was up in Dublin for some shopping.'

'It's probably better for him down there. Peaceful,' Stephen said, and they watched as the nanny turned across the terrace and passed behind the jumble of statues and fountains. He had a glimpse of her face, but only for a moment, and at this angle it was still hard to tell.

'It's not her,' he said in a bantering tone.

'Sweetheart, I was at school with the girl. I should think I'd know her when I saw her.'

'You're having me on,' he said, but when he glanced again at the terrace, he saw something that made his heart turn cold. A slight figure was standing on the terrace, wearing a grey overcoat and a black homburg. Even though he couldn't make out the nanny's face as she passed behind him, he could see this man's because he was staring straight at him. Narrow features and sharp eyes – but it was more the shape of him that was familiar. Stephen was sure it was him, and would have been sure even if he hadn't limped forward a

111

few paces and pushed his hat up, tipping the brim with his finger.

'We have to go,' Stephen said, jumping up suddenly.

'Go? Go where?' Lillian stood up as well, taking his arm again. The abrupt change of mood had alarmed her. Was this another one of his turns?

'That man is following us,' he nodded towards the terrace as he started to lead her away, 'we have to get out of here.'

'Who?' Lillian craned her head around. 'Him? But he's been following us for ages.'

'What?' Stephen was striding along the path, pulling Lillian along by the arm. 'Since when?'

'Since this morning. I saw him just after we left the hotel, and then again at the gallery. Why? What—'

'Why the bloody hell didn't you say something?' he demanded through gritted teeth, and regretted it in the same instant. Lillian wriggled out of his grip and stopped dead, planting her hands on her hips.

'I didn't say anything because you were clearly unwell. And, besides, I thought he was only one of those Special Branch men you told me about. Now, I'm sorry, Stephen, but I'm not going one step further until you tell me who that man is and why you seem to be so frightened of him.'

Stephen could see the terrace behind her and it was empty – even the nanny had moved out of sight.

'I'm not frightened of him,' he said automatically, sullenly. Nevertheless, it was true; he wasn't afraid of Garvey for his own sake. It was Lillian he was worried about. 'And he's not Special Branch, either – far from it. His name is Vincent Garvey and he's a very dangerous man who has a grudge against me.' He put out one arm, pointing along the path. 'Now, if I tell you what I know, will you walk with me?'

When they got back to the hotel, they packed their things in silence and then Stephen looked at his watch. It was three o'clock, so they had a little time in hand if they were to catch the night train to Holyhead.

'We'd better go back to Cadogan Gardens, first,' he said. 'I should tell somebody where I'm going.'

Lillian snapped shut her Gladstone bag and then sat down on the edge of the bed. 'Stephen, are you sure you're not being a bit hasty? I mean, he probably doesn't even know where we are, and–'

'Lillie, sweetheart, I told you, he's dangerous,' Stephen said, going to the window and looking down into the bustling street. He had told her that Garvey was an informer and that he had been banished from Ireland by the IRA. He had left out the fact that he was a murderer, that he had killed at least one woman and that he had come damn close to killing Stephen's brother as well.

'Well, he doesn't *look* dangerous,' Lillian said, but she stood up and took her bag from the bed. She knew Stephen probably wasn't telling her the whole truth, but this only made her more certain that it was best to do as he wanted. He wasn't easily rattled, and if he was this disturbed by the sight of that ridiculous little man in the park then there must be something to it.

Stephen came around and picked up his valise. 'It's for the best,' he said, and kissed her before opening the door.

They took another taxi to Cadogan Gardens, with Stephen fidgeting and peering out the back window every few seconds. He was sure Garvey had been watching him for a while – but was he watching only him, or the whole delegation? Was there something else going on, something larger? He didn't know, and part of him didn't care. If Garvey was involved, it was dangerous, and he wasn't having Lillian in the middle of it.

'Well, this looks nice,' Lillian said, as the cab pulled up in front of the house in Cadogan Gardens.

'I'm sorry we can't stay long,' Stephen said and, telling the driver to wait, he ran up the steps and opened the front door, ushering Lillian into the living room. The house was dark and empty – almost everybody had taken the weekend off and wouldn't be back until Sunday evening. But as he ran up the stairs to his room he met Dalton coming down, a relieved smile on his face.

'Thank Christ you're here,' Dalton said. 'It's bloody typical! War breaks out and nobody's home.'

'I can't stay,' Stephen twisted past him on the stairs, 'I've got to go to Dublin.'

'Dublin? But you can't go now – you're needed here. All hell's breaking loose.'

'What? Why?' Stephen stopped, dumbfounded, with one hand on the banister. In all the weeks he'd been here, he'd never been needed for anything. 'What happened?'

'The German police have arrested a ship full of arms which they claim was heading to Ireland, and which the British are claiming is a flagrant breach of the truce. As well as that, the cops in Wales have discovered what they claim is an IRA bomb-making factory and, to top it all off, there's some sort of bloody stupidity going on about telegrams to the Pope. I'm sorry, Stephen, but you're not going anywhere. There's an emergency meeting up in Hans Place in an hour and after that you'd better get in touch with your friend Cope.'

'Christ almighty,' Stephen muttered, and he looked down into the hall. The living-room door was open and Lillian was sitting just inside. 'Come up here and I'll tell you what happened.'

Dalton followed him to the landing, where Stephen told him about seeing Garvey in the park, and how he'd been following them all morning.

'I know Vincent Garvey,' Dalton said darkly. 'He's a vicious little bastard – and he's got an axe to grind with both you and your brother.' He looked down the stairs and thought for a moment. 'You're right, it's probably best to get her out of his way, but I can't let you go with her. I'm sorry, Stephen, I just can't.'

'Look, Emmet, I'm here voluntarily. I can–'

'I don't like it any more than you do, Stephen, but this is exactly what you came here for. You can't go home now. Anyway, I think I know what to do. Erskine Childers was here not ten minutes ago to collect some papers. He's going back to Dublin tonight to brief the Cabinet about what's happened. Why not send her with him? If you hurry, you can catch him at Euston and be back at Hans Place for the meeting. You can trust Childers – you know what he's like. He'd stop a bullet before he'd let any harm come to her.'

Stephen knew he was right. He didn't like it, but he nodded and then brought Dalton downstairs and introduced him to Lillian. She was pleased to meet him, but taken aback to have to bid him goodbye almost in the same breath, and even more so when Stephen told her about the change of plan. By then they were back in the taxi, which was hurrying to Euston Station.

'Well,' she said drily, 'I must admit, you certainly know how to show a girl a good time.'

'I'm sorry, Lillie. I know it hasn't–'

'No, Stephen, that wasn't fair of me.' She reached up and kissed his cheek. '*I'm* sorry. I know it's not your fault. Anyway, it will almost be worth it if I'm to go home with Erskine Childers. I absolutely loved *The Riddle of the Sands* – my father used to read it to me when I was a little girl. Do you know it?'

Stephen nodded. He'd not read it when he was younger, but when he had met Childers in the flesh a few weeks ago he'd been intrigued enough to go to Hatchards and buy a copy.

'He's a remarkable man, you'll like him,' he said, but in a distracted way, staring out the window. She took his hand and squeezed it.

'Is it very bad, Stephen?'

'It must be pretty bad if they need me to stay,' he admitted.

'Well, there is one good thing; with all this hullabaloo I've managed to forget all about Mr Keach.'

'I haven't.'

Another squeeze of his hand. 'You must talk to Billy about it at the first opportunity. He'll soon put a stop to his gallop.'

'I will, of course.' He nodded slowly and gave her a knowing look. 'But I have other plans, as well. I think I have an idea how to take Mr Keach down a peg or two.'

He just had time to explain his idea before they reached Euston. By then the weather had started to turn; rain speckled the windows of the taxi and they had to dash through a gusting wet breeze to reach the shelter of the station. It was more crowded than Stephen would have liked, but the platform for the Dublin boat train was almost empty, and he quickly spotted the slight figure of Childers walking down the length of the train, a briefcase in his hand and an overcoat folded over his arm. They dashed past the guard and were all but running to catch him up when he turned at the sound of hurrying steps.

'Stephen,' he began, surprised, and Stephen hastily introduced Lillian, who gave him a breathless how-do-you-do. Then Stephen explained in a whisper what they wanted, and Childers's craggy face hardened, his thick brows knitting together and his eyes growing flinty. With his stiffness and his very English manners, Stephen always found it difficult to gauge his humour, and he was relieved when Childers's face cleared and he smiled at Lillian. It wasn't the warmest of smiles, but it was a smile nonetheless.

'Of course. It will be my pleasure, Miss Bryce.' He looked significantly from her to Stephen. 'I'll wait for you on the train, shall I? May I take your bag?'

Childers took the bag and climbed up into the carriage. Lillian waited until he was through the door before she gave Stephen an anxious look.

'He seems a bit ... stern, don't you think?'

'He's always like that at first. But he'll warm up, don't you worry. And he's a good man, he'll keep you safe.'

'I'm not worried about myself, Stephen. You're staying here. Promise me you'll be careful.'

'Of course–' He broke off as the guard's whistle shrilled and doors started to slam shut along the train. The engine let out a piercing shriek and a burst of steam. 'You'd best get on. Write to me the moment you get home.'

He gave her a hasty kiss, and helped her up into the carriage as the wheels ground and squeaked and the train started to inch along the platform. Stephen followed it until it started to pick up speed and then stopped and waved as she leaned out the window, waving back. Then the long train slowly curved out of sight and the last carriage rumbled past, leaving him aware of a great void where the train had been. He watched until the last carriage had snaked round the curve and then thrust his hands into his pockets and walked slowly back along the platform, lost in thought.

VI

Billy Standing sat at his desk and looked at the envelope in front of him with a mounting sense of dread. He knew what it contained because he had already opened it, read the letter and taken one sickening glance at the photograph that was clipped to the back. Then he'd hastily stuffed everything back into the envelope, mortified. His mind flashed back to Saturday morning, to the grubby flat in Soho. Grimy windows and a musty smell, as if the place had hardly been lived in. Manning snoring in the bed beside him. Guilt, regret. He'd crept out with his shoes in his hand, thinking it would be simpler ... and, by Christ, how bloody wrong he'd been!

He had hardly moved a muscle since then. He was afraid to even touch the envelope, but he knew he had to do *something*. Inside his head, he was growing frantic. Who had sent it? Manning, possibly, but he thought there was more to it than just Manning – if that was even his name. Somebody else had to have taken the picture. Worse still was who had seen it? The seal had been intact when he had opened the letter but that didn't mean anything. Everybody knew that the British read all the mail that came to this house. Billy had a vision of a locked room in a basement somewhere, a secret policeman with a steaming kettle having a good smirk before he passed it to his superiors.

This thought brought blind panic bubbling up again, and it was only with a great effort that Billy managed to control it. Slowly, gingerly, as if he were approaching a deadly spider, he made himself reach across, turn over the envelope and open it again. The letter was on a single sheet of cheap notepaper with the photograph attached by a wire paperclip. He carefully detached one from the other, trying not to look at the image as he slid it back into the envelope, and held the page up in his shaking hands. The letter was written in a round, uneven hand, in black ink:

Mr Standing,

There's plenty more where this one came from. If you don't want your friends to see them in the papers, then bring £200 to the Marble Arch at 3 p.m on Sunday. Come alone and don't be late.

A Friend

Reading it and rereading it didn't make it any better, but the letter wasn't the worst part. He was about to pull out the photograph again, when the door burst open and Stephen came in. Billy jumped about a foot out of his chair and automatically shoved the note underneath the envelope. Stephen was in his vest and trousers, with a towel draped around his shoulders and white dabs of shaving soap under his ears. He had something in his hand, too, an envelope. Billy's heart sank inside his chest.

'Morning, Billy,' Stephen said, dropping the envelope and his wash bag on to his bed and taking a clean shirt from the wardrobe. 'You were up early.'

And just as bloody well, Billy thought to himself. He'd got up early so he could go down to the study and prepare his notes for today's session at the Admiralty. When he was halfway down the stairs, the post had slithered through the letter-box and Mary, the young housemaid, came running out to fetch it.

'Here's one for you, Mr Standing,' she'd said, as he reached the bottom of the stairs, and Billy had taken it and slipped it into his pocket without a thought. But then some niggling doubt had made him take it out again as he stepped into the empty study. A letter? Who would send him a letter here in London? He'd opened it there and then, but less than a minute later he was back in the privacy of his own room, his hands shaking and his breath coming short.

Stephen was buttoning his shirt in the mirror on the back of the wardrobe door, but Billy, half-twisted in his chair, couldn't take his eyes off the envelope that lay on his bed.

'What's that you've got?' he asked in a strangled voice.

'It's a letter from Lillie,' Stephen answered cheerfully, pulling on a tie and starting to knot it. 'I asked her to write when she got home. I thought I'd read it over breakfast.'

Billy felt a tightness in his chest as Stephen came and looked out the window while he straightened his tie. He was whistling a faint, untidy little tune and peered out at the gauzy grey street, oblivious. Billy, rigid with fear, held his sweating hands over

121

the envelope. He knew he would have to show someone, he would have to say something. But Stephen? No, that was unthinkable. He couldn't let him see it. He couldn't.

But what else could he do? Where on earth was he going to find £200 by Sunday? Not that that would be the end of it. He'd seen a few blackmail cases in the courts and he knew the victims always paid up at first, only resorting to the law when the demands became more outrageous. How far was he prepared to go? One way or another, the truth would come out in the end – it was only a matter of time.

Yes, time; time was the thing. There wasn't just himself to think about, there were the Treaty talks, too. If this came out now, the scandal could bring the whole thing crashing down. The anti-Irish press would have a field day – as if things weren't already bad enough with all the shenanigans about arms shipments and bomb factories and telegrams. And then there were the bloody unionists: Puritans and Presbyterians, half of them, thundering fire and brimstone. God help him if they ever got hold of it… No, he would have to pay – he had no choice. The blackmailers might squeeze him until he burst, but if he could only string them along until the Treaty negotiations were over…

Billy cut that thought off before it was fully formed. He couldn't do it; it wasn't possible. Even the money … at a pinch, he might be able to scrounge up two hundred pounds, but after that… No. He couldn't bear it. The strain, the deception, he was no good for that sort of thing. He was bound to crack. His only hope was to get help from somewhere, but where? The circle of people whom he could trust – whom he dared to trust – was limited to precisely one man, and that one man had already pulled on his waistcoat and was combing his hair in the mirror on the wardrobe. In a few moments he would go down for breakfast and it would be too late. The day would have begun and Billy would have his own business to take care of. He still had to prepare for the meeting at the Admiralty, he still had to brief Collins and the others. And Stephen had been out a lot lately. He could be sent off somewhere and he might not see him again until late, or perhaps not even for days.

But still, Billy hesitated. He couldn't find the breath to say what he would have to say, never mind the words. Looking up with a sort of dread, he watched Stephen take his jacket from the hook and put it on.

'Are you coming down for breakfast, Billy?' Stephen asked, and Billy just shook his head mutely. He couldn't tell him. He couldn't. Even though Stephen knew what he was like, was the only one here who knew. He'd known for years. But knowing was one thing, seeing was another.

'Suit yourself,' Stephen said amiably, and opened the door.

'Stephen,' Billy said suddenly, and the word came out as more of a squeak than he would have liked. He cleared his throat and looked at his friend, who was standing with one hand on the door, a quizzical look on his face. Billy managed a wan smile, though his heart was hammering.

'Can you close the door, please? I need to talk

to you about something.'

Dear Stephen,

Well, here I am, safely home in Dublin. After all the excitement in London, our journey home was most uneventful. The only trouble we had was a rather choppy crossing from Holyhead, but since Mr Childers and I are both seasoned sailors I believe we found it rather less trying than the rest of the passengers.

Part of me wants to tease you for making much ado about nothing, but I know you only had my safety in mind, so I shall say thank you instead. In fact, I must say thank you again for sending me with Mr Childers – and please extend my thanks to him when you see him, as he said he would be heading straight back to London tonight. What a fascinating and charming man he is! I must admit, I was quite in awe of him at first, but once I told him how much I loved his book when I was little he warmed to me considerably. Which is not to say he is vain – Mr Childers is possibly the least vain man I have ever met – rather, it was a shared love of the sea that got us talking at first. From then on he seemed eager to talk and I suspect he was glad to have a travelling companion who was not of a political persuasion (or at least one who would keep her political opinions to herself).

I'm sorry to see that some of the problems that kept you in London appear to be gathering momentum. I

124

have not heard anything at all about that ship in
Hamburg, but everybody is talking about the bomb
factory in Cardiff. And as for that silly telegram to the
Pope! It seems like such a storm in a teacup to me, but
the papers are all full of it. And things seem to be
taking an even more sinister turn, too. People are
saying that the Government might lift the stay on
executions of some of the Republican prisoners as a
sort of tit for tat. I would not say that the city is in
uproar over it just yet, but people seem to be fearful. We
have all grown used to the peace these last few months,
and I think everybody is afraid that this could spell the
end of the truce. Certainly we are waiting with baited
breath to see what the British will do. I only hope that
you and your colleagues in London will be able to
stave off disaster!

And I'm sorry to say that that is not the end of all
my bad news. I'm afraid that Dr Dunbar has been
taken to hospital. Please, don't panic! It was all done
in a very orderly fashion. It seems the doctor was taken
poorly last night and asked his housekeeper to call a
taxi to take him to Mercer's Hospital. I know Patrick
Duns is just down the road, but he wasn't having any
of it and said some things about the doctors there that
don't bear repeating. (You can probably gather from
this that he is not yet at death's door.) Anyhow, the
head man at Mercer's is a friend of his – or at least
someone he trusts not to accidentally do him in – and
he told Mrs Brady that Dr Dunbar is in no danger for
the time being. Since I still have tomorrow off, I will
pop over to see him in the morning. I will also go and
see Professor Barrett tomorrow evening and tell him
about what happened with Keach, so my next letter
should contain news of both.

125

*Do give my regards to Billy and tell him I am sorry
I wasn't able to see him when I was over. I shall leave
it to your own imagination to explain why I had to
leave in such a hurry! Please also give my regards to
Mr Childers and all your other colleagues, and the
very best of luck in their work. To you I send my love
and my deepest wishes that you will come home soon.*

With fondest kisses,

Lillian

The fog was back on Wednesday morning; thick
and sulphurous and filling the streets like cotton
wool. But it was not solid. It shifted and rolled
and was pierced now and then by the sun, whose
yellow rays cast weird shadows and lit passing
shafts of clear air.

Stephen went into the park and sat on his usual
bench. He was early, but he needed a few minutes
to himself; he needed to think. Billy's sexual tastes,
his *inclination,* had been no secret to him, but it
was something they had never ever talked about.
The love that dare not speak its name, he thought. To
be confronted with it like this was unsettling, the
more so because he had never really considered
the physical aspect – though he supposed Billy
must have had the same carnal urges as anybody
else.

But what disturbed him most of all was the
meticulous planning that had clearly gone into
the blackmail. It was obvious that it had been no
accident; that Billy had not been merely unlucky,
he had been targeted. Stephen couldn't help

wondering if there was more at stake here than just two hundred pounds.

As he sat on the bench and thought, the fog played tricks on his eyes. Trees and bushes loomed up and then slowly disappeared, and the air itself seemed to tumble and scrape over the grass. It was like being enclosed by a curtain. He could see almost nothing, but every sound was amplified by the fog. The clop-clop-clop of horses' hooves on the street, the squeal and thump of a sash-window opening. The distant rumble of traffic in Sloane Square was soon broken by the steady cadence of a clanging church bell. Ten o'clock. Cope would be here any minute.

By then, he was considering Garvey. Was it a coincidence that he had shown up just as Billy was being blackmailed? Should he even tell Cope about him? But then he heard footsteps on the pavement outside. Familiar footsteps and the tap-tap of an umbrella on the flags. The park gate screeched open and a few moments later a giant shadow materialized in the fog, slowly shrinking down until the compact form of Cope appeared just a few feet away.

'Good morning,' he said, sitting down beside Stephen without any ceremony. This was their third meeting in as many days – between one thing and another they'd been having a very busy week.

'Good morning.'

Cope planted the tip of his umbrella between his feet and placed both hands on top of it. 'And how are things in the Sinn Fein camp this morning?'

'Not much calmer than they were yesterday

127

morning,' Stephen answered. 'Even Griffith is like a cat on hot bricks, and the hardliners are pushing to break off the negotiations and go back to Dublin.'

Cope hunched his shoulders and ground the umbrella deeper into the gravel. 'What did they bloody expect?' he asked. 'How can they claim to be honouring the truce when they're making bombs in our own backyard and trying to run guns in from Germany? Eh? And that's to say nothing of that bloody ridiculous telegram to the flaming Pope!'

Ridiculous it might have been, but this last part was the most serious issue of all. A simple message of encouragement from the Pope to the King had degenerated into a full-blown diplomatic row over whether the troubles in Ireland were the fault of the Irish and whether the Irish themselves were subjects of the King. Another telegram, this time from President de Valera, had explained to his holiness that neither was the case. Unfortunately, it had done so in language that even the more liberal-minded elements of the British press found offensive and an affront to their king. The whole episode would have been farcical had it not come so close to causing the Treaty negotiations to break down.

'Griffith said he didn't send that telegram.'

'I know he didn't,' Cope sighed, his irritation dying away.

'In fact, he said he'd bloody strangle de Valera.'

'He's not the only one.' Cope twisted the umbrella deeper into the gravel, shaking his head. 'Look, I'm sorry, but there are going to be sanctions. I've managed to put a lid on this arms shipment – it all happened in Germany, so we can plead ignorance – but the press has got these other things in their teeth and they're not letting go. The PM is under huge pressure to show that we mean business, and with this bloody unionist conference coming up he's got to let them know that we're not above boxing Sinn Fein around the ears if they step out of line.'

'What sort of sanctions?'

'I don't know yet. Something short and nasty, I'd imagine – show of force sort of thing. He's got to be careful because the truce has held up very well until now and he doesn't want to upset the apple cart. But he has to do something, and it won't be pretty – so I'm afraid you're going to have to get your lot warmed up to that fact.'

Stephen nodded uncertainly. 'I'll try, but I can't make any promises.'

'Which of us can?' Cope stood up to leave and Stephen looked up at him. Even in the fog, the strain was plain on his face. Bags under his eyes and a grim set to his jaw. 'I'll know more to-morrow. Same time suit you?'

'There's something else,' Stephen said, and then hesitated. He remembered the fear in Billy's eyes; the effort it had taken to convince him that Cope could be trusted. 'It's rather confidential. Something that might turn out to be a personal matter, but I suspect it's not.'

'Go on.' Cope nodded brusquely, and Stephen took the note from his inside pocket and handed it to him. He read it without so much as a blink, then folded it and handed it back. 'When they say

129

there's more where this comes from, what are they talking about?'

'Photographs.'

'How bad?'

Stephen shook his head. He'd seen only a corner before Billy snatched it away, tears streaming down his face. Later, after Billy had gone to work, he'd seen a grey curl of fresh ash in the bedroom fireplace. 'I don't know. I didn't see the one they sent, but it frightened the shite out of Billy. It's probably safe to say they won't do our cause any good if they appear in the papers.'

'You can say that again.' Cope sat down once more. 'The way things are just now the slightest whiff of scandal would blow us all out of the water. I mean, it's bad enough that Mr Collins insists on knocking around with Lady Lavery, but this–' He looked directly at Stephen. 'I take it your friend isn't of the marrying sort.'

Stephen inclined his head. 'I suppose that's one way of putting it.'

'Well, that's all we bloody need! You know how those unionists love their scripture. We'll be up to our eyes in Sodom and bloody Gomorrah before we know it. And it would be the end of the talks, for certain.'

'That's why I don't think it's a personal matter. There's more at stake here than just Billy's reputation.'

'You're right,' Cope said, after considering for a moment. 'And for that reason I'll do everything I can to sort it out. In the meantime, I suggest Mr Standing starts thinking about where he can find two hundred quid.'

'You think he should pay?'

'I think he may have to. If nothing else, it might buy us some time.' Cope stood up, clearly more agitated than when he'd come into the park. 'Anyhow, I'll see what I can do. Same time tomorrow?'

'Same time tomorrow,' Stephen agreed and, with a tip of his hat, Cope was gone.

He could hear them praying in Whelan's cell. Him and the priest together. He knew they would be kneeling on the floor, heads bowed, murmuring to God. That's why he couldn't make out the words except when they came to an end and both pronounced 'Amen'. And then on again until the next one. Amen, amen, amen. It was like they were counting off the last few minutes he had left.

Joe lay on his bunk and stared up at the ceiling. They had left the gas on tonight and the unaccustomed light was trying his nerves. He tried to sleep but every time he closed his eyes he found himself following the murmurs from next door, waiting for the pause and then mouthing the 'amen' along with them. When he opened his eyes the hissing of the gas light seemed to grow in volume, blotting out the prayers, so he closed them again and listened.

At some point, sleep must have crept up on him. He woke with a start, sitting right up. The gas was still hissing but there was a faint light at the window. The silence from next door frightened him. Had he missed it? Was Whelan gone? He was burning to talk to him, to have some sort of last contact with him. Then he heard a voice, but it wasn't Whelan's. It was the priest.

131

'Do you want me to hear your confession now, Pat?'

The stool scraped on the floor. In his mind's eye Joe saw the stole kissed, the sign of the cross and the bible clutched in one hand. Whelan would be kneeling and offering up his sins for absolution. Joe covered his ears. He didn't want to hear, he couldn't bear it. He knew there was one sin that wouldn't be absolved, because it wasn't Whelan's to take with him.

When he took his hands away there was silence from Whelan's cell, but he could hear another sound. Distant voices chanted something to a pause and then a single voice intoned a few words before the chanting went on again until a final emphatic 'amen'. He rolled off the bunk and climbed up to the window. The night sky had faded to the light grey of day but he could make out nothing other than the usual jumble of black rooftops. Then he heard it again, more clearly. It was coming from outside the front gate. A crowd had gathered to keep a vigil and dozens of voices were saying the rosary. No, hundreds, and they were growing louder and louder all the time.

Moments later, he heard the sound he dreaded: the rattle of keys in a lock and then the squeal and bang of the gate on the landing. The tramp of feet and the clink of keys. Then they stopped outside Whelan's cell. Joe hung with one hand on the window bars and listened. Their voices were muted, respectful. Another rattle of keys before the cell door opened and then the priest spoke up in a louder voice: 'Our Father, who art in heaven, hallowed be thy name—'

132

Joe jumped down and went to the door. He pressed his ear over the peephole and heard the rattle of chains. They were putting him in leg irons for the walk down to the chamber.

'Pat!' he shouted, and pounded the door with his fist. 'Pat! I'm sorry!'

'Stay easy in there,' a gruff voice responded.

'Don't worry, Joe,' Whelan called back. 'It's all right. Say a prayer for me, now.'

'I can't–' Joe began, but he broke off, choking. Tears were streaming down his face, wetting the door. 'I don't know any prayers.'

'Yes you do, Joe. Now take care of yourself and don't be worrying about me. I'm off to a better place.'

The chain rattled and a boot scraped and then footsteps passed his door, heavy and slow and with the clink of the chain in between. He wanted to say something else but he couldn't find the words, so he pounded the door until the landing gate clanged shut over the distant whistles and calls of the men on the other wings.

'Good man, Pat!'

'We're proud of you, Pat. You're a hero!'

'God save Ireland!'

Joe pushed himself away from the door and sat down heavily on his bunk. The shouts soon died down and a solemn silence pervaded the prison. The only sound was the swelling murmur of the vigil outside the gates, growing louder as the sky lightened. He wondered if Whelan could hear it. The chamber had only a few small windows and it was a big, echoing place. He had looked inside one day when they had left the door open. He'd got a glimpse of a stout timber frame and some steps in the shadows. They'd have the lights on now, and the hangman they'd brought over from England would be waiting.

All at once, the crowd outside the gates fell silent and the sudden stillness pierced him to the heart. Joe felt sick and giddy, hot and anxious. He put his face in his hands and started to rock back and forth, whispering something to himself, anything to break the silence. He knew what was happening, he knew, he knew. The walk up the steps and the prayers coming all the time. The hood and the rope, Christ almighty! He was nearly suffocating and he squeezed his eyes shut, squeezed and squeezed, but all he could see was the bedroom door that morning. White-painted wood and a shiny brass doorknob. Voices on the other side, a woman's laugh. It was just another peaceful Sunday morning – but here was he, prowling up the stairs with a gun in his hand.

He couldn't shake it. The silence was killing him. He lay over on the bunk and curled up in a ball, covering his head with his hands as if he could protect himself. He could see Bagely's wife sitting in the bed, the look on her face terrible and accusing at the same time. The noise of the shots was still in the room along with the stinging smoke. She had seen him, she'd looked right in his eyes. She must–

The bell in the Bon Secours convent across the road started to ring out a single steady, plaintive note. Joe froze. He knew what that meant, even before the praying started up again. It was done. The drop and the snap. His throat felt tight and silent tears streamed down his cheeks as he sat up, feeling wrung out and wretched. The sound of the vigil grew louder, rising with the sun that was edging up, sending orange light oozing in the window. After a minute the convent bell died away, but it was replaced by another sound; the distant clank of a tin cup on the stone floor. Then came another, ringing along in time, and another, and another – until the sound echoed up and down the wings and all around the circle. Joe joined in, stamping his feet at first and then banging his cup on the iron frame of the bunk. He banged and banged and banged until the cup was dented and bent and the twisted handle was cutting into his fingers. He banged long after everybody else had given up, but he couldn't beat away the silence from the cell next door.

Stephen was in Hyde Park again, only there was no water in sight today. He and Billy were sitting near Speaker's Corner, facing out on to Park Lane and with the Marble Arch visible to Stephen's left. It was further away than he would have liked and he had to admit that the blackmailers had chosen their spot well. The arch stood at the junction of three busy streets and was far enough from the park for it to be impossible to get any closer than this without standing out.

Stephen was watching everything, trying to see through the façade of Sunday afternoon in the park. So far, he'd noticed nothing out of the ordinary, just nannies and mothers pushing prams, young boys in short trousers and girls in pinafores. Courting couples floated by, holding hands and smiling to each other, and whole families together, fathers walking stiff and erect and nodding solemnly as they passed. Behind them, a small crowd had gathered to hear a speaker who was just getting into his thundering stride in the corner.

'Brothers and sisters, we are all SINNERS!'

'Oh for Christ's sake!' Billy muttered, twisting around to look. 'That's all we bloody need.' He shifted his gaze a little to glare at Stephen, 'What are you laughing at?'

'Well, if you think about what we're here for, it's pretty apt, isn't it?' He shook his head, laughing helplessly.

'Hellfire and eternal DAMNATION awaits us all!'

'Well, I'm glad one of us finds it funny,' Billy said angrily, turning away from the preacher and folding his arms. Nevertheless, Stephen was glad of the distraction. Billy had been under strain from the moment he got the letter, and it had been growing and growing on him with every passing day. When they'd finally left Cadogan Gardens he had been white-faced and silent, his eyes darting everywhere and a noticeable tremor in his hands. He had hardly said a word all the way over here and Stephen was wondering if he still had the bottle to go through with it. Well, he thought, he'd better go through with it now. Andy Cope had walked past a few minutes ago. He hadn't uttered a word or even looked in their direction, but that was the signal that all his men were in place. Stephen twisted his wrist a little and looked down at his watch. Ten to three. Another few minutes and it would all be over.

'Relax,' he said to Billy. 'There's plenty of time yet.'

Billy found it very hard to relax. He was as stiff as a board, crossing one leg over the other every minute or so. His mind was in a whirl and he was already sweating a little under his collar. He unfolded his arms and did his best to emulate Stephen's comfortable slouch, but it didn't come off and he sat up straight again. Relax? That was easy for him to bloody say.

'I wish they'd bloody hurry up,' he said, pulling out his pocket watch and flipping it open for the tenth time.

'REPENT! We must all repent now!'

'Stop looking at your watch,' Stephen said. 'And stop getting your drawers in a twist. We've talked about this. You know what you have to do.'

'I know, I know. I just can't stand this bloody waiting,' Billy sighed, and looked sideways at his friend. It was all right for him – he didn't have to do the deed. And he'd been in the army – he must be used to this, and much worse. But still, how could he be so bloody calm? It was unnatural.

'Have you got a gun?' he asked and Stephen turned his head and frowned at him.

'Where the hell would I get a gun?'

'I thought you still had your service revolver.'

'It's back in Dublin.'

Billy shifted uncomfortably again. 'Do you think they'll have guns?'

'I doubt it,' Stephen replied calmly, though he was pretty sure that the men they were meeting *would* be armed. Cope had managed to find out who was behind the blackmail, and he had con-

137

firmed Stephen's worst fears.

'It's a cabal,' Cope had said. 'Some of them used to work for Colonel Winter's intelligence operation in Dublin and some were Auxiliaries. All of them have a grudge against the IRA and want the war to continue so that they can have their revenge. They're nothing out of the ordinary, I suppose. Every time a war ends, you'll always get some johnnies who want to keep fighting. But this lot have a couple of rather interesting bedfellows. One is a man called Mercer who used to be fairly high up in Dublin Castle and who, shall we say, has reason to blame Mr Standing for his recent fall from grace. The other is a man called Garvey–' Cope broke off deliberately, watching Stephen closely, but he didn't betray any sign of recognition. 'I understand he may be known to you – or at least to your brother. He's ex-IRA, banished from Ireland after some pretty unsavoury business that seemed to have a lot to do with your brother.'

'I believe he was an informer,' Stephen said curtly.

'He was,' Cope said, without batting an eyelid. 'But I believe even Winter's mob were wary of him. My sources tell me he's a dangerous lunatic and you'd do well to keep him far from your friends and family.'

Far from his friends and family. Stephen reckoned he was right about that much, and he had no reason to suspect he was lying about the rest, either. Ex-intelligence men almost certainly would have guns and would not be slow about using them.

'They wouldn't dare shoot you with so many

people about,' he told Billy in a calming voice. But then he couldn't resist. 'Not until they get the money off you, anyway.'

'What a comfort you are, to be sure,' Billy said acidly, but there was a frightened squeak in his voice and Stephen felt a little bit ashamed of himself.

'For when that day comes, we will all be JUDGED!' shouted the preacher, his voice rising once more to a furious pitch. 'JUDGED, I tell you, and not one of us will escape.'

'What did you make of the writ?' Stephen asked, keen to keep Billy talking. Keach had made good on his threat and a writ for libel had arrived via his flat in Dublin, where Lillian had picked it up and sent it on. She had also enclosed a note explaining that she had not received a writ for her part in the affair. Stephen had a feeling that this had enraged her even more than if she *had* been sued.

'Well,' Billy composed himself for a few moments and seemed to shrug back into the persona of a lawyer with a case in hand, 'it's all pretty cut and dried, I'm afraid. You shouldn't have written that note – it really was very rash of you–' he felt the look Stephen gave him, and had the decency to blush. 'All right, all right. I know I'm the last person to lecture you on rashness, but you know what I mean. I'm sorry to say he's got you by the short and curlies.'

'And what about Lillian?'

'I checked. There's no mix up. She hasn't received a writ because he simply hasn't issued one. From what you told me, I'd say he's got her in just as tight a corner as you, but he seems to

139

be keeping his powder dry.'

'And why would he do that?'

'For several reasons. In the first place, slander is trickier to prosecute than a written libel. Things can be said in the heat of the moment and there can be provocation, and so forth. Then you must remember that Keach would hardly look very gallant taking a case against a woman who called him names. Finally, the threat of an action can often be of greater use than the action itself. Remember, Lillian works for him, so he might be of a mind to hold it over her head and use it against her on an ongoing basis. Better again, he can hold it over *your* head. He's going to try and administer punishment to you through the courts, and I imagine that if you start to cut up rough he'll threaten to drag Lillian in there as well.'

'Charming,' Stephen said, sneaking another glance at his watch. 'But the question is, what can we do about it?'

'Well, that's the tricky bit, isn't it? The trouble with libel is that the burden of proof is on the defendant. That means Keach doesn't have to prove anything to win his case. On the other hand, if you want to get out of it with a whole skin, you're going to have to prove that what you wrote in that note is the truth, the whole truth, and nothing but the truth.'

'And how the hell am I supposed to do that?'

'Best case? Prove that Lillie wrote that paper. Since we've already agreed that's impossible, the next best is to show that she's *capable* of writing it. Past work, exam results, peer witnesses like your chum Professor Barrett – that sort of thing. That medal she has from the college would go down a treat as well, make a jury wonder why such a clever girl would even want to pass somebody else's work off as her own – which is what Keach's claim amounts to. Meanwhile, we work on Keach from the other direction. You said he has a bit of a history of this sort of thing. What about that chap he had sent down from Cambridge?'

'He's dead,' Stephen answered. 'I checked up on him. Apparently, he joined up during the war and was killed at Arras.'

'Ah. Well, that's unfortunate. Still, our best bet would be to pick holes in Keach's record as a mathematician – or his lack of one. It'll be a bit of a battle, however, and I wouldn't–'

Billy broke off as a clock started to chime somewhere out on Park Lane. Three o'clock. Stephen stood up quickly, relieved at the interruption. Even talking about the case gave him the willies and he regretted his earlier dig at Billy. By the sound of it, he would need all the help he could get from that direction.

'We can talk about it later,' he said. 'Let's get your problem sorted out first. Remember what I told you – make sure you see the photographs before you show him the money, and don't forget the negatives. Don't let him bring you anywhere and don't lose sight of me. I'll be right here.' This was all exactly what Cope had told him to say, but he transmitted it with as much authority as he could muster.

'You're sure about this, Stephen?' Billy asked, getting up and brushing down his overcoat. 'You're sure this is for the best?'

141

Stephen nodded, but he was far from sure. He knew Cope had Special Branch on standby to raid the houses and flats of all those they knew were involved – but that wasn't to say there wasn't somebody they didn't know about, and that wasn't to say that they hadn't already made copies of the photographs. As Cope himself had said, it wasn't watertight – nothing could be guaranteed.

'It's the best we can do,' he said, and Billy gave him a grim smile and a nod. Then he turned and walked the short distance to the narrow gate that led out on to Park Lane. Stephen sat back down on the bench and watched him walk up the street and cross the road to the island where the arch stood. There was a smattering of applause from behind him, and when he turned he saw that the preacher had finally run out of fire and brimstone and the small crowd was starting to break up and drift away.

Billy had almost reached the monument. Stephen could see him silhouetted against the light coming through the central arch. He walked clean under the arch, causing Stephen to sit bolt upright on the bench, but after looking from side to side, Billy walked back out into the light. Stephen kept his eyes fixed on him, but he suddenly got the feeling that it was *he* who was being watched. There was a man coming towards Billy, walking across from Oxford Street, but Stephen couldn't rid himself of that nagging skin-crawling feeling. He watched the man for as long as he could, until he was almost at the arch, but then he couldn't stop himself from glancing over his shoulder – and he saw Vincent Garvey standing there, not fifty yards away.

There was no doubt – not even much surprise. Garvey wore the same grey overcoat and black homburg he'd had on the previous week. But he was much closer; close enough for Stephen to see the inches-thick sole of his orthopaedic boot. He had his hands in the pockets of his overcoat, a thin smile on his face as his eyes met Stephen's. Probably there for a while, Stephen thought. He must have been watching all along, blending in with the crowd for the preacher. Stephen didn't want to take his eyes off him, but a hasty glance told him that the man walking from Oxford Street had stopped beside Billy. A look back; Garvey was coming towards him.

Stephen sat tensed on the bench, ready to fly. He knew Garvey probably had a gun in his pocket but he had to keep his eye on Billy. He was talking to the other man, shaking his head. The other man was tall, fair-haired and well dressed. Stephen thought he might have seen him before, but he couldn't be sure at this distance. At last, he reached inside his overcoat and pulled out an envelope. Billy took it and peered inside. Stephen flashed another hasty look over his shoulder. Garvey had covered about half the distance between them, his head darting from side to side as the last of the preacher's crowd slowly wandered away. Stephen knew he would have to move soon. Then a shout from the monument made them both look in that direction. A third man had appeared and had pinned the tall man against the white marble of the arch. A fourth was running around from the back of the monument while Billy backed clear of the scuffle. Stephen's eyes went to Garvey; he had frozen like a startled cat, with a ludicrous expression on his face. Then he turned and started to run.

Stephen was up and after him like a shot. Garvey had no great turn of speed with his bad leg, but Stephen had a bad leg of his own and his wounded knee soon began to protest at this unaccustomed exercise. In any case, Garvey hadn't been far from a pedestrian gate and even with his lumbering, ungainly stride he was quickly out through the railings and lurching into the traffic on Park Lane. Stephen kept after him, ignoring the pain in his knee and feeling the tails of his overcoat flapping behind him. He felt the cold black iron of the railings under his hand as he swung out through the gate, but Garvey was already halfway across Park Lane, running diagonally towards Oxford Street.

He saw Billy out of the corner of his eye as he ran across Park Lane. He also saw the two Special Branch officers leading the tall man away, his hands cuffed behind him, but he could feel Garvey slipping away. He reached the far kerb and turned towards Oxford Street, but Garvey was already there. He had plunged straight into the busy traffic, sending cars screeching and horns honking, and then had darted behind a van. The traffic was moving again by the time Stephen reached the same spot, and he had only a glimpse of Garvey on the other side, like a man across a river. Panting and weak-kneed, Stephen ran into the road, only to jump back as a taxi came roaring towards him, its horn blaring. Then an omnibus rumbled past, followed by a flurry of bicycles, and Stephen felt his heart sinking at the delay. He dodged another motor van, smelled the rank sweat of a horse that towed a carriage across in front of him, and finally made it to the far pavement.

But Garvey was gone. Not a sign. The maroon red of the underground station glared at him only a few yards up the street and he walked along and stared down into the gloomy ticket hall. Nothing. Not a soul in sight until the turnstiles started to clank and ring and a fresh tide of people flowed up the steps towards him.

The house was quiet when he got back. There was nobody in the sitting room, but from the kitchen came a faint light and the rattle of crockery as tea was prepared. Stephen went upstairs and sat on his bed, stretching out his leg and rubbing his tender knee. He had been limping when he went to meet Cope at his club and had to explain how he had chased and lost Garvey. Nevertheless, Cope had been pleased; they had nabbed everybody else and the photographs and negatives had been safely destroyed. Furthermore, Cope believed he could invoke the Restoration of Order in Ireland Act to keep the conspirators under lock and key for as long as the Treaty negotiations lasted.

'Give the beggars a taste of their own medicine,' he'd said, grinning slyly. 'Now, if only our lords and masters would stop bickering and start talking, everything would be coming up roses.'

But Stephen knew that everything was most certainly not coming up roses. The sanction that Cope had warned him about had proved to be the hanging of an IRA man, and it had not gone down well particularly with Collins. He was reminded of this when he heard the rumble of a motor car pulling up outside. The doors slammed and then Collins's voice echoed loudly around the empty street. He was shouting in his fury.

'He didn't say that, Emmet. He said he would try, and you know damn well what that really means. Well, you would if you'd seen the smug look on his bloody face when he said it. He has a forked tongue, that fella, and he's been waiting for his chance ever since–'

His voice died away as they came in through the front door, but it carried in a more muffled form up the three flights of stairs to Stephen's room.

'–him and his ... what did he say? The sinews of war. I'll give him the bloody sinews of war. I'll show–'

Stephen was aware that there had been some informal talks that morning, but he hadn't expected them to last this long. And they hadn't been that informal, either, by the sound of it. The men went into the sitting room, their voices growing more faint as Collins made his way to the office at the back of the house. Stephen frowned. Sunday night was Collins's night off, when he rolled up his shirtsleeves and had a few drinks with his pals, maybe even a singsong. It didn't sound like there would be much of a singsong tonight.

After a few minutes he got up and changed his shirt. Some of the excitement was still fizzing inside him and he felt restless. He was hungry, too. Perhaps if he got something to eat it might take the edge off the excitement and he could settle

146

down to read or work, do something to find his equilibrium. He had just finished knotting his tie when he heard a step on the landing. There was a gentle knock at the door, and Dalton stuck his head into the room.

'Ah, there you are, Ryan. I was hoping I'd find you in. Where's your pal?'

'At the theatre,' Stephen answered, feeling the hairs prickle on the back of his neck. He'd bought Billy the ticket himself, just before he left him to go and meet Cope. It had been the best thing he could think of to keep him out of the way until his obvious relief and excitement had passed. But he wondered if they'd been rumbled anyway. Collins was no fool and he had people everywhere. Cope might have been discreet, but he could hardly vouch for the Special Branch—

'Oh, well, it's no matter. It's yourself that Mick wants to see, if you have a minute.'

'Of course.' Stephen went downstairs with Dalton, through the sitting room and dining room, where the tea had been laid out on trays on the sideboard. Dalton stopped at the last door, knocked politely, then opened it and ushered Stephen in with a jerk of his head.

Collins was sitting in his chair, his jacket off and his shirt open at the neck. He had a glass of whiskey in his hand and a murderous look on his face. Dalton followed Stephen into the room, gently closed the door and then took a step to one side, standing with his hands clasped together and his head slightly bowed. Stephen was reminded of their first meeting in Dublin several weeks before, but on that occasion Collins had not glared at

147

him with quite so much ferocity.

'Emmet tells me that you're a dead shot – a sniper.'

'What?' Taken aback, Stephen looked from Collins to Dalton. Dalton's face was grave, unreadable. 'Well, I–' he began but Collins didn't let him finish.

'Emmet's not bad himself – he commanded a sniper school for a while, but he says you're something special, that you had a bit of a reputation in France. He says you once shot a fella from a mile away. Is that true?'

Collins's voice was quiet but insistent. He clearly wasn't joking. Stephen felt his cheeks go red.

'Not exactly, no–' He glanced again at Dalton, who clearly knew more about him than he had ever let on. But then, Dalton had been on the staff in France near the end of the war, and he must have heard some stories. No doubt they had become more and more lurid with every telling. 'As a matter of fact, it was only three quarters of a mile.'

Out of the corner of his eye he saw Dalton's cheeks crumple as he tried to hold in a laugh.

'Oh, is that all?' Collins's stony face broke briefly into a grin. 'Sure, if I'd known it was only that far, I wouldn't have bothered you at all.' His eyes darted in Dalton's direction and his face turned grave again. 'But then again, I remember Dick Mulcahy telling me another story about you – about how you went to Mayo to bury your grandfather and the crew of Auxiliaries that was terrorizing the place mysteriously got shot up by a sniper. Did you ever hear that story, Emmet?'

148

Dalton nodded solemnly. 'I did.'

'I'd say you have a talent, Mr Ryan. A very rare talent.'

'I wouldn't call it that,' Stephen answered stonily.

'That's as may be,' Collins stood up and drained his glass. 'But all the same, I have a job for you.'

'What sort of job?' Stephen asked, his hackles rising again.

'I want you to shoot somebody for me. Emmet thinks Birkenhead might be the man, but I say Churchill. Churchill's got it coming to him.'

Stephen's eyes widened. He knew Collins could be cold-blooded, but he had never expected this. A glance in Dalton's direction didn't offer much comfort. He was as hard and cold as a statue.

'Is this a joke?' Stephen asked, but Collins shook his head gravely.

'It's no joke. They've just executed one of our lads in Dublin to show us that they mean business, so I want to show them that we mean business too. A little taste of what they'll get if we can't come to an agreement. What do you say?'

Stephen didn't answer at first and the room was so silent that he could hear the long-case click ticking out in the hall. Part of him still clung to the idea that Collins was joking, but he was fairly sure he wasn't. This was a man known for audacity, for daring.

'I say no,' he answered sharply. He wasn't one of Collins's gunmen, to be ordered around. Collins looked stung, then glanced into the bottom of his glass as Stephen pressed on. 'It would be suicide. Even if I wanted to, which I don't, how the hell do you think you could get away with it?'

'If you do it at long range you won't be caught,' Collins answered, in a barely restrained voice. 'You can do it out at his country house. We can get you the gun and set everything up. It just needs to be done differently to our usual style. Two men with revolvers would be a dead giveaway, and they'd probably get caught as well. But a single shot that nobody would ever see coming, well, that would be something else. It would show them that no-where is safe.'

'It would show them that you can't be trusted,' Stephen answered slowly. 'And it would kill the talks stone dead.'

'Not necessarily. If we did it right, they'd have a hard time tying it back to us.'

'Are you mad?' Stephen asked, now angry rather than apprehensive. 'You just said you wanted to prove a point, send a message. Of course they will tie it back to you. If they caught a Chinaman with the gun on him, they'd tie it back to you. Everybody knows what Churchill and Birkenhead are involved in at the moment. Everybody knows what their opinions are. Who else would bloody want to kill them? But that's beside the point. I said no, and I mean no. I didn't come here to kill anybody. I'm on a safe conduct pass the same as the rest of you and I'll honour it even if that means you have to send me home.'

'Well,' Collins threw back his head and looked him directly in the eyes, 'in that case, we've noth-ing else to talk about.'

He jerked his head and Dalton stepped over to the door and opened it. Confused, suspicious, and with his cheeks still bright red, Stephen turned and walked back into the dining room. The door closed behind him and he stopped. He suddenly felt overwhelmed, and his hands were shaking, his head spinning. He walked into the sitting room and sat down in one of the armchairs. The front door opened and he heard laughter in the hall. The other men were coming back, probably from the pub, and he prayed they wouldn't come in here. He was relieved when he heard them thumping up the stairs.

After a few minutes, he felt calmer. Still no sign, no word from the back office. Maybe it was a joke, after all. His hunger came back and he went into the dining room again, helping himself to some bread and meat from the trays on the sideboard. He had sat down to make himself a sandwich when the office door opened and Dalton came out. He smiled when he saw Stephen.

'Good idea,' he said, closing the door behind him. But he only took a cup of tea before he sat down beside Stephen at the long table. 'How are you feeling?'

'Confused,' Stephen admitted, looking at him a little sullenly. 'I thought we came over here to talk.'

'We did – and we still are,' Dalton told him. 'As a matter of fact, we'll be back in Downing Street tomorrow, business as usual. It's just that Mick gets a bit upset sometimes. And who can blame him? Pat Whelan was a good friend of his and he doesn't like leaving him behind and just carrying on as if nothing happened. But that's what he has to do and that's what he's going to do. He just had to get it out of his system, is all,' Dalton swirled the tea in his cup and looked at Stephen over the rim. 'By the way, you did right in there, standing up to him. He needs that, sometimes, and he respects it, even if he won't admit it. He'll be as right as rain in the morning, and he won't think any the worse of you for what you said. Quite the opposite, in fact.'

'He sounded pretty angry to me,' Stephen said, glancing at the door.

'It'll pass soon enough,' Dalton said, and then he grinned. 'But, all the same, you might want to stay out of his way for a little while.'

VII

Midnight came and the deep bronzy tones of Big Ben rang out over the rooftops of Whitehall. In a large room at Number 10 Downing Street, Stephen stood up, stretched, and walked as far as the door. Then he turned, thrust his hands into his pockets and slowly worked his way back to his chair, studying the portraits of prime ministers as he went. After the sound of the bells died away, his shoes sounded very loud on the polished floorboards, but the noise did not seem to disturb his companions. Cope sat on one side of the room and Childers on the other. Both were hunched tensely in their chairs and both had glassy, faraway looks on their faces.

When Stephen reached his chair he sat down again. In the hour he'd been there they had not been disturbed except when a maid brought in a tea tray. No sign, no word of anything, and he was beginning to wonder whether Billy had been too quick off the mark. But he'd been in high spirits when he'd come back to Cadogan Gardens in a motor car. He had burst through the front door and charged halfway up the first flight of stairs before changing his mind and coming down to stick his head into the sitting room. Stephen was sitting by the fire and had been drowsing over a newspaper before all the commotion woke him up.

'Stephen! Get your coat and come with me!' he cried, and darted up the stairs again. Stephen had to throw down his paper and hurry out into the hallway.

'Why? What's wrong?' he called up the stairs. He had feared something might happen. Everything had been quiet these last three weeks – perhaps too quiet. Not a word about blackmail, and Collins had been as sweet as you like. Even the negotiations seemed to be back on track, and the atmosphere in the house had changed from gloom to a sort of determined optimism. He had not had to meet with Cope in over a week and had been making progress with his mathematical work. But now...

Billy's beaming face appeared over the banister. 'Nothing's wrong, Stephen. In fact, it's quite the opposite. I think they're going to sign!'

He disappeared again, but Stephen didn't move. He was rooted to the spot. They were going to sign? He could hardly believe it. After all these weeks, after coming so close to disaster...

'Come on, Stephen.' Billy came thundering

down the stairs again, a bundle of papers clutched to his chest. 'Don't just stand there gawping. Get your coat and come with me. Don't you want to be there when history is made?'

But the closer they got to Downing Street, the more Billy's mood dampened down. When Stephen remarked that agreement seemed to have come about very suddenly, he had nodded sombrely.

'Lloyd George is playing hard ball,' he whispered as the car hummed down Whitehall. 'He's put his final offer on the table and we can take it or leave it. If we take it, we'll have to accept an oath to the King as the head of the Commonwealth and the loss of Ulster – for the time being, anyway. Ulster will have to vote on whether or not they want to come into the Free State.'

'Bloody hell,' Stephen said in a shocked voice. It was indeed a hard bargain. He knew the delegates had been sent in the hope of negotiating full independence for Ireland. It had always been a slim hope, but independence for only three-quarters of the country and an arrangement where an English king remained the head of state was a very long way from the cherished republic. 'And you think they're still going to sign?'

'The alternative, to use the Prime Minister's exact words, is immediate and terrible war.'

'Christ! Do you think he really means it?'

'Do you want to find out if he's bluffing?' Billy looked grim. 'Personally, I think he's serious. He's gone about as far as he can politically, and certainly far enough to satisfy public opinion. If we refuse this carrot he's offering, then he'll be perfectly justified in using the stick.'

The slamming of a distant door brought Stephen back to the present. Carrot and stick, he thought, looking from Childers to Cope. It wasn't hard to tell which was which. Cope was all about conciliation and compromise, but not Childers. Childers had come for a republic and would rather suffer immediate and terrible war than take anything less. And he was not the only one. Many men had fought and died for an Irish Republic and many more were still in jail – Stephen's own brother among them. What would they think if the delegates came home with anything less?

After a few minutes, Cope took out his watch and looked at it.

'The mills of God grind slowly,' he sighed, and Childers smiled his bleak smile but did not say anything. He leaned forward and wrung his hands together, looking down at the floor. The tension was palpable.

A short time later, there was a knock at the door and Billy came in. Stephen looked at him expectantly, but all he got was a barely perceptible shake of the head.

'Mr Childers? They're asking for you now.'

Childers stood up and fastened his jacket. 'If you will excuse me, gentlemen,' he said, and with his back ramrod straight and his shoes ringing on the floor, he marched out with Billy.

'There goes an unhappy man,' Cope muttered, after the door had closed. 'I can't be sure, but I believe he was sent out here to cool his heels.'

'I can imagine,' Stephen said. If the tension out here was bad, it must have been unbearable in the conference room. He had a mental picture of Collins's wrath breaking like a wave against the hard rock of Childers's intransigence.

'But what do you think?' he asked Cope. 'Will they sign?'

'Not if Mr Childers has his way, they won't.'

'You didn't answer my question,' Stephen pointed out.

Cope shrugged and smiled. 'I know, and I apologize. It's not that I'm trying to be evasive; it's just that I don't know. I certainly hope they'll sign, but part of me is afraid that Mr Childers isn't the only one who won't find the terms acceptable. I believe the Prime Minister when he says he's gone as far as he can, but I think he's leaving it a bit thin for your lot. Remember, they've still got to ratify the Treaty when they go home, and God only knows how that might end.'

God only knows, Stephen thought to himself, but he didn't say any more. Minutes stretched into an hour. Big Ben boomed out again at one o'clock and then there was the sound of movement outside. A door opened somewhere and many feet came drumming down the hall. Then Billy burst in, beaming.

'They've gone and done it!' he said. 'They've signed. It's done.'

Stephen and Cope looked at each other, neither of them sure what to say. Then they both stood up and shook hands.

'Congratulations,' Stephen said.

'Well, at long last–'

'Mr Cope?' One of the British secretaries was leaning in through the open door. 'The Prime

Minister would like to see you.'

'Thank you, Stephen,' Cope said, clasping his arm. 'Thank you for everything.'

Stephen followed him as far as the door. Secretaries and clerks were walking quickly up and down, some of them laughing and clapping their hands and all of them clearly excited.

'What now?' he asked Billy.

'Well, it's back to Hans Place for me – a few loose ends to be tidied up, telegrams to be sent and so forth. You'd best go and pack. I imagine we'll be going home tomorrow.'

'All right.' Stephen took his overcoat from the stand near the door and started to put it on. Just then there was a crash up the hall as another door was flung open and then heavy footsteps came towards them. The Irish delegation appeared, with Collins in the lead.

'Congratulations–' Stephen began to say, but the word died on his lips as Collins glared at him. His face was pale and his lips were thin and he stalked out into Downing Street looking fit to do murder.

Joe was out in the yard when the word came down. He had it to himself that morning because the frost was so hard there was ice on the wire and the bitter north wind was cutting a sharp swirl inside the walls. Still he was out in his overcoat, his collar turned up and his boots slipping on the rime as he walked and walked and walked. Ten times around every day – he'd done it with Whelan and he did it now. Come rain or come shine, ten times around.

On his eighth turn he heard cheering coming

157

from the wing. It echoed and tumbled inside and only spilled out the door in a confused babble as he passed. Around he went again. On the ninth turn Jimmy O'Dowd was standing in the doorway, stuffing his pipe and grinning at him. He was in his shirtsleeves, but he didn't seem to mind the sharp breeze, only putting his back to it to light the pipe.

'They done it, Joe.'

Joe stopped and pulled his hands on his pockets to blow on them and wring some heat into them. 'They done what?'

O'Dowd clucked at his pipe a few times and then chuckled out a long puff of sweet-smelling smoke. 'They signed a Treaty with the Brits. Mick Collins and those boys over in London done it last night. Your brother's over there with 'em, isn't he?'

'He is.' Joe nodded, blowing again into his cupped hands. He felt a little dart of pride at the mention of his brother, but otherwise not much emotion. He was more curious than elated. 'What did they get? Is it a republic we have now, or what?'

'I dunno.' O'Dowd shrugged and clenched the stem of his pipe in his teeth as a particularly vicious gust whirled in, nipping at Joe's ear and blowing out the pipe. 'All I know is we're getting out of this place. There'll be an amnesty now, that's for sure.' He shivered and clasped his arms around himself. 'Jesus, Joe! It's like the North Pole out here. Will you not come inside?'

'I'll be there in a minute.' Joe nodded out into the yard. 'I've one more to do.'

'Well, mind you don't freeze to death before

they let you out,' O'Dowd muttered and ducked back inside. Joe put his hands in his pockets and continued on his way, head down, nestling deep into his overcoat. Still he felt no emotion, not even at the thought of getting out. He reached the outside wall and turned along it. Outside was just over there, just a few feet away. In his mind, he saw himself walking on the other side. He'd be near the canal, maybe a barge would be puttering past, maybe there'd be ice in the reeds. But would it make any difference? He wouldn't get the time back. He knew he'd been luckier than most in that respect, with not even seven months in the lock-up. But it felt like longer, and it felt like it had left its mark on him. All the loneliness, all the boredom, all the despair, it was on him now and he'd never get rid of it.

He walked along the wall, hunched into the wind, and slipped one hand out of his pocket to brush the stone from time to time. 'Stone walls do not a prison make', that's what Whelan used to say. He used to know who said it, too, but Joe had to rack his mind even to scratch up the second line; 'nor iron bars a cage'. That was it. But it seemed to Joe that there was more to it than stone and iron. There were all these memories that were penning him in here and always would, even after he got out. There was the morning when they took Whelan away, the rosary and the silence that came after it. Then the day when they moved him off D wing – they said it would be cruel to leave him there on his own and he'd shouted at them to fuck off and made them drag him out. After that, they put him in the medical block for a few days until

159

he calmed down. And the doctor came and told him not to worry and the chaplain came and told him not to worry and–

He was lost in himself as he marched along. Faster and faster. Ten times around, that was what he had to do. He didn't even see the ice, though it must have been there the other nine times. His foot went out from under him and one hand came out of his pocket almost by itself. His shoulder hit the wall and then the other foot went as well. In a reflex, he tried to catch himself with his free hand but it was no use. Nails and knuckles scrabbled at the wall but still he went down, landing hard on his side and jerking his head so hard he saw stars.

Nobody saw him, nobody shouted, nobody came running. The fall knocked the breath out of him and he lay where he was for a moment, wheezing and cursing at the pain in his hand. That felt like the worst of it; the knuckles skinned off him on the stone. But the sudden jolt had knocked something else inside him, had upset some delicate balance. Suddenly he could feel all that weight, everything on top of him, pressing him down. It was as if there was some sort of hole in him and all his strength was flowing out. He felt too weak to get up, or even to roll over, and he lay his head on the ground and pushed his face in against the wall until he felt the cold stone on his forehead. It wasn't long before the tears started, and the heat of them seemed to burn him, so he wiped them away with his bloody hand, but more came, and more, and suddenly he was sobbing and crying so hard he couldn't even feel himself.

The sharp wind blew in from over the sea and carried with it the smell of salt and the threat of snow. Despite the cold, Stephen had come out on deck and was leaning on the rail of the Dublin packet. He'd been cooped up on a train all day and he craved a bit of solitude. Some of the others had been drinking since they left London, and now they were going from rowdy to melancholy. He didn't blame them. In fact, he felt a bit melancholy himself. It was like the end of a holiday, a return to the everyday. Only none of them were sure what would be waiting for them when they got home, or even if they'd be welcome.

Still, he was keen to get back to Dublin. Whatever troubles were waiting for him there, he knew somebody would be happy to see him. But as he peered over the rail, he had a feeling it would be a while before they saw Dublin. They were still in Holyhead harbour, and there was wreckage drifting and bumping along the side of the ship. The sailors had rigged a big acetylene lamp on the bridge and by its light he'd seen some planks, a wooden fish crate, and a black oilskin jacket floating in the water.

A door crashed open behind him, jerked out hard by the wind, and Billy came out and wrestled it closed.

'What the bloody hell happened?' he demanded, coming up beside Stephen and peering over the rail. 'What was that bang? Have we run aground or something?'

Stephen had felt the bang, too, but that had been nothing compared to the jerk as the engines were thrown into reverse, churning up muddy foam and making the deck vibrate and rivets rattle.

'I think we've hit a fishing boat, look.' He pointed to another piece of blue-painted planking, drifting back along the steel side of the ship, trailing a long skein of netting.

'Bloody hell! That's all we flaming need!' Billy fumed. 'Look, I'd better tell the others. I'll be back in a tick.' And he went back inside just as another fishing boat came surging and bobbing into the harsh white circle of light thrown out by the acetylene lamp. As the choppy water sparkled and flashed, he saw it was rainbow-coloured from a thick film of oil.

Even though he knew what had happened, he got a shock when he saw the body. He saw the feet first, heels up, and he thought first of all that it was just a pair of boots floating along with the wreckage. But then he saw the legs, and the ghostly white of a knitted jersey with the arms outstretched, then black hair bobbing through the oily surface.

The door banged open again, making him jump. Billy came up, holding on to his hat in the breeze.

'Collins has gone to talk to the captain,' he said, and then he saw the body. Two men on the fishing boat had snagged it with boathooks and were hauling it up the side, the limp arms dripping water and oil. 'Oh, God love us, that's the last thing we bloody need! They'll never let us go now.'

Stephen shot him an angry look. 'For Christ's sake, Billy, the man is dead.'

'I can see that. But what can we do for him, eh? Nothing, that's what. But we'll still be stuck here until tomorrow while they sort it all out.'

162

'Yes, and then we'll get to Dublin tomorrow evening instead of tomorrow morning,' Stephen retorted. 'What difference does it make? Collins doesn't seem to be in any rush to get back anyway.'

To Stephen's eye, Collins had looked the most melancholy of all, even though he hadn't been drinking. His mood had not improved since Stephen had seen him at Downing Street, and a few of the others had been whispering that he thought he'd signed his own death warrant.

'The Treaty is bigger than Collins and it's bigger than that poor blighter over there. Whether Collins likes it or not, the thing is signed and now we have to get it ratified. It'll be all over the morning papers and if we don't appear in Dublin to stand behind it, we'll look like we don't believe in the thing ourselves. Our opponents will have a bloody field day.'

'Our opponents?' Stephen gave him a sideways look. 'Already we have opponents? The ink's hardly dry.'

'I know, but apparently de Valera is furious that we signed anything without referring back to him, and he's not the only one. The minute it gets out that we haven't got the full republic, all the fight-to-the-last-breath merchants will be down on us like a ton of bricks. I mean, there's even a rumour going about that de Valera has had warrants drawn up to have us all arrested for treason the minute we land in Dublin. And, as if that isn't bad enough, we've already got Childers and Barton muttering about it – and Barton is one of the ones who signed the bloody thing!'

Just then, the fishing boat backed away and the

acetylene lamp blinked out. Suddenly it seemed very dark, and the sweeping beam of a distant lighthouse threw only a faint light on their faces.

'We were never going to get the full republic,' Stephen said quietly. 'Never in a million years. I think we got the best we could have hoped for, and probably more than the British wanted to give. And at least it's a start. We might not have a republic yet, but at least we have some chance of getting one in the future.'

'That's pretty much what Collins said,' Billy answered, as the deck started to vibrate under their feet and the ship nosed slowly forward, heading out to sea between the winking green and red lights at the harbour entrance. 'And for all his moping about it, I think he believes in the Treaty and he'll fight like a lion to have it ratified. But you can see why he's so bloody miserable, can't you? It's his men who fought and died for the republic, and he's the one who sent them out. Now he's got to go back and convince them to take something else. I don't envy him, Stephen. Those men have already spilled blood for the republic. Why would they stop now? Why would they stop until they get it?'

The line of them straggled across the yard, every man standing with his brown paper parcel clutched in his arms. They were all behaving themselves; no pushing, no shouting, no stares, just a hopeful look on their faces, that the wait was finally over. Even the screws were in good humour. They were supposed to be guarding the line, but they just lounged over against the wall, neither

164

moving nor raising their guns. Most of them looked even happier than the men in the line.

'Go on, then, Paddy. Give your missus a kiss from me,' one called out, and the reply was lost in peals laughter from the others.

Joe didn't smile or say anything. He kept his eyes fixed straight ahead, past the man in front of him, past the screws, firmly on the gate. He wasn't sure what he felt or what it meant. He wasn't even sure where he would go when he got outside. All he knew was that he had to get to the gate and walk out. After that, it was another world.

The line twisted across the yard and passed a window where a screw was giving out travel passes and ticket money. Every time a man reached the window, the line shuffled forward a step, squeezing up like a caterpillar. Then the wait, then another step. Every time they stopped, the men stood quietly, heads bowed, hands in front. They were not out of prison yet.

'Name?' the screw behind the window demanded, and he ran a stubby finger down his list when Joe muttered his name. 'Where are you going?'

Joe didn't know what to say. He tried to think of his address, the house on Gardiner Street where he'd been living, but he couldn't remember.

'Dublin,' he said at last.

'Tram fare, so,' the screw said. He whisked a few coins off the little stacks he had and slid them under the open window. 'Next!'

Joe shuffled towards the wicket gate under the arch. He'd often looked in this direction, often wondered what it would feel like. There was a screw standing there with a clipboard.

'Name?'

Joe said his name again and kept staring at the gate as the screw ran down his list. He could hear people outside; laughter, conversation, even a crying baby being shushed.

'Don't hurry back, Joe.' The screw grinned as he pulled open the wicket. It squealed as if it had never seen much use and through the opening he saw light and cobbles and a child running past. He had to duck down to get through. He almost felt like holding his breath.

A dozen men had gone out before him so he didn't get much of a cheer, but a girl ran up and kissed him on the cheek and some men he didn't know shook his hand. He blinked in the light and looked around, but he didn't know what he was expecting to see. He certainly wasn't expecting to see his brother, but there he was, coming towards him with half a smile on his face: friendly, but somehow constrained. They shook hands and then it seemed they didn't know what to say to each other. Stephen thought his brother had lost weight. He looked gaunt, and he had been able to feel the bones in his hand.

'How did you know we'd be getting out?' Joe asked. Even he hadn't known how quickly it would happen. The Treaty wasn't even two days old, but instead of roll call this morning they'd been told to pack up their stuff and get ready to leave.

'A friend tipped me off,' Stephen admitted. A telegram from Cope had been lying on the door-mat when he let himself into his flat that morning, carrying his bags and still yawning after his night on the Holyhead packet.

'Great friends you have,' Joe said, and the sneer in it wasn't lost on Stephen. He knew when Joe was spoiling for a fight, but he'd already made up his mind not to give him one.

'You're probably sick of that prison food,' he said. 'I thought we might go for something to eat?'

'No, thanks,' Joe said, without moving. What the fuck did he know about prison food?

'Well, what about a drink, then? A pint to celebrate. I'll tell you what went on in London.'

'I know what went on in London,' Joe ground out. 'We heard all about what you did.'

'What we did?' Stephen demanded. 'What the hell is that supposed to mean?'

'You know damn well what it means, and you know damn well what you did over there. You've got some neck on you, showing your face here today.'

'What?' Stephen was flabbergasted. 'What the hell are you talking about? What we did over in London just got you out of prison.'

'Yeah, by pissing away everything we done to get in there in the first place. What bloody use is us getting out when you gave the whole fucking country away?'

'Oh, don't you bloody start!' Stephen put his hand to his head. 'What did you think would happen? Did you think we'd just go over there and they'd give us everything we asked for? Don't be so fucking thick! We got more than we had before – much more. And we were lucky to get it because the only other thing they were offering

167

was total war. Is that what you want? Is that what you'd do to the people you're fighting for? You wouldn't last a fortnight. I know – I fought in a war. I've seen what they can do, and I wouldn't wish it on anybody.'

'Yeah, you fought for *them*,' Joe spat. 'You never fought for your own country, did you? So don't tell me about the people. I think we both know who your fucking people are. I'm sure they'll look after you now that you've made your bargain with them. Me? I'd rather be back in there.' He pushed past his brother, jerking his arm away when Stephen tried to stop him.

'Joe, for God's sake–'

'Get your fucking hands off me,' Joe growled, and he clutched his brown paper parcel to his chest and walked away as fast as he could.

Part Two

DUBLIN

VIII

There were still a few signs of Christmas in the comfortable houses along Adelaide Road. As Stephen and Lillian walked together towards Earlsfort Terrace, they saw flashes of tinsel, candles in the windows, even an occasional tree. But the holidays were nearly over. The New Year had begun and everybody would be going back to work in the morning.

Everybody, that was, except Stephen. Just after Christmas, he had received a letter from the college board. They had felt compelled to write to him in connection with his legal dispute with his head of department. In light of this fact, they said, they thought it best to extend his leave of absence until the matter was resolved. Keach was behind it, of course. A clever little move, Stephen had to admit – the perfect riposte to Billy's attempt to delay the court case for as long as possible.

'They had no right to do that,' Lillian exclaimed. 'And certainly not without even hearing your side of the story. What did Billy have to say? Did you show it to him?'

Stephen had shown it to Billy, but he didn't think there was much he could do about it. Besides, Billy had other things to keep him occupied. While Stephen's involvement with the Treaty had ended the moment he stepped off the Holyhead packet, Billy had been retained to advise the Dáil on the legal niceties of the agreement.

'I did, but I don't think he's had a chance to do anything. He's been really busy since we got back.'

'Well, I've a good mind to give them what for tomorrow. It's bad enough having to go back and look at Keach's smug face, but that holier-than-thou old fool of a provost–'

'Now, Lillie–' Stephen pulled her up short as they reached the corner of Earlsfort Terrace. They could see the National University Building across the road, a crowd still gathered outside it, despite the cold. 'We talked about this. Remember the plan? You know what we have to do and you know it's not going to do us any good if you tear a strip off the Provost.'

'I know, sweetheart. But it'll make me feel better.' She smiled and kissed him. 'You and your plan. You know it's cracked, don't you? He'll never bite.'

'Of course he'll bite,' Stephen said, with a good deal more confidence than he felt. 'What did I tell you about fishing? It's all about how you present the bait.' He nodded across the road. 'Come on, let's go and see what all the fuss is about.'

They threaded their way through the crowd at the gate and went up the steps of the university building, showing their passes to the tough-looking man who was guarding the door. The passes had been issued and signed by Michael Collins as Minster of Finance and had come with a note explaining that they were a small token of his gratitude. The man at the door peered at them closely, then nodded and stood aside to let them in.

172

The broad foyer was almost empty. A few journalists sat at side-tables, scribbling in notebooks, and perhaps a dozen men and women were scattered around in knots of two or three, deep in conversation. The atmosphere was serious, almost grim.

'Billy said he'd come out and meet us at three,' Stephen said, glancing at his watch. He was not very hopeful – Billy was never on time for anything – but as he turned around he saw him coming across the foyer, looking harassed but smiling when he saw them.

'Stephen, there you are. And Lillian! My dear, you look delightful,' a kiss, 'how lovely to see you again. I'm sorry to rush you, but we must be quick. It's nearly over, you see. If they can last the next half-hour without an adjournment I believe they may finally take the vote.'

'How does it look?' Stephen asked as they climbed up the broad stairs and then hurried down a carpeted corridor.

'Not good, as you've probably already gathered. I'm sure there's been nothing else in the newspapers.'

They both nodded. Practically the whole country was waiting with baited breath as the Dáil debated the Treaty, which it had been doing almost since the day it had been brought from London. Even allowing for the Christmas break, they had been arguing over it for more than three weeks and were still nowhere near a consensus. If Billy was right in what he said, they were finally coming close to a vote on the Treaty, but which way it might go was anybody's guess.

173

'The Cabinet is about evenly split,' Billy said. 'And even after all this interminable palaver, the same is true of the Dáil itself. Fifty-fifty, almost straight down the middle. It's a right old bloody mess, I can tell you.'

'But they have to ratify the Treaty, don't they?' Lillian asked. 'I mean, what on earth will happen if they don't?'

'I shudder to think.' Billy stopped in front of a pair of tall double doors and turned to face them. 'Well, here we are. It's standing room only, I'm afraid. You can stay as long as you like, but if it does come to a vote, they'll clear the chamber first.'

He pushed open one door and ushered them inside. The council chamber was a room of quite impressive proportions, but it was so packed with people that it looked cramped. Most of the floor space had been covered with long wooden benches, and these were filled with men and women whose focus was entirely on the dais at the far end of the room. Here, the Cabinet sat – at least Stephen supposed it was the Cabinet, for he knew only some of the faces. President de Valera sat in the centre, and on one side Stephen recognized Collins and Griffith, while on the other he spotted Robert Barton, who had been another of the delegates in London. However, he did not know the man who was speaking. He was a small man, middle-aged, but very trim, and possessed of a passionate energy that carried his words clearly down to where they stood.

'The members of the Headquarters' Staff were the best men we could get for the positions; each of them carried out efficiently the work that was entrusted to him; they worked conscientiously and patriotically for Ireland without seeking any notoriety, with one exception; whether he is responsible or not for the notoriety, I am not going to say–'

'Shame,' one of the men on the benches called out.

'Get on with the Treaty!'

'Who is that man?' Lillian asked.

'That's Cathal Brugha, the Minister of Defence,' Billy whispered.

Brugha was not easily put off by the hecklers. He was in a fine flow of feeling, beating time with the rolled-up papers in his hand. 'There is little more for me to say. One member was specially selected by the Press and the people to put him into a position which he never held; he was made a romantic figure, a mystical character such as this person certainly is not; the gentleman I refer to is Mr Michael Collins.'

A chorus of booing and shouts of disapproval came from some of the benches, while there was cheering from others. Collins himself looked unperturbed, but the feeling of tension in the room was palpable.

'I take it he doesn't get on with Mr Collins,' Lillian observed.

'No, and he never did, apparently,' Billy said. 'The Treaty has brought out their old animosity, with Collins standing for it and Brugha very much against.'

'What about de Valera?' Stephen asked. He had been watching the President sitting in the middle of the dais. He looked strained and troubled, but his thin lips rarely opened. 'Where does he stand?'

'He's against it, too – very much so – but he has to be careful. I think he's aware of how precarious things are and he's trying to avoid a rift in the party. So he lets Brugha do most of the shouting and only puts his oar in when he has to.' Billy's eyes roamed around the room for a moment and then he nudged Lillian with his elbow. 'But as far as hating the Treaty goes, both of them are only in the ha'penny place compared to our friend Childers over there.'

'Mr Childers?' Lillian's eyes widened. 'But he's such a lovely man. Is he really a zealot?'

Childers wasn't a member of the Cabinet, but Stephen had spotted him on one of the benches near the front, his face as hard and cold as ever. He seemed to be made of stone. While there was a fair bit of jostling going on all around him – men nudging each other, waving their arms in approval, or even just applauding or shaking their heads – Childers hardly moved.

'Oh, he's a zealot all right,' Billy whispered. 'But he's also so damned cold-blooded you wouldn't believe it. With Brugha there is a certain amount of passion, as you can see. He gets so carried away that you could believe he lets his animosity towards Collins cloud his feelings about the Treaty. But not so Childers. Childers objects to the Treaty purely on moral and political grounds and he's the most implacable enemy it will ever have. He's against it and nothing will ever put him off – nothing. It's just not in his nature. I mean, you saw him arguing in London, Stephen. You know what he's like.'

'I know,' Stephen agreed. Implacable was the word, all right. Childers was against the Treaty and he would fight it until his dying day.

At this point de Valera slowly got to his feet. He stood stooped like a broken man, hesitant, almost as if he didn't want to get up at all. The whole room fell quiet as he cleared his throat and then started to speak with great deliberation – his barely audible voice giving the sense of a man who was tired beyond the bounds of human capacity.

'I say that the Irish nation will judge you who have brought this Treaty,' he said, his voice cracking with emotion. 'If it is approved, they will judge you by comparing what you got for the Irish people–' He gasped and his voice trailed off. He was clearly overcome, unable to speak. Seconds passed in total silence before Collins got to his feet.

'Let the Irish nation judge us now and for future years,' Collins said in a gruff voice. He too, sounded tired but also deeply affected. 'Let us have the vote now.'

Collins sat down the moment he finished speaking, catching everybody unawares. De Valera turned a little and looked to the speaker.

'Very well.' The speaker started in his chair, and then rapped on the table with his gavel. 'Very well, we will take a vote in the usual way by calling the roll. The vote is on the motion by the Minister for Foreign Affairs that Dáil Eireann approves of the Treaty. The clerk will call the roll after the stewards have cleared the chamber.'

'Out we go, I'm afraid,' Billy said, ushering them back towards the door. They didn't go far –

just to a chaise longue in the corridor outside – but Billy wouldn't sit down. He hopped from one foot to another and then paced up and down with his hands in his pockets. Eventually he said he was going to see the clerk and left them alone to stare anxiously at the door.

'Seriously, Stephen, what if it doesn't pass?' Lillian asked.

'Then God help us all,' he answered, thinking of Lloyd George's threat – immediate and terrible war. What would he do then? He would have to fight. He could hardly stand back now, claiming he'd done his part.

A door opened down the hall and he heard somebody walking towards them. Out of the corner of his eye he saw a soldier in the green uniform of the Irish Republican Army, complete with Sam Browne and creaking cavalry boots. He paid little attention, however, and got quite a start when he realized the soldier was Emmet Dalton.

'They're still voting,' Dalton said, in answer to their questioning looks. Then he smiled apologetically at Lillian. 'I'm sorry, Miss Bryce, but do you mind if I borrow your fiancé for a minute?'

Lillian's questioning look fell on Stephen, who shrugged but got up and followed him a few yards down the corridor.

'I hear you're out of a job, Stephen,' Dalton said, turning to face him and thrusting his hands into his pockets.

'Not exactly,' Stephen replied evasively. He wondered if it was Billy who had told him about the letter from the college.

'Well, let's just say you're at a loose end for the

time being. The point is, I'm not. I'm still in the army and whichever way things go in there,' he jerked his head towards the council chamber, 'I'm going to be kept very busy for the next while. We need an army, Stephen, and an army needs soldiers. Particularly officers, and ones with experience are worth their weight in gold.'

'I'm not a soldier,' Stephen said bluntly, and cast a significant glance in Lillian's direction. 'Not any more.'

'Rubbish. You'll always be a soldier, whether you like it or not,' Dalton answered, a faint smile coming to his face. 'I know you better than you think, Stephen. I fought in that war, too, remember? I know what it did to you, but I also know what you can do. I even looked up your citation in the *London Gazette*. "His gallantry and determination set a fine example to his men." Ring a bell, does it? You don't change that just by putting on a civilian suit.'

Stephen didn't answer. *Whichever way things go in there.* What if it didn't come to a war? What if the Treaty was accepted? That wouldn't get him off the hook, either. He could hardly just walk away and leave them to it. Whether he liked it or not, he was part of it now.

'Look, you don't have to answer straight away,' Dalton went on, his voice lower, an insistent whisper. 'I know you'll need to talk about it. But we *want* you, Stephen. Our terms would be generous. You can start with the same rank you had when you were demobbed – captain, wasn't it? And it would be a short commission; you can resign if you get your old job back.'

'General Dalton!' a shout came from back down the corridor. Somebody had leaned out of a doorway and was beckoning furiously.

'Well, think about it anyway,' Dalton said as he turned to leave. 'We need men like you.'

'What was that about?' Lillian asked when Stephen sat back down.

'I don't think you want to know.'

Before she could press him further, Billy reappeared. He was walking slowly and looked dazed.

'Well?' Stephen asked. 'Have they finished the vote?'

'They have,' Billy sat down heavily on the end of the chaise. 'It passed.'

'Oh thank God!' Lillian laughed, relieved.

'It passed, but only by seven votes,' Billy went on, despair in his voice. 'Sixty-four to Fifty-seven. The Dáil is split – the country is split. Christ, what a mess!'

At that moment the doors to the chamber burst open and the deputies came streaming out. To a man they looked shocked and angry. After the first rush the crowd thinned and Stephen could see the dais at the far end of the chamber. He saw Collins standing up, his head cocked towards Emmet Dalton and his face stern and forbidding. His back was turned to Eamon de Valera, who was still slumped in his chair, his face in his hands and his whole body heaving with sobs.

By early March, Dunbar had taken a private room at a nursing home in Rathmines. The hospital had diagnosed liver cancer and said there was nothing they could do for him. There wasn't much the nursing home could do for him either, but it had its advantages.

'I'm back on the morphine,' he said dreamily, when Stephen came to visit him one day. When he opened his eyes and saw the look on Stephen's face, he laughed. 'Oh, don't look so fucking glum! I'm not injecting myself – the nurse gives it to me whenever I need it. Anyway, it's hardly going to kill me *now*, is it?'

Stephen sat down beside the bed. He knew Dunbar hated morphine with a passion that only a reformed addict could have – a passion that he understood because he had once been addicted himself.

'Is it working?'

'Oh yes. I feel rather fuzzy. There's nothing like it for easing a chap's progress to the next world.'

This time it was Stephen who laughed.

'The next world? I thought you didn't believe in any of that.'

'I'm hedging my bets.' Dunbar slipped a packet of Woodbines from under his pillow. 'Get the door, will you?'

As he did on every visit, Stephen closed the door and opened the window while Dunbar lit a cigarette. After he lifted the sash, Stephen stayed by the window and looked out over the long garden. Spring was coming and the peeping heads of daffodils and crocuses had added a kiss of colour to the dull tones of the winter garden. A few of the more adventurous patients had decided to take the air and were walking unsteadily around the damp lawn in their pyjamas and nightgowns.

'Well, what's happening in the world?' Dunbar demanded, picking a stray shred of tobacco from the tip of his tongue. Stephen could tell by the stack of newspapers that he was already well up on what was happening in the world, but he knew it wasn't just information that Dunbar wanted; it was talk, stimulation. Apart from Mrs Brady, his housekeeper, he and Lillian were the only visitors Dunbar ever had.

'There's trouble in Limerick,' he answered, watching as an ancient man stopped in the middle of the lawn and squinted into the watery sun, smiling at it like an old friend. Politically, the country was coming apart at the seams; after losing the vote on ratification, de Valera had resigned as President and a provisional government had formed under Arthur Griffith to implement the terms of the Treaty. However, the southern division of the IRA had broken away from the Government and there had been skirmishes in Limerick as pro-Treaty and anti-Treaty elements fought over possession of the barracks vacated by departing British troops.

'There'll be plenty more where that came from,' Dunbar predicted. 'This bloody army convention that the anti-Treaty crowd are talking about is really putting it up to the Government.'

Stephen nodded. The most dangerous thing of all was the rift in the army, which was widening every day. The anti-Treaty faction, who also refused to recognize the authority of the army GHQ, wanted to call an army convention where they hoped to secure the IRA's allegiance to an anti-Treaty Army Executive. The Government had banned any such convention, but they were threatening to go ahead anyway. If they did, Stephen couldn't see it ending in anything other than war.

'It's only half the army,' he pointed out. 'A lot of the troops in Dublin are still loyal to the Government.'

'And what about you? Are you loyal to the Government?'

Stephen grunted. He didn't know who was more persistent, Dunbar or Dalton.

'He asked me again, you know. He came around to the flat last week in a staff car and in full uniform. That's the second time. He must think I'm bloody Achilles or something.'

'I dare say you are, compared to what he's got to work with. I mean, half of those buggers probably think the wide end of the rifle is for hitting you with,' Dunbar took a long drag on his cigarette and lay back against the pillows. 'Anyway, what did you say?'

'I said I'd think about it.'

Dunbar chuckled. 'You've had two months to think about it.'

'I know, and I admit I'm tempted. I'm so bloody bored these days, it's driving me up the wall.' Stephen walked back around the bed and sat down. All his life he'd been in school, college or the army; he'd had a routine. Now he had nothing. He was still working on the zeta function but it was a lonely existence, spending all day in the basement flat, without even Dunbar upstairs to talk to. 'And Billy thinks it would be a good idea, too. He's trying to have the case heard in Dublin and reckons it'll look good if I show up in uniform. Plus, it's a paying job. God knows how long this legal business will take and I'm getting nothing from the college.'

'What does Lillian think?' Dunbar asked, narrowing his eyes through a cloud of his own smoke.

'She's not mad about it – she still remembers the last time I put on a uniform – but she thinks it would be the right thing to do.'

'And what about you? Do you think it's the right thing to do?'

Stephen shrugged. He'd known the answer to that the first time Dalton had asked him, but he hadn't wanted to admit it.

'I suppose it is. I think it's my duty. This is my country after all, and I support the Treaty. If they need soldiers to fight for it then that's what I should do.'

'Then what the bloody hell are you waiting for?'

Stephen threw up his hands. 'Oh, I don't know. I suppose I've got this niggling feeling that it's not my fight. It was something my brother said to me – that I'd never fought for my country. Well, he's right, isn't he? The army's made up of all these men who've been fighting for Ireland since the Easter rebellion and here am I, coming late to the party. Six years late *and* I used to fight for the flaming British.'

'Balls!' Dunbar exclaimed and the smoke seemed to catch in his throat. He was seized by an explosive coughing fit that doubled him over in the bed, hacking, wheezing and choking. Stephen jumped up and tried to calm him, patting his back and taking the flattened stub of the cigarette from his fingers. He was struck by how bony and frail

184

Dunbar felt under his pyjamas. He could feel his shoulder blades and see the yellowish tint to his skin as he leaned forward into the sunlight.

'Easy, easy,' Stephen said, pushing him back against the pillows and pouring him a glass of water as the coughing subsided. 'Here, drink this. Maybe it *is* time you gave up the fags.'

'Balls,' Dunbar wheezed again. A swig of water seemed to clear his throat, and he went on, breathing hard. 'Double balls. It's too late for the fags to kill me now, and of course it's your bloody fight! It's been your fight ever since you went off to Turkey. How many of those poor bastards you left behind at Suvla went out there on John Redmond's say so? Eh? How many of the men we buried in France died fighting for Home Rule? Well, they're not here to see it–' Dunbar winced, shuddered, and arched his head back against the pillows as a spasm shook him. 'Looks like I bloody won't be, either, but you will. The thing they all died for is right here under your nose, and if you're not careful it's going to slip away again. They're not here to fight for it any more, but you are, Stephen, you are. So you're going to have to fight for them and don't let those fucking idiots balls it up... Oh, Christ! Get the nurse, will you?'

The ladies' common room was silent except for the scratching of pens. Summer exams would begin in just over a month and half a dozen young ladies were crowded around the table, hard at work.

Lillian sat a little apart from them, in an armchair by the window. This was where she worked

185

if she wasn't lecturing or giving a tutorial and she quite liked it here. The mathematics common room might have been more convenient, but Keach was often there and she wanted to steer clear of him – now more than ever.

She finished reading her paper and made a few notes in the margin. It was almost ready. She would show it to Stephen first and then ... absently, she glanced at her watch and jumped straight up. She would be late! The young ladies all looked around at her as she hastily screwed the top on her pen and shoved the paper into her bag.

'Going somewhere, Miss Bryce?' one of them asked, while the others tittered. They all knew she was engaged to Stephen and they all knew about the trouble with Keach ... and now Stephen had joined the army. They thought it was very romantic.

'He's getting his uniform,' she explained, hurrying into the corner to fetch her hat and coat from the stand. 'I promised I'd be there for the fitting.'

'Oooh lovely! A uniform!' one of them whispered, and then there was a heavy knock and the door creaked open.

'Is Miss Bryce here?' a gruff voice bellowed from out in the hallway. The young ladies all laughed.

'You can come in, Mr Hopkins. We won't bite you.'

Hopkins advanced a step but barely came in through the door. He was one of the older porters and also the most old-fashioned. Lillian leaned out to show herself as she pinned on her hat. 'I'm here, Mr Hopkins, but not for long. I'm just going out.'

'Parcel came for you, miss.' He held up a small box wrapped in plain brown paper and tied with twine.

'Oh?' She came around and took the parcel, frowning as she did so. She'd had letters at college before but never a parcel – and certainly not without a stamp. 'Where did it come from?'

'A boy brought it, miss. Said he'd been given a shilling to deliver it to you. Only I wouldn't let him in the gate, so I says I'd bring it to you myself.'

'How kind of you, Mr Hopkins. Thank you very much.'

Hopkins bowed and left and Lillian turned the box over in her fingers. This was most unusual and she was aware of the young ladies jostling around the table behind her, practically climbing over one another to get a look at what it might be.

'What is it, miss?' one of them asked, only to be shushed by the others. Lillian was sure it was from Stephen – her birthday wasn't far away – but why not give it to her himself? And that wasn't his handwriting on the brown paper. Then again, if he was trying to surprise her he might have disguised his hand, and even deliberately misspelled her name with only one 'l' in the middle.

Without turning around, she plucked at the string and the paper fell away. The box inside was just as plain and when she pulled the top off she found it was stuffed with cotton wool. But there was something in there, something small and heavy. She turned the box upside down and a bullet fell out into her palm.

'What is it, miss?' one of the young ladies asked again. She heard them standing up, coming

187

around to have a look, and she quickly slipped the bullet into the pocket of her coat.

'Nothing,' she said, turning around and stuffing box, paper and twine into her bag. 'Nothing. It's just a little joke. Now, I must dash – I'm late as it is.'

Before she knew it she was out of the common room, out of the college and practically running across College Green. The thing had given her such a fright that she could hardly think. She could feel the weight of it in her coat, and recoiled at the deadly little shape of it when she put her hand in her pocket. Only when she stepped off the pavement and almost into the path of a tram did she come to her senses. She jumped back and took a deep breath, then forced herself to look around. Whoever had sent it clearly knew where she worked – they might be watching her even now. She doubled back a little, then crossed at the bottom of Grafton Street and went up Dame Street instead. She still felt exposed. Stopping suddenly, she turned and looked at a shop window, watching her own reflection in the glass but also the whole street behind her. Nothing. Another tram clanged past. She was being an idiot. What did she think, that she was in some silly penny dreadful? She turned and walked on. She would be late.

She *was* late, but by the time she got to O'Callaghan's the little bullet in her pocket felt much heavier than her bag. The sensation of being watched had overcome her twice more on the way but she had stopped twice more and seen nothing. The second time was in the middle of Grattan Bridge. It was a particularly busy spot, with people hurrying back and forth on their lunch hour, and she suddenly realized that any of these people rushing past her could have been the one who sent it – any of them. She turned and put her back to the rail and felt in her pocket for the bullet. It was like a curse on her, she thought, a little pill of malice. She wanted to throw it in the river but she stopped herself. He would want to see for himself. It might even tell him something.

Stephen stepped out of O'Callaghan's just before she reached the door. He was wearing a dark green uniform and cap and had a brown-paper parcel tucked under his arm. When he saw her his face cracked into a grin and he raised his arms and gave her half a twirl.

'What do you think?'

She was so relieved to see him that she almost ran the last few yards.

'Oh, Stephen. I'm sorry I'm late!'

His grin faded to a frown that stayed in place even after she kissed him. 'What's the matter?' he asked.

'Nothing. It's nothing, sweetheart. Now let me have a good look at you. I must say, I like the green – it's much nicer than khaki.'

She could feel him watching her as she walked around him. 'What's the matter?' he asked again.

'It's nothing to worry about, really,' she said, though she felt so much safer when she looped her arm through his. 'I'll tell you when we're in out of the way.'

She made sure that they got a quiet table at the hotel where they went for lunch. Even so, she could see some of the other customers staring at

Stephen's uniform. Some were simply curious but some looked hostile. Stephen, however, was looking at her. She could feel the question coming again.

'Stephen, before I say anything, I want you to promise me that you won't ... overreact.'

He was looking at her so mildly that it seemed impossible to think his reaction would be anything but calm and measured. But she knew him better than anybody else. Sweet and gentle he might be, but he could also be deadly hard and dangerous. She had seen that side of him once before, in Mayo. He was easily capable of killing people who threatened him, and he wouldn't think twice about it if it were she who was threatened.

'I promise,' he said, and smiled.

She took the bullet from her pocket, reached across and dropped it in his palm. His reaction was much as she had expected. No shouting or exclaiming, no histrionics; just a tightening of his jaw, a hardening around his eyes.

'It came for me at college,' she said. She was already looking in her bag for the box and wrapper. She took it all out and gave it to him.

'When?'

'Just now, before I came out.'

'Did you see anything – anybody hanging around?'

'No.'

Stephen studied the bullet, rolling it slowly between his fingers. It was a small-calibre pistol bullet, which struck him as odd. There was something almost personal about it – but it was dangerous, nevertheless, dangerous and deliberate.

She needed protection, but how could he protect her when the army could send him anywhere at a moment's notice? His eyes darted up. The waiter was coming towards them, carrying their plates. He closed his hand on the bullet and quickly slipped it into the breast pocket of his tunic.

'What do you think?' Lillian asked, leaning forward so that she could whisper. 'Should I go to the police?'

He shook his head. The old police forces were gone now that the British were pulling out and he didn't think much of this civic guard the provisional government had set up.

'It's your birthday soon, isn't it?' he asked, unfolding his napkin. The waiter set down their plates and vanished with a murmured *bon appétit*. Lillian frowned at him.

'Yes it is, in a couple of weeks.'

He gave her a knowing smile. 'I'll get you a present.'

They had to use a van to open the gates. Then the van wasn't strong enough so they all got behind it and pushed. The tyres squealed on the wet cobbles and the chain hummed under the tension and eventually something snapped behind the groaning gates and they swung open.

Joe was with the first group into the courtyard. The nights were lighter now that summer was nearly on them and he could see the massive copper dome of the Four Courts silhouetted against the stars. Nobody troubled them as they moved along the east wing of the building, no lights, no shouting. A small side door gave in to a few good kicks and then they were inside. But the noise brought the night watchman running. They heard him first, his boots clattering across the marble floor. Then they saw his lamp and pressed themselves in against the walls. When he was almost on top of them, O'Connor stepped out and the light gleamed on the brass buttons of his uniform. It also showed the big revolver in his hand.

'You'd better get out,' he said quietly. 'We don't want to harm you.'

The elderly watchman was startled by the gun but stubbornly stood his ground. 'Who the hell are you?' he demanded, looking around at the shadowy figures, all of them armed.

'We're the forces of the Army Executive and we're taking over this building.'

'The Army Executive? You're against the Treaty, are you?'

'We are,' O'Connor's gun didn't waver.

'Shame on you, so. That Treaty is good enough for me, so it is.'

'Well, it's not good enough for us.' O'Connor jerked his pistol towards the open door. 'Go on home now, you're not wanted here.'

They kept the watchman's light and added a few torches and bicycle lamps of their own. Joe had his rifle slung over his shoulder and walked quickly down the long corridor, following the beam of the man in front of him. He felt a familiar sort of excitement, something that he'd given up on in prison, but it was tamped down in him, restrained. Part of him felt like he wasn't really here, like he was standing in the shadows, watching himself marching through the dark, but not really sure where he was going.

When they reached the end of the corridor, they came to a broad space that they could barely see across. Their lights swept across the mosaic floor and eventually picked out doors and columns and walls that curved right back around to where they stood. This was the great round hall, the very heart of the building, and Joe had a sense of great space above him. A few of them looked up, turning slowly in wonder, and their lights picked out gilded cornices and alabaster statues and then the latticed belly of the dome curling up to a single spot of pale moonlight high above them.

'Right lads,' O'Connor came out all business, walking in the light of a storm lantern and holstering his revolver, 'we're in. Now we need to make the place secure. Gather round.'

He detailed them off to various places: the courtrooms, the basement and all the exits. Ammunition had to be brought in, the gates barricaded and kitchens set up. Joe was sent with a man called Mahony to find a way out on to the roof.

It wasn't as easy as he'd thought. Behind the courtrooms there was a labyrinth of judges' chambers and cells and clerks' offices, all connected by narrow stairs and corridors. There were no lights and Mahony's acetylene lamp seemed to blow out every time he turned around.

Joe had a small electric torch, so he left Mahony fumbling for matches and went on by himself. He came to a spiral stairs and climbed up, his boot nails scraping on the iron treads, until he stepped up on to bare floorboards. The torch showed a narrow attic with curving walls and no sign of a window. Stacks and stacks of paper lined the room; man-high piles of files and folders, some of them tied with ribbon, some with dusty wax seals. They seemed to absorb all sound and it was so quiet up here that he felt like he'd stepped right out of the world. It felt so peaceful that he switched off his torch and shut his eyes and let the silence wrap itself around him. He liked it here. He liked the warm dark and the smell of cobwebs and dust, and the only thing that disturbed him was the squeak and scratch of a mouse.

A few moments later, he opened his eyes again and saw the faint outline of a square on the ceiling above him. It was pitch-black in here, but lighter outside. It could only be a trapdoor.

He had to drag over a small table so that he could climb up to reach it. Then he found it hadn't been opened for so long that the latch was stiff and he had to beat it with the end of his torch. When it fell open a gush of cool air and the hum of the city seemed to fall in on top of him. He pocketed his torch and hauled himself out through the hole. The ghostly green shape of the dome soared up to his left and there was a solid stone parapet to his right. He stood up and leaned on the parapet and looked out across the city. He could see the river below him and the bridges and the lights on the other quay. He could see the square tower of Christchurch and the low humps of the Dublin Mountains to the south. It was a good vantage point, all right. When the attack started, they'd see them coming.

He knew that they would be attacked here. They all did – that was why they were occupying the place. But would it be the British or their own troops that would attack them? Or would this election solve everything before it came to that? He didn't think it would. The men downstairs who were barricading the doors and blocking up the windows were past elections now. They were hoping that the British would try to drive them out of here. If the British attacked them then the pro-Treaty part of the army would surely come to their aid. They would unite against the old enemy; the rift would be healed and they would be one republican army again, fighting for the true republic.

But what did the people care for the true republic? Their lives still went on down there. They would wake up in the morning and eat and drink and go to work, and never even notice that the Army Executive had taken over the Four Courts. He thought of what the watchman had said to them; the Treaty was good enough for him. It was probably good enough for most of them, too. It made no odds to them if they lived in a republic or a free state. They only wanted peace, and the Treaty promised peace.

But sometimes Joe still felt the urge to fight. It came on him now and again like a rage. To hell with peace. What right did they have to accept the Treaty? Which of them spoke for the dead? Who was standing up for the men who had fought and died for a republic? None of them had any right, and yet they were prepared to shake hands with the British and take their guns and money and swear allegiance to their king. It made his blood boil. Men had died to get them this far – they couldn't stop now. To hell with the people who didn't give a damn, who just wanted to get on with their grubby little lives, wearing out the days until death. And to hell with the lickspittles and their Treaty–

He heard a bump behind him and looked down in that direction. His fists were clenched and he realized he'd been talking to himself. A light flashed up through the trapdoor.

'Joe, is that you?' Mahony's voice came up in a fearful whisper. Joe had to clear his throat before he could answer.

'Yeah.'

'They want us to come down and give them a hand with the barricades.'

'Right. I'll be down now.'

But before he left he took one last look over the parapet, letting his eyes sweep right across the city. It was very quiet, very peaceful. Most likely, nobody even knew they were in here. But they would. They'd wake up to it, and then they would come. Probably to talk at first, then to fight. But he didn't mind that. He wouldn't shirk it. He was not afraid for himself.

OUR PURPOSE

The Treaty is in existence. Use it for Freedom.

It can be used for that purpose
It ought to be used for that purpose
It WILL be used for that purpose

VOTE FOR THE TREATY

Stephen's polling station was in a school in Rathmines. Lillian had come with him that far, but she wouldn't come inside. She was still fuming over not being able to vote.

'Just promise me you won't chain yourself to the railings,' he joked as they parted.

'Oh-ho! Listen to him!' She gave him a playful shove towards the door. 'You shouldn't mock those less fortunate than yourself. Now hurry up and cast your vote and don't keep me standing here all day.'

It didn't take long. After all the fuss about this election, all the pacts and promises and threats and accusations, it was very civilized in the end. Candidates and canvassers were polite and good-humoured and the allegations of treason or war mongering had been confined to the handbills left scattered around the floor.

'Well, that was painless,' he remarked to Lillian as he came out, pausing to settle his cap back on his head. It had been his first time voting; for the 1918 election he'd been stuck in France, sharing a freezing army hut with a dozen other unlucky sods. 'What time is our meeting with Mr Noyk?'

'Three o'clock – there's plenty of time.'

They turned to go and all but collided with Billy Standing, who was coming in through the gate. He looked distracted and was pleasantly surprised to see them.

'Where are you two off to, then?'

'To see your friend Mr Noyk.'

'Oh?' Billy's brow wrinkled but he said no

more. Stephen had asked him to recommend a good solicitor but had told him not to ask why he wanted one. Billy suspected it had something to do with the libel case Keach had taken against him but didn't press the issue. He had bigger things to worry about these days and, besides, the last thing he'd done in that case had been to lodge papers at the Four Courts. Now that the courts had been occupied by the Army Executive those papers were well and truly in limbo, and Keach's case along with them.

'Well, and did you cast your votes?' Billy asked.

'He did,' Lillian said. 'I wasn't allowed.'

Billy frowned. 'Why on earth not?'

'What do you mean, why on earth not? Haven't you heard?'

'No.' Billy looked perplexed, his eyes darting from one to the other. 'I was in London all week. Just got back this morning, as a matter of fact. I thought I'd cast my vote before I went back to the office. What's happened?'

'There was some problem with the register of electors not being updated,' Stephen explained. 'A lot of women who should have been able to vote weren't registered.'

'Oh dear.'

'So much for universal suffrage,' Lillian put in, in a flinty voice.

'Well, on behalf of the Government, I do apologize.'

'Government my foot! They couldn't even organize–'

'What were you doing in London?' Stephen cut in, to defuse the situation.

'Trying to convince the British that we will win this election and keep our part of the bargain by implementing the Treaty. They have their doubts, of course. This business with the Four Courts is particularly embarrassing.'

Stephen could understand that. In the weeks since the Army Executive had taken over the Four Courts they had been sending out patrols and foraging parties, and had occupied half a dozen other strong points around the city. So far, the Dáil had not moved against them – they had been content to let them stew rather than provoke an open fight – but there was only so much they could ignore. These men were going about armed to the teeth and were openly commandeering cars and seizing foodstuffs in the name of the Army Executive. They were preparing for a siege and at the same time trying to provoke the Government into making a move against them.

'Maybe they'll clear out after the election,' Stephen suggested. 'If the people come out strongly in favour of the Treaty, they won't have a leg to stand on.'

'That never bothered them before,' Billy pointed out. 'This is the fight-to-the-bitter-end crowd we're talking about. They're zealots and they're convinced that they are doing what's right for the people, whether they know it or not.'

'Oh, now Billy, surely they're not that bad,' Lillian said. 'The people are getting their chance to vote on the Treaty and de Valera himself always said he would obey the will of the people.'

'I'm sure he did, when he thought the people would follow him,' Billy answered, not without some bitterness. He'd had a hard week in London. 'However, to be fair to Mr de Valera, I suspect the matter is slipping from his grasp. It's the Army Executive itself that's calling the shots now. Rory O'Connor and Liam Lynch and the like – they're the real die-hards. Not to mention Cathal Brugha and Erskine Childers. Compared to them, de Valera begins to look rather mild.'

Stephen had already heard these names being bandied about in Army HQ. What amazed him was that they were spoken of not as the enemy, but as old friends, as comrades. They were all respected – some of them were even revered – and Stephen knew that the reluctance to bring them to a fight was not entirely due to political expediency.

'Well, here's hoping they'll see sense after this election,' he said.

'Hear hear,' Billy agreed, and he took Stephen by the arm and led him away for a few paces, whispering as he went. 'Listen, Stephen. You should be aware that something's going to happen very soon. The fact is we're going to have to move on the Army Executive – we don't have a choice any more. The British are putting us under immense pressure to do something. They say it's intolerable that the Government is not allowed to govern and, to be honest, I can't say I disagree with them.'

'So, what do you think will happen?'

'Well, we're going to have to show that we can keep our own house in order, aren't we?' Billy said. 'The army's going to have to get them out of there – because if they don't do it, the British certainly will.'

IX

FREE STATE AND BRITISH ALLIES

General Macready is at the offices of the Provisional Government, directing the campaign against the Irish Republican Army.

They have sent an ultimatum to the Four Courts, giving them two hours to clear out before bringing their biggest guns on to them.

Artillery for this purpose is supplied to the Free State Army by the British, and British Army instructors are assisting in manning these big guns.

WHAT DO YOU THINK OF THAT?

It was mid-morning by the time he got back to Winetavern Street. As he came down the hill from Christchurch he saw soldiers crouching in doorways, and more of them hiding behind the armoured car that was parked at an angle across the street. Only Dalton was out in the open, standing in the gap between the armoured car and an eighteen-pound gun with his field glasses trained on the Four Courts. Bullets were sparking and pinging off the cobbles nearby but Dalton paid them no attention.

Stephen walked out and stood beside him. 'Four more shells per gun,' he reported. 'That's all they'll give us.'

Dalton took down the glasses and rubbed his eyes tiredly. They had both been up all night, supervising the collection of the field guns from the British depot in the Phoenix Park.

'Well, I suppose that's better than nothing. You told them high explosive, not shrapnel?'

'I did, but they said beggars can't be choosers.'

'Cheeky sods.'

The turret of the armoured car rang like a bell as a flurry of bullets struck it. Dalton brought up his glasses again and gazed across the river at the green dome of the Four Courts, carefully studying the granite rim just below the copper.

'What's going on here?' Stephen asked, glancing down at the pool of fresh blood under the breech of the eighteen-pounder.

'They've got a sniper,' Dalton said. 'Or else they're just lucky. In any case, they got two of the gun crew here and one on the far side of the river, all in the space of about five minutes. Needless to say, it put the willies up the rest of the crews, which is why I'm standing out here like a bloody idiot, trying to show them it's safe.'

A bullet clanged against the shield of the eighteen-pounder and went whizzing away. Another one cracked smoke off one of the cobbles between them. Stephen felt his muscles start to tense.

'It's probably not,' he pointed out.

'I know, but if I can't get these bloody crews to fire their guns, we'll have to starve the bastards out. Here, have a look, will you?' Dalton handed him the field glasses and then broke off to pound on the back door of the armoured car. 'You in there! What the hell are you waiting for? Return fire, for Christ's sake!'

There was some scrabbling and shifting inside the car and then the machine gun opened up in a long, tearing burst. Stephen covered his ears and watched the tracer rounds arcing through the grey sky as the firing went on and on and on.

'Stop, stop! Cease firing, for Christ's sake!' Dalton pounded on the door again. The firing stopped, though it sounded like the gun had jammed. 'Short bursts! Short bursts! God, give me fucking strength!' He turned around and started barking orders to the men hiding behind the armoured car while Stephen scrutinized the Four Courts through the glasses.

The building was huge, and built like a fortress. It looked on to the river and stretched all the way from one bridge to the next, with thick granite walls and dozens of windows. The sniper could have been behind any one of those, but if he was able to strike on both sides of the river he was most likely high up. Stephen focussed on the high dome in the centre, inching his gaze around the parapet, studying every granite block, every seam of cement, every shadow. He had swept almost as far as he could before he stopped at a dark patch just below the rim of the parapet. It could have been a water stain or some damage to the block work, but even as he watched he saw a flash and a bullet whizzed directly overhead.

'I think I've got him,' he said, taking down the glasses. But as he did, he saw something else happening in Chancery Place, directly across the river from where he stood. They had another eighteen-pounder in there, right up close to the east wing of the Four Courts. 'What the bloody hell do they think they're doing?'

'What is it?' Dalton demanded and Stephen pointed across the river. It was close enough for him to see clearly without the glasses, though he couldn't understand what was going on.

'Over there, look at the gun crew.' He was pointing to the knot of uniformed men who were bodily lifting the muzzle of the eighteen-pounder high in the air. They had already knocked the wheels off the carriage and appeared to be propping the gun up with baulks of timber so that the barrel was nearly vertical.

'What in the name of God–?' Dalton muttered as a man went scurrying up to the gun with one of the precious shells cradled in his arms and slid it into the breech. Then the whole crew ran clear as the gun captain hauled on the lanyard. The gun went off with a shattering blast that dug cobblestones out of the road and sent the timber baulks flying in every direction. Straight away, the crew was back at the gun, but the barrel was too hot to lift so they crouched in behind the shield and tried pot shots with rifles and revolvers.

'This is a bloody shambles,' Dalton exclaimed and leaned in behind the armoured car. 'You there! Go across and ask Mr O'Neil what the hell he thinks he's doing with that gun.'

'I think they put that one right through the copper dome,' Stephen observed, shielding his eyes with his hand. 'There's a hole in it now.'

By the time Dalton's runner got across the bridge, creeping along in the shelter of the balustrade, the gun crew had got their piece back up on its blocks. This time, the gun captain sighted carefully along the barrel before the shell went in and he fired.

'They missed altogether that time,' Stephen said. 'You know, I think they're trying to hit the sniper.'

'Nothing would bloody surprise me,' Dalton said, and when the runner came back and reported that that was exactly what they were doing, he just rolled his eyes. 'Stephen, you'd better get over there–'

'General Dalton, sir!' A young lieutenant had crept down the road behind them and was shouting from the shelter of the nearest doorway.

'What is it?'

'It's the British, sir. They've sent a message down from Kilmainham. They want to see you right away.'

'Well they'll just have to bloody wait.'

'They said it's urgent, sir, and the message is signed by General Macready himself.'

'That's all I bloody need,' Dalton said, turning to Stephen. 'I'd better go and see him – and you'd better come with me. Between the two of us we might be able to give the impression that we know what we're up to.'

Most of the British Army had already withdrawn from Ireland, but the remaining garrison had its headquarters in the Royal Hospital in Kilmainham, about a mile upriver from the Four Courts. Stephen knew it well; he had attended medical boards here during the war and felt a familiar twinge in his knee as they drove in through the gate. He got an altogether different familiar feeling when a shell whistled over the car and exploded above the lawn, the shrapnel shredding the leaves clean off a small tree.

'Oh Jesus Christ almighty!' Dalton put a hand over his eyes. 'I'll fucking murder O'Neil.'

'Do you want me to go back and tell him to stop?' Stephen asked. The car was pulling up in front of the adjutant's house where a small band of British officers waited on the steps. A few yards away, pacing angrily up and down, was General Macready himself.

'No. I need you to keep the others off my back. Send the car – send a note: cease all firing until further notice. Then go and make small talk with Briand and his chums while I grovel to Macready.'

'Small talk?' Stephen muttered to himself, but as Dalton got out he hastily scribbled a note and sent it back with the driver. When the car drove away he found himself alone and facing the officers on the steps. The khaki uniforms looked familiar but the faces were stony and hostile. Briand was at the front and he came down the steps quickly, his veiny jowls quivering.

'Well now, this is a pretty pass, is it not?' he said, and before Stephen could get in a reply, he went on, 'We loaned you those guns in good faith, young man. The express purpose was to get those beggars out of the Four Courts and what do we find? That you've turned them on us!'

'I beg your pardon, Colonel,' Stephen said, darting his eyes in Dalton's direction. By the look of it, he was getting much the same lecture from Macready. 'There has been a mistake, that's all.'

'A mistake?' Briand's jowls quivered again. 'A

mistake, you tell me? Well, you do still have the guns, don't you? You haven't let them slip through your hands, have you? I hear there's been a lot of that going on, you know.'

'We still have them, Colonel,' Stephen said, more stung by this comment because it was quite true. There was a steady trickle of National Army men defecting to the anti-Treaty side, and more often than not they brought guns or materials with them. 'It's just that our gunners are having particular trouble with a sniper and they're letting their enthusiasm run away with them.'

Well, that's one bloody way of putting it, he thought, though Briand seemed somewhat mollified.

'A sniper, you say? Well, you don't use artillery to deal with them, young man. The best thing for a sniper is another sniper. That's what we always used to do in France, and it worked very well. Give 'em a drop of their own medicine, you see.'

'Thank you for the advice, Colonel.' Stephen answered drily, putting on a false smile. 'I'll be sure to bear it in mind.'

'Hmmm.' Briand rocked back on his heels and nodded, as if to say; just you make sure that you do. Out of the corner of his eye, Stephen was relieved to see Dalton shake hands with Macready and turn back towards him. And at least no more shells had landed since they had arrived, though he suspected that O'Neil had simply run out of ammunition.

'Colonel Briand, nice to see you again.' Dalton nodded curtly and took Stephen firmly by the arm, walking him out of earshot. 'Well, that's it,' he whispered, 'we've been given an ultimatum.'

'What did he say?'

'He says we're on borrowed time. He's already had orders from London to move on the rebels and he's doing us a favour by staying out of it. But he can only hold out for so long, so he's given us until tomorrow night to get those boys out of the Four Courts, otherwise he'll do it for us. And I don't have to tell you what happens the minute the British get involved.'

Stephen nodded. If the British stepped in, the whole game would be up. The Treaty and the provisional government would both be null and void.

'We'll need more men and more shells if we're to do it by tomorrow night,' he said.

'Let me worry about them. Macready's already promised me enough shells to start a full-scale bombardment tonight. Once the walls are breached we'll mount an attack in the morning. What I need you to do is leave me clear to use my guns. I want that sniper, Stephen. I want him gone, and I want you to bloody well get rid of him for me.'

It had gone so quiet that Joe was starting to wonder if they'd given up. No shelling for the last couple of hours and not much in the way of rifle fire, either. After a while, he pushed himself up and looked out through the loophole. The opening wasn't very big, but it offered a surprisingly good view of the bridge and the streets below. Through it, he could see that they'd built a barricade down in Chancery Place and moved another armoured car into the end of Winetavern Street. Plenty of men were moving down there, and he'd been hearing the rumble of lorries all afternoon. They hadn't given up at all. They were just getting ready to push even harder.

When he looked up from the loophole, he could see down the river towards the docks and the city centre. He knew there was another stronghold down around Sackville Street but he didn't think they'd be much help now. The boys were all full of talk about a link-up, about reinforcements pushing up to them at night, about breaking the siege, but Joe knew better than to believe that. They'd always known the National Army was stronger than they were, they'd just hoped that they didn't have the will to come against them. But clearly they were coming against them with a vengeance now. There were no two ways about it; they were cut off.

There was a noise behind him and he turned to see Flaherty crawling out through the trapdoor, pushing the rifle case in front of him. It was a fancy case in polished tan leather, and there was a fancy gun inside it – a hunting rifle with a telescope. Flaherty had picked it up when they raided some big house for guns and he brought it everywhere with him. Nobody minded because he was the best shot in the garrison. Just that morning, he'd managed to pick off three men in the gun crews before the rest of them bolted for cover. Joe had spelled him for a few hours while he went downstairs to get some sleep, but now he was back for the evening shift.

'Well, Joe. How does it look?' he asked, crawling along the gutter on all fours.

'It's been quiet for a while,' Joe said. 'There were

a couple of officers standing out in Winetavern Street earlier on, but I haven't seen them in a while. The rest of them have been keeping their heads down since you got them fellas in the gun crews.'

'What the feck happened there?' Flaherty asked, nodding up at the ragged hole in the copper near the top of the dome.

'They took a few shots at me with one of the big guns down in Chancery Place.'

'Jaysus.' Flaherty shook his head and grinned, 'I must have stirred them up something rotten earlier on. Did you try a shot yourself?'

'I took a few at them two officers, but I didn't hit either of them.'

'Sure that's an awful long shot over open sights.' Flaherty peered out through the loophole and patted his rifle as he slid it out of the case. It was a deadly looking thing with a beautiful walnut stock and a long blue barrel. 'Maybe I'll have more luck with this girl, if they come back before dark.'

Joe wished him luck with his work and crawled back to the trapdoor. When he dropped down into the dusty attic he paused for a few moments before going down the stairs. It wasn't the same as it had been here on that first night. It felt like all the noise and passing people had shaken something out of the air. A breeze blew down through the trapdoor and he could see shafts of light coming in through the holes where the shell had passed through the roof. It was a pity, he thought; it had been so peaceful here before. Then he pulled his rifle down after him and shouldered it and went down the spiral stairs.

The floor of the round hall was scattered with lumps of plaster that had fallen down from the dome. Traces of gold gleamed through the dust, but it had long since lost its sparkle. Everybody just stepped over the biggest lumps and went about their business. The atmosphere was tired and tense. They'd been preparing for this attack for weeks but had always hoped that it would never start. Now that it *had* started, they just wanted it to be over. This second silence was killing them. They knew another attack was coming, but it was hard waiting for the hammer to fall.

The smell of soup wafted out of one of the courtrooms. Joe hadn't realized how hungry he was, but he'd had nothing since yesterday and his stomach suddenly grumbled. He went in to the steam and clatter of the kitchen and came out with a mug of soup and a lump of stale bread. Short rations already. Even after two months of foraging they'd not been able to put much by. He stepped over the legs of a young man sleeping with his rifle clutched in his arms and sat with his back against the wall, easing himself down and using his own rifle as a crutch.

'Wanna smoke?' one of the lads sitting next to him asked, offering a battered pack of cigarettes.

'Thanks.' Joe took one and put it behind his ear while he dipped the bread in his soup and wolfed it down.

'Where's your post, then?' the lad asked, lighting his own.

'Up on the roof.' Joe gulped down the last of the soup and wiped out the mug with the crust off the bread.

'Can you see anything?'

'Not much. It's fairly quiet out there.'

His companion blew out a stream of smoke and grinned at him. 'You think they're gonna let us get away?'

'No,' Joe shook his head, 'it's not that quiet.'

'Then we're fucked, so. Because that tunnel's no fucking use.'

It was only then that Joe noticed his companion was covered in mud up to his waist. He had taken off his boots and draped his socks over them to dry. Joe had heard they were digging a tunnel but he hadn't quite believed it until O'Connor took him down to the basement and he'd seen the pile of mud and rocks, and lights jiggling about at the end of a dark hole in the wall.

'No go?' Joe asked, putting the cigarette between his lips and lighting it from the end of his companion's.

'Not a chance. We're too close to the river, boy. Fecking thing fills up every time the tide comes in.'

'It's death or glory for us, so.' Joe took a deep drag from his cigarette and leaned his head back against the wall.

'Sure who'd have it any other way, boys?' a voice asked, and they looked up as Liam Lynch walked towards them. He was a rather slight figure, with a thin face and round, wire-rimmed glasses, but Joe liked him. He'd done great things commanding the Second Cork Brigade during the war against the British, and even though he'd strongly disagreed with the tactic of taking over the Four Courts, he'd come in with them anyway.

Joe pulled in his legs as Lynch stepped over him and lightly kicked the boy who was sleeping in the rubble on his other side.

'Hey, Sean, get up; wake up out of that. Come on, Father Albert is saying Mass in a few minutes. You said you'd go.'

The boy stirred, looked up at Lynch, and then curled up smaller.

'Go away,' he muttered, but Lynch only kicked him harder. 'Come on, up you get. I promised your ma you'd go to Mass and that's a promise I'm keeping. Come on, up with you now.'

'Where's the Mass?' Joe asked.

Lynch pointed to one of the doors on the other side of the hall. 'Over there in courtroom three. Father Albert said he'd be starting at five o'clock.'

'I'll go,' Joe said, and he stood up, dusting the plaster off his trousers, and nodding to his companion. 'Thanks for the smoke.'

He walked across the rotunda and stood his rifle against the wall outside the door, sliding the handle of his mug down over the barrel. When he went in, Father Albert was stretching an altar cloth over the bench where the judge would have sat. Father Albert was a tall man and very thin, and yet he seemed to fill his habit, which he wore belted at the waist with his rosary looping down to his knee. He had a voluminous beard and warm brown eyes, and he was still wearing a band on his arm painted with a red cross.

'Are you here to serve?' he asked, and it was only when he realized that he was the first man in that Joe understood what he meant. He'd been going to Mass regularly since he got out of jail

213

but he didn't think of himself as religious. He wasn't even sure if he believed in God; he was still feeling his way, groping in the dark for that certainty that Whelan must have had. He certainly wasn't ready for *that*.

'Oh no, father. I won't if it's all the same.'

He took a seat in the jury box and watched as the others filtered in by ones and twos. They were mostly men, but it looked like a few of the Cumann na mBann girls had sneaked back in, even though they'd been sent home days ago. The girls were the only ones in uniform; the rest wore the same suits they'd had on for weeks, though most had at least made an effort to clean themselves up. A comb had been passed around and what ties and collars there were looked startlingly clean against the dirty suits and grimy shirts.

Eventually, every available seat was full and some of them were sitting cross-legged on the floor in front of the altar. It was very quiet, an anticipatory silence. Joe thought if he closed his eyes he might be at Mass in any normal church on a peaceful summer evening. Then Father Albert came out with his vestments on over his habit, kissed the makeshift altar, and intoned:

'*In nomine Patris, et Fili, et Spiritus Sancti. Amen. Introibo ad altare Dei.*'

'*Ad Deum, qui laetificat juventutem meam.*'

The response had hardly died away when there was a loud crash that shook the walls. Dust and plaster drifted down and everybody looked up fearfully. The hammer was falling.

Three floors above Chancery Place, Stephen lay

against the slope of a slate roof with an army blanket over his head and his rifle resting in the crook of a chimneystack. He didn't like it up here. Even though he was lying behind the chimney-stack, his chest, head and shoulders were exposed to the dome of the court building and he could clearly see the loophole that the sniper was using. The only cover he had was the blanket, which was more or less the same colour as the roof, and the fact that he was far enough behind the firing line for the sniper not to think of looking for him here.

He didn't like the timing, either. He would have preferred to come up under cover of darkness and to catch the sniper in the morning, when the rising sun was shining right into the loophole, but that didn't fit with Dalton's schedule. The shelling would commence at five, and the bells of Christchurch had already chimed out the hour. The gunners were late, but so was the sniper. He hadn't taken his eyes off that loophole for the last half hour, and he'd seen nothing.

He shifted his weight a little and tried to let some more air at his face. It had been a dull day, but very humid and the air was warm and close and crackling with the threat of thunder. It would have been hot enough without having his head wrapped in a blanket, he thought, trying to ignore the mad-dening itch where it rubbed the back of his neck. Just then, an eighteen-pounder went off directly below him, and the noise of it reverberated off the walls and rattled the slates around the chimney stack. He saw the shell strike a wall and go off with an orange flash and a puff of black smoke. As the crack of the detonation rolled out across the rooftops, bits of shattered masonry showered down into a courtyard. Stephen steadied himself and focussed on the loophole, staring at it over the sights of his rifle. If that didn't bring him out–

Something moved behind the loophole and Stephen snugged his cheek against the stock of the rifle. It hadn't been much, just a flicker in the shadow, but he knew what it meant. He didn't take aim but watched intently, both eyes open. A loud thump from across the river, and a shell blew smoke and splinters from the front façade of the courts. Boom! Another from Chancery Place went in through a roof and the explosion that followed blew half the slates off. He could imagine the chaos, pandemonium, screams and noise. It would be getting pretty hot in there now, and he couldn't help wondering how his brother was holding up.

Stephen was well aware that Joe was inside the Four Courts. Dalton had told him out straight before the siege even started. They'd had long enough to watch the place – they knew very well who was in there and who wasn't. Dalton hadn't said it in so many words, but Stephen knew he was offering him the chance to pass, to take a post somewhere out of range of his own brother. Stephen didn't even acknowledge it. His last memory of Joe was that day outside Mountjoy Prison. His brother was clearly prepared to lie in the bed he'd made – well, he would damn well do the same.

Nevertheless, it bothered him. Another one of those shells could go through the roof, could burst inside and kill his brother stone dead. Or it could be Joe who was behind that loophole – he could be drawing a bead on his own brother.

But when he thought about it, he knew he could rest easy on that score. Joe was a terrible shot. They'd never put him up there as a sniper – he hadn't the patience for it. Their grandfather had tried to teach them both together but Joe had never found the knack. He'd been persistent, though; bull-headed, even at that age. He hadn't liked the noise or the kick of the gun, but he'd stayed at it. He kept trying. Even when the kick of the gun bruised his shoulder, even when there were tears of frustration blurring his eyes, he kept trying. He was driven to it by anger – anger at himself for failing and anger at his brother for succeeding.

Stephen hoped it wasn't anger that was driving him now. If Joe was in there because he believed they could make things better, that was one thing. If he was in there because he'd rather die than live with the bitterness of not getting what he wanted, that was another. He'd hoped it would never come to this – he'd hoped they'd see sense after the election. The people had spoken and they'd said they wanted the Treaty. Why would these men not listen?

Another flicker of movement behind the loophole. He'd picked this spot carefully and, dull though it was, the setting sun was lighting the loophole from behind. Closing one eye, Stephen took aim on the square of light he could see, waiting for it to fill again. The eighteen-pounder boomed out below and he felt the vibration through the roof. *Steady, steady.* His focus was on the loophole and on the rifle he held in his hands.

It was just a question of bringing the two together – that's what his grandfather had always taught him. Make everything small and be easy with yourself. Stephen clenched his hand on the stock, twisting it slightly and feeling the curve of the trigger meet the bend of his finger. It was an ordinary rifle, but it would do the job at four hundred yards. He'd tested it, sighted and cleaned it before coming up here and he knew that it shot true. All he had to do was wait for the right moment.

He tried to settle his breathing but suddenly he could hear his heart beating inside his chest. He gripped the rifle again, tilted his head a little and willed the sniper to appear. Suddenly, the light in the loophole was gone, then it reappeared, then it was gone. Something moved in front of the loophole and his heart gave a leap. It was hard to be sure in this light, but he thought it was the barrel of a rifle. The hole must be tiny, less than a foot square. Letting half his breath out he held the rest and started to gently squeeze the trigger. It gave way almost imperceptibly and then the rifle banged and bucked hard against his shoulder.

The beaten men were ordered to parade on Ormond Quay. It wasn't much of a parade; they were pushed and jostled into a line along the quay wall, standing with their backs to the river. Every one of them was filthy, hungry and near falling down for lack of sleep. Sullen white eyes stared out of grimy faces.

Their captors didn't look much better. Green uniforms had all been blackened by soot, some splashed with blood and salted with white plaster dust. The National Army men looked edgy, uncertain, as if they couldn't believe it was all over. Some of them gave out cigarettes, but some glared threateningly or aimed a kick at their enemies. Armoured cars patrolled up and down along the quay, their guns swivelling along the line as they passed.

Joe sat down on the edge of the pavement and lit a cigarette. The boy sitting beside him had a bloody bandage around his head and was crying his eyes out. Joe handed him the cigarette.

'Stop crying,' he said. 'Don't give them the satisfaction.'

The boy sniffed and wiped his eyes with his sleeve, clearing a broad white streak across his face. Then he put the cigarette to his lips with a shaking hand.

'What's going to happen to us?' he asked. 'Do you think they'll shoot us?'

'Not at all,' Joe answered, though he wasn't so sure of that. They might not be executed, but he didn't like the look of some of those boys going around with Thompson guns. They were angry, and they had some right to be. Anticipating that the building would be stormed, O'Connor had ordered dozens of mines to be placed. Some had been defused but half a dozen had gone off. The biggest one hadn't even been a mine – a shell must have hit the ammunition dump in the basement and set off the tons of captured gelignite they'd had down there. The blast had blown out windows all along the river and set some of the nearest houses leaning drunkenly on their foundations. Joe's ears were still ringing, and he could

219

tell by the look of them that some of the National Army soldiers were still smarting. It wouldn't take much to set them off.

An open car came slowly along the quay and Joe watched it approach before he suddenly dropped his head and looked down into the gutter. A few of the National Army officers going around looked vaguely familiar, but the man in the back of that car was very familiar. Paddy Daly was one of Collins's right-hand men and had once been Joe's commanding officer. He had a lot of brass on him now but Joe knew him for a dangerous hard bastard, and had no reason to think a bit of braid had made him any softer.

Joe cocked one eye up when the car had gone by safely. Its slow passing brought tensions to a head a bit further down the line.

'Go on out of that, you fucking traitor!' one of the lads shouted.

'You watch your mouth!'

'Look at him. He's riding around in a British car!'

There was some jostling, then the crack of metal on bone. A cry of pain and a curse. The captured men grumbled angrily and some threw dangerous looks at their captors until one of them cocked his Thompson gun. That quick metallic snick stopped everything dead.

'Steady boys. Just keep quiet, now.'

The car had stopped near the corner of Chancery Place and Daly was out and shaking hands with some officers who came over to greet him. They walked along the quay, past the mound of rubble where the front wall had been breached.

Flames were still crackling up out of the basement and now and then a twist of the breeze blew smoke over them as slivers of ash and burnt paper drifted down like snow. It stuck in Joe's craw to watch them wandering along like they were out for a Sunday stroll. Some men had died in there and others had run mad with fear when the shells blew the roof in and machine-gun bullets whipped and bounced around the rooms like angry wasps. He didn't feel any shame that they had surrendered. They'd lasted as long as they could – they'd been down to drinking rainwater to slake their thirst – but it saddened him to think that they'd never had a chance. It had all been for nothing.

After standing and admiring the destruction for a while, Daly and his lackeys turned and started to walk slowly along the line of captured men.

'Fucking peacocks, they're worse than the Brits,' somebody muttered, and when he saw them coming close, Joe lowered his gaze again. A minute later a pair of shiny brown boots came into his field of view.

'Are you Joseph Ryan?' a voice asked.

Joe was surprised when the boy who was sitting beside him, who had been bawling his eyes out a few minutes ago, suddenly jumped up and pushed the officer away. 'No, he's not. Now fuck off!'

The officer pushed back, and Joe heard him open the catch on his holster. 'I wasn't talking to you. Now get out of my way.'

Joe took a deep breath and stood up slowly. He looked into the eyes of the officer, a young man with ginger hair and not much chin. It could have been worse; when he saw the boots he'd been half expecting his brother. Looking over the officer's shoulder, Joe could see Paddy Daly leaning with one hand on the car, staring at him. No point in playing dumb, then.

'Are you Joseph Ryan?' the officer repeated in a clipped voice. He still had one hand on his holster, as though he were making sure his gun was still there. Joe looked him directly in the eye.

'Lieutenant Joseph Ryan, Second Battalion, Dublin Brigade, Irish Republican Army.'

'Follow me, please,' the officer said, and Joe straightened his back and lifted up his head and marched after him to the waiting car.

X

WHAT IS AN IRREGULAR?

An irregular is one who fights without Pay for the Old Cause which will never die.

WHAT IS A NATIONAL SOLDIER?

A National Soldier is one who fights to establish an English King and an English Constitution in Ireland.

For all the noise and tumult of battle, sometimes there were moments of eerie calm. Stephen experienced one such in the sweet shop on North Earl Street. They'd fought their way in there and were waiting for the eighteen-pounder to fire again. Those few minutes seemed so strangely quiet that he knew he would remember the scene. His men lay in the dust and the broken glass and all he could hear was their harsh, excited breathing and the crackle of flames from across the street. He opened his revolver, tipped out the empty shells and reloaded. Sergeant Johnson reached up to a broken jar on the counter and stuck a liquorice stick into his mouth. Nobody spoke. They just looked at each other and gathered themselves, getting ready to move. They all knew what they had to do.

The eighteen-pounder was at the end of Henry Street, firing diagonally past Nelson's Pillar at the hotel on the corner. The Hammam Hotel. He tried to remember if he'd ever been in there. Not that he ever would now; the place was blazing like a torch, having been set on fire by the shells. In fact, the whole block was burning but there were still men inside and they were still shooting. When Stephen leaned out to look through the splintered door of the shop, a bullet whipped past him and shattered the ornamental mirror behind the counter.

'There's bad luck for somebody,' one of his men said, and just then the gun in Henry Street roared and went screeching backwards across the cobbles. The shell struck with a flat thump and blew in the second-floor corner of the hotel, showering the street with brick and broken timber.

'Let's go,' Stephen said, and he went out the door and ran straight for the hotel. He didn't even have to look to see if the others were following him. Dalton had been as good as his word; he'd promised a handful of good men and these six were as good as he could have hoped. Some, like Johnson, were clearly trained soldiers and some of them were more enthusiastic than disciplined, but not one of them was afraid of a fight. When he reached the far pavement he threw himself down behind the stone pedestal of the railing outside the hotel and they all dropped down after him. A rifle cracked out somewhere over their heads and was answered by a short burst from the Lewis gun they had left in the sweet shop.

Stephen raised his head a little so that he could peer down into the hotel basement. His plan was already set – half his men would go in that way and attack from below while he took the rest in through the lobby. There was already smoke pouring out of the lobby windows, and the sound of groaning and shattering glass inside, but he didn't think he had much choice. There were still men in there, and if the fire wouldn't force them out, he would have to do it.

'Get ready with those Mills bombs,' he said, and then he felt a hand tugging at his sleeve.

'Sir, there's a civvy here.'

Stephen rolled half over and saw a man crawling towards him on his hands and knees. He wasn't quite a civilian, but a St John Ambulance man with his cap pushed back on his head and his first-aid bag dragging along beside him.

'Where the hell do you think you're going?' Stephen demanded.

'Are any of your men wounded, captain?'

'No.'

'Well, I'll have a look in the hotel, then.'

'No you bloody well won't!' Stephen pushed him back and then ducked as another shot whizzed past and kicked chips off a kerbstone. This bloody do-gooder wasn't the first civilian he had seen, though he was probably the most foolhardy. There were firemen fighting the fires a few blocks down and a whole crowd of onlookers had turned out to watch the fighting from the bottom of Sackville Street. 'Sergeant, keep him behind us.'

Johnson grabbed the ambulance man by the scruff of his uniform and hauled him into cover. He grinned at him with liquorice-blackened teeth.

'Stay there, chum, and we'll get you a few customers in a minute.'

'Put those bombs in,' Stephen ordered, and ducked his head as another shell thumped into the wall of the hotel and showered them all with dust and bits of masonry. The pins came out and two Mills bombs were lobbed through the shattered basement windows. Two flashes and then hot air and glass blasted out over them. The men jumped up to run down the steps, but froze when a shout came out from the hotel.

'Don't shoot! We're coming out.'

Stephen looked up at his men, jerked his head, and they dropped down again. Then he crawled along to the corner of the pedestal wall so that he could see through the shattered frame of the revolving door. It was dark and smoky inside, but he could see a white sheet hanging from a rifle held up over the reception desk.

'Do you surrender?' he shouted in.

'Yeah.'

'How many of you?'

225

'Six that can walk. Two wounded.'

'What's your name?'

'I'm Commandant Dan O'Byrne.'

Stephen leaned back and made a few quick signals to Sergeant Johnson. Two of the men who had been poised to go into the basement got up, dashed across the doorway, and slid into cover on the other side.

'Well, come out where I can see you, Commandant O'Byrne. Just you. No guns, and keep your hands up.'

There were footsteps inside, the crunch of broken glass. Then a man stepped out through one of the empty window frames. He walked to the centre of the steps and stood facing across the street with his hands up. Stephen stood up from behind the wall, holstered his revolver, and walked up the steps to where he stood. Even with all his men covering him from behind the wall he felt the hairs on the back of his neck prickling. One shot was all it would take.

O'Byrne wore a suit that was almost black with soot. His eyes were very white in his grimy face and he wore an empty holster slung on a strap across his shoulder. He looked incredibly young to Stephen, but also incredibly tired, his head drooping between his upraised hands.

'You can put your hands down,' Stephen said quietly, and O'Byrne nodded his acknowledgement as he lowered them. 'My name is Ryan, by the way.'

'You fight a hard fight, Captain,' O'Byrne said with a wry smile, looking up over his shoulder as something came crashing down inside the hotel

226

and sent a shower of sparks shooting out one of the upstairs windows.

'As do you,' Stephen acknowledged. 'I wouldn't have thought anybody could last that long in there.'

'Well, we've had enough and we're coming out. I must warn you that I don't speak for Mr Brugha, however.'

'Cathal Brugha?' Stephen asked. He'd been warned that Brugha might be inside this block, but then he'd been warned that a whole slew of people might be inside – including de Valera.

'He told me he'd hold his fire until I got my men out, but he's not coming out himself. He said you'll have to come in and get him.'

'Well, we'll just have to see about that,' Stephen said. 'Still, I accept your surrender, commandant. You'd better bring all your men out before they suffocate. I can have some of my men help carry your wounded if you will give me your word that Mr Brugha won't fire on them.'

'That won't be necessary,' O'Byrne said grimly, and went back inside. Stephen stood his ground in front of the steps, feeling the eyes of his men on him. O'Byrne came out leading his men, who looked even more shattered and filthy than he did. Between them they carried the two wounded men on blood-spattered bed sheets. Stephen detailed one of his men to bring them back to Sackville Street and then crouched down again behind the pedestal wall.

'Cathal Brugha's still in there,' he told Sergeant Johnson.

'Oh aye?' Johnson's face, despite being leathery

and covered in grime, was remarkably expressive. His scowl conveyed intense disapproval. 'Are you thinking of getting him out?'

Something else came crashing down inside the burning hotel and a gust of hot air, smoke and sparks blew out through the gaping door.

'No, sergeant. It's not worth it for one man. I think we'll wait here. He won't stay long with the place on fire around him.'

'That's exactly what I was thinking, sir,' Johnson said, and with a satisfied smile he fished the un-eaten half of his liquorice stick out of his pocket and started to chew on it. Then the St John Ambulance man popped up behind him, looking indignant.

'You can't do that! You can't just leave a man in there to burn to death.'

'I can if he's threatening to shoot any of my men I send in after him,' Stephen said, and glared at him. 'And why the hell didn't you go with the wounded?'

'There's a first-aid post just around the corner,' the man answered, looking as if his professional integrity had been impugned. 'Why don't you let me go in and talk to him?'

Stephen looked back through the doors. The fire had reached the far side of the lobby and he could feel the heat on his face. He mightn't have liked this first-aider, but he had to admit he wasn't lacking in courage.

'Go ahead,' he said. 'See if you can talk sense into him. Tell him we won't shoot if he comes out unarmed, but don't stay too long – that ceiling could come down any minute.'

'He's a proper little hero, isn't he?' Sergeant Johnson grinned, watching him walk up to the doors. 'The boy stood on the burning deck, his pockets full of crackers...'

'St John Ambulance!' the ambulance man shouted through the door, and then stepped inside, shielding his face with his arm. 'Hello? Is anybody here?'

He was gone a good deal longer than Stephen would have liked – particularly since he was the one who would have to go in after him. He couldn't send any of his men – it was far too dangerous. Even in the time they waited part of the roof fell in and one of the walls cracked with an ominous ground-shaking thump. Still, he didn't see that he had much choice. He had pushed himself to his knees when he saw something moving on the stairs at the back of the lobby. When he saw the flash of a white cap band he was relieved, but it was hard to make out anything else. A window blew out on one of the floors above and showered him with glass and ash and as the heat grew more intense he had to shield his eyes with his hand.

'Come on, for Christ's sake!' he muttered. At last he was able to make out that there were two of them. The ambulance man seemed to be helping somebody along with an arm around his waist. 'Thank Christ for that,' he muttered, but as they came closer to the door, the ambulance man seemed to lose his grip on his patient. The two figures parted and Brugha – Stephen recognized him even with all the soot and smoke – came charging forward in an awkward run. The ambulance man came after him, pulling him by the arm

229

and almost bringing him down, but Brugha slipped away again, and it was only when he burst out through the door, soot blackened and streaming smoke from his clothes, that Stephen saw the gun in his free hand.

Stephen had holstered his pistol, and was fumbling for it when Brugha brought up his gun and fired. It was a big Mauser pistol and it was close enough for him to touch. Brugha wouldn't have missed if the ambulance man hadn't tried to grab him again just as he pulled the trigger. The bullet went whizzing past Stephen's ear and he ducked automatically, bringing out his pistol and cocking it in one motion.

'Mr Brugha, Mr Brugha!' the ambulance man was shouting, and Stephen managed to lunge and get hold of the strap of his first-aid satchel, pulling him away just as Brugha spun around and fired again. The bullet went wide, but Brugha was already past them, out in the road and reeling like a drunk.

'*Éirinn go bràch!*'he shouted, and brought up his heavy pistol to fire again, just as Stephen brought his up. But neither of them got the chance. The Lewis gun gave a burst from across the street and felled Brugha like a tree.

Joe heard them coming before he saw them. Heavy boots in the hallway, then the door crashed open and two of them were in on top of him. No talk, no questions; just a hard kicking to keep him quiet when they lifted him up by an arm each and dragged him outside.

They took him down to the basement – the stairs

230

were murder on his bruised ribs – and pushed him into a chair in the bare room they used for interrogation. Then they went out, closing the door behind them, and left him sitting under the naked light bulb. Nothing. Time passed, and he heard the drumming of feet on the floorboards over his head, a flurry of shouting, and then a scream. Then more silence, until a distant telephone started to ring. Closer by, there was a squeak, and then the hasty scratching of tiny claws behind the skirting board. Were they watching him? He was sure of it, but he didn't care. Let them watch him. He didn't move, didn't give them anything to think about. He sat slumped in the chair, his head bent, feeling too far gone to even care about what was to come. One of his eyes had already closed up from the beatings, but through the other he could see his own shirt front, stained with blood and sweat and God knew what. He could smell himself sometimes, too. It was days since he'd had a wash, and that out of a cold tin bucket inside the Four Courts. How many days it was, he didn't know. He'd lost track of time – of day and night, even. That's what they wanted, of course. They wanted him in the dark: alone, confused and afraid.

After a while he started to pray. He prayed to God even though he wasn't sure if he was listening. It wasn't the sort of prayer he'd been taught at school and nor was it a desperate plea to be rescued. It was more like an examination of the situation, of what he had already endured and what he was sure was to come. And in examining it, he felt like he was putting it away from himself and offering it up to God. He was asking Him to take away the pain.

The door opened and a man came into the room. Joe didn't look up, but he knew it was Hughes. He could tell by the smell of his cologne. Hughes had always been a dandy, always with his hair oil and his tie pins and his shiny shoes. But even though he knew what it meant, Joe enjoyed the first waft of perfume. It was like sweetened oil, like chrism, and it smelt so sweet and so clean that it could hardly be evil.

But Hughes was no angel. 'Well, Joe,' he said, and hit him in the ribs with the leather blackjack he always carried. It was no casual shot; he'd been working on that spot for days and the pain went through Joe's chest like a spear. 'Sit up, Joe. Sit up. Let me see your face.'

Joe sat up, grunting and gasping with the pain, but he kept his head bowed, and tried to sit so that his ribs were protected by the back of the chair. Hughes walked around him, gently tapping the blackjack on the seam of his trousers.

'You know what I want, don't you, Joe? I don't even have to ask the question.'

'I don't know,' Joe mumbled. But he did know. For all the beatings and the shouting, the only one who'd got information out of this interrogation was *him*. He knew from Hughes's questions that some of the senior men from the Four Courts had managed to escape from Jameson's distillery, where they'd been locked up after the surrender. What he didn't know was where they'd gone, and that was what Hughes was after.

'What was that?' Hughes asked, and he put the

end of the blackjack under Joe's chin, and lifted his head. 'Speak up, I can't hear you.'

'I said, I don't know. I don't know where they are, I don't know anything.'

'Oh come on, Joe, you're cleverer than that.' Hughes took away the blackjack and went pacing again. 'At least, I thought you were. But I'm getting tired of it now. I'm beginning to think you don't want to help me.' He stopped pacing, and stood behind the chair, so Joe could feel his breath on the back of his neck smell the cologne. 'Is that how it is, Joe? Do you not want to help me?'

Joe heard him draw another breath, felt him move and braced himself for the blow. But all Hughes did was kick the chair, jerking Joe's head back and jangling his ragged nerves.

'All you have to do is tell me where they are, Joe.'

'I don't know where they are,' Joe repeated. He was telling the truth. They could have gone to any one of a dozen safe houses but they wouldn't have stayed long, and by now they would be long gone. They could be down in the south or even gone to England and Hughes knew this as well as he did. But that was beside the point. What Hughes really wanted was to break him, to get something out of him – anything at all, no matter how small or trivial or out of date it might be. Because once he told them that one thing, once he did that, they would own him.

'But you *do* know where they are,' Hughes was behind him again, menacing. 'You just don't want to tell me, do you? Go on, Joe, tell me, please. Tell me what you know. It'll be better for all of us in the long run.'

Joe heard a sliding step and knew what was coming. He tried to brace himself for it but Hughes was too quick. He feinted one way and Joe ducked to try and protect his head. But in doing so, he left his ribs exposed, and the blackjack found its mark. The shock of it drove all the wind out of him. He tried to cover himself with his hands, but the blackjack caught him on the side of the head, stunning him. He fell off the chair in a heap, and Hughes went for him again, again, again. Chest, kidneys, head. Joe curled up in a ball, try to protect himself as best he could, but it went on and on until Hughes's strength failed him and he eventually stopped, bent over with his hands on his knees and panting for breath.

'By Jesus, I'm sorry, Joe. You know I didn't want to do that, but you didn't leave me any choice, did you?'

Joe could hardly hear him. His ears were ringing, and he felt lightheaded and weak. Every nerve was screaming with pain. His hands were shaking and he could taste blood in his mouth.

'God will forgive you,' he mumbled, blood and spit dribbling out over his swollen lips.

Hughes came around in front of him and pulled a handkerchief from his pocket as he hitched up his trousers and hunkered down, mopping his brow.

'What was that Joe?'

'I said God will forgive you.'

'Ah, now, Joe, there's no need to go bringing God into it, is there? He's not here. He's not coming to help you. Now, why don't you just tell me what I want to know, and then I won't have to hurt you any more.'

Joe looked up into his face. Hughes was smiling, but it was a false smile, lips pulled back, showing his teeth. He could see right through him; he knew Hughes was enjoying this. There was no connection there, no love. And he was wrong. God was here; He was everywhere. Even through the veil of pain, even lying on this cold stone floor, with blood and sweat running down his face, he knew the truth of that, and he knew that Hughes was wrong. Hughes would never understand, and would be forever damned by his own ignorance.

'You're wrong,' he whispered, and turned his head to smile up at Hughes. Then he covered his face as Hughes jumped up and came at him again.

Billy stopped at the college gate and looked back at the man who had just walked past him. He'd been so lost in thought that he hadn't even noticed him coming towards him but then something flashed in his memory and he stopped in his tracks. He studied the figure as he disappeared towards Grafton Street but he still couldn't quite place it. A black homburg and a brown raincoat. Nothing out of the ordinary there, except that he was an unusually small man and he walked with a limp. Billy tried to remember his face but he couldn't. He was sure he knew him from somewhere but, no, it just wouldn't come.

He shrugged and went on into the college, grinning to himself as he passed under the gate and tipped his hat to the porter. He'd laughed out loud when he heard that they'd billeted Stephen here. Lord, of all the places they could have put him! Still, at least it was during the summer vacation, and he'd be less likely to bump into anyone he knew.

But as Billy walked into Front Square, heading for the cluster of soldiers he saw standing outside the chapel, he spotted another figure striding hastily towards the gate. Could that be the litigious Mr Keach? He certainly matched Stephen's description very closely. Well, he wouldn't be very happy – not after the mess the republicans had made of the Four Courts. His whole case had literally gone up in smoke and it would take months to sort everything out now. For this reason, Billy's grin was even broader as he approached the soldiers and heard Stephen's voice in the middle of them all, rapidly giving out orders.

'...I want a guard on the gate, lieutenant, changed every four hours. Sergeant, you will need to speak with the college cook about provisioning...'

Billy waited a few yards away until he had finished. As the crowd of men gradually thinned he felt as if Stephen was emerging from the throng, and thought how strange it was to see him once more in the place where they had first met. But this Stephen Ryan was not the same one he had met ten years ago. This was a soldier, who commanded respect and whose men saluted him smartly before they dashed off to carry out his orders. At last, when they had all gone, Billy cleared his throat and Stephen turned towards him. He smiled, but his face was grimy and smudged with soot, and his uniform spattered with brick dust.

'You look like you've been in the wars, Stephen.'

'You could say that. I'm just back from Sackville Street. We've managed to clear them out of the hotels but the whole place is a shambles.'

'I dare say.' Billy nodded. He'd seen the smoke and heard the firing. He'd once wondered if Collins and Mulcahy and the others would have the stomach to take on their old comrades, but not any more. 'Is it true that Cathal Brugha was killed down there? I heard a rumour.'

'He pretty much killed himself,' Stephen remarked bitterly, 'And he damn near killed me while he was at it.'

'He martyred himself,' Billy said. 'But then, a man like him was always going to do that. I shouldn't be too upset over it.'

'Who said I'm upset?' Stephen asked, giving him a look that clearly showed that he was. 'Anyway, what brings you down here?' He loosened the collar of his tunic and ran two fingers underneath to ease the chafing. He'd been hoping to have a wash and then go up to Lillian's for his tea. There weren't many advantages to fighting a war in his hometown, but he was determined to make the most of what there were.

'I have some news of your brother.'

Stephen froze, and the look on his face made Billy quickly put up his hands.

'Don't worry; it's not bad news. Well, not that bad, anyway. He's still alive. He was captured after the Four Courts surrendered.'

Stephen looked relieved but then stiffened into

a more formal attitude as a soldier came running up to him and saluted.

'General Dalton's compliments, sir,' he said, and handed Stephen a long chestnut-coloured leather case. 'He wanted you to have this.'

'Thank you, corporal,' Stephen answered absently, frowning at the case, which was highly polished and clearly quite heavy. He brought it over to a nearby bench and opened the straps that held it shut.

'What the devil is it?' Billy wondered aloud, and then Stephen lifted the lid to reveal a beautiful-looking rifle with gleaming walnut woodwork and a long blue barrel.

'A shooting prize,' he said, picking up the note that lay inside and handing it to Billy. The note simply read: *'Victori Spolia Ire.'*

'All I ever got was a tin of biscuits,' Billy grumbled, but he watched approvingly as Stephen pulled the rifle from the case, looked expertly along the barrel, and snapped the telescope into place on top.

'Perhaps it's more of a *memento mori*,' he remarked, turning the gun to show Billy the long scar on the stock. It was clearly very fresh; a deep white furrow through the glossy walnut, travelling along the top of the stock to the point where the shooter's face might have been.

'I shudder to think,' Billy remarked and then reminded Stephen of what had brought him here. 'Anyway, about your brother?'

'Where are they holding him?' Stephen asked, slipping the rifle back into the case and swiftly fastening the straps. 'I heard they were going to

238

put those men in Mountjoy. Is that true? I suppose he'll feel at home there.'

'He's not in Mountjoy, I'm afraid,' Billy said, and the tone of his voice was glum enough to make Stephen straighten up slowly and forget about the rifle. 'They've taken him to Oriel House.'

Stephen couldn't hide the dismay that came over him. He knew about Oriel House and about the men who worked there: secret police by any other name. Many of them had worked in Collins's counter-intelligence unit in the war against the British and now they were using British tactics against their new opponents. Everybody knew about the beatings that went on in there; some said that prisoners were tortured, and Stephen had even heard of men being killed and their bodies dumped in the mountains.

'How the hell did he end up in there?'

'Apparently, one of his old chums was down at the Four Courts and spotted him. You know how he was part of that crowd before the split. I mean, apart from any information he might have, you can bet they'd want to show him what they think of one of their own who turned against them.'

'Christ almighty!' Stephen's dismay deepened. Billy was quite right; they would certainly go much harder on one of their own. But what could he do? Oriel House was a law unto itself. What little authority he had as a captain in the army would carry no weight at all in there. Dalton might be able to do something, but it might take days and even then there was no guarantee.

'I've got to get him out of there,' Stephen said. 'They'll bloody kill him.'

239

Billy knew the time had come to play his ace. He slipped an envelope from his inside pocket. 'Use this.'

'What's that?' Stephen asked, looking at the envelope as if it might bite him.

'It's a release order signed by the Minister for Home Affairs. It requests that he be released into the custody of a Captain Wallace. For our purposes, that would be you. Once you have him, you can do what you like with him. Since there is no such person as Captain Wallace, there won't be any questions asked.'

'But how on earth did you get that?'

'Never mind how I got it.' Billy smiled mysteriously. 'Let's just say that Mr O'Higgins believes it would suit us better if Joe remains in the land of the living. He seems to think we might find a use for him later on.'

Stephen had been on the point of taking the letter, but he hesitated. He knew Billy was working for the minister and didn't doubt that the letter was genuine. But it was still a *fake* release order. Why go to all that bother over his brother? He eyed the envelope suspiciously.

'Go on, take it.' Billy shook the envelope at him. 'Take it and we'll call it quits.'

Stephen frowned. 'We'll call what quits?'

'Stephen, surely you haven't forgotten that business in London?'

'No, of course not. But I mean, that was nothing. It was—'

Billy shook the letter again. 'It was something, Stephen. And so is this. It will get him out. Take it, Stephen. At least let me do this for you.'

'All right,' he said, and took the envelope. 'We're quits.'

The pain was waiting for him when he woke up. It drove into his ribs the moment he moved, and he grunted in surprise and snapped open his eyes. He was in a strange room and the light streaming in the window hurt his eyes. He wasn't used to waking up in daylight, and it was like needles in his eyeballs. Closing his eyes again, he tried to rub them with his hand. He wished he could stay asleep. He was so tired and this bed was so soft and warm, but even moving his hand a few inches sent shafts of pain spearing through his chest again. He groaned.

'Are you all right?' It was a woman's voice, soft and concerned. He felt a cool hand on his forehead.

Joe opened one eye, slitting it against the sun, and he saw a young woman leaning over him. She looked familiar, with a pleasant face and kind eyes behind her spectacles.

'Sit up, now, and I'll give you something to drink,' she said, and pain speared through his ribs as she helped him up and put a pillow behind his back. He was still dazed and in pain, and hardly knew what was happening when she put a glass to his lips and helped him drink. The cool, clean water relieved the parched feeling in his mouth and throat and seemed to clear his head. He got his other eye open and looked at her as she set down the glass and sat in the chair beside the bed. Her hands were folded in her lap and she was smiling at him.

241

'Do you remember me?' she asked. 'I'm Lillian, Stephen's fiancée. I don't think we've ever been introduced.'

'You were in court one day,' he said, and the words sounded very loud inside his own head. But talking seemed to bring some relief to the tight feeling inside his chest.

'I was,' she answered, and when she saw the way he was peering around the room, bewilderment on his bruised face, she added, 'you're in Stephen's flat on Northumberland Road. Well, his old flat. He lives in the barracks now. But it's safe here. You can stay until you're better.'

Safe. The last thing he remembered was the cell door opening and the feeling like lead in the pit of his stomach. He knew he couldn't take another beating. He would tell them what they wanted to hear – tell them anything to make it stop. But the kicking hadn't come, even though he had curled up in a ball, tensed against it. They'd picked him up and put him on a chair they brought in. Then one of them held his head while another one wiped his face with a wet cloth, washing away the worst of the gore. Then they buttoned his shirt and lifted him by the elbows, helping him now, not dragging him. Down the hall and out past the front desk. It looked surprisingly normal; green walls and a wooden chair and a telephone. But there were sandbags around the door and two soldiers standing there, waiting for him.

'Would you like a cup of tea?' Lillian asked, and she jumped up without waiting for an answer. 'And what about something to eat? Could you manage that? I'll make you some toast, shall I?'

She went out and Joe let his head fall back against the pillows. His brother had come to get him. He couldn't believe it – it was so unexpected, he hadn't even recognized him at first. Then, when he did open his mouth to say something, Stephen had cut him off, seizing him roughly by the arm.

'Right then, Ryan, let's be having you.'

The other soldier had opened the door and suddenly they were out on the street. It was a warm summer evening but thick clouds were threatening rain. A sluggish breeze stirred the humid air, but it had never felt better to Joe; the air had never been so sweet. He tried to draw in a deep breath but a broken rib stabbed at him and he stumbled on the step. His brother held him up.

'Keep walking,' he whispered out of the side of his mouth. 'Just as far as the car.'

The car was parked just up the street. The second soldier – a sergeant, Joe had noticed – had got in front of them and was opening the door. He straightened himself and walked as steadily as he could towards it. His legs were weak and he leaned heavily on Stephen's arm. When they finally got there, he could hardly raise his feet to climb into the car. His brother practically lifted him in, as the sergeant ran round and quickly started the engine. It was an open car, and Joe flopped back in the seat and stared up at the open sky. The cloud was swirling, rolling, threatening to douse him, but he didn't care. He felt light-headed and strangely giddy, but at the same time he wanted to sleep.

Stephen came around and got in the other side. He leaned forward and said something to the sergeant and the car started to move down the

243

street. Joe was aware of Oriel House going past but he didn't look, didn't even turn his head.

'Jesus Christ,' Stephen said, looking him up and down. 'What the hell did they do to you?'

'They had a few questions they wanted to ask me,' Joe mumbled, but he felt so tired he couldn't say any more. He swallowed painfully. His throat felt constricted and suddenly everything seemed to hurt. Every bump, every jolt of the moving car, even the force of the air blowing on his face. It was as if his body couldn't take all these new sensations and every stretched and shredded nerve was screaming. He slumped against the side of the car and shut his eyes against it, willing it to stop.

He heard a step in the next room and then the rattle of crockery. Lillian came into the room, carrying a tray. Joe felt his stomach tighten at the smell of buttered toast. He couldn't remember how long it was since he'd had any solid food.

'How are you feeling?' Lillian asked, setting down the tray and pouring him a cup of tea. His hand shook as he took it.

'Weak,' Joe said, and winced as the hot tea stung some of his broken teeth. He blew on the cup. 'Sore.'

'Stephen said he gave you an injection last night, to help you sleep.' She handed him the plate of toast, already cut into fingers. 'Do you think you can manage on your own, or would you like me to help you?'

Joe needed no help to dispose of the toast, broken teeth or not. Lillian went out again and came back with more. Joe ate more slowly then, feeling as if he was coming back to himself.

Lillian sat quietly by the bed and watched him.

'Where did he go?' Joe asked, after he had swallowed another finger of toast. His stomach suddenly felt heavy and distended, and he took another sip of tea to try and wash the greasy taste of the butter from his mouth.

'He had to go back to the college. He's commanding a detachment of soldiers there. They were involved in the fighting on Sackville Street.' Lillian looked down at the floor quickly, as if she realized she had said too much. When she looked up again, she smiled at him. 'He said he'd come back this evening, if he could get away.'

Joe had some idea how the fighting had gone in Sackville Street. Apart from Hughes bragging about how the anti-Treaty forces had been routed, he'd been able to hear the sounds of battle all day and through the night; the deep earthy boom of field guns and the lighter rattle of gunfire. His brother must have been in the thick of it.

'He took a big chance, getting me out, didn't he?' Joe said.

'He's your brother,' Lillian said, looking at him steadily. 'And he's a good man. He wouldn't leave you, no matter what your differences.'

Joe knew she was right, so he just nodded and looked down at the plate. The nail of his thumb was split and bruised but he couldn't feel any pain from it – at least, no more than from anywhere else. He felt ragged and broken, a shell of a man.

'What will you do now?' Lillian asked quietly. 'It's not safe for you in Dublin – in Ireland, even. Maybe you should go away for a while.'

'I can't go away,' Joe answered. 'Where would I go? There's nothing else for me. This place is all I have left.'

XI

A searchlight pierced the darkness and swept across the sea just as Stephen came up from below. The white beam dazzled him, but it lit up the whole ship, casting weird shadows from the armoured cars and eighteen-pounders that were chained to the deck. It also showed Dalton standing over by the port rail with the ship's captain and a man holding a signal lamp.

'What's going on?' he asked, shielding his eyes as the searchlight swept around again. The ship's engines had stopped and they lay rocking on the gentle swell. The light went out just as suddenly as it had come on, but before it died he had a glimpse of a long black shape lying on the water a few hundred yards away. 'What's that?'

'A British patrol boat from Haulbowline, come to ask us what the devil we think we're up to,' Dalton answered, and nodded to the man with the signal lamp. 'Tell him we already have a pilot aboard and we mean to proceed into Cork Harbour.'

'I don't trust that bugger of a pilot,' the captain muttered as the signal lamp started clacking.

'Neither do I,' Dalton admitted. 'But we don't have any choice. We can't afford to heave to until morning. He's taking us in tonight, mines or no mines.'

'Mines?' Stephen said. It was bad enough that they were running without lights on a moonless night – not to mention the fact that they had a second ship following close astern. Somewhere ahead was the open mouth of Cork Harbour and Stephen had not liked the look of it on the ship's charts. It wasn't so much a harbour as a big bay, deeper than it was broad and filled with islands and bars and narrow channels.

'The Irregulars have mined the passage,' Dalton took him by the arm and led him towards the cabin where he had set up his headquarters, 'and apparently they've also sunk a block ship. It turns out our arrival by sea is not quite as un-expected as I would have liked.'

Stephen followed him through the low door, blinking in the dim electric light. He glanced at the chart spread out across the table and then felt the deck vibrate beneath his feet as the engines came to life and the ship slowly gathered way once more.

'And you don't trust the pilot not to run us into one of these mines?'

'I don't.' Dalton sat down, pulled off his cap and ran a hand through his hair. He looked strained and tired. 'As a matter of fact, I think he helped lay the bloody things. That's why I've got Liam Tobin up in the wheelhouse with him, holding a gun in his back. If that bugger sinks the ship, he won't have to worry about getting into a lifeboat.'

Stephen leaned on the table and ran his eye over the chart. Cork Harbour led to Cork City

247

and Cork City was right in the heart of enemy territory. Now that the Army Executive forces had been driven out of Dublin, they were falling back on their strongholds in the south. Three fighting columns had been sent out from Dublin to take control of the southern counties, but they were meeting heavy resistance. A seaborne landing in the enemy's rear could prove to be a decisive blow. Not only would it give the Government a base in the south, but it would also relieve pressure on the columns and deal a heavy blow to morale on the anti-treaty side.

It could also, of course, be a complete disaster – and nobody knew this better than Dalton. It was his plan; he was the one who had put it to Collins, he was the one who had asked for the precious field guns and armoured cars to be borrowed from the columns and he was the one who had all but guaranteed that the plan would work. Stephen watched him out of the corner of his eye as he studied the chart. He was staring morosely up at the light, his eyes vacant.

'This channel looks very narrow,' Stephen said, pointing to the long strip of water that threaded between Great Island and the shore. It was only a few hundred feet across, and there was no other way to get to Cork. 'They couldn't have asked for a better place to lay mines.'

'I know,' Dalton lowered his gaze towards the chart and he seemed to come alive as he focussed on it, 'but we don't have to go all the way through. See here,' his finger went to Passage West, a village on the landward side of the channel. 'There are quays where we can land our men and unload the cars and guns.'

Stephen nodded. It was only a few miles to the city from there. If they were able to land un-opposed, they could be in Cork by breakfast time. But that was the thing; even a few men would be enough to keep them off if they were properly placed.

Dalton seemed to have read his mind. 'The only problem is this.' His fingernail tapped at a large building that stood right on the corner where the passage opened. According to the chart, it was a granary. 'Our intelligence says the rebels have got a post in this place. As you can see, it covers our approach and the quay itself. I don't need to tell you what they could do to us if they have a machine gun in there.'

'Then why don't we send a boat in?' Stephen pointed to the shoreline south of the granary. 'A small party could go ashore here and take them from the rear.'

'Hmm.' Dalton's face brightened, but he studied the map closely before he went on. 'All right, that's a good idea. We'll send a boat. I want you to lead the party, though.'

'Well, all right,' Stephen said reluctantly. He'd only said it on the spur of the moment, and now he wasn't so sure.

Dalton looked up at him keenly. 'But you have experience of this sort of thing, don't you?'

'Experience?' Stephen laughed. 'I did it once, years ago. There were ten thousand other men with me and we had the British Mediterranean Fleet behind us.'

'Well, it's still a damn sight more experience

than anybody else has,' Dalton countered. 'I mean you've seen what we've got below decks.'

He was right. The army spread very thin. Most of the experienced men had been promoted and sent with the land-based columns. First up, best dressed, as Dalton himself had said. The men on these ships were mostly raw recruits, and Stephen had been below for most of the voyage, trying to show some of them how to handle a rifle.

'I'm sure they'll be fine,' Stephen said, though he knew they'd be in trouble if they met any sort of organized resistance.

'God, I hope so.' Dalton sat back and yawned, stretching his arms. 'Sometimes I think head-quarters wants me to balls this up.'

Before Stephen could say any more, there was a knock on the door and a young sailor stuck his head inside.

'General Dalton, sir. Captain sent me to tell you Roches Point is on our beam. We're coming into Cork Harbour.'

'Right,' Dalton stood up and put his cap back on, 'I'm going up to the bridge. I'll tell the captain we need a boat. You'd better go down and pick your men.' He held out his hand. 'Best of luck, Stephen. I'll see you ashore.'

Stephen shook his hand and watched him go out, heard his boots ringing on the stairs going up to the bridge. 'I bloody hope so,' he muttered under his breath.

The college was eerily quiet, even for the summer vacation. There wasn't a soul to be seen in the Front Square and it looked so peaceful that Lillian

250

hesitated under the front arch, afraid to disturb the scene. The soldiers had left and the students wouldn't be back for another month, and all she could see were green uncluttered lawns and the vibrant red and yellow bands of the flower beds. The taller trees waved lazily in the light breeze and the sun sparkled on the windows. It all seemed so tranquil, and yet, when she thought of what she had come here to do…

'Is Mr Keach here?' she asked the elderly porter who had opened the wicket gate to admit her. He had already locked it again, as if to keep the world safely outside, and was puffing back to his kiosk with a ponderous, heavy tread.

'Yes, miss. He come in about half an hour ago. Don't know if he's staying long, though. Says he's off on his holidays tomorrow.'

'Well, I'd better hurry, then,' Lillian said, though she first went and left her bag in the ladies' common room and then fairly dragged her feet all the way across the square. Maybe Stephen was right, she thought. Maybe she *should* wait until he came back. But no, she knew she was right. She rehearsed in her mind the argument she'd had with Stephen before he'd left. He hadn't been able to tell her where he was going, but she knew now that he was in Cork; that they'd landed from the sea. And God knew how long he'd be down there. Even if it was only for a week, Keach would be gone by the time he got back, and then they'd lose another month. In any case, she had argued, it wouldn't look right if Stephen was the one to do it. It was her paper; it had to be she who made the offer.

'It's all about how you present the bait,' she murmured to herself, looking up at the front of the mathematics department. Keach had taken over Professor Barrett's office and she could see the window from where she stood. She knew the office; she'd been in there often enough, but not since Keach had moved in. Nevertheless, if that's where he was, that was where she had to go. She took the folder from under her arm and looked at the half-dozen pages one more time, as if to make sure that it was all there. Then she took a deep breath and went up the steps.

It felt strange to be inside with the place so quiet. During term you could always hear the buzz of voices from the common room downstairs, or the rumble of feet going to lectures or the library. She went down the hall and up the stairs. Her own footfalls seemed so loud that she went almost on tiptoe. At the top of the stairs she stopped and paused to let her eyes adjust to the gloom. It was stranger still to have no expectation of seeing Professor Barrett's animated face when she knocked on his door. Even the thought of meeting Keach made her skin crawl, and she had a sudden urge to turn and go back, back out into the safety of daylight and the warm August sun.

She heard the tread of a shoe inside the office and a floorboard creaked. He was in there, in any case. She could hardly back down now. Steeling herself, she went up and knocked firmly on the door.

'Come!' came Keach's voice, and she pressed the handle and plunged inside. For a moment, she was disconcerted; the room was not as she

252

remembered it. Keach had put his stamp on the place by moving the desk, rearranging the bookcases and introducing some potted palms. Professor Barrett would have been horrified.

'Miss Bryce!' Keach was standing behind his desk, leaning over something. He peered at her over his spectacles, his guarded look at odds with the warmth he tried to inject into his voice. 'What an unexpected pleasure.'

'I beg your pardon, Mr Keach. I'm not disturbing you, am I?'

'No, not at all.' Keach looked down at what he'd been writing. 'Just some last-minute paperwork, that's all. I'm going on holiday tomorrow. Please, come in. Come in and tell me to what I owe the pleasure.'

'I wondered if I might be able to speak to you on a delicate matter,' Lillian said meekly, shutting the door behind her. She had hardly taken a step towards him when he came around the desk and gestured to the two chintz armchairs arranged beside the fireplace at the far end of the room.

'Please, please, let's not be formal. Let us sit down together and have a chat. It's been a while since we had a good chinwag, you and I.'

Lillian sat down on the edge of one of the armchairs with her folder balanced on her knees and her hands folded on top. Keach didn't take the other chair but went to the small table in the corner.

'Will you join me in a sherry?' he asked, looking at her sideways. 'I know it's early, but I won't tell if you won't.'

He gave a false laugh that set Lillian's teeth on

edge, but she looked around and smiled at him. 'Why, I suppose it's no harm. Just a small one, please, Mr Keach.'

'Excellent, excellent!' Keach poured two glasses of sherry, handed one to Lillian and then sat down and crossed his legs. The chairs were very close together and Lillian shifted a little, trying to avoid touching his knee with hers. She held the folder in her lap, as if trying to shield herself with it. It took an effort to move it away, to reach out and place it on the side table by the fireplace. Keach's eyes lingered on it for a few moments but then returned to hers with an indulgent smile.

'Now, Miss – ah, really, I hate to be so formal. Do you mind if I call you Lillian? Or would you prefer Lily? It's such a lovely name.'

'Lillian,' she answered, with a smile as false as his.

'Very well, Lillian it is. Now then, ah, Lillian – what exactly is it that you wanted to speak to me about?'

'Well, it's rather a delicate matter, Professor.' Lillian cleared her throat and took a sip of sherry. 'I'm afraid I'm not quite sure how to put it. It's about your case against my fiancé.'

There was very little else that it could have been about, but Keach did his best to look surprised and a little dismayed. 'Ah,' he said, pursing his lips sadly. 'I'm sorry, but I'm not sure that we can really talk about that. We've both placed the matter in the hands of our lawyers, as you know.'

'Please, Mr Keach, hear me out, I beg you.' Lillian took another sip of sherry. The glass was already more than half empty.

'My dear girl,' Keach leaned forward, 'are you feeling quite well?'

'Yes, I'm fine, thank you.' She cast her eyes down and fiddled with the stem of the sherry glass. *Liar,* she said to herself. But her greatest worry was that she was laying it on too thick. He was so close, his face just inches from hers, that he was bound to notice. 'It's just that I'm very worried about Stephen. He's gone away – with the army, you know. You've heard that he joined up again, I'm sure. After what happened with his suspension ... he well, you know...'

'Yes, I had heard something like that,' Keach said sourly, and he leaned back a little – much to Lillian's relief.

'I didn't think it would come to anything,' Lillian pressed on quickly. 'I mean, I didn't think he'd have to fight. It was so hard the last time, I'd never have let him join up again if I thought it would be this bad. But I'm sure you saw what went on in Sackville Street, and the Four Courts. It's dreadful, and terribly dangerous.'

'Oh, terribly,' Keach agreed, without much enthusiasm. 'But I'm sorry, Lillian. He's made his choice – I don't see that there's anything I can do about it.'

'But he would leave the army if he got his old job back. It's only a temporary commission. They will release him if his suspension is lifted. And with the new term starting in a few weeks, I thought...'

She brought her head up to face him and caught a strangely cold, calculating look that made her feel suddenly fearful.

'I see.' Keach looked away quickly and then

jumped to his feet. He set down his sherry glass and walked to the window with his hands clasped behind his back.

'Well, you know, I'd *like* to help,' he said. 'Really, I would. But I'm sorry to say that might not be so easy to do at this point. You know there are lawyers involved, and writs have been served, to say nothing of the damage to my reputation if I were to withdraw my claim.'

He was standing behind Lillian, so that she had to twist around in her chair to see him. He had turned away from the window and was facing her, silhouetted by the bright summer sunshine outside. She reached for the folder lying on the side table.

'Well, I'm sure I could make it worth your while, Mr Keach. If you would care to look at this...'

'Make it worth my while?' Keach asked. Three steps and he was there, standing behind her, leaning on the back of her chair, leaning close. She could feel his breath on her neck. 'Yes, I believe you could, Lillian.' His hands were on her shoulders and the touch of them made her start. She dropped the folder and the pages sprayed out across the carpet. 'I'm sure we could come to some arrangement,' he whispered, and slipped his hand down, cupping her breast.

Lillian struggled against him, trying to wriggle free, but he held her with his other hand on her shoulder, pinning her into the chair.

'Mr Keach, no!'

'Oh come on, Lillian. We both know why you really came here.'

'No!' her voice cracked out. He was squeezing

256

her breast and she could feel his breath hot on her face as he tried to kiss her. But to do so, he had to loosen his grip on her shoulder and she managed to break his grip, twisting down out of the chair and then jumping up to face him. 'How dare you!' she said, her face flushed and her breath coming hard. Fury won out over fear and disgust when she saw he was smirking at her. 'How dare you!' she said again, and she turned on her heel and ran out of the room.

It was turning into a beautiful summer's day. The sky was pure blue with hardly a cloud, and the early morning sun threw a broad silver band for miles across the sea to the south. Birds sang in the hedgerows and the golden stalks of ripe barley nodded lazily in the first stirrings of the breeze.

Stephen decided to stop in the barley field to straighten his line. Not that it was much of a line; Dalton had only been able to spare him four men, all of them raw, and nervousness was making them clump together.

'Spread out!' he ordered, going down on one knee. While they waded away through the whispering barley, he twisted his body so that he could look back the way they had come. Cork Harbour and the Great Island lay below them. He couldn't see the ships any more, but now and again the distant roar of a diesel engine told him that the armoured cars and eighteen-pounders were still unloading. For all Dalton's apprehension, the landing had gone without a hitch. No mines had been struck and even the granary had not put up much of a fight; just a single ragged volley as

Stephen's party burst in, and then the Irregulars had fled through a side door. If it were all this easy, he thought, he'd be home by the weekend.

When all he could see of his men were four heads bobbing above the barley at long intervals, he turned and studied the ground ahead. They had just reached the brow of a hill and from here the ground dipped a little and then climbed back up towards the band of tall leafy trees that lined the road into Cork. A scout had reported a roadblock along here, and Dalton had sent Stephen to flank it before he tried to bring his cars and guns up the road. He could see no sign of the roadblock – no sign of life at all, except for a thin plume of smoke rising up from the small cottage at the top of the next field.

'Right, lads, forward,' he called, and his men rose up with him and continued their swishing march through the barley. Another fifty yards and they came to the edge; the ground changed to lumpy furrows and limp green leaves. A turnip field, and it was rising, too; curling up towards the road. Stephen lengthened his stride, anxious to get to better cover. Out of the corner of his eye, he saw his men were starting to bunch up again.

'Spread out–' he began, but he was cut off by the rat-tat-tat of a machine gun. He instantly dropped to the ground and the two men nearest to him did the same. But the next one seemed to have been stunned by the sudden noise. He looked around as if he was trying to see where it had come from and then took off at a run for the safety of the standing barley.

'Get down!' Stephen bellowed, but it was too

late. The machine gun barked again and he went sprawling. Cursing under his breath, Stephen pressed himself hard into a furrow, smelling the sharpness of crushed green leaves amid the mouldy odours of earth and manure. The echo of the shots rolled away across the hillside and then everything was silent save for the swish of the breeze and the hesitant twitter of a blackbird in the ditch.

His nearest man was only five yards away, shaking in the dirt, sweating, clearly terrified.

'Did you see where they're shooting from?' Stephen asked.

'The cottage, I think.'

Stephen raised his head a couple of inches until he could see the tin roof of the cottage through the nodding leaves of the turnip plants. It was about two hundred yards away and he cursed himself for not being more wary of it. It covered the whole of the field they were in, and now it had them pinned down in the open.

'Right, throw me your rifle,' Stephen told him, laying his head back down, and when the man wriggled off the strap of his rifle and threw it over, a shot zipped straight between them, cutting the stalks off a few turnips.

'Oh, Jesus Mary and Joseph!' the man panted, curling up in a ball.

'Stay calm, now, and lie flat.' Stephen pulled the rifle in by the strap, opened the bolt and checked it, all without raising his head from the ground. Whoever was in that farmhouse was clearly waiting for them to move and he didn't fancy his chances with one magazine and two men who were frightened out of their wits. On the other hand, he didn't have much choice. If they waited, they'd be picked off eventually.

'Do you see that wall over there?' he asked in a steady voice, hardly raising it above a whisper. There was a dry-stone wall running up the edge of the field, about thirty yards behind where the two men lay. They turned their heads, looked and nodded.

'I'm going to start covering fire and when I do, I want the pair of you to get up and run like hell for that wall. All right? Here we go. One, two, three–'

He came up on his knees and loosed off two shots at the nearest window of the farmhouse. He felt as much as heard the men getting up behind him and charging for cover, then he saw the flash of a muzzle in the window as the machine gun started after them. He fired again, three shots, and then flopped down and crawled as flat as he could, hearing bullets whipping and whizzing overhead. He'd made it into the ditch when the machine gun stopped suddenly and he heard the click and the clank of an empty pan being changed on a Lewis gun. That was what he'd been waiting for. He jumped to his feet and scrambled over the wall before they could get another shot off.

'Right, then, so far, so good,' he said, trying to appear cheerful to the two men cowering on the other side. They were all he had left. He'd seen one man knocked down on the run and had just crawled past the one they got with the first burst. Then again, he knew where that machine gun was now, and this wall would give him cover all the way up to the farmhouse. Adrenaline was flowing and his blood was up. He felt focussed and clear and he knew exactly what he was going to do.

'Reload this,' he said, thrusting the rifle back at its owner and pulling his revolver from its holster. 'Are either of you carrying any bombs?'

'Here.' The second man fumbled a Mills bomb out of his pocket and almost dropped it because his hand was shaking so much.

'Calm down, take a deep breath,' Stephen told him, slipping the bomb into his pocket. Had he ever been that nervous? He tried to remember the first time he'd seen action. Another bright, sunny day like this one, only instead of green and gold fields it had been amid sand and scrubby rock in Turkey. He hadn't had the time to be nervous – or the sense. It had been such a great big adventure back then.

'Right, follow me,' he said, and led them in a low crouch along the wall until it hit a corner and turned away from the cottage. The gap was only about twenty yards; they were so close he could hear voices coming from inside. He placed his men there and moved a few yards further on, so he would be out of their line of fire. When he straightened up and peered over the wall, he could see the barrel of the machine gun sticking out of the nearest window. Down again. He checked his revolver, looked at his men and gave them the signal to fire.

They jumped up and blazed away gamely, breaking glass and chipping flakes of whitewash off the stone front of the cottage. Stephen rolled over the top of the wall and dashed across the gap to the corner of the cottage. He was coming into his own men's line of fire, but he didn't have far to go. The machine gun started up again, spitting fire from only a few feet away, and he flattened himself against the wall of the cottage and crept closer and closer. The firing stopped. His men had dropped down into cover and he heard muted laughter from inside the house. Close enough. He pulled the pin on the bomb, counted three and lobbed it in through the window. Scuffling, curses, from inside. He rolled himself away from the window but still felt the flat crack of the bomb and the heat of the blast as fire and smoke shot out through the window beside him.

Half an hour later, Dalton drove up to the cottage at the head of a convoy of three armoured cars, each one towing an eighteen-pound gun. Stephen and his men had already cleared the roadblock, which had consisted of nothing more than a table, a bicycle and a few other bits of furniture from the cottage jumbled into the middle of the road. Dalton's car stopped and he stood up in his seat and surveyed the scene. He saw the two National Army men who had been killed crossing the field laid out beside the two Irregulars who had manned the machine gun. The gun itself leaned against the wall of the cottage. It looked battered and blackened, but still might be serviceable.

'Well,' he said, as Stephen came out of the cottage and saluted him. 'It looks like you've been in the wars.'

'I'm sorry to report two men killed, sir.'

'That's not your fault.'

'Yes, it is. I let them walk right in to it.'

Dalton's eyes narrowed. He'd been in Stephen's position himself often enough. He knew what it was like after action – the doubt, the depression. He also knew the bill might have been much higher if he'd sent anybody else.

'You're never going to be bloody happy, are you?'

Stephen didn't answer, but instead looked over his shoulder at the four corpses, at the blood and glass on the ground, at the charred whitewash and the gaping windows. This had been somebody's home, but you wouldn't keep pigs in it now.

'Come on,' Dalton jerked his thumb over his shoulder, 'hop in. I'll give you a lift into Cork.'

The Army Executive forces had not quite disappeared from Dublin. Many had been arrested and more had fled south to continue the fight in the country, but a few were still at large in the city. They lived a necessarily secretive existence, staying in safe houses, moving often and rarely coming together. When meetings such as this one were called, they arrived discreetly, in ones and twos, mostly coming in through the back kitchen after leaving their bicycles outside.

Joe wasn't really sure if he was one of them. He left his bicycle in the back garden with the others and Mrs Humphries greeted him warmly as he came into the kitchen but, as he followed her down the hallway, he felt apprehensive. What was he doing there? After his bruises had gone down, he'd left his brother's flat and gone to Kirwan's pub on Parnell Square. Shay Kirwan was dead

263

against the Treaty and he'd put him up, giving him bed and board in exchange for lifting a few barrels in the cellar. That's all he'd been doing for the last few weeks; working in the cellar and keeping his head down. It was Kirwan who'd told him about the meeting. He'd given him the time off and all but sent him here, so Joe had come on a borrowed bicycle. But he wasn't sure if he was even supposed to be here, and he had the feeling that he might not be welcome.

This became more apparent when Mrs Humphries showed him into the dining room. It was the only room in the house big enough to hold them all, and these tough-looking men made a curious sight sitting around the gleaming mahogany table, amidst the bone china and silverware. They were chatting with the voluble intensity of men who didn't get much company when Joe came in, but all talk stopped when they saw him. Most were Dublin men and many of them old acquaintances, but that wasn't the way they looked at him. A few uneasy nods and a couple of open stares were all he got. He knew what they were thinking. They were all on the run and some of them had even escaped from captivity. But not one of them had walked straight out the front door of Oriel House – and not one of them had been sprung by his brother. Even if he still had a few scars to show for it, he wasn't surprised that they didn't trust him.

Nevertheless, they pushed up and made a space for him near the door. The conversation never recovered, however, and there was a general sense of relief when Ernie O'Malley came in. O'Malley was the senior officer at large in Dublin since

Liam Lynch had escaped to the south to organize the new Army Executive headquarters. O'Malley had been in the Four Courts and was one of the senior officers who had escaped afterwards. He was a young man with a rather square face, wide-set eyes and a mop of curly hair. Joe remembered him as brave, serious and a bit of an intellectual. Even after the shelling had started he'd often been seen going around with a book in his hand, giving out orders and encouragement and the odd bit of Latin while he was at it.

'Right, lads, I suppose we might as well get started,' he said, taking off his raincoat and draping it over a chair. They could all see the butt of his pistol sticking out from under his jacket. 'First of all, thanks for coming along. I know how hard it was for all of you to get here tonight and how dangerous it is for many of you to stay in the city. Much as I hate to admit it, the National Army has control of the capital and it would be foolish of us to pretend that we can win the war on the streets of Dublin–'

There was a murmur of discontent and even disbelief. O'Malley was one of the hardest of the die-hards. Defeatist talk was not what they expected to hear from him. But he grinned as he stuck the stem of his pipe between his teeth and held up his hand to stop the muttering.

'Don't get me wrong. I'm not suggesting for a minute that we abandon Dublin. But we have to face the fact that the main fight has moved elsewhere – for the time being, anyway. Our comrades in the south are engaging the National Army now, and I'm sure we all hope that they

265

may have better luck than we did. Our job must be to give them as much support as we can, and that means becoming a thorn in the backside of the National Army.'

That was more like it. The men were laughing and some of them even banged the table, but O'Malley wasn't finished. He took the pipe from his mouth and looked around the room, his eyes shining and a smile twitching at his lips, like a magician waiting for the right moment to turn his trick.

'Now, I'm sure you will all agree that we got the worst of it when we brought the Free Staters to open battle on the streets here. We got the worst of it when we did the same with the British, and what did we do then? We went into cover and we sniped at them and harried them until they were mightily sick of us. We made our small numbers an advantage, and that's what I'm saying we do here. No open attacks, but small little pinpricks; shootings, bombings, robberies. Anything we can do to tie up National Army troops here in Dublin while our pals knock the stuffing out of them down in Limerick and Tipperary and Cork. What do you say to that, then, eh? Let it be hit and run for us, boys. Nip and tuck and we'll see who has the most fight in them!'

He had them now. The air was electric and the men around the table were smiling and laughing, their faces alive and attentive.

'Good man, Ernie,' somebody called out, and hands drummed on the table. O'Malley tried to quieten them by waving down the noise with his hand. He had just restored silence when there was a heavy knock on the door behind him. When the door opened a head popped inside and Joe half turned to see who it was. His jaw instantly clenched and his hands curled into fists. Vincent Garvey's eyes swept around the room, settled for a moment on Joe's face, but then moved on again as if he didn't know who he was.

'Good evening, lads, sorry to interrupt you now.' Garvey's grin looked false on his narrow face. 'Ernie, do you think I could have a quick word with Austin?'

Austin was Austin Stack, O'Malley's deputy and quartermaster. He was half out of his seat before O'Malley waved him down again, looking vexed. 'Can it wait a minute, Vincent? We'll be finished shortly.'

'Sure, there's no rush.' Garvey's head bobbed. 'Take your time. I'll wait inside in the living room.'

He closed the door softly and Joe stared at it for a moment, half wondering if he'd really seen him.

'Well, as I was saying...' O'Malley scratched his head and paused for a moment, trying to gather his thoughts.

'Sorry lads, excuse me,' Joe said abruptly, and he got up and walked out into the hall.

Mrs Humphries's living room was long and high ceilinged and furnished in an old-fashioned style with Turkish carpets and lots of mahogany and velvet. Garvey was sitting in an armchair in the far corner. He had one hand in the pocket of his raincoat and was watching the door intently when Joe came in.

'Well, well, if it isn't my old pal Joe Ryan? You're looking rough, Joe. Were you in the wars?'

'What the hell are you doing here?' Joe demanded. He didn't come very far into the room, making sure to leave the door open and stopping well short of Garvey. If he knew him at all, he had a gun in that pocket.

'I'm here on business, Joe. Not that it's any of yours, but sure I'll tell you anyway. You boys need guns and bullets to keep up the good fight, and I'm the man who can get them for you. I've got contacts now, in England–'

'You shouldn't even be in this country,' Joe spat. 'You were told what would happen if you ever came back.'

Garvey just threw his head back and laughed. 'Ah Joe, did you not hear? Things have changed. Mick Collins is the man who put that sentence on me, and your pals in there don't like him any more. So as long as I keep them sweet I can come and go as I please. They help me if I help them. That's how it is nowadays, Joe, it's business.'

Joe's hands were down by his sides, his fists clenched so hard the nails were cutting into his palms. He hated Garvey. Maybe he would never know exactly what he'd done to Maggie but he knew that he'd taken her away from him. Garvey had killed her, and for that Joe hated him with a fury that he could barely contain.

'I know what you're thinking, Joe,' Garvey told him, with a wink. 'But if you were going to kill me, you should have done it when you had the chance. You should have done it when you and your brother had me that time. But that's your problem, see, you're too soft.'

There was a noise outside. The dining-room

door had opened and, from the noise of the voices, it sounded like the meeting was breaking up. Joe glanced over his shoulder and Garvey saw his chance; he jumped to his feet and crossed the room to where he stood. Despite his bad leg he was surprisingly quick and quiet, and he managed to do it without once taking his hand from the pocket of his raincoat.

'But don't you worry,' Garvey stopped next to Joe, close enough for him to feel his breath on his cheek, 'I'm not going to kill you. Not yet, anyhow. Maybe I'll do your brother first. Or, better yet, I'll do that girl of his. Have you ever seen her, Joe? Nice-looking bit of stuff, she is. Bit on the lanky side for some people, but she's real posh. I bet she'd—'

'You shut your fucking mouth.' Joe turned on him. Gun or no gun, he didn't care.

Garvey was smaller than he was, but he was quick. Before Joe could lay a hand on him he had slipped away and stood half behind the open door.

'Ah Joe, when are you going to learn that you can't protect the women?' he said contemptuously. 'Look at the state of you. You can't even protect yourself.'

'I'll kill you,' Joe whispered. 'If it's the last fucking thing I do, I'll see you dead.'

'What's going on here?' O'Malley demanded, stalking into the room.

'Me and Joe were just catching up,' Garvey said, slipping around behind him. 'Is Austin free now? I'll just pop in to see him. I won't keep him long.'

He limped down the hall and O'Malley quickly

269

closed the door. Then he stared at Joe, putting his hands on his hips. 'What the hell was all that about?'

'That man's a tout and a murderer,' Joe answered, looking at him sullenly.

O'Malley just shrugged. 'He may well be, Joe. But he's also the only one who can get us guns without having to steal them from the National Army. We have to be practical.'

'Practical? Where is he getting the guns? Eh? Have you thought of that? Do you not think it might be from the sort of people who'd sooner see us killing one another than getting along?'

'You're starting to sound like a Free Stater,' O'Malley said quietly.

'Practical, my arse! That fucker would sell us all out as soon as he'd look at us.'

'Well, for fuck's sake, Joe, what else are we going to do? Do you not know that beggars can't be choosers? I don't like him either, and if half the stories about him are true, then he's not to be trusted. But I don't have any choice. We must have guns to fight and I don't care where they come from. All that matters is that we win the war. When we've done that, then we can sort everything else out.'

'It's as simple as that, is it?' Joe stared at him in disbelief. Seeing Garvey had affected him deeply, and rage still seethed inside him. But there was something else as well. Was it disappointment? No, it was worse; betrayal. Was this what they had fought for? Was this why he had gone to jail? Was this why Whelan had died? When he was in Oriel House he'd despised Hughes and all the others because he could see what they'd become. But were his own side any better?

'Win the war, whatever it takes?' he asked, disgusted, and pulled the door open. But he stopped on the threshold and shook his head. 'I'm sorry, Ernie, but if that's what it takes, maybe the war's not worth winning.'

XII

Imperial Hotel,
Cork,

21 August 1922

My darling Lillie,

Thank you for your last letter, even though I was never as sorry to receive one from you. It saddened me to hear that poor old Dunbar has lost his last fight and I will miss him very much. I suppose it was not unexpected, but still, he was the very best sort of friend and the world will be much poorer without him.

But at least this cloud has some scrap of a silver lining. The moment I got your letter, I went to Dalton and asked if I could go to Dublin for the funeral. It seems there is an armoured car that needs to be sent back, so he has put me in charge of the detachment that is driving up. All being well, you should see me before you see this letter, but I will post it anyway since I face a long drive right through the middle of 'bandit country' and there is no telling how long it might take.

You will be interested to hear that Michael Collins has just arrived. He is not in good form. He looked unwell and was very subdued, which is never a good sign with him. Then again, the weight that has been placed on his shoulders must be immense. For poor Arthur Griffith to die so suddenly was a terrible shock for everybody, but none more so than Collins. Of course, Griffith is not the only friend he has lost. You may remember Harry Boland, who was killed in a shoot-out in Skerries a couple of weeks ago. Even though he fought for the other side, it seems that he and Collins were once the very closest of friends and Collins is still not the better of his loss. He was another thoroughly decent man, by all accounts. With all these good men dying, I sometimes wonder who will be left to pick up the pieces when this horrible war is over.

Anyway, enough of this endless talk of death. I do have some good news, which is that I've been promoted. Dalton has made me a commandant (that's a major in the old style). We had a drink with Collins to celebrate but, as you can imagine, our joviality did not survive for very long. To be fair, Collins was not the only one with a long face. Dalton was just as gloomy, despite the fact that his seaborne attack was a complete success and the City of Cork is now ours.

His greatest problem is what to do next. True, we have taken the city, but what do we do now that we have it? We sit on our hands while the Irregulars melt away into the countryside. They are setting up to fight us from the ditches and hedges as they fought the British before us, and I'm afraid that if we give them the space to start that business then we are done for. Not to sound too bloodthirsty, my dear, but if we are to win this war then *we must strike hard and strike fast. The longer the other lot can drag this out, the more we look like ogres, motoring around in our armoured cars, and terrorizing the countryside. The fact that we got these armoured cars from the British is one that Mr Childers and his propaganda machine are not slow to point out, and it is not too difficult for them to convince the people that we are nothing better than British stooges. As you can imagine, the longer we delay, the worse it gets.*

I know Dalton has been pressing for another blow, for more landings and more round-ups to try to take some of their key men out of circulation, but the Government will not wear it. They are afraid of appearing too heavy-handed, and I cannot say that I can blame them. This thing is all about the people, not the politics. If we go at it too hard then we could lose the support of the people. Not hard enough and we will still lose the support of the people, only more slowly.

Well, there I go again, getting maudlin. It seems I can't help myself. On the bright side, there is something of a hooley going on in the bar downstairs. They have taken the opportunity of Collins coming to visit (the Commander-in-Chief, no less – only God almighty ranks higher for us army men!) to throw a party. I suspect this is partly to try and put a smile on Collins's face, and partly to celebrate the taking of Cork – which, up to now, we were not sure was worth celebrating. I don't know whether Collins will stay very long, as he plans to be off early in the morning. He is making a tour of West Cork, which did not sit well with Dalton, who thinks the idea is foolhardy. Collins might have been born and reared in West Cork, but the place is now quite a stronghold for the Irregulars, and for Collins himself to drive out there is

273

a bit too much like putting his head in the lion's mouth. But, despite his ill-humour, Collins has lost none of his self-confidence, and he will not be put off. He has said that they would never shoot him in his home county, and he rather brusquely told Dalton to stop clucking over him like an old mother hen!

Well, it seems I spoke too soon. The noise from downstairs has stopped, and I suspect that Collins has gone to bed. I think I will avail of the respectful silence to get some shut-eye myself! I shall be thinking of you as I go off to sleep, and I look forward to seeing you again soon. I remain,

Yours ever,

Stephen

It was getting dark by the time they drove into Portobello barracks. Stephen had ridden in the touring car and his face was sunburned, his eyes gritty with dust and his backside sore from two hundred miles of bad roads. Nevertheless, he was glad he hadn't gone in the armoured car, which could only have been worse. He looked at it in some distaste as it rattled to a halt outside the barracks stables and the crew wearily climbed out. Three times the bloody thing had held them up: once with a puncture and twice through overheating. No wonder Dalton had been so keen to get rid of it. Even when the damned thing was working it was barely able to break thirty miles per hour, and had trailed slowly along in their dust, grumbling and swaying its snout like some cranky green beast.

Stretching some of the stiffness out of his limbs and back, he told himself to stop being so flaming bad-tempered. He was home now, and he had made the entire trip without once hitting a road-block or a blown bridge, without once being shot at or ambushed. Lillian was only ten minutes away and the night was young. A quick wash and a change and he would nip around and surprise her.

After he had paraded his men and dismissed them, he took his valise from the touring car and walked around to the officers' quarters. It was good to see the barracks so busy on a Tuesday night. In the half-light he could make out men darting in and out at the double, and dozens more marching smartly across the barracks square. He'd only been away for a fortnight, but there was a noticeable improvement, and the National Army was finally starting to look like a proper military force.

But it was only after he had unpacked his kit and had had a wash and shave that he realized that something was amiss. As he buckled on his Sam Browne, he stood and looked idly out the window of his room. It was now almost completely dark, and yet men were still being drawn up by platoons, orders were barking out, squads were being de-tailed off to draw food and ammunition. Some-thing was definitely afoot. Dalton was still in Cork with Collins, but there was bound to be somebody in the adjutant's office who could tell him what was going on.

He was halfway across the square when he saw a figure coming in through the gate. It was too dark to make him out clearly, but he knew that walk well enough.

'Billy!' he called out, and Billy stopped and looked around. Stephen picked up his pace. 'Do you know what's going on?' he demanded, jerking a thumb over his shoulder. 'What's all the excitement about?'

'Stephen? Oh, thank God!' In the faint light from a nearby window, the relief was clear on Billy's face. He patted his pockets, pulled out a cigarette case and lit one hastily. 'Thank Christ you're here! I thought you were still in Cork.'

'No, I drove up today. Just got back, as a matter of fact. Why? What's the matter in Cork?'

'It's ... well ... but haven't you heard?'

'Heard what?' Stephen glanced over his shoulder, to where the men were still assembling in the barracks square. He was starting to get a bad feeling. 'Billy, what's going on? Has something happened?'

'They got Collins,' Billy blurted out. He looked aghast. 'I thought you knew. I thought you were down there.'

'They got him? What do you mean? Has he been kidnapped?'

'They shot him, Stephen. He's dead.'

'That's impossible,' Stephen said flatly. But even as he spoke, his stomach turned over and he had a sudden light-headed, unreal sensation. It couldn't be true, but, somehow, he knew it was. He remembered leaving the hotel that morning, just as Collins came out; the grim look on his face, the way he walked as if he was hardly aware of his surroundings. Not a word, not a smile. 'But how?' Stephen asked, 'Where?'

'Somewhere near Bandon in West Cork. They ambushed his car when he was driving back into Cork City.'

'But it was an armoured car, for God's sake. I saw him drive off in it this morning. He can't be dead – it's ridiculous.'

He remembered the solid clank of the door closing after Collins had got in, then the smooth rumble of the engine and the blue smoke chugging out on the still morning air. He'd envied Collins because he had an armoured Rolls Royce, while he had to drive all the way to Dublin with that rattling bloody Lancia.

'He *is* dead, there's no doubt about it,' Billy said firmly. 'I just got off the telephone with Emmet Dalton. He was standing right beside him when it happened. Apparently, some men started shooting at them a few miles outside Bandon. The road wasn't even blocked and Dalton ordered the driver to run them out of it, but Collins insisted on stopping to fight. He got out of the car and started shooting back with a rifle but he was hit in the head a few minutes later.' Billy took a nervous drag of his cigarette. His face looked drawn, his eyes darting everywhere. 'He's dead, Stephen, no question. The bastards killed Michael Collins.'

Everything was wreathed in black: black flags and black crêpe on the trees and lamp posts, black coats and black hats filling every inch of space in between. Black armbands on the soldiers. Black shawls and black lace mantillas on the women. Six days had gone by since Collins had been shot and now it was time to bury him.

It seemed like the whole city was coming out to mourn his passing.

Stephen was marching in the cortege behind the gun carriage. The one splash of colour he could see was the green, white and orange of the tricolour draped over the coffin, with the pale drooping heads of some lilies lying on top. Bands had been playing mournfully all along the route, but they stopped as the cortege finally neared the cemetery. Stephen felt like he was marching through a sea of silence. Heads were bowed as he passed; signs of the cross were made. The only sounds he heard were the steady tramp of feet and the click of rosaries and murmuring prayers.

He saw the cemetery gates just as the black-plumed horses began their slow turn towards them. This was the second time he had been here within the week, but there had been no such pomp and ceremony for poor old Dunbar. Nevertheless, there had been a good turnout; more than a few former patients, medical colleagues, as well as a sprinkling of soldiers. Dunbar himself might have cracked that they were mostly there to make sure he was dead, though perhaps only to hide the fact that he was flattered. Cynical and cantankerous he might have been, but he would also be missed.

Stephen couldn't help wondering what Dunbar might have made of today's spectacle. For a start, he might have protested that somebody was walking on his grave – though it could hardly be avoided, the cemetery being so packed with people. As he passed through the gate, all Stephen could see was a sea of black coats and top hats that spread all the way to the walls, filling every available space between the yew trees and gravestones. He had not gone very far in before the gun carriage stopped and the coffin was carried the last few yards on the shoulders of six National Army soldiers. Stephen joined the ranks that formed a green square around the open grave. He found his eye drawn to the gleaming coffin, poised above the gaping earth while the priests and bishops came forward, each in turn, and said their words. Then the firing party formed up and raised their rifles for the volley. There was a shout, and the guns cracked fire into the blue sky. Rooks cawed and flapped out of the trees, but the silence that followed seemed even deeper. Another volley, and another, and a cloud of gun smoke drifted across the grave. After the last volley, the rifles were shouldered and a solitary bugle sounded the reedy notes of the Last Post.

Then it was over. The firing party was marched away and the remaining soldiers were dismissed. Everybody seemed at a loss as to what to do next. Stephen was waylaid by Dalton, who introduced him to a few of the other officers, and by the time he got clear the crowd had started to thin appreciably. He had arranged to meet Lillian at the cemetery gate and he soon saw her standing a little to one side, letting the throng stream out past her. He raised his hand to wave, but then he noticed somebody else out of the corner of his eye. It was only a glimpse, a solitary figure almost lost in the crowd, but when he turned his head to look, he was sure. It was Vincent Garvey.

Stephen stopped dead in his tracks. Garvey had

been watching him from the other side of the gravel road, standing under the wings of a great stone angel and staring straight at him. But as Stephen's eyes met his, he took his hand from his pocket and turned towards Lillian. His hand came up and made the shape of a gun; two fingers straight out and his thumb cocked up like the hammer. Then it jerked back as if he had pulled the trigger.

Stephen went straight for him. Even though he didn't have his service pistol, he was wearing a sword and that would bloody do if it came to it. But he never had a chance; a solid stream of people was flowing along the road, shuffling slowly towards the gate, and he had to shoulder his way through. Garvey had chosen his spot carefully, with a smaller pedestrian gate at his back. The moment Stephen started towards him, he was gone, darting back and weaving through the scattered mourners. There was a small queue at the gate and Stephen had a moment's hope as Garvey seemed to get stuck there, just within reach. But with one push and a duck of his head he was in the opening and then gone. Stephen dragged himself clear of the crowd on the road and started towards the gate, but then he stopped and looked in Lillian's direction. Better be safe than sorry.

'He'll be long gone, anyway, Stephen,' a voice behind him said. He looked around and saw his brother walking towards him from under the shade of a stand of yew trees.

'What the hell is *he* doing here?' Stephen demanded.

'Watching you.' Joe stopped a few feet away. He

was in his shirtsleeves with a jacket folded over his arm.

Stephen's eyes darted to the gate and then back to his brother. Then he pulled off his cap and ran his hand through his hair. Something was going on here, and he didn't like it.

'All right, then. What the hell are *you* doing here?'

'Watching him.'

'I thought you said he could never come back to Ireland?'

'Things have changed.' Joe nodded back towards the spot where they had just buried Collins. 'All bets are off.'

You can say that again, Stephen thought. Then he took a good look at his brother, squinting against the strong sunlight. He looked fit and healthy – much better than the last time he had seen him. But behind Joe he saw a bunch of soldiers coming down the road, plenty of brass amongst the green. Any one of them might recognize his brother, and might not be averse to dragging him back to Oriel House.

'Are you sure it's safe for you to be here?' he asked, nodding towards the soldiers.

'Not really,' Joe glanced over his shoulder, then grinned and closed the gap between them, 'but I'm not staying. I've already paid my respects.'

'To Collins? I didn't think you'd have much respect for him.'

'He was a good friend and a brave man.' Joe shrugged. 'He always said he'd die for Ireland, only I don't think he ever thought it'd be an Irish fella that would do him in. Still, the place will be poorer without him.'

'It will,' Stephen agreed, looking over his shoulder towards Lillian, who had seen him and was waving. He waved back. 'Listen, do you want to come somewhere with Lillie and me? Maybe go for a drink or get something to eat? I don't have to be back in barracks for a while.'

He knew what the answer would be before he even opened his mouth, but it was something at least that Joe looked disappointed.

'No thanks, Stephen. It'd probably be better for both of us if I don't.' Joe stuck out his hand. 'Give her my regards, though, will you? Tell her I was asking for her.'

'I will,' he promised, and they shook hands before they parted, Joe walking towards the small gate that Garvey had gone out through. Stephen hadn't taken three paces before he heard his brother calling him again.

'Stephen!'

'What?' He stopped and looked towards him.

'Look after her. She's a nice girl.'

Part Three

GRACE DIEU

XIII

The MINISTER for DEFENCE (General Mulcahy):
Anything that will shock the country into realization of what a grave thing it is to take human life is justified at the moment.
Speech to Dáil Eireann, November 1922

The guard carried an oil lamp that rattled and squeaked as he walked down the passageway, throwing weak yellow light on the slimy walls and rusty doors. They didn't even have gas down here, and there was the feel of the crypt about the place, with its dank air and the cold seeping up through the floor.

They stopped at the last door and the guard rattled the key in the lock, pushed it open and then set the lamp down inside.

'There you are, sir,' the guard said, and Stephen nodded as he ducked into the cell, taking off his cap.

'Thank you, corporal.'

Childers was sitting on the edge of his bunk, hands braced on his knees, ready to stand up. He had a hunted look on his face, which changed to a frown and then to a guarded smile when he realized who it was.

Stephen merely nodded. 'Good evening, Mr Childers. How are you?'

'Mr Ryan,' he said, standing up and, after a slight hesitation, shaking Stephen's outstretched hand, 'what an unexpected pleasure.' He peered more closely at Stephen's uniform. 'Or should that be Commandant Ryan?'

There was just enough light for Stephen to see bruises on his face, the torn collar of his shirt. Still, he did his best to smile. 'I'd prefer it if we weren't so formal.'

'Please sit down.' Childers gestured at the rickety chair that stood in the corner, the only furniture he had apart from the narrow bunk bed. Stephen sat down, and, after a moment's hesitation, so did Childers, perching on the edge of the bunk and crossing his legs. As his eyes got used to the flickering yellow light of the lamp in the corridor, Stephen saw how drawn he looked. He had always thought Childers's face so hard and flinty that it might have been chiselled from stone, but it seemed to be crumbling under the strain of these last few days. And who could blame him? He had been caught in unlawful possession of a pistol. Under the new Army Emergency Powers act, that was a capital crime.

'Are they treating you all right?' Stephen asked self-consciously. He'd already seen the bruise on his face; now he saw the skinned knuckles and the overly stiff way Childers was sitting. Somebody had given him a hell of a beating.

'Most of your comrades have been very civil,' Childers admitted, but then he gave Stephen a wan smile. 'Some of them, however, seem to think I'm the devil incarnate and have tried to knock the evil out of me.'

'I'm sorry to hear that,' Stephen said. But he wasn't surprised. The Government had demonized Childers, painting him as the malign Englishman, hell-bent on wrecking the Treaty. He was the bogeyman, which made him a much better catch than de Valera. De Valera was a hero of the Easter Rising, had once been president of the Dáil and was still idolized by half the men in the Government. If they caught *him,* they wouldn't know what to do with him. But Childers was different. He had few friends, he was prickly and unyielding and, above all, he was British. They would have no trouble playing rough with the devil on de Valera's back, the one who kept whispering him on.

'Well,' Childers sighed. 'I suppose it's nothing compared to what they've got in mind for me.'

What they had in mind for him was a firing squad.

'It might not come to that,' Stephen suggested. 'I understand it's under appeal.'

'My appeal will be denied,' Childers said bluntly. Stephen knew he was probably right – it was a vain hope. Not that Childers had ever been enthusiastic about an appeal in the first place. He had refused all along to lodge one, because to do so would mean recognizing the legitimacy of the court and, therefore, of the Government. His lawyer had only persuaded him to go ahead on the basis that if his appeal was successful, it might save the lives of eight other men who were facing execution.

They sat in silence for a minute before Childers smiled bleakly.

'You know, when I saw the uniform, I thought you were bringing me some rather bad news.'

'I'm sorry about that.' Stephen's cheeks flushed a little. There couldn't be many reasons why a Free State officer would come to see him at this late hour. 'As a matter of fact, I came to ask if there was anything I could do for you. You obliged me once in London. I wondered if I might return the favour.'

Childers's face brightened at the memory. 'Ah yes, your charming fiancée. I trust she's well?' Then another thought occurred to him. 'Or is she your wife by now? Are you married?'

'No, not yet.'

Childers laughed, a curiously boyish trill that seemed out of place in this gloomy cell. 'I hope you're not stringing the poor girl along,' he chided.

'No, not at all – it's quite the opposite, in fact. She's the one who wants to wait.'

Another laugh. At least Childers seemed to be coming out of himself.

'Does she really? Well, she did strike me as a very modern young lady.'

'She is that all right,' Stephen admitted, smiling. But he quickly returned to his question. It was a matter of some urgency. They were moving Childers from barracks to barracks to forestall any attempt at a rescue, and he might not see him again. 'Honestly, is there any thing I can do for you? I can carry a message to your family if you wish.'

'Thank you, Stephen, but I fear you wouldn't be allowed to deliver it in that uniform. I'm

288

afraid Molly would have at you with the garden shears.'

'Well, perhaps I could telephone.'

'Perhaps,' Childers chuckled, but then his smile faltered and his face turned grave. 'Seriously, Stephen, I appreciate your offer. And, as it happens, there is something you could do for me. I've asked if I could be allowed to see my son. The request was taken civilly enough, but I have no idea if it fell on deaf ears. So, if you could see your way to...'

'Of course.'

'Even if you were able to put in a word with the powers that be, it might help...'

'I'll do everything I can. You have my word on it.'

'Thank you,' Childers said, and he looked down at the floor, clearly moved. Stephen decided it was time to take his leave.

'I'd best be getting on,' he said, standing up and offering his hand.

'Yes, of course. Well, give my regards to Lillian, won't you?'

'I'll be sure to.'

'And thank you for coming. I only wish–'

Childers didn't say what he wished, just smiled and clasped Stephen's hand in both his. Stephen nodded and turned on his heel and walked back out into the passageway.

OGLAIGH NA h-EIREANN
(Irish Republican Army)
GENERAL HEADQUARTERS, DUBLIN.

30th November, 1922.

GENERAL ORDER.
TO:
  O/C., All Battalions.

"ENEMY MURDER BILL".

1. All members of Provisional "Parliament" who were present and voted for Murder Bill will be shot at sight. Attached find list of names.
2. Houses of members of Murder Bill, Murder Gang and active supporters of P.G. who are known to support Murder Bill decision will be destroyed.
3. All Free State Army Officers who approve of Murder Bill and are aggressive and active against our Forces will be shot at sight; also all ex-British Army officers and men who joined the Free State Army since the 6th December 1921.
4. Individual action on paragraph 2/3 will be ordered by Brigade 0/C.
5. To be duplicated and transmitted to 0/C., all Units.

Liam Lynch, General.
Chief of Staff.

They didn't have lunch in the country, General Hales had told Billy; they always had dinner at this hour. Dinner now and tea later on, O'Maille had chimed in, explaining the phenomenon as if it was some obscure mystery. And they both agreed that the Ormonde Hotel did a fine dinner. Bacon and cabbage; hot and steaming, and lots of it. Two pints of stout to wash it down and all three of them were in fine form when they stepped out on to Ormonde Quay. Hales raised his hand towards a sidecar that was parked over by the quay wall and the driver tipped his hat and cracked his whip to stir the horse in their direction.

'Are you sure we can't give you a lift, Billy?' Hales asked. He was a big man, bluff and hearty, but no bumpkin. He had a wise old face and eyes like chips of granite. 'We can drop you to your office before we go back to the Dáil.'

'No, thank you,' Billy pointed up the river, towards the Four Courts. 'I think I'll take a stroll up to see how the rebuilding is coming along.'

The truth was he didn't want Hales and O'Maille bending his ear all the way up to Merrion Square. They'd had their time with him. They were both important men – Hales was a member of the Dáil and O'Maille was the Deputy Speaker – but Billy was just as important in his own way. As secretary to the Minister for Home Affairs he had the ear of one of the most powerful men in the Government and this wasn't the first time he'd been treated to lunch by men who wanted things spoken about in Cabinet meetings.

'Well, good luck to you, so,' Hales shook his hand, 'and don't forget to mention me to Mr O'Higgins.'

'I won't. But don't you forget to keep an eye out,' Billy told him with mock seriousness. He turned and shook hands with O'Maille, a quieter, much more soft-spoken man. 'Both of you. Remember you're legitimate targets, now.'

'Ah, legitimate, my arse.' Hales opened his coat and showed Billy the gun thrust into the waistband of his trousers. 'If Lynch's boys come looking for me they'll only find trouble. Isn't that right, Liam, eh?' Hales winked at O'Maille as the sidecar crunched and rumbled around to the kerb. 'Come on, now. We'd best get back to running the country.'

Billy waited until they were settled on the sidecar and then waved them off and turned towards the Four Courts. A cold drizzle had started and was being carried down the river by the sharp breeze. He wondered briefly if he shouldn't have taken that lift, but then shrugged and fastened the neck of his overcoat, putting his head down against the rain.

'I beg your pardon—' he said, as a man brushed past him in a rush, catching his jutting elbow. He had half turned when he saw a second man running down along the quay wall, pulling something from his pocket.

'General Hales! General Hales!' the first man called as he caught up to the sidecar, which was just pulling out into the road. Hales jerked his head around in surprise and started fumbling at the buttons of his overcoat.

'Liam Lynch says hello!' the man shouted, and raised his arm. There was a double crack and the horse bucked and leaped, jerking the sidecar a few yards down the road. In a flash, the driver was gone, jumping down and running for his life, but the two men paid him no attention. They ran after the sidecar and then they both fired together and

Hales fell out of his seat and sprawled on the cobbles. The horse bolted across the road, crashing the shaft of the sidecar into the quay wall, and one of the men ran over and fired at O'Maille, still sitting slumped in his seat. The other stood over Hales, pointed his gun very deliberately, and shot him in the head.

'Oh my God!' Billy said, feeling his knees go weak and his bowels turn to water.

'Come on, Paddy!' one of the shooters shouted, and they fled down the street beside the hotel.

'Oh my God,' Billy said again, and he took a few paces towards the prostrate body of Hales, lying face down in the road. He couldn't take his eyes off him, but his legs would hardly work and he was shaking with fright as he edged closer, almost afraid to go any further. He could see blood pooling out and flowing through the cracks between the cobblestones. 'Help!' he said in a wavering voice, and looked around at the sound of footsteps coming towards him. But his relief was short-lived; two hard-faced young men in raincoats were bearing down on him.

'Who are you?' one of them asked, thrusting his face close to Billy's. Billy had noticed they both held one hand inside the pockets of their raincoats. He thought his legs might collapse under him.

'I'm—' Billy began, but fear had constricted his throat and he almost choked on the words. 'I'm nobody.'

'What business had you with them pair?'

Billy could feel the heat of his breath, and something hard jabbed him in the belly. 'I ... I—'

he began, but he was saved by the other one.

'Come on, Tom,' he urged, grabbing his companion by the arm and pulling him away. 'Come on, let's go. The army'll be here any minute. We'd better get out of here.'

'You saw nothing!' the first one spat, and then they were gone, running, and Billy slowly turned and looked at the scene. The horse was still bucking frantically, whinnying and bumping the splintered shaft against the quay wall. O'Maille had fallen sideways in his seat, his face to the sky, and Hales lay in a pool of blood on the road. Billy could hardly take it all in. His arms hung limply by his sides and his knees were shaking. He thought he was going to be sick.

He had sore eyes and a sour taste in his mouth. A throbbing headache and the feeling that his skull and bones were made of eggshell. When he stepped out of his quarters, the frosty air hit him like a splash of cold water. Stephen winced as he gently settled his cap on his head. Then he set off for the officer's mess.

It was strange to think that Dalton would not be there. He was gone; he'd had enough and had resigned his commission. Last night had not been the first time that Stephen had stayed up drinking in Dalton's office, but it would be the last, and he was glad. Apart from the aftereffects, it had been painful to watch Dalton sink lower and lower, night after night. It had been hard stretching him out on his couch, pulling off his boots and leaving him with a blanket draped over him. Above all, it had been distressing to watch him tearing himself apart.

Collins's death had been the catalyst, of course. Dalton had been standing right beside him when he was killed, had put the bandage on his head even though he knew it was no use. Stephen had told him it wasn't his fault, that there was nothing he could have done, but he knew Dalton would never accept that. He blamed himself, and guilt had worked on him and weakened him. Slowly, the strain of his turbulent life – the years of fighting, going right back to the Somme – had started to overwhelm him. And then the executions had been the final straw.

For Stephen's part, he was just glad that he didn't know most of these men. For him, it had been bad enough when they shot Childers. It had shaken him to the core, even though he'd always known it was bound to happen. For Dalton, it must have been worse because he knew the others as well – O'Connor and McKelvey and all the rest. He had been friends with them and had fought alongside them against the British.

'Look what they make you do,' he'd said to Stephen, the night after the first executions. He'd been drinking hard, but it hadn't seemed to have had any effect on him. There were tears welling in his eyes. 'It's too much, Stephen. Christ almighty, it's not enough to kill your enemies. You have to kill your friends as well.'

Stephen was halfway across the barracks square when he decided that he couldn't face the mess after all. The thought of greasy bacon and fried bread made him nauseous, and then there would be the noise and the chatter, talk about the war, business as usual. He veered off towards the orderly room. He could probably wangle a cup of tea in there, and at least it would be quiet.

He had almost reached the orderly room door when he heard his name being called. The voice was familiar but the sharpness of it pulled him up with a jerk. He turned and saw Billy closing a door after himself. Stephen knew that door. It led to General Mulcahy's office – the office of the Commander-in-Chief and Minister of Defence. Billy was breathing some very rarefied air indeed.

'Good morning, Billy.'

'Good morning.' Even as he closed the gap between them, Billy looked him up and down. 'You're looking a bit peaky.'

'I had a late night.'

'I bet you did.' Billy looked over his shoulder, as if to make sure that nobody was listening, and dropped his voice to a whisper. 'So, is it true, what Mulcahy just told me? That your pal Dalton has resigned his commission?'

Stephen immediately resented Billy's tone. For some reason, he particularly bristled at him referring to Dalton as his pal.

'That's right,' he said stiffly.

'Bloody cheek,' Billy said, raising Stephen's hackles even higher. 'Though, if you ask me, it's good riddance. The man's a wreck. More trouble than he's worth, going around moaning about the executions. Putting the wind up half the bloody men while he's at it. I thought he was a proper soldier–'

'He *is* a proper soldier,' Stephen cut across him angrily. 'And I happen to think he's right.'

'Oh, don't you flaming start,' Billy warned. 'I'd have thought *you*, of all people, would understand the necessity of pressing home an attack.'

Stephen was astounded. 'Pressing home an attack? Is that what you call it? You're shooting prisoners. If the Germans had done that you would have called it an atrocity, and you would have been right!'

'Balls, Stephen! Don't talk to me about atrocities. I've seen what the other lot do with my own eyes. I was there when they shot Hales – I saw them execute him in the bloody street, and I was damned lucky they didn't plug me while they were at it. And as for the rest – I'm sure you heard what happened to McGarry's son?'

Stephen nodded uncomfortably. Sean McGarry was a member of the Dáil who had supported the Emergency Powers Act. The anti-Treaty forces had burned his house down as a reprisal. McGarry had escaped, but his seven-year-old son was burned to death.

'I met that boy, once, Stephen. An innocent child. For the love of Christ, don't talk to me about atrocities! These people are savages. They don't have the support of the people and even their own church has thrown them out, but still they go around murdering folk for upholding the law, murdering democratically elected representatives of the people they claim to be fighting for. What are you saying? That we should just let them run around murdering people without any form of reprisal?'

'Reprisals are what the Auxiliaries did, remember? And everything you just said is what the

British used to say. Is that what we are now? Are we the imperial power?'

'We're the bloody *power*, is what we are. We're the ones the people elected to do what we said we were going to do, which is to implement the terms of the Treaty.'

'They didn't elect us to shoot prisoners,' Stephen said hotly.

'No, they elected us to govern – by whatever means necessary.'

It was only then that Stephen realized that their voices had risen in pitch and volume. They were practically shouting at each other.

'Well, it's a sorry sort of Government that has to govern by shooting its enemies,' he said in a quieter tone. 'And if I were you, I'd watch my step. It's getting pretty hard to find men for firing squads.'

Billy was incensed. 'Watch my step? Was that a bloody threat?'

'No, it was a bloody warning! We're soldiers, Billy, not executioners. You can talk all you want about how necessary these executions are, but you're not the one who has to pull the trigger. It's all very well on paper, but half the men have no stomach for it, and if you keep making them shoot their prisoners, then you'll soon have a mutiny on your hands.'

'They'll do what they're damn well told,' Billy warned, and made as if to walk away. 'They're soldiers of the Free State, and if they can't do the hard thing when it's needed, when the future of the whole country is at stake, then they've no business being soldiers at all. So they'd better do their bloody duty – and so had you, Stephen. There can be no wavering, not from you and not from anybody else. If we don't hold our nerve now, the criminals will win.'

He walked away and Stephen turned after him. Maybe it was thanks to Dalton's influence, but he'd not yet been ordered to command a firing squad. However, he knew it was only a matter of time. If they kept up the current rate of executions his turn was bound to come. And he wouldn't do it; that was all he knew. He'd told nobody, not even Lillian, but his mind was made up. If he got that order, he would resign on the spot.

'Criminals go to jail when they're caught,' he called after Billy.

'And soldiers do their duty,' Billy called back, turning round and wagging his finger. 'Just you remember that, Commandant.'

XIV

Conspiracy to Murder

THE
Provisional Government

HAS SENT AN AGENT TO THE SOUTH

**To assassinate
Eamon de Valera**

THE NAME OF THIS AGENT IS KNOWN

Is this done by the Will
of the Irish People?

The journey from Dublin should have taken a couple of hours but it took twelve. All day, they'd been rolling slowly between the wintry fields, stopping, starting, backing up. The Irregulars had torn up so much track that it was impossible to go anywhere in a straight line, and it was long after dark by the time the train finally puffed tiredly into the station.

Stephen gathered his things and stepped down into the steam that billowed along the platform. He carried his valise over his shoulder and the gun case in his free hand. The handful of other passengers who had stayed the journey hurried past him, heads down against the rain that was drumming along the roof of the train and splashing in the station gutters. The sign on the wall said 'Cahir'. He had arrived in Tipperary.

The stationmaster watched him from the station-house door, standing with a red flag tucked under his arm. He shot Stephen a dirty look as he bowed his head to light a cigarette but Stephen ignored him and walked towards the turnstile. He was still slightly dazed by his arrival. It was only yesterday morning that he'd been summoned to General Mulcahy's office. This in itself had not been unexpected, since he'd been working on Dalton's staff and, with Dalton gone, he was now at a loose end. But as he marched into Mulcahy's office, he'd had a sense of foreboding. Was this it, at last? Were they putting him in charge of a firing squad? He hadn't seen Billy since they'd had that row before Christmas, and he knew he had influence. Would he do it out of spite? But Mulcahy had smiled warmly when he came in, had stood up and shaken his hand.

'We're sending you to Tipperary,' he'd said without preamble, and then had led Stephen to the map, where he jabbed with his finger at a brownish area on the border of Cork, Tipperary and Waterford. 'The Knockmealdown mountains. We believe that's where the Irregulars have their headquarters.'

Stephen had already heard as much. The Irregulars were fighting a guerrilla war; playing hit and run, burning barracks and houses and mining roads and railways. They operated in small groups, just as they had against the British, but they still had a central command, which was widely believed to be moving between three or four strongholds in the south, of which the Knockmealdowns was the largest.

'Are we planning an attack, sir?' Stephen asked.

'In due course, yes – but we want to isolate them before we make our sweep. We've got a ring of posts around these mountains. Kilworth Camp, of course, in Cork, and on the Waterford side we've got Commandant Donovan at Capoquin – do you know him?'

Stephen nodded. He had met Donovan when he was in Cork. He'd thought he was a good soldier and a charismatic leader, and if anybody was familiar with the Irregulars' tactics, it was

Donovan. He'd learned his trade leading a flying column in the war against the British and had ended up with a heavy price on his head. But once the British had left he had come out in favour of the Treaty and was just as ruthless against the Irregulars as he had been against the British. Old comrades or not, if they stood against him he would show them no mercy.

'Good. Our weak spot, then, is here to the north, on the Tipperary side – and that's where you come in. We have a company stationed here, right on the northern edge of the mountains. They're billeted in a big house just outside the village of Castlegrace, a place called Grace Dieu... What's the matter, Ryan?'

Stephen was frowning. Grace Dieu? The name sounded familiar to him, but he couldn't place it.

'Nothing, sir. I was just wondering what the weakness is.'

'It's more a question of strength on their part and weakness on ours. The Irregulars are particularly active in that area. They're well organized and well led and they're not afraid to take us on. They ambushed one of our patrols a few days ago and killed the garrison commander, a Captain O'Carroll.' Mulcahy walked back to his desk and leaned on his hands. He looked at Stephen frankly. 'Far be it from me to speak ill of the dead, but, in my opinion, if we had a weakness in that area it was Captain O'Carroll. He was not what I would call a very active officer. That's why I'm sending you to replace him. I want you to reorganize that outpost, give the Irregulars a flea in their ear and get ready to tighten the noose on those mountains.

Think you can manage that?'

'Yes, sir.'

And that was that. He got a twelve-hour leave and travel orders for the next day. It was better than a firing squad, but it wasn't half as cushy as what he'd grown used to. As Lillian herself had jokingly pointed out, it was a long way to Tipperary – and he had no idea when he might be back. Again, Stephen had wondered if Billy had anything to do with it. True, they had had a blazing row, and Stephen had probably said some things he shouldn't have. But was Billy this petty? Would he send him away just to pay him back?

But for now he had other things to worry about. He may have reached Cahir, but it was another twenty miles to Castlegrace. Twenty miles at night, and across country that was more or less hostile. Even if he could find a car to take him, it would be safer to stay put, to find a hotel and try to telephone in the morning. But as he walked out of the station he saw the long, unmistakeable shape of an armoured car parked down the street, its steel sides shining black and slick in the rain. He turned towards it and a moment later the door of the pub across the street banged open and a man came running, taking a last drag from a cigarette before throwing it into the gutter. With a final skip on to the pavement, he drew himself up beside the armoured car and gave Stephen a sloppy salute as he arrived.

'Commandant Ryan, sir?' he asked, breathlessly.

'That's right.'

'I'm Lieutenant Walsh, Peter Walsh. I'm the ...

303

well, I suppose I'm *your* second in command now.'

Walsh was holding out his hand but Stephen hesitated before he shook it. He knew he was probably being grossly unfair, since it was dark and he was tired, but he had taken an immediate dislike to Lieutenant Walsh. He wasn't sure whether it was the fact that he'd come running out of a pub, the slovenly salute, or the slightly mocking tone of his voice, but he didn't like the look of this man, not one bit.

'I'm pleased to meet you, Lieutenant.' He let go of Walsh's slightly limp hand. 'Have you been waiting long?'

'Ah, no more than a few hours,' Walsh answered cheerfully. Stephen looked significantly at the armoured car. There were only a dozen of those in the whole army and this man had left one parked outside a railway station for half the day. Stephen felt the stir of an angry retort, but he held his tongue as the far door clanged and the driver came around, saluted and stood looking at him expectantly.

'Is this really necessary?' Stephen asked instead, nodding at the car.

'It is, sir,' Walsh answered and then his expression changed as it dawned on him that Stephen was questioning his judgement.

'The Irregulars are divils for ambushes, sir. They got Captain Carroll in one last week, and I thought if they got word you were coming they might have a go at you as well.'

Stephen looked from Walsh to the driver. Armoured car or not, with just the three of them, they'd still be buggered if they drove into any sort of half-decent ambush.

'Well, then. I suppose we'd better get going.'

The armoured car had not been built to carry either passengers or their luggage. They had to stuff Stephen's valise beside the driver while Stephen climbed in and sat in the gunner's seat, with his gun case standing between his knees and his head sticking up into the turret.

'Mind your head, sir. You're a bit tall for this old girl,' Walsh remarked, and Stephen tried to turn the turret slightly so that the butt of the Vickers machine gun wouldn't hit him in the face if they came to a sudden stop. As it was, the gleaming brass cartridge belt swayed and clacked against his shoulder as the driver started the engine and they pulled out into the narrow street, rumbling and splashing over the cobblestones.

There was an observation slit in front of Stephen and he could see the headlight beams flicker past the pubs and shop fronts of the town before his view suddenly changed to parallel bands of hedgerow, wet and nodding in the slanting rain. He hoped the journey wouldn't take long. The car was a Rolls Royce, but it was far from luxurious. In fact, it was hot, noisy and reeked of petrol, and it was so cramped that Lieutenant Walsh pressed and bumped against him every time they went around a bend. He was also proving to be more talkative than Stephen was in the humour for after such a long day.

'Is that your own gun, sir?' he asked, nodding to the long leather case that stuck up between his knees. Even in the dim yellow light inside the car it looked elegant and expensive.

'Yes, it is.' Stephen nodded, shouting over the roaring of the engine. Then, since Walsh was obviously trying to be nice, he added, 'It's a rifle.'

'Is that the one you used to shoot Cathal Brugha?' Walsh asked.

'The one I what?' Stephen demanded incredulously, and it came out unusually loud as the driver slowed to a snail's pace to negotiate a narrow bridge.

'Are you not the fella that shot Cathal Brugha?' Walsh asked in a disappointed voice. 'When the lad in headquarters called to say you were coming, he said you did. He said they were sending you down here to plug de Valera as well.'

Stephen would have laughed if Walsh hadn't looked so serious. Instead, he just shook his head. 'I didn't kill Cathal Brugha,' was all he said.

They drove on for a few miles in silence.

'How many men do we have?' Stephen asked when the engine noise died away again. They had crested a hill and the driver was letting the heavy car coast down the other side, only touching the brakes now and then as they rolled into the bends.

'Fifty, all told,' Walsh answered. 'The men are billeted in the outhouses, but Mr Devereux lets the officers stay in the house. Not that that's such a good thing. He's a bit of an odd fella, is Mr Devereux, though his sister is very nice. She looks after him, see, on account of he's a cripple...'

'Devereux?' Stephen cut across him, 'Did you say Devereux? Devereux owns the house?'

'Yes, sir. Alfred Devereux. He lives there with his sister, though I think he was from Dublin originally.' Walsh's face brightened as he made a connection. 'Why, sir? Do you know him?'

'Christ almighty!' Stephen muttered to himself. Alfred bloody Devereux! He knew him all right, but that was such a long time ago now. And now he knew why Grace Dieu had sounded so familiar to him. It would have been familiar to Billy, too, he thought, and now he was certain that Billy had had a hand in this posting. How it would have amused him to have Stephen billeted with Alfred Devereux, of all people.

'Do you know him, sir?' Walsh pressed him again.

Stephen didn't answer at first. He had bent forward to the observation slit, suddenly keen to see where they were going. The car was slowing again and as it turned sharply, the headlights swept across a stout granite pillar and the bars of a black iron gate. They were nearly there.

'I used to know him,' he said as the tyres crunched slowly and smoothly up a gravel driveway. 'We were in the army together.'

'Oh? I didn't know he was in the army.'

'He was,' Stephen answered. 'The British Army.'

It was snowing on Marlborough Street when Joe came out of the Pro-Cathedral. It was the evening of Little Christmas and the air was frigid, with a sharp breeze that swirled the snowflakes through the globes of yellow gaslight and sent them scurrying in little clouds along the pavement. Joe stopped in the church portico and turned up his collar against the cold. He pulled his cap down around his ears and wondered if he wouldn't be better off staying inside. It wouldn't be much

307

warmer, but at least it would be peaceful.

As he bent his head to blow some warmth into his hands, he looked at the motor car parked across the street. He'd noticed it a few times in the last couple of days and he knew they were watching him. They already knew where he lived, so there wasn't much point in trying to be clever. Just go home and sit in front of the gas fire for a while. If they wanted him, they knew where he was. But what he couldn't understand was why they were bothered. If they'd been watching him at all, they'd know he was no use to them any more.

Thrusting his hands into his pockets, Joe started down the steps. Just as he reached the pavement the back door of the motor car opened and a familiar figure stepped out. Joe stopped in his tracks. Another man was getting out of the front of the car and from the way he held his hand inside the front of his overcoat, Joe knew he had a gun in there. But Billy Standing had a smile on his face. He said something to the man with the gun and then came across the street on his own.

When he reached the pavement, Billy held out his hand, but Joe ignored it. He nodded to the other man, still standing beside the car, still holding his hand inside his coat.

'Who's your friend?'

'He works for me,' Billy said, turning and making a small gesture. The man stared at them for a few moments longer, then opened the door and got back into the car.

Joe made no remark at this display, just hunched his shoulders as a flurry of snow came blowing down the street and speckled the thin material of his suit. This was no weather to be out without an overcoat. 'What do you want?'

'I want you to do something for me,' Billy said. 'You know, I was just thinking how everything has changed. The shoe is on the other foot now, isn't it? Remember when you used to be the one who asked me to do things?'

Back when Billy had worked for Frank Mercer in Dublin Castle, Joe had worked for Michael Collins. Billy's job had been to track down the bank accounts where the republicans hid their funds and Joe had been ordered to stop him. Instead, Joe had managed to turn Billy, and had run him as a mole inside Dublin Castle.

'That was a long time ago,' Joe said warily. 'The Brits are gone, and now your lot have taken their place.'

'Well, that's one way of looking at it,' Billy agreed, and braced himself as another gust of wind hit them. The snow was falling harder now, and starting to drift against the steps of the church. He'd hardly been out in it for a minute but already the astrakhan collar of Billy's coat was turning white and he could hardly feel his ears. 'Listen, there's no point in us both freezing to death. Why don't you come over to my car so we can talk? I'll drop you home, if you like.'

'No thanks.' Joe thrust his hands deeper into his pockets and stamped his feet firmly on the slick pavement. 'I prefer it out here.'

'All right. Then here's what I want you to do. I want you to find Liam Lynch for me.'

Joe snorted. 'Why? So you can have him shot like all the others? Find him yourself.'

'I don't want to have him shot. In fact, I want to put an end to all that. I don't need to know where he is; I just need you to bring him a message from the minister. Tell him that we want to make peace.'

'What are you asking me for?' Joe gave Billy a wary look as he stamped his feet again and hugged himself for warmth. His cheeks were burning in the freezing wind. 'Last I heard, he was in the south somewhere. I wouldn't even know where to look.'

'Perhaps not, but you can find out, can't you?'

'I'm not an informer,' Joe got out. His teeth were starting to chatter.

Well, isn't that very noble of you? Billy thought. You who used informers left, right and centre, and now you're baulking at becoming one yourself. But he didn't say it aloud.

'I'm not asking you to be an informer. I told you; I don't need you to tell me where he is. I just want you to take a message to him.'

'What makes you think he'll listen to me?'

'He knows you. If I'm not mistaken, he was in the Four Courts with you. And with a record like yours, you're bound to be trusted.'

No, I'm not, Joe thought. After that evening in Mrs Humphrics's house he'd had no more invitations to meetings, no more contact with any of that crowd. They were prepared to trust Vincent Garvey as long as they needed him, but not Joe. He was on the outside now, and no mistake.

'I'm not the man you want,' he said, and made to move past. But Billy caught him by the elbow.

'Yes, you are,' he said. 'Who the hell else am I

310

going to send?'

Joe stopped and thrust his hands back into his pockets. 'If I could find him, what would I tell him? What terms are you offering?'

'We'll stop the executions in return for a cease-fire and we'll start releasing prisoners if he agrees to peace talks.'

Joe looked sceptical. The Irregulars enjoyed the odd local victory, but every week saw the Free State government strengthen its grip on the country. Under these circumstances, Billy's terms sounded too good to be true, but he slipped an envelope from the pocket of his overcoat and held it out to Joe.

'It's all in here, and it's a genuine offer. Can you take it to him?'

'I don't know,' Joe was still wary, 'I'll have to ask around.'

'Take it.' Billy thrust the envelope towards him. 'Take it to him yourself. He'll know it's genuine then, and you're the only one I can trust.'

Reluctantly, Joe took the envelope. 'I'll see what I can do,' he said, slipping it into his pocket. 'And if I am able to get it to him, where should I bring his reply?'

'I have an office on Merrion Square. You can bring it there. Just ask for me.' He saw Joe's eyes dart back towards the car. 'Don't worry. No harm will come to you. I'll put the word out.'

'I'll see what I can do,' Joe said again, and he walked away through the snow. Billy watched him until he turned the corner and then walked across and got back into his motor car.

'Will he do it?' the driver asked, twisting

around from the front seat.

'Oh yes. He'll do it all right.'

'And what do you want us to do?'

'Keep an eye on him. I want to know where he goes and who he talks to. In particular, I want to know when he goes down to the south.'

'All right,' said his companion, and he turned around and pressed the starter, and the car rumbled into life.

Grace Dieu,
Castlegrace,
Co. Tipperary
9 January 1923

My Darling Lillie,

You will never guess who was here to greet me when I arrived at my new billet. None other than my old chum, Alfred Devereux! Remember you told me he had a big house somewhere down in the country? Well, I appear to have stumbled upon it. It turns out Grace Dieu *is his family estate and he lives here with his sister.*

I'm sure you're surprised – I can tell you I was, particularly as I only learned the identity of my host about a minute before I landed on his doorstep. Thanks to the efforts of the Irregulars, I was rather late arriving but both he and his sister had waited up to welcome me. He didn't seem terribly surprised or put out to see me, but it was hard to tell because his face is still rather badly disfigured. Also, he is still confined to a wheelchair, but he does seem to have improved a bit in other ways. He has recovered a certain amount of his speech,

312

though I think it will take a bit of getting used to before I can understand even half of what he says. However, his sister, Susan, seems to understand him perfectly and she fills in the gaps. Needless to say, he still relies very heavily on her, and I'm afraid she looks rather worn out after nursing him for all these years.

However, the years might also have mellowed him, because he seemed much more agreeable than I expected. Almost the first words he spoke to me were in the way of a compliment – he said he was glad to see they'd finally sent a proper soldier. I'm not sure if this reflects as much on me as it does on my predecessor, but it's more than I had expected from Devereux.

He also told me – with his sister filling in – that my opponent in these parts was also in the army. His name is Quinn and his father had a labourer's cottage on this very estate. Young Quinn joined the Munster Fusiliers as soon as he was old enough and saw quite a lot of fighting in France. He must have learned a thing or two over there because when he came home he led the British a merry old dance during the Tan war. It seems he knows this area – and particularly the mountains – like the back of his hand and Devereux reckons it will be the devil of a job to catch him. Quinn and his men live in the mountains and only come down to carry out a raid or attack before bolting back into safety. They have already burned a few houses, shot up the police barracks and had a go at blowing up a bridge over the river Suir. As is often the way with these characters, he is very popular with the locals and apparently they call him 'The Fox' on account of his red hair and his cunning.

Since I don't think I could sleep just yet (I felt tired earlier on, but meeting Devereux again has woken me up a bit!) I might as well describe my new billet, which is very comfortable as these things go. My room is quite large and well furnished, though slightly damp and a bit gloomy, as these big houses often are. Devereux's room is directly below mine – it used to be the billiards room, but the table has been replaced with a special low bed designed to make it easier for him to get in and out. His sister has a suite of rooms on the west side of the house, while Lieutenant Walsh (my second – more of him anon) is somewhere at the back. Our men are billeted in the stables, which are behind the house. With the weather turning cold, I wasn't sure how humane this was, but Devereux assures me that their accommodation is better than much of what we had to put up with in France. I intend to see for myself in the morning.

Of course, you must think that Devereux is uncommonly generous to put us up like this. But there is method in his madness. As you know, the Irregulars have started burning big houses because they believe their owners are Free State sympathizers. Since Grace Dieu is the biggest house for miles around, I'm sure Devereux realizes that they will get to him eventually. So, what better way to avoid having your house burned down than to have a lot of Free State soldiers staying there? We might cause him a little inconvenience with all our tramping about and noise and mess, but I dare say we're preferable to a visit from 'The Fox' and his friends!

Well, that's all I can say for tonight. I'm sure once I've seen the place in daylight I'll be able to give you a much better picture of how things stand. For now, all I can say is that I miss you already. Please make sure to keep your 'birthday present' with you at all times,

314

and don't forget the permit I got you as well. I have a feeling this war is coming to a head, and I'm afraid that things might get even more dangerous before we are finished. Please keep yourself safe and write soon to let me know how you are. For now I send you all my love and kisses.

Missing you very much,

Stephen

He was up before it was fully bright. A quick wash and he came downstairs through the gloomy house, then out through the front door into the biting chill of the morning. Everything was grey, but getting lighter in the gathering day. Ghostly rooks cawed softly in the bare branches of the oak trees and a silvery band of frost stretched away across the lawn. The air was so calm and still that it seemed a shame to shatter it.

He walked around the house and into the stable yard, his feet crunching so fast on the gravel that he was halfway across the yard before they realized who he was.

'Christ almighty!' came in a clear whisper as he strode into the stables. More muttered curses and they scattered before him like fish fleeing a shark. He didn't stop, didn't speak, but strode straight through with his hands clasped behind his back. He saw blankets and bedrolls spread out on the straw, bits of kit scattered around and half-dressed men rubbing sleep out of their eyes. He passed on without a word.

After the stables he followed the smell of frying

bacon across the yard. The kitchen was well laid out and busy, full of steam and smoke, and the cook at least managed to straighten up when he saw him, wiping his hand on his apron before saluting.

'Carry on,' Stephen said, and when he came back out a ragged line of men had formed down the middle of the yard, being barked into shape by a sergeant who instantly spun around on his heel and threw out a bone-snapping salute. Better and better.

Stephen returned the salute and then passed quickly along the line. Some of them were still half-buttoned and perhaps one or two were still half asleep, but he was well aware that what he had done was not quite fair, and at least they were up and showing willing. Not a total loss, he thought, though there was still no sign of Lieutenant Walsh. He turned around and walked back to the sergeant, who was standing rigidly straight with his eyes boring into the whitewashed wall on the far side of the yard.

'Good morning, Sergeant–?'

'Coakley, sir. Good morning, sir.' Coakley's accent was undoubtedly Irish, but there was a very peculiar twang to it.

'Were you in the army before, sergeant?'

'Yes, sir. Five years in the Sixty-ninth Infantry Regiment.'

Stephen frowned. The Sixty-ninth? He'd never heard of it. But a moment later the penny dropped.

'Ah – the American army, was it?'

'Yes, sir.'

This was unexpected but hardly a disappointment. Coakley looked like there was more to him than just a smart salute. He had an intelligent face, with a broad forehead and sharp blue eyes. A broken nose lent him a slightly pugnacious air and Stephen reckoned he had probably seen action with Pershing's Expeditionary Force. If he had, that would make him invaluable.

'Well, sergeant, I wonder if you can tell me what arrangements have been made for mounting a guard over this house and the grounds?'

Stephen thought he knew the answer to this before Coakley ever opened his mouth. When he saw Coakley's eyes break their rigid stare and flicker briefly in his direction, he was sure of it. Again, it wasn't fair, but it had to be asked.

'None, sir.'

'I see.' Stephen made sure to show his disappointment, but was careful not to labour the point. This wasn't Coakley's fault. 'Well, from now on, we *will* have a guard. I want a permanent sentry on the front gate and three men patrolling the perimeter of the house and gardens. We will be secure in our own base, if nothing else. Is that clear, sergeant?'

'Clear, sir.' There was something like relief on his face, and Stephen had the feeling that Coakley was very much of his own way of thinking.

'Very well, you may let the men have breakfast, but be advised that I will be making a full inspection in one hour. Carry on, sergeant.'

'Yes, sir!' Another cracking salute and Stephen left him rattling off orders fourteen to the dozen. By the sound of it, he could rely on Coakley.

317

Lieutenant Walsh, on the other hand... It was already eight o'clock and there was still no sign of him – and he could hardly have slept through the racket that had just been going on under his window. He was mulling this over as he walked back around to the front of the house, and then Susan Devereux hailed him.

'Good morning, commandant. Did you sleep well?' She was standing at the bottom of the front steps, with a bicycle leaning against her hip as she fastened her hat with a long pin.

'Very well, thank you.' Stephen closed the gap between them. 'Are you going out?'

'Yes, I'm popping over to Curaheen House. I promised I'd call in to see my friend Fiona Mandeville.' She smiled at him. She might not have been especially pretty, but she had a broad, friendly face and there was genuine warmth in her smile. 'She's been having a bit of a bad week, I'm afraid. Her husband's stuck in London, you see, and it would be bad enough being here on her own with two small children without some of Mr Quinn's men paying her a visit a few nights ago.'

'Really? How far away is this?'

'Oh, about five miles, that way,' she pointed to the east, where the edge of the watery sun was peeping weakly through some misty trees.

'Did she say what they wanted?'

'Food and guns, I think. That's usually what they're after. God, can you imagine what it must be like living up in the mountains in this weather? They must be starving. Anyway, they didn't get anything off Fiona. She chased them away with a shotgun.'

'Really?' He smiled. That might not have been advisable, but it conjured up an amusing image. 'She sounds rather formidable.'

'Oh, she's not really. Her bark is worse than her bite. But you'll meet her soon enough. I'm going to invite her to dinner when I go over.'

Stephen looked uncertainly at her bicycle as she finished pinning her hat and took hold of the handlebars, placing one foot on the pedal.

'Are you sure it's safe to go over there on *that?*'

'Oh, yes, it's perfectly safe. You hardly ever see them down here in the daytime, and they would never do any harm to a woman. They're very *gallant,* don't you know.'

'I'm sure they are,' he agreed, though he didn't think that laying ambushes and burning houses was all that chivalrous.

'Well, goodbye,' Susan said, and she pushed the bicycle forward, skipped on nimbly and pedalled down the drive, wobbling through the gravel as she picked up speed. 'Oh, and don't forget to have breakfast,' she called back. 'Don't bother waiting for Alfie – he always sleeps late. Just help yourself; you'll find everything in the dining room.'

'I will,' he said, waving her off. But when she had disappeared between the trees he turned away from the house and then walked out across the lawn, following a mossy stone path until it dropped through a terrace in three shallow steps. He stopped here and turned around. Now he could see not only the whole front of the house, but what lay behind it as well. The mountains reared up like a wall. They were no great height but they seemed to rise from directly behind the

319

house and their steep sides stretched away to the
east and west. The ground was all heather and
rock, curving from one peak to the next and cut
by gorges, gullies and streams. The peaks were
dusted with snow and took on a faintly rosy tint
in the light of the rising sun, with the cloud just
kissing some of the higher ones.

The longer Stephen studied them, the more his
heart sank. Quinn's hideout was up there – somewhere – and with only fifty men at his disposal,
he had little hope of finding it. Even if Commandant Donovan had twice that number on the
far side, they would hardly be able to mount a
decent search…

A soft thump from the house broke his chain of
thought and drew his eyes down. He saw Lieutenant Walsh standing outside the front door,
stuffing something into his mouth and licking his
fingers. As he ambled down the steps, Stephen
hurried back up the path to cut him off.

'Right,' he said under his breath, 'I need a word
with you.'

XV

**Zeitschrift für Angewandte
Mathematik und Mechanik**
Akademie-Verlag

*A new method for the derivation of inhomologous
Lorentz transformations from the theory of special
relativity.*

By J. G. KEACH
Trinity College, Dublin (Ireland)

*Mathematics Department,
Trinity College,
Dublin.*

1 February 1923

Dear Dr Bernard,

It is with great regret that I must bring to your attention a paper published in the German Journal of Applied Mathematics & Mechanics (Zeitschrift für Angewandte Mathematik und Mechanik – see copy enclosed).

This paper, which has been published by Mr Keach of this department and of which he purports to be the sole author, is identical to a paper that I wrote last year. I regret to say that I have not been consulted in this matter by Mr Keach and nor have I been cited as an author. I must therefore assume that Mr Keach is attempting to pass my work off as his own.

As you are no doubt aware, this is not the first time that Mr Keach has committed such an act. I'm sure you will agree that such a state of affairs is completely unacceptable and I trust you will deal with the issue as a matter of urgency. I look forward to meeting with you in the very near future in order to discuss the matter further.

Yours sincerely,

Lillian Bryce,
Lecturer in Mathematics

The cold wind had dulled Joe's senses so much that it took him a while to realize that there was a light in front of him. He stopped and blinked and wiped some melting snow out of his eyes. There was a cluster of buildings up ahead; black against the white of the snow, and in the middle of them was a single yellow light. It was hard to make out through the gathering dark, but surely they were too big to be a farm? He beat his arms across his chest and then stuck his frozen hands in his armpits for a minute. Even if it was a farm, he thought he'd risk it. Night was coming on fast and the wind was picking up, rattling dusty snow through the bare bushes of the ditch and cutting him to the marrow. He only had an old overcoat and a threadbare scarf and his cap wasn't much use in this weather. His ears were numb and his bare fingers were curling into claws with the cold. Even if it wasn't the monastery, that light meant shelter and warmth, and he knew if he didn't get in somewhere soon he'd be in trouble.

He put his head down and trudged towards it. Even as he walked, he was still hugging himself, trying to squeeze some warmth into his hands, and his boots slipped and skidded on the icy road. He felt so tired now he could hardly find the strength to move his legs, and every jolt and slide seemed to shake his very bones. Two weeks, it had taken him to get this far; two weeks, and he still wasn't even sure where he was going.

The first week, in Dublin, had been the most dangerous. The circle of men he knew – or who knew him – was getting smaller and smaller, and as more of them were arrested or shot by the Free Staters, the ones left behind were becoming more and more suspicious. Most of the men he had known in the Four Courts were gone now, and even O'Malley was in the bag; riddled with bullets when he tried to shoot his way out of a Free-State raid on Mrs Humphries's house. Joe had mostly been met with hard stares and suspicion. He'd been passed from one man to another, questioned, even threatened.

Eventually he was given a scrap of paper with an address in Limerick City, though getting there was no easy job either. The envelope he carried didn't protect him from the Free-State soldiers who stopped and searched him any more than it did from the Irregulars who pulled up the railway tracks and blew up the bridges. When he eventually got there he was sent on again to Ennis, then to Mallow, then Clonmel. Sometimes he got a lift in a lorry and sometimes the loan of a bicycle, but most of the time he walked. After the first day he'd had blisters the size of shillings on both his feet; now he had blisters coming up under the blisters.

Once he reached Clonmel, he knew he was getting close. The town was crawling with Free-Staters, but they didn't look half as comfortable as they had elsewhere. He'd had to duck into a pub to avoid being arrested by a patrol that seemed to be grabbing every man who happened to walk down the street, and when eventually he reached the address he'd been given, he was told it wasn't safe for him to stay. The Staters had already raided half a dozen houses in the town and they might strike again at any minute. They told him to get to the monastery at Mount Melleray and put him on a milk cart that would take him to Capoquin, the nearest village. That had been the previous night, and he'd been on the go ever since.

With his head down against the wind and his arms wrapped around himself he had managed to lose any sense of movement. His feet kept moving, his legs kept complaining and he could feel the cold eating into him, but he didn't know if he was getting anywhere. He didn't care. He was too cold and too tired. Then there was a loud clang just in front of him and his head jerked up. The sound of a bell rang around the snowy hills, and then it tolled again. He could see the shape of a church just a few yards ahead and even see the dim glow of a stained-glass window, all red and green and blue. There were other buildings behind, and a tall window showing that single yellow light he'd seen from down the hill. A third time, the bell tolled and he straightened himself up and shook some life into his tired limbs. He was here, he had made it.

He was tempted to go into the church, just to sit down for a minute, to warm himself and to try to restore some feeling to his face before talking to anybody. But as he came closer he heard the hum of chanting voices, sounding strangely warm and sweet as it drifted through the freezing air, and after listening for a moment he turned away and went towards the light.

The yellow light he had seen was burning in a window with no curtains. When he looked inside he saw a very long table set for a meal, with mounds of cut bread piled on plates and benches running down both sides. Food and warmth. That was all he needed to see. He went along to the door and hammered on it until his fist tingled and pricked as the blood flowed back into his frozen fingers. Eventually, he heard footsteps, then the bolt was shot and a gust of air enveloped him that was so warm and so rich with the smell of food that he suddenly felt giddy.

The man who had opened the door was dressed in a monk's habit, but he wasn't like any monk that Joe had seen before. He was over six feet tall, rail thin and completely bald, with big, slightly protruding eyes. He inclined his head towards Joe.

'Can I help you?' he asked, in a very soft voice.

'Michael Byrne sent me,' Joe got out, though he had not, as far as he knew, met anybody by that name in the last two weeks. That was just what he had been told to say. The monk didn't bat an eyelid, but opened the door and beckoned him inside. Joe had never been so glad to walk into a room in his life. The door opened directly into the kitchen and there was a log fire blazing in the fireplace, and the smell of cooking food coming thick from the stove.

'Warm yourself,' the monk commanded, and Joe hardly needed to be told. He shuffled towards the fire, fumbling at the buttons of his overcoat as he went, and felt the heat stretching the skin of his face when he was still five feet away.

'Have you come far?' the monk asked, busying himself at the stove.

'I left Clonmel last night,' Joe answered, finally getting his coat open and stretching out his hands to warm them. He could feel the life coming back into his tired limbs already, but the smell of food was giving him a strong empty ache in his stomach.

'A hard journey in this weather,' the monk said, and he brought a bowl of steaming stew that Joe set in his lap and ate hungrily while the monk excused himself and went out for a time. He wasn't gone more than a minute, but Joe was wiping his bowl with a crust of bread when he came back.

'I take it you are wanting to go into the mountains,' the monk said, standing in front of him and folding his arms up the sleeves of his habit.

'Is that where Liam Lynch is?' Joe asked.

'I don't know who is up there and who is not. We don't ask. They send a man down every few days with messages for your friend Mr Byrne. In this weather he's been coming less often, but you shouldn't have to wait more than a couple of days. You're welcome to stay here until he comes. It's perfectly safe provided you stay inside. The Free-State soldiers come around from time to time, but they never intrude.'

Joe had the feeling he had made this speech before, which was odd. The church was no friend to the Irregulars. It had come down firmly on the side of the Treaty and a pastoral letter from the bishops had all but excommunicated anybody who fought against it.

The monk must have noticed the puzzled look on his face. He smiled.

'Our superiors may indulge in politics, my friend, but we do not. Out here, one weary traveller is the same as another. You are welcome to stay for a few days and no harm will come to you as long as you are here. Now, you must be tired. Come along.'

Joe got up and followed the monk out of the kitchen. After the heat and the food he had started to feel sleepy, but he was aware of the chill as they passed out into a long stone-flagged corridor, and hugged his arms to himself again when the monk stopped to light a candle stuck in an old-fashioned sconce. The air was cold and he could see his breath frosting on it as the candle flickered into life. They went on again by the light of the candle and stopped at a small wooden door, which the monk unlocked with a key from the bunch on his belt.

'We live simply here,' he said, pushing the door open. 'I'm sorry if it's not quite what you are used to, but I believe you will be quite comfortable.'

327

Joe peered inside. The room was very small and very plain. The ceiling was barely high enough to stand under and the only furniture was a low bed and a simple wooden chair and a crucifix hanging on the whitewashed wall. It looked like nothing so much as his cell in Mountjoy.

'I'm sure I will,' he agreed, and took the candle. 'Thank you, brother.'

Billy's office looked out on to Merrion Square. In the summer he had been able to see nothing but the green canopy of the trees in the park, swaying and rustling and shot through with sunlight. To-night, however, everything was bare and white. Below the half-closed blind he could see snow-flakes twisting through the lamplight and the only sound was the steady burr of the paraffin heater beside his desk.

When he reached the end of the report he was reading, he uncapped his pen and made a short note at the bottom before putting it into the tray for the minister's attention. Then he pulled out his watch and checked the time. Perhaps one more before he went home, he thought, and his hand was on the next report when there was a polite knock on the door and Diffney came in with a telegram.

TO: W. STANDING DEPT H AFFAIRS
YR MAN PASSED CAPOQUIN THIS MORN-
ING BOUND FOR MELLERAY. I AWAIT YR
ORDERS.
DONOVAN, COMMDT.

Billy read it, then let it fall on his desk and took a cigarette case from the drawer. He lit a cigarette and savoured the taste of it as he felt that feeling start again in his stomach. It was the same thing he used to get when he was in the castle, when he'd been passing information to the IRA – a sort of painful fluttering just under his ribs. It was uncomfortable, but pleasurable at the same time. The strange thing was, he didn't enjoy it now but he knew he'd miss it when it was gone.

'Will there be an answer?' Diffney asked.

Billy shook his head, blowing out a thin stream of smoke through his lips and pushing up his spectacles so that he could pinch the bridge of his nose and ease the incipient ache that was growing there.

'No,' he said 'Not right away. He's not there yet.'

Grace Dieu,
Castlegrace,
Co Tipperary,

1 February 1923

My darling Lillie,

I was very pleased to receive your last letter and the copy of the article. I told you he would take it! I simply knew he would be too cocky to refuse. He thinks he's won after the last time, but I believe he's about to get his comeuppance. You must hold your nerve. I know the hearing is at very short notice but I also know you have nothing at all to worry about. Just make absolutely

329

certain that Mr Noyk is there on the day. Everything hinges on him, so he must be allowed to attend. Accept no argument on this point. If he is sent out, then you must leave also. The board may not like it, but they are not going to like what Mr Noyk has to say either!

I'm only sorry that I won't be there myself. I have sent off a request for leave but I doubt I will get it because I've hardly been here a wet day. As well as that, things are beginning to warm up in these parts. Well, some things are – the weather certainly is not. We have had quite a bit of snow, which makes things difficult for us but even more so for the Irregulars, so I am not complaining. Despite the snow, I have been keeping the men very active and they are shaping up quite nicely. We have just had a hectic week of raids, patrols and searches and, between us and the weather, I'm sure the Irregulars are starting to feel the pinch.

The only fly in the ointment, then, is Lieutenant Walsh, who is proving more trouble than he is worth. I can't make up my mind as to whether he is just incompetent or if there is something more sinister going on. As far as incompetence goes, it is not that he is stupid – though he sometimes carries on that way – but there is a sullen stubbornness about him that can be very disagreeable. If he does something wrong (which happens more often than I'd like), he absolutely refuses to acknowledge the fact until I point it out to him and then, of course, he becomes resentful – and he's not slow to show it. More than once he's been as near openly insubordinate as makes no difference and I strongly suspect he is playing up to the men. He puts himself across as the local man, while I am only a blow-in from Dublin and, worse, I used to be a British soldier, the old enemy.

On the other hand, I'm beginning to suspect that he

isn't entirely true to our cause. Devereux is convinced of it. He neither likes nor trusts Walsh, and has already hinted that he had something to do with the ambush that killed my predecessor. This is awkward to say the least, as I spend half my time watching Walsh like a hawk. I would dearly like to get rid of him, but to do so I should need some solid proof that he is up to no good. Even then I could find myself at a sticky wicket because about a dozen of the men served with him during the Tan war and even if they aren't as sympathetic to the Irregulars they might resent my sending him away. If I'm not careful, could end up making things worse for myself.

On the credit side, Sergeant Coakley is proving to be invaluable. Being American-trained, I'm sure he found some of my habits as odd as I did his, but now that we have got used to each other I believe we will make a good team. He is reliable and clever and, though they make fun of his accent behind his back, the men regard him with that mixture of fear and respect that is the mark of a good sergeant. If I only had a half dozen more like him I believe I could sweep the whole lot of the rebels out of those mountains and be back home to you in a flash!

Well, it's nearly time for dinner, when I must button up my tunic, put on my Sam Browne and go down and make myself agreeable for an hour. To be honest, it's not that bad. The food is generally good and Susan Devereux is a very pleasant hostess. Her brother, though it can sometimes be very hard to understand him, can also be very amusing in a rather cynical way. Even Lieutenant Walsh tries to be sociable, though I believe Devereux has detected the tension and throws out the odd wicked little barb to try and provoke a row

331

between us.

Tonight, however, we must endure a fresh horror in the shape of Lady Fiona Mandeville, the chatelaine of Curaheen House. She is a neighbour of sorts, though Devereux cannot abide her. Perhaps it's not a good sign that I find myself so often in agreement with him, but I have to say that I don't care for her much, either. She is a horse-faced creature, very brash, very English, and very much of the old-style 'whip them, flog them' type. Much as she grates on my nerves, however, I have to admire her fortitude. While Lord Mandeville seems to be permanently established in London (officially taking care of his 'business interests', although Devereux believes these run to a passion for cards and a string of mistresses), Lady M remains here, twenty miles from the nearest town and with two small children to take care of. She has already had one brush with the Irregulars and while she seems to think they are afraid of her, I'm firmly of the belief that she is the one who should be afraid of them. The more we tighten the noose on the Irregulars, the more attractive an easy target like her will become.

Now I must finish. The gong is clanging downstairs. I would much rather stay here and keep you in my thoughts, but I must go down. If it's not too horrible or protracted, I will give you an account of the meal in tomorrow's letter.

Until then, I send you all my love,

Stephen

It had started to snow again. Large wet flakes patted and thumped against the French windows and fluttered down through the dim light that filtered out on to the terrace. Stephen was at the desk in the library, which was the room he used as his office. It was at the west end of the house, next to Devereux's bedroom and was lined with bookshelves and filled with old-fashioned mahogany furniture, with Turkish carpets scattered on the floor.

He finished reading the last page from the pile in front of him and then leaned back and rubbed his eyes tiredly. This was the reality of command; provisioning bills, intelligence summaries, readiness reports. Aside from his other failings, Captain O'Carroll had been lax with his paperwork and there had been a pile of it to sort out. Still, at least it was done now. He pushed his chair back and walked to the window. The house was silent save the ticking of the old clock on the mantel. All at once it seemed to pause, then it whirred loudly and marked midnight with twelve tinkling chimes.

Stephen looked out across the snowy lawn. There was no moon, but everything was so white that he could see the muted curves and folds of the ground right down to the dark line of the trees. Apart from the falling snow, it was very still. He wondered if it was snowing in Dublin, and thinking of Dublin brought Lillian to mind. It was at times like this that he missed her most of all. When he was busy, the work and everyday worries absorbed him, but when it was this quiet he could feel her absence like an ache.

As his mind turned he thought how quickly time was passing. Already he had been in the army for a year. He missed the academic life, though he often thought that he hadn't engaged with it seriously. It had been barely a couple of years, between one thing and another, and, even though he'd enjoyed it while it lasted, he had to wonder if he was really suited to it. He didn't want to simply make a living out of it; he wanted to excel, to succeed. He knew he had the ability, but he wasn't sure if he had the commitment. Great work in mathematics required an almost religious devotion, and he felt as if he had allowed himself to be too easily distracted.

But as he looked at himself reflected in the glass, at his uniform, he also knew that he wasn't really suited to this life either. He might be good at it, but it was no way to make a living. It was no way to live a life.

A groan from the next room startled him. He turned his head and looked in the direction of Devereux's room, but nothing followed and he went back to staring out across the lawn. It had been a night like this when Devereux was wounded. Snow blanketing the ground and turning everything white and ghostly. Time's passing had dimmed many memories from the war, but not that. He could see it as clearly as if he was there now: the bone-biting cold on a crystal-clear night, ice on the wire and rime on the clothes men stood up in. The shattering noise as the Germans opened up on Devereux's patrol with everything they had...

Another groan, lower, but somehow more anguished. Clearly, Devereux's memories were working on him as well. Stephen knew very well that he had them, though he never spoke of them. The other evening at dinner, Lieutenant Walsh had asked him what the war was like. The question had been perfectly polite, a genuine enquiry from one soldier to another. Devereux had just glared angrily at him.

'Well,' Susan Devereux had said, as an uncomfortable silence descended on the table. 'That was a long time ago. I'm sure he can hardly remember, can you Alfie?'

Devereux had turned his gaze on his sister – if anything, looking even angrier. Stephen had looked on apprehensively as Devereux's head jerked a few times, his jaw clenching the way it always did when he was working up to say something.

'I remember,' came out quite clearly at last, and then he'd nodded at Stephen. 'He remembers, too. Never bloody forget. Never.'

He was right. Stephen would never forget the smell of singed hair and scorched flesh from one of Devereux's wounded men. The heat and the blast from a shell that landed as Stephen ran out to help them. The way Devereux had writhed and brayed with pain in the Aid Post afterwards. It all came back to him now, on a quiet night in the country, as he looked out at the snow falling. And it made him miss Lillian even more. Everything did.

Stephen yawned and stretched and glanced over at the clock on the mantel. Time for bed. He had started to turn away from the window when something caught his eye. It was far down near the edge of the lawn, but he could clearly see it was the figure of a man. He stopped and watched steadily for a moment. His first thought was that it was one of the sentries, but this man wasn't moving. He was just standing there, and he appeared to be watching the house. In fact, Stephen had the feeling he was looking straight at him. Was he seeing things, or was it just some shadows in the trees? But it was definitely a man...

'No, no!'

The shout came so clearly from Devereux's room that Stephen jumped where he stood. He shivered and looked around automatically. The memories certainly were eating him tonight. But once again, silence followed. His nightmare had probably woken him up. Well, Stephen knew well enough what *that* was like. He listened for a few moments, as if to make sure, and then he turned back to the window and looked out across the lawn again.

The man he had seen down there was gone.

XVI

He made his men cover the last half-mile on foot so that they wouldn't hear them coming. When they reached the ditch enclosing the cottage, Stephen split them up, sending Sergeant Coakley around behind the cottage to block any escape. They were so used to this now that it could all be done in total silence – just a few nods and hand signals. Then Stephen crouched down in the snow and waited. He could see the cottage through the bare branches of the hawthorn bush. He could

see its white walls looming out of the early morning dark and a tendril of smoke twisting up from
the chimney. But he could hear nothing.

When he thought Coakley had had time to get
into position, he looked along the line of his men.
They were all crouched down behind the ditch,
watching him expectantly as he raised his hand.
Two quick jabs towards the cottage and they
were off, piling through the gateway and fanning
out in front of the cottage. Then two darted forward, kicked in the door and disappeared inside.
Stephen went in after them with his pistol drawn,
but he knew the moment he walked inside that
there was nothing here. This was a labourer's cottage and only had two rooms. It had a packed
earth floor and billhooks and other tools hanging
from the bare beams of the thatched roof. There
was nowhere to hide and nobody here.

'Search the place for arms,' he said to his men,
and went to the fireplace at the end of the main
room. Turf was still smouldering in the grate and
the kettle hanging over it was hot to the touch. A
table had been pulled up to the wooden settle
beside the fireplace and there was food on it,
bread and cheese, freshly cut, and two mugs set
out beside a corked bottle of milk.

Sergeant Coakley came in, slinging his Thompson gun over his shoulder. He looked disappointed.

'There ain't nobody outside, sir.'

'They were here.' Stephen nodded at the table.
'Looks like we just missed them again. Did you
see any tracks?'

'Two sets heading up the hill. They're fairly

337

clear in this snow – do you want us to follow, sir?'

Stephen shook his head. Two men could mean anything. They could be a foraging party come down from the mountains or they could be outsiders, trying to break through to the Irregulars' headquarters. Then again, they could just as easily be a couple of Quinn's men trying to lure them into an ambush. Whoever they were, they had at least a ten-minute head start.

'No, sergeant. They have the better of us this morning. We'd better–'

'Sir,' a soldier came running in, 'sir, there's something you should see. We've just spotted smoke. Looks like it's coming from down the road.'

Stephen followed him outside without a word. He saw the smoke straight away – he could hardly have missed such an enormous cloud, even if the sky was still a little dark. But he had to climb to the brow of the small knoll in front of the cottage before he could see where it was coming from. There was hardly a breath of breeze, so it was rising up in a straight black pillar from a wooded area about two miles to the east. In the darkness of the trees he could see a dull orange glow lighting the base of the pillar.

'Christ almighty!' he exclaimed as Coakley came up beside him.

'That's Curaheen House, sir.'

'I know it is. We've been had, sergeant!' He turned and shouted to the rest of the men, 'Clear out! Everybody back to the tender!'

It took them barely five minutes to cover the half-mile of rutted track back down to the road.

It took another ten to drive the three miles to Curaheen House, Stephen fuming and urging the driver to go faster, faster – even though he knew it was already too late. All the way there, he was thinking of Lieutenant Walsh. He was the one who dealt with the informers; he was the one who'd got the tip. Well, it was a bit too much of a coincidence that this last tip had sent them creeping around an isolated cottage while the Irregulars were burning Curaheen House...

He smelled the fire before he saw it. As they swept through the gate in a spray of gravel and roared up the drive, they were engulfed by the thick cloud of smoke that was swirling through the trees. By the time the smoke cleared they were nearly at the top of the drive and he had a clear view of the house. About half of it was on fire, with the roof already fallen in and flames billowing from the windows. The other half was smoking ominously, but the doors and French windows were open and a few men came running out with their arms full of furniture and books before dumping it on the lawn and hurrying back inside.

'See what you can do to help,' Stephen shouted to Sergeant Coakley as the tender skidded to a halt and the men piled out on to the drive. He hurried over to the mound of furniture that had already accumulated on the lawn. There were women there, still in their nightclothes, clutching two small children to their hips and shushing them as they cried.

'Lady Mandeville?' Stephen asked, but she was not there. A stout old woman with wisps of grey hair sticking out from under her nightcap just jerked her chin towards the house. At almost the same instant he heard Lady Mandeville's shrill voice, imperiously ordering two of his men to be careful with that cabinet, and he saw her bodily dragging a sofa out through the French windows.

'What happened?' Stephen asked the old woman. 'Who did this?'

'It was Quinn, sir,' the old woman answered, pressing the younger Mandeville boy to her as he started bawling again. 'Quinn and his men came in the middle of the night. They had guns, sir. They told us to get ourselves and some things for the children out and then they emptied paraffin all over the place and burned the house. It was dreadful, sir, dreadful. The poor children is terrified…'

'Mr Ryan!' Lady Mandeville's voice cut sharply through the dull roar of the fire. Stephen turned his head and saw her bearing down on him across the gravel drive. She was wearing a housecoat over her nightdress and her face was smudged with soot and wet with tears.

'Lady Mandeville, I'm terribly sorry–' Stephen began, but she slapped him with all her might across the face.

When they stopped for a rest he could see the monastery down below them. Between the sky and the snow everything was bright blue or white but it lay down there in the valley, greyish black, like a polished pebble. Joe's eyes were watering and his throat was raw with the freezing air, but it was so clear that morning that he could see everything; he could see the church and the tower, the sheep pens and the vegetable garden. Even though he'd only been there a few days, it felt very familiar to him and he was sorry to be leaving it behind.

A puff of smoke blew past him and he turned around and saw that O'Leary had lit another Woodbine. He smoked them constantly, although they didn't seem to slow him down. Joe couldn't believe it was possible to walk so fast, through knee-deep snow and up such a steep hill, but O'Leary could do it. But then he was a proper mountain man – tall and rangy, with wild hair and flinty eyes and a face so weathered and leathery it was impossible to tell what age he was. He wore a belted overcoat and wellington boots and stood in stony silence while Joe panted and tried to get his breath back.

'Smoke?' he asked at last, but Joe just shook his head and tried to suck in some deep breaths of freezing air. He flopped down in the snow and rested his arms on his knees and then looked down at the monastery again. It looked as peaceful as he remembered, and as his breathing eased he thought of waking in the dark on his first morning and hearing the shuffle of feet outside, the faint clack of rosaries and the distant tolling of the bell. It was the middle of the night and at first he thought that he was dreaming, but then he heard the soft chanting again, the same he had heard when he first arrived, and he lay his head back and listened to the sweet unintelligible song of devotion.

He'd carried that sound with him for the rest of the day. When the silence returned and then the light increased and the day started to fill with the sounds of work, he found himself humming the cadence, though he did not know the words. He still had it with him now, ringing around inside his head, a reminder.

'Are you right?' O'Leary asked, and he flicked the butt of the Woodbine away so that it hissed in the snow. Joe scrambled to his feet and kicked a couple of steps up the hill, showing willing.

'Is it far?' he asked.

'Five miles,' O'Leary answered, and Joe's heart sank. But then O'Leary turned and nodded up the hill. 'It's easier once we get to the top of this.'

He might have been right, but by the time they reached the top of the ridge Joe needed another rest. With the sun beating on his back and the glare of the snow he felt hot under his coat and he could feel the sweat trickling down his chest. But his feet were like blocks of ice and his hands were wet and raw. At last, the slope lay back a bit and he could at least walk more or less upright, his boots crunching through the frozen crust of the snow and plunging deep in the soft stuff below. O'Leary had stopped again and was lighting another Woodbine, cupping the match in his hands to hide it from the breeze that was blowing harder now. Joe stopped beside him and put his hands to his aching back as he caught his breath. From up here, they could look north across the Golden Vale of Tipperary, half the county laid out below them like a tapestry, all patches of green and white and golden brown.

'Holy God,' Joe said, pushing his cap back on his head and blowing on his hands to warm them. 'There's a view for you.'

'It is that,' O'Leary agreed, an unmistakeable

note of pride in his voice. 'That's what we're fighting for.'

Joe didn't say anything for a few moments. This was the first time O'Leary had said anything to him about the war, or even hinted at his allegiances. He had come unarmed to the monastery and, as far as Joe knew, he was just another one of the people who were helping him to get to where he wanted to go. In fact, ever since he'd started this journey, he'd felt as if he was skirting around this war rather than taking part in it. He was navigating his way past obstacles that the war threw in his path, dodging it and trying to stay out of its way. But now that he was nearly at the end of his journey, he could see that he wasn't skirting around it but was right in the middle of it. It was impossible to avoid it; it was everywhere.

'Do you think we can win?' he asked eventually.

'Not at all,' O'Leary said, and shrugged deeper into his overcoat. 'But it's not about winning, is it? It's about standing up for what you believe in.' He nodded out over the countryside. 'It's about doing what you think is right.'

A gust of wind came booming up the slope, rolling a flurry of snow in front of it. It was strong enough to rock Joe on his feet and he half turned, holding up his hand to shield his face. Then it was gone as quickly as it had come and Joe looked out over the plains again.

'What's that?' he asked, pointing to the column of smoke that was rising up from the plain a few miles to the north. 'Looks like trouble.'

'It's trouble, all right.' O'Leary hawked and spat in the snow, then took a long drag from his

343

cigarette. 'It's trouble for the Staters, is what it is. Our boy Quinn's been up to his tricks again.'

'Quinn?' Joe asked, turning up his collar as the wind gusted again. The cold was getting into him now, and he was starting to wish they would get moving again. 'Who's Quinn?'

O'Leary took another drag from his cigarette, then carefully pinched it out between his bony fingers and slipped it back into the pocket of his overcoat.

'He's a slippery hoor, is what he is.' O'Leary grinned and turned west along the ridge. 'But you'll meet him soon enough.'

When the senior fellows came in they sat at a long table across the top of the hall. They all wore their full regalia of hoods and gowns, and there was so much scarlet silk and gold lace on show that it lent them an almost festive appearance. But there was no levity in their faces; they were universally solemn and took their seats with an air of grave purposefulness.

Lillian faced them from a table near the middle of the hall.

She was wearing her plain black master's gown and felt very much as if she was sitting her *vivas* again. No, it was worse than that. It was more like the morning of Stephen's brother's court martial; grim and officious. The only friendly face she could see was Professor Barrett, and he looked distracted and uncomfortable. He was limping heavily and he had to be helped to his seat by a porter.

It took a long time for the fellows to settle

344

themselves. While she waited, Lillian glanced at Noyk, the solicitor, who was sitting beside her. He, too, looked rather grave, though he cracked a warm smile and a nod, as if to say he was ready.

Lillian had been trying not to look at Keach, but she couldn't help it. He was sitting by himself at a table a few feet away. He had not said a word to her or even acknowledged her presence since he had come a few minutes before. This was the closest that Lillian had been to him ever since that day in his office six months before. Even being this close gave her a bit of a chill, and she looked away quickly when his eyes darted in her direction.

'Now then,' Dr Bernard began, looking up and down the line of the senior fellows. Then he peered over his spectacles at Mr Noyk, as if he had not noticed him before. 'Miss Bryce, before we begin, can you please tell us who is this gentleman you have brought with you?'

Lillian stood up. 'This is Mr Noyk, Provost. He is my solicitor.'

There was a murmur of discontent amongst the fellows. Dr Bernard's jowls shook as he conferred with the two sitting nearest to him. Then he frowned at her.

'Miss Bryce, I thought I made it clear that our hearing today is purely to assist in establishing the facts of the case. Furthermore, I can assure you that it will be conducted with scrupulous regard to the finest academic traditions, of which this college is justly proud. Without wishing to offend Mr Noyk, I see no need to have an outsider here. This is not a legal matter, there will be no cross-examination.'

345

That's what you tell me now, Lillian thought, but she stood her ground. 'I appreciate that, Provost, and I mean no disrespect to either yourselves or the college. Mr Noyk is not here to enter any sort of legal plea and nor does he intend to cross-examine anyone. He will, however, make a statement on my behalf that I believe will clarify the facts of the case beyond any possible doubt.'

These last words were spoken with such conviction that she felt Keach staring at her as she sat down again. However, they also had the desired effect upon the fellows, who whispered to each other and then slowly began to nod together.

'Very well,' Dr Bernard said unhappily. 'We will suffer Mr Noyk to stay in order that he may make his statement. However, we will not allow him to question or cross-examine Mr Keach in any way. If there are any questions to be asked, we shall do so. Is that understood, Miss Bryce?'

'Yes, Provost.'

'Very well. I'm sure we're all well acquainted with the events that have brought us here today. However, as a means of laying out the facts of the matter as they currently stand, I shall summarize. In this letter to me, dated the first of February' – the provost held up a copy of the letter – 'Miss Bryce alleges that a paper published in a respected academic journal under the name of Mr Keach was, in fact, written by her. Is that correct, Miss Bryce?'

'That's correct, Provost.'

'And do you stand by the allegations made in that letter, Miss Bryce? I should remind you that these are very serious allegations indeed.'

'I do.'

'Very well,' the Provost shifted his gaze to Keach. 'Mr Keach, you have read this letter, have you not?' He raised one shaggy eyebrow, and when Keach nodded, he went on, 'Having read the letter, how do you respond to the allegations that were made therein?'

Keach slowly got to his feet and looked along the line of the fellows with a faint smile on his face and a slight, almost suppliant stoop to his back.

'Well, gentlemen, I deny them absolutely, of course. They are completely untrue, and may I remind you that this is not the first–'

'Do you have any proof that it's yours?' Professor Barrett cut across him. His voice was a little slurred, but those few words came out clear enough. Keach stared at him for a moment and then smiled ingratiatingly at the Provost.

'I beg your pardon, sir, but if I may say so, I don't believe the burden of proof lies with me. Miss Bryce has made this groundless allegation, surely it lies with her to produce the evidence to support her claim.'

'I believe it does,' the Provost said, and turned towards Lillian again. But Professor Barrett was not about to let him off that easily.

'I knew you were not much of a mathematician, Keach,' he drawled, seeming to choke on the last word and producing a handkerchief to dab at the sagging corner of his mouth. Keach started to protest, but Barrett managed to cut him off again. 'But I did not think your grasp of logic was quite so weak. Do you seriously mean to ask Miss Bryce to prove that you did not write this paper?'

This question was so obtuse that it made the Provost frown and look in Barrett's direction. But it also knocked Keach off his balance. He frowned and looked down at his feet for a moment and Lillian tried to hide the smile that was spreading across her lips. This was the old Professor Barrett she knew and loved.

'Yes, of course.' Keach shook his head impatiently. 'But Provost, may I say that I object–'

'Yes, you may,' the Provost answered testily. 'But just this once, Mr Keach, and I might add that *I* object to this quasi-legal tone that you are adopting. I might have expected that from Mr Noyk, here, but not from you. Professor Barrett, do you have a *point* that you wish to make?'

'Mr Keach claims that Miss Bryce has cast the first stone. But surely it is he who has done so by putting his name to that paper. Surely we should require him to produce proof that it is his.'

This was a subtle argument, and one that appeared to rely upon mathematical rather than legal logic. Nevertheless, Lillian could hardly have hoped for better. The point seemed to be well received by the other fellows, who nodded their agreement.

'Very well,' the Provost said in a weary tone. 'Mr Keach, can you provide any proof that the paper is, in fact, yours?'

'Of course,' Keach said quickly, but then he paused, and those few seconds of silence told Lillian everything she needed to know. 'The work developed from an earlier paper on the Lorentz transformations. It was, therefore, developed in a very short time, over a period of just a few weeks, in fact–'

'When?' Professor Barrett barked. Lillian felt a little flutter in her stomach; her mouth was already dry. This was the critical point.

'In August of last year. I had some thoughts during my summer vacation, in fact, and I wrote them up in my notebook, which I have here.' Keach held up a foolscap book. 'When I had progressed the work to a certain point, I took the liberty of sharing some of it with Professor Lorentz himself. I wrote to him in October of last year and he very kindly wrote back to me with some thoughts on the matter. I have his letter here, as well.'

He held up a sheet of paper with a triumphant flourish and then bowed his head to the Provost.

'There is my proof, Provost. And I must say, I object to the tone of Professor Barrett's questions. This really is most unseemly.'

'Yes, it is.' The Provost shot an angry glance at Barrett, who was staring down at his hands. He looked exhausted. 'Miss Bryce, will you please explain your claim, in view of what Mr Keach has just said.'

'Sir, I believe a statement from Mr Noyk will explain everything.'

'Very well,' the Provost huffed, clearly annoyed.

'Your ... erm... Gentlemen,' Noyk began, rising to his feet and holding up a heavy manila envelope closed with a thick wax seal, 'I have here a set of documents that I cannot make any claim to understand. They consist of mathematical workings that were entrusted to me by Miss Bryce over a period of several months, with each item being duly dated and initialled by me. The final

349

instalment is a mathematical paper that, I am told, is almost identical to the one that is in dispute. However, I can only vouch for its authenticity and provenance. I must leave it to you, learned gentleman, to confirm any similarity.'

Professor Barrett looked up again, a new light in his face. 'As Emeritus Professor of Mathematics, I would be happy to examine the papers and confirm if they are similar, Provost.'

'I'm sure you would, professor.' The Provost shot him another angry glance. Lillian could tell by the look on his face that he already knew where this was going. 'Mr Noyk, you mentioned a period of several months. Can you tell us precisely when these items were given to you by Miss Bryce?'

'The first pages were deposited with me more than a year ago, on...' Noyk consulted his diary, open on the desk before him, 'December the eighth, 1921. The deposition was arranged and was witnessed by Miss Bryce's fiancé, a Mr Ryan, who had just returned from London. The final completed paper, which was signed by Miss Bryce in my presence, was deposited with me on the sixteenth of June last year. I remember it quite clearly, sir, because it was the day of the election.'

It took a few moments for this to sink in. According to those dates, the paper that Keach claimed to have worked on in his daybook and about which he had corresponded with Professor Lorentz, had been completed two months before he had ever thought of it. Furthermore, Lillian knew that the envelope contained notes, drafts and revisions that mapped the development of the paper from its inception almost to the day she had brought it to Keach's office. By itself, this would have been enough to prove that the paper was hers, but since Professor Barrett had forced Keach to say *when* he had written his paper, the dates were doubly damning.

As Noyk sat back down beside her, Lillian stared straight ahead. She didn't say a word. She could feel Keach staring at her openly, but she wouldn't look at him. There was consternation on the faces of all the fellows except for Professor Barrett, who gave her a crooked smile and the very faintest of nods.

'The day of the election, indeed,' The Provost muttered, and his gaze moved to Keach. He looked as if he was going to say something else, but decided against it. Instead, he took off his spectacles and rubbed his eyes. Some of the other fellows were looking at him, some at Lillian, but most of them were staring at Keach.

'I see we have only raised even more questions than we had hoped to answer,' the Provost said at last. 'Not least of which is why a member of the staff of this college felt compelled to deposit her work in escrow with a solicitor. However, I think a period of reflection is required, during which I trust that Professor Barrett will confirm if there is indeed any similarity between these papers.' He looked up and down the line. 'Mr Noyk, Gentlemen, I thank you for your time. That will be all.'

Chairs scraped and the fellows stood up. Lillian kept her seat for a few moments, but Keach did not. In a few angry strides he was in front of her, leaning down over her table, his face close to hers.

'You think you're fucking clever, don't you?'

'I beg your pardon?' Noyk said, rising up indignantly. 'That is no way to speak to–'

'I have nothing to say to you, Mr Keach,' Lillian answered coldly. 'I believe I will save it until I am called to give evidence in your libel action against my fiancé.'

'That's what you think,' Keach spat. 'You haven't heard the last of this you know. I'll bloody show you!' And he stalked off, without even bothering to take his notebook and his letter from Professor Lorentz.

On the table before him lay a letter to General Prout, head of the Southern Army Command in Cork. The letter was short, but it had taken him all evening to write. This was his third attempt. His first had been very harsh and the second not much better. His anger must have cooled a little in the writing because the tone of this one was more moderate. The crux of it was still there, however: he could no longer accept Lieutenant Walsh under his command. His difficulty lay in explaining why not without condemning Walsh to a military prison or perhaps a visit to Oriel House.

Then again, he reflected, Walsh had done himself no favours. He'd smiled insolently and said he couldn't remember the name of his informant – this when Stephen was just back and still reeking of smoke from Curaheen House. A polite enquiry had quickly turned into an all-out shouting match and had ended with Stephen confiscating Walsh's sidearm and confining him to his quarters. Now he wanted to be rid of him.

After all the noise earlier on, the room was

silent. No sound save the ticking of the clock on the mantel and the soft burr of the lamp. Stephen signed the letter and was blowing on the page to dry the ink when there was a gentle knock on the door. Sergeant Coakley came in and saluted.

'Sorry to interrupt, sir, but there's a fella just come to the gate and he's asking to see you.'

'To see me?' Stephen looked up from stuffing the letter in an envelope. It was nine o'clock at night, the temperature outside was well below zero and the roads were covered in ice. Somebody wanted to see him very badly indeed. 'Who is it?'

'I don't know, sir. He wouldn't give his name and he said he'd only talk to you.' An uneasy look came over Coakley's face. 'I think he's an informer, sir.'

Stephen thought he'd had enough of informers for one day. He didn't like them, didn't trust them, and they'd caused him nothing but trouble so far. But they were a necessary evil, and with Lieutenant Walsh on his way to a military court in the morning, he'd have to get used to handling them himself.

'All right, send him in.'

'Yes, sir.' Coakley saluted and turned smartly.

'And sergeant?'

'Yes, sir?'

'Search him first.'

Coakley nodded grimly. 'Right you are, sir. I'll leave a man outside the door as well.'

The informer proved to be a young man with thinning fair hair and a wispy moustache. He came in crushing his cap between his hands and looking nervous and uncomfortable. Stephen decided to be brisk.

'Good evening,' he said, standing up from behind the desk. 'Before we go any further, I need to know your name.'

'McGuinness, sir. Brian McGuinness. I'm from Bohergaul, over near Newcastle way.'

Stephen knew Bohergaul; it was a townland not far from Curaheen House. At a good five miles each way, it was no easy journey on a freezing evening like this. He gestured to the chair on the other side of the desk. 'Very well. Please, sit down, Mr McGuinness.'

McGuinness sat as directed but managed to retain his hunched and hunted look, perching uneasily on the edge of the chair and darting his eyes all over the room.

Stephen thought about offering him a drink, but sat down and got straight to business. 'Now, then, what did you want to see me about?'

'Is it true that you pay money for information?'

'Yes, if the information proves to be valuable.'

'How much?'

Stephen smiled. 'That depends on the information.'

This seemed to stop McGuinness in his tracks. He looked like he was about to say something but stopped himself and looked down at the floor. Stephen leaned forward. Either this man was a consummate actor or he had some very valuable information.

'Do you have something you'd like to tell me?' he prompted, as gently as he could.

'My wife's expecting,' McGuinness said, raising his head a little and looking at him from under his brow.

'I see.'

'He sent me down so I could look after her but I don't want to stay here. I don't want my child to be born in this place. All I've ever known is trouble.'

Stephen felt certain of it now. McGuinness knew something. If he wanted to leave, then he'd need money for a fresh start. And he was no fool, either. He knew as well as Stephen did that informers would always be found out eventually. Maybe it would take months or maybe it would take years, but in a small place like this – even in a small country like this – the truth had few places to hide. Stephen tried to overcome his distaste at the situation. He might not like it, but he sensed an opportunity. Here was a man who had already made up his mind to leave behind everything he knew; he was just trying to work up the courage to burn his bridges.

'Who sent you down?' he asked, though he already knew the answer.

'Quinn. I used to be with him up in the mountains.'

'So you know where his hiding place is.' Stephen did his best not to sound too keen, but McGuinness looked up at him sharply, then lowered his head again and nodded.

'It's not just one place. There's three or four spots spread over about a mile of the mountains. There's a cave, a cottage and a couple of old sheep pens that they covered in.'

Stephen nodded. He had the satisfying feeling that the veil was being drawn aside at last, and what McGuinness was telling him made sense. From what he said, Quinn would hardly be comfortable up there, but he and his men could survive easily, and with four positions spread out like that it would be hard to spring any sort of surprise on them.

'How many men has he got up there?'

'It changes. Fellas sometimes come in from other places, and he sent a few home for the winter. When I left he had about twenty with him, but that was without the headquarters boys.'

The headquarters boys? That was interesting, but Stephen decided to draw him out slowly.

'Twenty men? Is that all? I would have thought there'd be more.'

'He gets more when he comes down to fight. The twenty he has with him now are only the ones who are on the run, but he's got people all over this district.' McGuinness shifted uncomfortably and looked over his shoulder as if he feared somebody was listening at the door. 'You'd be surprised where he's got people. Mostly they're just eyes and ears, but a few of them will fight, or hide weapons or men if he asks them.'

Stephen leaned back in his chair. 'And what about these headquarters boys? How many of them are there?' he asked, trying to sound disinterested.

'No more than ten, though you rarely see them all together. They come and go in twos and threes. They always keep moving and they never get together unless they've got something to talk about.'

Stephen folded his arms and considered Mc-

Guinness for a few moments. His gut feeling was that the man could be trusted – but this was no trustworthy act. He was selling his friends for money. The clock on the mantel ticked and Stephen's eyes bored into McGuinness, searching for some sign, some clue as to his true intentions. McGuinness must have felt his stare, because he looked up defiantly.

'They're up there now,' he said.

'Who are?'

'The headquarters boys. Two of them came in yesterday before I left. They said the others were on their way to meet them.'

'Why?'

'I don't know. They said something was coming down from Dublin.'

Stephen's mouth was dry and his heart was thumping in his chest. Here was either the biggest coup he could have wished for or else an even more elaborate trap than the one he had walked into that morning. But he had made up his mind at last.

'Would you be able to guide us to these places in the mountains?'

'No,' McGuinness answered, jumping back in his chair as if he'd just been stung. 'I'll show you on a map, but I won't go with you. It's more than my life's worth. It's more than my wife's.'

Stephen glared at him across the desk. The clock on the mantel ticked.

'Give me a map and I'll show you,' McGuinness offered. 'But I won't go. You can pay me after, if you want, but I won't go.'

It could easily be a trap, Stephen thought, but

it was still an opportunity he couldn't pass up. He would just have to take his chances.

'All right,' he slipped open a drawer and unfolded a map of the mountains, 'show me.'

Half an hour later he let McGuinness out through the French windows. Then he went to the door and told the sentry to fetch Sergeant Coakley.

'Yes, sir?' Coakley asked, coming in a few minutes later.

'Have one of the tenders brought around,' Stephen told him. 'I need to go to Capoquin.'

'Tonight, sir?' Coakley looked unhappy. Apart from the risk of an ambush, the roads would be treacherous.

'Yes, sergeant. I need to see Commandant Donovan urgently. I'll take six men with me. I'm leaving you in charge here. I want you to issue rations and ammunition and have the men ready to go at a moment's notice. We may have some work to do tomorrow.'

XVII

It felt like he'd hardly been to bed at all. He'd come back after midnight and spent an hour going through the plan with Sergeant Coakley. Now it was just gone six in the morning and he was up and moving again. But he could feel something he hadn't felt in a while – excitement, anticipation. After weeks of sitting here under the mountains, waiting for the Irregulars to make their next move, they were finally going on the attack. He yawned as he came down the stairs, his eyes still half-gummed with sleep; but he felt alert and ready. Today was the day.

Commandant Donovan had agreed that they had to move fast. He was as keen as Stephen to strike at Quinn and he thought that the informer's tip was at least plausible – not least because his comments about the headquarters staff coming together seemed to tally with information he already had.

'Somebody came through here a few days ago,' he'd said, and he gave Stephen a sidelong look. 'I was told to keep an eye out and report back to Dublin when he showed up. Then this morning I received orders to stand by to make a sweep through the mountains.'

'Really?' Stephen frowned. As the commander of a significant section of the cordon around the mountains, he would have expected to have been informed of any such plan. 'I've had no such orders. Surely they would–'

Donovan was giving him another strange look. 'These orders didn't come from Army HQ,' he said bluntly. 'They're from the Department of Home Affairs. This is their operation and it's very hush-hush. All I have from HQ is a letter signed by Mulcahy himself, telling me to give them any and all assistance that may be required.'

It was still odd, but Stephen didn't have much time to think about it. Donovan gestured at the map spread out on the table between them.

'I think your plan is good. If we come at them

from both directions we should pinch them between the two of us. I've more men, so I'll do the
sweep, but you need to get in and drive them out
of their hidey-hole.' Donovan nodded to himself,
a fierce look coming into his eyes. 'If this weather
holds they'll never get away from us, Stephen.
They'll have nowhere to hide if it stays clear.'

If it stays clear. The weather was everything.
Stephen peered up into the still-dark sky as he
came out of the house. He was heartened see the
stars pricking the lightening purple of the night.
That was good. There were a few smudges of
cloud, but the day promised to be as clear and
sunny as the one before. He backed up a few yards
so he could see the tops of the mountains looming
ghostly white behind the house. In his mind's eye
he could see them in full daylight, blinding white
under a pure blue sky, their rounded slopes as
smooth and hard as porcelain. Donovan was right:
there would be nowhere to hide up there.

When he went around to the stable yard he
found everything was as he expected. The
engines of the two tenders and the armoured car
were warming up and his soldiers were all busy
drawing ammunition and extra rations as the
smell of breakfast wafted out from the mess.

'Morning, sergeant,' he greeted Coakley, returning his salute. 'Is everything in hand?'

'Good morning, sir.' There was a note of excitement in Coakley's voice. 'Yes, sir, we're as ready
as can be. The lads don't have much in the way
of winter clothing, but we're making the best of
what we have.'

'Very well. Have the vehicles brought around to

the front of the house and then let the men have their breakfast. We'll parade at oh seven hundred. All right?'

'Yes, sir.' Coakley nodded, and Stephen saw a dark look come over his face. Following his gaze, he saw a dark shape standing at one of the windows in the back of the house. He couldn't make it out clearly in the dim light, but he knew that was Lieutenant Walsh's room.

'Carry on, sergeant,' he murmured, and walked back around to the front of the house. He'd been thinking about Walsh ever since he'd left Capoquin. The plan he'd hatched with Donovan called for every man he could muster, and a second officer would be especially useful. But Walsh was simply not to be trusted. He would have to stay behind, but even the thought of leaving him here was giving Stephen the willies. He decided he would leave a few men to keep an eye on him. He could hardly afford to spare them, but he didn't see that he had much choice.

As he came back to the front steps he found Devereux sitting there in his wheelchair. He was still in his pyjamas with a blanket draped around his shoulders and down into his lap.

'Mornin', Ryan,' he drawled as Stephen came up the steps. 'You're early 'day. P-p-planning raid?'

'We're making a sweep through the mountains,' Stephen admitted. 'I'll be taking most of the men with me. We should be back before dark.'

'Wha' 'bout Walsh?' Devereux asked, a grin turning up one corner of his mouth. No doubt he'd heard the row through the library door, and noticed that Walsh hadn't joined them for dinner

361

last night.

'He won't be joining us, and he won't be staying, either. I'll be sending him to Cork as soon as I come back tonight.'

''Bout bloody time,' Devereux said, nodding jerkily. But then his eyes narrowed. 'How many m-m-men you leaving?'

'Five,' Stephen answered, wincing a little as he said it. He knew it was risky. If Quinn or any of his men managed to escape, they would know he'd thrown everything into the attack. 'That's all I can spare. Look, maybe it would be safer if you and your sister went and stayed in the village, just until–'

'No runnin'!' Devereux ground out. Then he spun his chair around deftly and jerked his head. 'F-f-follow me.'

With one good push he wheeled himself up the ramp and into the gloomy hallway. Stephen followed him to a door that stood opposite to the one to the library. He realized that he'd never been in this room, though it wasn't locked. Devereux turned the handle with his good hand and then wheeled himself inside. It was a large room with a desk near the window and some comfortable armchairs on either side of the fireplace. It looked very much like a gentleman's study, though to judge by the dust and the smell of must, it didn't see much use. Devereux rolled across the room and stopped in front of a heavy oak cabinet that looked as if it was bolted to the wall.

'K-k-key on top,' Devereux said, rolling his eyes in that direction. The cabinet was too tall for Stephen to reach, but he pulled over a chair and climbed up, feeling around in the dust until his fingers found an old-fashioned iron key. Devereux just nodded as he brought it down, then moved his eyes towards the lock.

Stephen opened the lock and swung the doors apart to reveal a rack of gleaming guns.

'Sue lock 'em up,' Devereux explained, and he shot Stephen a knowing look. 'You kn-kn-know why.' His lips twisted into a lopsided grin, but then he nodded jerkily. 'Shh-shotgun.'

Stephen reached in and took the shotgun from the rack. It was an expensive-looking fowling piece with a walnut stock and beautifully engraved barrels. Devereux took it from him with his good hand and rested it across his lap.

'Cartridge,' he grunted, and managed to trap the barrels under his limp arm and push the lever to break the gun with his good hand. When Stephen handed him the box of ammunition he thrust it under the blanket covering his lap and brought out two shells between the fingers of his good hand. His hand was shaking badly, but he managed to get first one cartridge, then the second, into the breech and snapped the gun shut again. Even that much was hard work for him and he had to bend to it intently, staring at the gun and grunting with the effort. When he finally lifted the gun and slid it down between his body and the arm of the wheelchair, he gave Stephen a broad, almost defiant smile.

'Breakfast!' he barked, very clearly, and he wheeled himself out of the room.

On the day after the college board, Lillian went

back in to work as usual. She knew that the board had gone as well as she could have hoped, that she had succeeded – and yet she didn't know what would happen next. She was a bundle of nerves as she pushed her bicycle through the college gate, though this had less to do with the college board than it did with the note that she'd found as she went out that morning.

It was so small that she had almost missed it: just a little slip of paper folded twice. She hadn't even noticed it until the draught from the opening door whipped it up and whirled it across the hall carpet. When she picked it up she wondered if the coal-man had left it, or Mr Donohoe from next door. But when she opened it she recognized the hand-writing instantly. There were only four words on the note, but she could tell that they had been written by whoever had sent her that box last year.

I'm Watching you, Lily

She hadn't shown it to her mother – she would have had a heart attack – but she hadn't thrown it away either. It was in her bag, in the basket of the bicycle, and she knew who had sent it – or she thought she did.

It had to be Keach, she told herself, but it couldn't be him. If it was, then he was the one who had sent her the bullet last year – but he wouldn't have done that, would he? These were the con-flicting thoughts she had as she pushed her bicycle across Front Square. Every time she glanced at the bag in the basket, she was sure it was him, and yet a second thought told her that it couldn't possibly be Keach. If she knew anything about him, she knew that he was, at heart, a coward. He would never have the courage to come to her house, still less to go up to the door. And then there was the bullet – where would he even get one? Of course, there was what had happened in his office that day but even though it appalled her to think of it, she felt it was in keeping with the man, vain, greedy and repellent as he was. This note was different. It was altogether more sinister, and it simply didn't fit Keach any more than the bullet did.

She was still trying to make up her mind when she reached the mathematics department in New Square. She stopped when she recognized the steps and the familiar door. What a fool she was! Her morning tutorial wasn't for an hour and she'd meant to go to the ladies' common room instead. Only she'd been so lost in thought that she had hardly noticed where she was going. She turned away, but as she did, she saw a movement at the window of Keach's office. It was Keach himself and he was standing there, looking at her. Their eyes met for an instant, but then he stepped away from the window, his face like thunder. Lillian thought of going in, of leaving her bicycle and marching straight up those steps with the note in her hand, but, once again, she thought the better of it. She pushed the bicycle away and went to the ladies' common room.

There was no sign of Keach when she went back to the mathematics department to give her tutorial. His blinds were drawn and the door to his office was closed. But there wasn't a single student absent for that tutorial, and quite a few others leaned out of the junior and senior common rooms to peek at her as she went up the stairs. She didn't respond to any of them; she made no sign or mention of it. Her students seemed disappointed when she went to the board and started talking to them about hyperbolic functions, and yet they knuckled down to work at it and it was she who started to drift. She simply couldn't focus on the work in hand. She could hardly remember her students' names and, more than once, she had to ask for a question to be repeated. In the end she apologized; she said she wasn't feeling well and let them out half an hour early. Then she went back to the ladies' common room and sat by herself for a while.

Her afternoon tutorial went a little better. She had made a point of reading her notes beforehand – if nothing else, it took her mind off other things – and she managed to lose herself for a while in the flow of talk and the questions and the refined argument that always grew up when a tutorial went well. And yet, at the back of her mind there was the thought that it was all so unreal. It was like watching a play that was going on all around her, but she couldn't see it all, she couldn't see what was going on behind the scenes. After everything that had happened the day before, and the note, and this strange atmosphere that seemed to follow her wherever she went, she knew something must have changed, something must be happening. And yet, nothing had been said. Not a word from the Provost or from anybody else, for that matter. Colleagues and students passed her by and nodded hello and smiled at her, but she knew they *knew*. In fact, they probably knew more than she did – it must be all over the college by now. And yet … she had heard nothing.

A porter was waiting outside the ladies' common room with a note for her when she went back to fetch her things. After her last tutorial of the day she usually stayed on in college to work on her research, but she had decided to go home early today. It just didn't feel right to be here, and she wondered if it ever would again. For a moment she feared the worst when she took the note, but she knew by the feel of the paper where it had come from. Two lines of elegant blue handwriting asked if she would see the Provost in his office at half past five. So much for going home early.

'Thank you,' she said to the porter, and then she sighed and went inside and sat down to wait.

Joe felt a hand shaking him by the shoulder and he woke with a start. He opened his eyes on stone walls and a mud floor, water dripping down from a corrugated iron roof. The little window was webbed with thick scales of frost but pierced by a bright, almost painful light.

'Come on, Joe.' Somebody kicked his feet. 'Up, up! We have to go.'

Joe pushed himself up and rubbed the sleep from his eyes. He was lying on one of the hard benches beside the fireplace. There was the dead stump of a candle on the mantle and a mound of white ash in the hearth, but all the other men were gone. All he could see was a rangy figure in a green greatcoat bent over the table near the door, rifling through a pile of papers.

'Come on, Joe,' the figure said without looking around. 'Up you get. We have to hurry, now!'

Joe finally recognized the voice. It was Liam Lynch.

'When did you get here?' he asked, sitting up and pushing his feet into his boots. 'And where's everybody else?'

'I stayed up the valley last night,' Lynch said, turning around and pushing his spectacles up on his bony nose. 'I hear you have a letter for me.'

'I do.' Joe fished the letter from inside his jacket and held it out. He was surprised at how easily it passed. There was no momentous feeling, no sense of relief. Lynch tore open the envelope and Joe went back to lacing his boots.

'Aye, that's it all right,' Lynch said, and Joe jerked his head up at the bitter note in his voice. 'That's why they're here.'

'Who's here?' Joe's eyes went to the window as a shadow moved past. He heard footsteps crunching in the snow, some urgent whispers from outside.

'The Staters. They're moving in from the west, coming up through the Vee. They knew this letter would bring us all to the one place.'

Lynch folded up the letter and slid it into his pocket and Joe watched it vanish with something like despair.

'No, it can't be. It's real – he told me himself. It's a genuine offer.'

'Tell that to the boys that are coming to get us,' Lynch said, and he pulled open the rickety door and went outside.

Two miles away, as the crow flies, Stephen was out in the snow, pushing and heaving with a dozen of his men as they tried to get the tail of the big tender out of a snow-filled ditch. The road into the mountains was bad enough in fine weather, but with an inch of ice it was treacherous and the tender had suddenly slewed sideways and dropped its back wheels in the ditch with a sickening scrape and a thud. They'd managed to back the armoured car up enough to get a chain on and now they were all grunting and shoving as both engines roared and the tender rocked and squeaked, until eventually the wheels bit and the heavy lorry slithered forward into the centre of the road.

'Right, all aboard!' Sergeant Coakley roared, his face red with exertion, and as Stephen climbed back into the cab of the tender he looked at his watch. It had taken them over an hour to get this far, but they were nearly at the top of the pass. Another half-mile and they would have to get out and walk anyway, but he wanted the trucks up there, and the armoured car for support. As he peered forward through the windscreen he became more and more suspicious that they might not get the day they had hoped for. He didn't like the way the weather was shaping up. The sky was still blue, but there were ominous clouds in the south and they had already been swept by a couple of rattling little showers of snow and sleet.

'Keep going,' he said to the driver, though it came out more grim than encouraging. 'Not far to go now.'

The tender ground slowly up the road, following the squat shape of the armoured car, which seemed better able to handle the ice. Stephen's eyes constantly moved across the horizon, scanning for any signs of trouble. As they rounded another hairpin bend, the gradient seemed to ease a bit. Gears clashed and the tender picked up some speed. Stephen could see Sergeant Coakley ahead of him; he was sitting on one of the benches behind the turret of the armoured car, his Thompson gun lying along his knees. Suddenly his arm shot up.

'Sir!' he shouted, pointing to something high up the slope above them. But it was almost in the eye of the sun and the glare was too much. Stephen shielded his eyes with his hand and heard a loud thud as something struck the body of the tender.

'Jesus,' his driver muttered, flinching, and then the windscreen shattered and showered them both with glass. The driver jumped back in fright, pressing his foot on the accelerator, and the wheel seemed to buck and jump in his hands. They shot forward, almost collided with the back of the armoured car, but slid past it and went nose first into the ditch. Despite trying to brace himself with his hand, Stephen was thrown forward and smashed his head on the remaining pane of the windscreen.

By this time, Joe was climbing again, but harder and faster than he ever had before. He had to get to the top of the ridge. That was all he could think of. It was above him, the white sharp against the blue. His breath was sawing in his throat and the muscles in his thighs were screaming, but he knew he couldn't stop. He went up and up, harder and harder, until his knees buckled and he collapsed in the snow. He rolled over to look back down at the cottage. Lynch and O'Leary were ahead of him and were already out of sight, but he could see a couple of the others climbing up the far side of the valley. They looked for all the world like flies climbing up a white wall and he watched their painful progress for a few minutes while he tried to get his breath back.

A couple of Quinn's men, he reckoned. The last of them had left the cottage just before he set off, although Quinn himself had been long gone. Joe only had a dim memory of him from the night before; a stocky man with red hair who didn't say much. According to Lynch, it was he who had raised the alarm, sending a man running up the valley when he found out the Staters were moving in on them. No sign of them yet, though. Joe wondered if it had been a false alarm, but then he heard a distant pop-pop-pop come echoing across the valley. Gunfire. Maybe Quinn was right, after all. Joe threw his head back and looked up the slope. It was still white against clear blue, but there was a thick belt of cloud rolling in from the west and the first tendrils of mist were creeping into the valley.

Cover, he thought. If he could get up there, he'd find some cover. He rolled on to his knees and then got painfully to his feet. His legs were shaking but he forced himself to take one step, then another, following the tracks that Lynch and O'Leary had made. Faster, faster, he said out loud, when he heard another volley crack out over the mountains. At last the ground started to lie back and he knew he was near the top. He plunged on, stumbling through the snow, and then threw himself flat and looked down into the next valley.

The cloud was getting thicker, but he could see the road zigzagging up through a pass and then running along the southern edge of the mountains. He could also see a small lake, pure black against the snow, but that wasn't what interested him. There, down on the road, three vehicles were stopped and men in green coats were spreading out from them. It was the Staters, all right, and they were firing up the hill at a string of black figures spread out just below the ridge. The two men he had seen climbing up from the cottage now joined them, sliding down and bringing up their rifles to shoot at the troops below. The sound of the shots came much clearer now, cracking through the thin air, and he could hear the angry, urgent shouts as well.

Joe stood up and looked at the tracks he had been following; they went along the ridge in the other direction, away from the fighting, and dropped down out of sight after a few hundred yards. Those men were probably covering for Lynch, so that he could get away. Joe hesitated, crouching down as a shot thumped into the snow not far from where he stood. He thought of going over to help, but what could he do when he didn't even have a gun? Another shot zipped through the air over his head, and he knew it wasn't a stray. They were bloody shooting at him. With one last look he turned around and followed the tracks away to the east.

Stephen was bleeding from a cut above his left eye and his ears were still ringing from the impact, but he had managed to pull the Springfield rifle out of its case and was firing at the black shapes up the mountain in between shouting orders to his men.

'Move forward!' he called out. 'Give covering fire by sections.'

Coakley had already got his men out of the ditch and had them spread out in a ragged line across the curving flank of the mountain. Stephen only had a glimpse of them before another snow shower swept across them and blotted them out. It fell over them like a blanket and stopped all shooting, replacing the crack of gunfire with the whispering of blowing snow. Stephen made the most of it and ran down the road, ignoring the jabs of pain from the old wound in his knee and urging the rest of the men out and up the mountain. Then back to the armoured car to order covering fire if the snow cleared. When it did, his men were a hundred yards up and moving in good order. He went after them, shouting encouragement and instructions and pausing to kneel and fire every few paces.

The telescope was disconcerting, being just strong enough to make those targets human. Without it they were nothing more than black specks, dotted around the top of the mountain, but when he brought up the rifle and took aim on them they grew arms and legs and had faces and warm breath streaming out on the breeze. He picked one out and took aim and when he squeezed the trigger he saw him spin around and fall down on his face. Another few yards forward, the snow getting deeper in the hollow of the hill and he knelt down and took aim again, but it was hard to

373

find a target. All he could see were two or three lying splayed out in the snow, the rest appeared to have broken back over the hill towards their base. He swept the whole line of the ridge and finally found one moving along the ridge, to the east. But he was a long way off – nine hundred yards at least. Still, the breeze had died and the air was clear. He might just make it. He brought up the rifle again, took aim and started to gently squeeze the trigger.

'Sir!' One of his men shouted, and he twisted his head away, lowering the gun. 'Sir, look!'

He was pointing back the way they had come, back down the road and out across the plane to the north. The lowlands looked quite dirty and brown, with only patches of snow here and there, but Stephen's eye was drawn to something else; a thick column of smoke was rising up from behind the flank of the mountain. The moment he saw it he knew, with a sinking feeling, exactly where it was coming from.

Lillian went to the Provost's office at a quarter past five. Even though she had been there before, she was slightly disappointed when she arrived. It always seemed much less grand than she expected; rather plain and dingy, crowded with books and piles of paper and lined with the same yellowing wallpaper that she had seen in the older parts of the college. The anteroom was the domain of Mrs Sheridan, who had been the Provost's secretary for as long as Lillian could remember.

'The Provost will be here shortly,' she said, eyeing Lillian coldly as she came in. 'Would you care to wait?'

'Yes, thank you.' Lillian sat down with her bag in her lap and pretended to study the titles of the books on the shelf beside her while Mrs Sheridan poked half-heartedly at a typewriter. Lillian knew she was being watched very carefully. After a few minutes a door slammed, footsteps came down the hallway, and the Provost appeared, clearly lost in thought. He ambled into the room with a slight frown on his face and then stopped and looked at Lillian as if he had never seen her before.

'Ah, Miss Bryce,' he said, looking vaguely uneasy, and then he gestured absently towards the door of his office. 'Come in, come in.'

The office proper looked much the same as the anteroom, only larger. The Provost's desk was stacked with books and scrolls of paper, fronted by a threadbare chair and glared over by an intimidating portrait of Dr Mahaffey, his predecessor.

'Please sit down.' The Provost firmly shut the door, gestured at the chair and then walked around the desk and settled into his own. 'Now then, Miss Bryce, I thought it was only fair to tell you that there has been a further development since yesterday's meeting of the college board. Mr Keach has tendered his resignation. I have accepted, and he will be returning to London shortly...'

Lillian pursed her lips. She'd been afraid it might come to this. Keach had been chosen and appointed by the college board, so they would have lost face if they had had to sack him. On the other hand, Keach wasn't the type to go quietly and she thought he'd probably been paid off. Still, at least he was gone, and the damage was done. He might say he had resigned, but the academic world was small enough for everybody to know what had really happened.

'...Of course, the events leading up to his resignation were regrettable, but we are prepared to overlook what happened in the interests of doing what is best for the college. I'm sure you were only doing what you thought was right and we are prepared to turn a new page–'

'Excuse me, Provost,' Lillian couldn't keep quiet any longer, 'are you criticizing what I did? Are you telling me I was wrong to expose a cheat and a liar at the head of my own department?'

'Well, no, of course not.' The Provost looked vexed. 'There is no denying that the outcome was for the best, but I must say your methods leave a lot to be desired.'

'My *methods?*' Lillian could feel the colour rising in her cheeks. She was furious, but partly she was furious at herself. Why on earth had she thought it would be different? There was a dreadful predictability about all this. Of course they were blaming her; of course it was all her fault. No matter what she did, she would never be right. She would never be a member of this club.

'Yes, Miss Bryce. Your methods were very dubious, not to say disreputable. In fact, the whole affair smacked of entrapment and may well have seriously damaged our reputation – and very unnecessarily, if I may say so. As I believe I said to you yesterday, I would very much have preferred it if you had kept this as a strictly internal matter.

Had you come to me earlier, I can assure you that you would have had my fullest support.'

'Oh really? And do I need to remind you that this is the second time that man stole my work? On the first occasion my fiancé quite rightly accused him of stealing and was dragged into a legal action that he could hardly afford – and what support did he get from the college? None whatsoever. You suspended him. You hung him out to dry and left us with no other option but to prove he was right by our own means.'

'Well, I...' the Provost stammered, but she knew she had him on the back foot.

'And speaking of that disgraceful episode, I assume that since Mr Keach will most certainly be withdrawing his libel action, you will now reinstate Mr Ryan to his previous position.'

'Certainly not!' the Provost exclaimed, his face hardening. 'As I understand it, Mr Ryan has taken a commission in the army. As far as the college is concerned, he has renounced all claim to his studentship.'

The colour drained from Lillian's cheeks. And yet, she was still not surprised. In all the years they'd been here she and Stephen had had to fight for everything, for the most basic rights that were automatically granted to that privileged group who fitted in, who belonged to the right social class or the right sex. No matter how brilliant they were, no matter how gifted, they would never be part of that class; they would always be excluded. Instead of anger at Keach, she now felt only cold loathing for this old man and everything he stood for.

'Well, that is a very great loss for this college,' Lillian said, standing up. 'I believe that in the fullness of time you will see exactly how great a loss. As for myself, it is clear that I am regarded as more of an inconvenience than an asset, so I'm sure I won't be such a great loss. You've already had one resignation, well, here is another – and I'm sure it's more welcome. I resign from my lectureship, Provost. Good night to you, now.'

She heard him stand up behind her, start to protest, but she walked out and shut the door on him. Never a glance at Mrs Sheridan, never a word to anyone as she fetched her bicycle from the rack and dropped her bag in the basket. The cobbles were treacherous and glazed with frost so she pushed the bicycle across the square. Out through the gate and around by College Green. She didn't stop, didn't look back. She was still too angry to feel upset. Perhaps she would be later, but for now she felt slightly relieved. It was over at last, for better or worse. She had liberated herself; her whole life lay ahead of her now and she could do whatever she pleased.

But as she walked around on to Brunswick Street, a feeling of loss suddenly overtook her. Ten years of her life had just ended. For ten years she had strove to be as good as the men, to show what she could do. She had given most of her adult life to that pursuit; she had endured insults and threats and she had put off her marriage so as not to jeopardize her goal. And what had any of that got her? Nothing. But self-pity soon gave way to self-loathing. She felt selfish and weak and she missed Stephen so much it hurt. She wished he were here now; nobody else could understand, nobody else could help...

She heard a footstep behind her and looked over her shoulder. She had been so lost in her thoughts that she had hardly noticed the snow starting to fall. The heavy flakes flickered in the globes of gaslight, a moving curtain that obscured almost everything more than a few yards away. All she could make out was the twin tracks of her bicycle tyres through the fresh snow and her own footsteps. She turned up the collar of her coat and continued on, but as she went she put her hand on her bag in the basket, as if to reassure herself.

She hadn't gone more than a few paces before she heard the steps behind her again and this time she didn't stop. She put her head down and went on as fast as she could, but the footsteps kept pace with her – if anything, they were getting closer. They had a strange, metallic sound and were curiously uneven. *Clack, clack-clack, Clack, clack-clack.* Closer and closer, they seemed to be right behind her, but she wouldn't stop. This was the darkest part of the street, all walls and yards, with little light and less life at this time of night. She stared straight ahead. Only another hundred yards and there would be houses and some hope of help.

'Hello, Lily, I've been watching you,' the voice was startlingly close, but she didn't recognize it. It was harsh and rather high, but definitely belonged to a man. She spun around to face him and found a short figure with a belted overcoat and a flat cap.

It was almost too dark to see, but he was holding something in his hand and pointing it at her.

'Don't make any noise, now,' he said, but Lillian grabbed her bag, dropped the bicycle and ran for her life.

There was the crack of a gunshot behind her. Fragments flew off the wall near her head and the bullet went whining away. She stumbled and fell and almost lost the bag, but picked herself up and darted into the safety of an alleyway. She ran on, feeling along the wall and clutching the bag to her as if it was the most precious thing in the world. A door, an opening, anything would do – but there was nothing, and when she looked back she saw him silhouetted against the curtain of snow falling through the dim light on the street. She ran on but then tripped over something. Her feet slipped on the snow and she stumbled against the wall, going down on her knees and dropping the bag. As she pushed herself up she looked again. He was coming towards her, limping, and holding the gun out in front of him.

'Now, now, Lillie, there's no need to be frightened,' he was whispering, coming slowly down the alleyway. 'We haven't even been introduced properly, have we?'

Lillian groped in the dark for the bag. She could feel panic mounting inside her and she tried to hold it down as she threw her hands in wider circles. Then her fingers brushed against something and she seized on it, pulling it open and feeling inside. She managed to twist around so that her back was square against the wall. He was getting closer and she couldn't find it. Her hand delved further into the bag and finally she felt the heft of the gun. Her fingers closed around the handle and she pulled it out and dropped the bag again. Both hands on the handle, she got her thumb on the hammer, just the way Stephen had shown her.

She had hoped that she would never have to use it. Stephen had bought the gun for her after she had been sent the bullet.

He had given it to her as a birthday present, had arranged a permit from army headquarters, and had shown her how to fire it. He'd said she was quite a good shot, but it was one thing banging away at bottles and old tins. This was quite another. Her heart was racing and she could hardly breathe, but she managed to get her gloved finger on the trigger. Then she waited. For all the times Stephen had shown her how to shoot, all the practice with bottles and tins, she knew she had to let him get close. Again, she wished Stephen were here now. She missed the feel of him standing behind her; his firm hand on her arm as he helped her aim. But she remembered everything he had told her. *Hold it in both hands; don't shoot until you're sure of the target...*

'Come on, now Lily,' Garvey was saying, creeping closer and closer. 'You've nowhere to go now, have you? There's no sense in making this any harder than it needs to be.'

Lillian held the gun up, looking along the stubby barrel. She could see part of him in the dim light coming in from the street – an arm, a shoulder. But the rest was dark. Then she saw the gleam of his gun, moving closer.

'Lillie, Lillie, come on now,' he whispered, and she squeezed the trigger just like she'd been taught. The flash blinded her and the noise was very loud in the alleyway, but it seemed to stop him in his tracks. He flinched but then stood there, not moving. She fired again blindly and he fell down in a heap, his gun clattering out of his hand.

It was late afternoon before Stephen got back to Grace Dieu. Even after he had seen the smoke, he'd pressed on with his attack. What else could he do? Even if he'd turned around straight away it would have taken them hours to get down and there was very little they could have done. So he'd brought his men up to the top of the ridge, but by the time they got there the cloud had blown in again and it looked like it was there to stay. They reached the crest in a near blizzard and found three dead Irregulars lying in the snow and a mess of footprints heading east, some of them sprinkled with blood.

'Do you want us to follow, sir?' Coakley asked, shouting over the wind.

'No sergeant.' Stephen straightened from rubbing his throbbing knee and shook his head. If the informer was right – and it looked like he was – the Irregulars' base was below them, in a deep valley on the other side of the ridge. He shielded his eyes against the blasting snow, but he could see nothing. Nevertheless, he pointed down that way. 'Let Commandant Donovan take care of them. We'll finish what we started.'

Down they went. The wind died away almost

the moment they dropped off the crest of the ridge and a few minutes later the snow cleared and he saw a small cottage below them. They plunged towards it, and quickly came to a small stream like a brown scar in the snow. Crossing it, they found grey footprints and muddy trails criss-crossing each other. One led to a low structure with a sod roof, another led further up the valley, towards a rocky outcrop standing stark and black against the snow. There was no doubt about it. This was the place, exactly as the informer had described it.

There was also no doubt that it was deserted. Stephen split his men up and ordered a search. As they set to work, he walked into the cottage, ducking his head under the low lintel. The mud floor was wet and spongy and the place smelled of damp and mould and burnt turf. Water dripped from the tin roof and a few blankets lay on the settles beside the fireplace. No way to live, he thought, and he ducked back outside again. The pile of rifles and revolvers, ammunition and food that was building up quickly told him how successful his attack had been. Maps and other documents he stuffed into his pockets as they were handed to him. He looked around the snowy slopes that surrounded them, at the cap of grey cloud. His job was done. He had chased the Irregulars out of their hideout and into the arms of Donovan. But he felt no elation, no sense of triumph.

'Burn it,' he said to Sergeant Coakley. 'Burn it so that we can get out of here.'

The smell of smoke was still with him even after

they climbed back over the ridge and dropped back down to the road. The aroma of paraffin and burnt wood hung about his clothes. The cloud lay low over the northern planes, but he knew there was more smoke up there, a thick pillar climbing up from Grace Dieu. He tried not to think about it as they worked to turn the armoured car around and pull the crashed tender out of the ditch. But in his mind's eye he could still see the orange flames that had flickered below them as they climbed away from Quinn's hideout. He could still hear the crackle of burning thatch and the crash as the roof of the cottage had fallen in. The pop-pop-pop of burning ammunition. This wasn't war; it was just destruction.

The worst of the smoke had dissipated by the time they drove through the gates of Grace Dieu. The fire had gutted the house, and the roof and upper floor had long since fallen in. Flames still spouted from a few of the ground-floor windows but there wasn't much left to burn by then. Stephen climbed tiredly out of the tender and looked up at the cracked and blackened walls. Even though he'd been expecting it, the sight dazed him. The scene in front of the house was not much better. There was a meagre pile of furniture saved, but not much, and most of the servants stood in a knot, talking amongst themselves and looking at him uncertainly. Susan Devereux sat on one of the dining-room chairs, her head in her hands.

Stephen was on his way over to her when he saw a body lying in the driveway, not far from the steps of the house. The green uniform drew his

eye and when he went over he saw it was Lieutenant Walsh. At least, it was Lieutenant Walsh's
uniform; the face was such a mess that it was
unrecognizable. As he was kneeling down to
check he saw a second body lying down the side
of the granite steps, half hidden by the baluster.
An Irregular this time, but he saw the flash of red
hair and crept as close as he could, shielding his
face from the heat with one hand. A stocky man
with red hair and a grubby overcoat. Probably
Quinn, he thought, though he didn't recognize
him. What he did recognize was the wound that
had done for him – another shotgun blast, but to
the chest this time.

Susan Devereux stood up as he came over to
her. She wiped her arm across her eyes but only
managed to smear the soot over her face.

'Miss Devereux, are you all right?' he asked,
and she nodded, though her chin was trembling.

'I'm fine, thank you. I must tell you that your
men gave a good account of themselves ... I wish
... I ...' She screwed up her face as tears came
streaming through the soot.

'Miss Devereux, Susan,' Stephen took her by the
arms, 'where is your brother? Where is Alfred?'

'He wouldn't stop shooting,' she cried. 'He
wouldn't. They said they wouldn't hurt him, even
after he shot Mr Quinn, but he wouldn't come
out. He said he would die fighting, and he kept
shooting, so they burned the house with him
inside. They killed him!' she wailed, and he felt
her whole body shaking with sobs as he pulled
her to him and let her weep into his shoulder.
'They killed poor Alfie!'

When Joe came down out of the cloud he was half frozen. He was staggering through the snow with his arms wrapped around himself and he could feel the ice in his eyebrows and hair. He'd long since given up trying to follow Lynch and O'Leary and just wanted to get down and get warm. Melleray would be best but anywhere would do.

The moment he could see where he was going he brightened up. Even with the gloom of early evening coming on he could see the green plain stretching away from the mountains. He could see trees and he could see houses and he could even see the odd speck of light here and there. Closer by, he could see a small stream cutting a black runnel through the snow until it disappeared into a glade of stunted trees. He turned towards it and quickened his pace a little, swinging his arms to try and beat some warmth into them.

His throat was parched and raw from the cold air and when he reached the trees he knelt at the stream and gulped down some of the icy water. It refreshed him, and he stood up and blew on his hands to try to warm them. Then he saw a flash of green – something moving in the trees below. He didn't even have time to move before he saw a second one, and then he heard the shot and a bullet went cracking through the branches just over his head. Joe turned and ran.

'Halt! Put your hands up!' came the shout, but Joe ignored it. He dodged through the trees, crouching as he ran, but out of the corner of his eye he saw more men coming across the slope towards him.

'Halt!' Another shot, and he felt it slam into his back and he fell forward into a patch of snow. He tried to get up, but he had no strength and he could feel cold spreading up his back. One leg wouldn't move, but he could kick with the other and he tried to push himself up the hill, straining for the opening between two trees. A small tear in the cloud was passing by, a tiny patch of beautiful blue, and he pushed himself towards it, clawing at the snow with his hands, heaving himself up the hill and panting and cursing under his breath with the effort. He pushed and pushed but it was no good. That tiny patch of blue sky passed by and there was only the grey cloud and the white slope stretching up and the cold.

He let his head fall down on his arms and let one, long, weary breath out. He could hear them coming up on him, feel the thump of their tread through the earth like a heartbeat, but that was all he could feel. He was so tired and so cold he could hardly lift his head when they stopped and looked down on him. He saw boots and leather gaiters and green trousers but that was all. Everything else was too far away, too dull. He let his head fall on his arm and tried to gulp in some air, but it was hard. There was blood in his mouth, he could taste it, he could feel it trickling out. The cold had spread right through him now. He felt like the snow was sapping into him, absorbing him, but he couldn't move any more.

'I got him, sarge,' said a voice, coming from very far away.

'You did, all right,' came the answer, even fainter.

'Is he still alive? What'll we do with him?'

'I'll take care of him, Pat,' said the second voice, and Joe heard the metallic snick of a gun being cocked. He closed his eyes and let the cold take him.

EPILOGUE

Soldiers of the Republic. Legion of the Rearguard: The Republic can no longer be defended successfully by your arms. Further sacrifice of life would now be in vain and the continuance of the struggle in arms unwise in the national interest and prejudicial to the future of our cause. Military victory must be allowed to rest for the moment with those who have destroyed the Republic.

PROCLAMATION TO ALL RANKS
OF THE REPUBLICAN FORCES
ISSUED BY EAMON DE VALERA,
24 MAY 1923

Billy waited until he heard the outside door close and then he got up and went to the window. He saw Stephen go down the steps and settle his hat on his head, then walk away towards the canal. It was strange to see him a civilian again but that was what he was. He had resigned his commission and now he was out of uniform, a free man.

Billy watched him until he was out of sight and then went back to his desk and picked up his glass. When Stephen had been shown in, he'd poured them both a whiskey to celebrate the end of the war. They had caught up with Liam Lynch eventually, and he'd been mortally wounded in a skirmish with Donovan's men in the Knockmealdowns. After that, the fight seemed to go out of the Irregulars and they had been ordered to dump arms and stand by until the situation was more favourable to them. A ceasefire by any other name, Billy always thought.

'To victory!' he said, but Stephen didn't raise his glass. Billy drank anyway and then sat in his chair and eyed his friend. Not much of a victory for him, he thought. He knew Stephen and his brother had never been very close, but still, Joe's death had hit him hard. Two months had passed, but he still looked slightly vacant, as if something was missing from inside him. He had come to see Billy of his own volition, but it seemed as if he didn't know what to say, and he'd just sat there for the most part, looking into his glass and speaking only when spoken to. Billy knew he was getting married soon and yet he didn't say a word about it. He hardly even mentioned Lillian except to say that she was fine, in good spirits, actually. The spark of friendship was gone and Billy had been almost relieved when suddenly he stood up and held out his hand.

'Well, I'd better be going, Billy. I'll be seeing you.'

'Of course you will,' Billy had answered, a little woodenly, and then he'd shown him to the door.

'Listen, Stephen. I'm sorry about what happened to your brother. Truly, I am. If it's any comfort, he was trying to bring an end to the war.

He was a good man, Stephen, and he was trying to do a good thing.'

'I know he was,' Stephen said, without looking at him, and he went out and took his hat and coat from the rack and gave a half-hearted wave as he went out the door.

'Well then,' Billy said to himself, and drummed his fingers on the desk. It was at quiet times like this that he missed the war. There was still so much to do, but somehow it didn't seem to have the same urgency, the same attraction as it did just a few weeks ago. He suddenly had doubts of his own, and wondered if Stephen wasn't doing right to get out now. What had he to look forward to from this office? Shuffling papers until retirement? A little power? Maybe even the chance to steer the country a little way, but really, not much. When it came down to it he would just be part of the machine. History would not remember him as it would the ones who were gone.

And now he was getting maudlin as well. It was time to go home – or perhaps to his club, to take his mind off things. Yes, his club, he decided, and put on his hat, though he left his overcoat on the rack. There was warmth in the air and a stretch in the evening. The war was over and summer was coming – he had every reason to be cheerful. Whistling a tune to himself, he picked up his briefcase and switched off the light.

Outside, it was just getting dark. The budding branches of the trees looked stark and black against the fading sky and there was a faint smell of fresh grass on the air. Billy came down the steps and turned up towards Stephen's Green. He hadn't gone far before he saw a man step out of a doorway up ahead and turn his head to look at him. Then he heard the scrape of a shoe and he knew there was someone behind him as well. He felt cold sweat break out under his collar and a bolt of fear in his gut. He kept walking, but stepped off the kerb and started to move diagonally across the street. All he could think of was the park; there were trees and cover in there. He kept walking but the man he had seen was walking towards him, crossing the street to cut him off. Then he saw another one, coming along the park railings, and his heart sank in his chest.

'Mr Standing!' somebody called from behind him, and he stopped and turned to face them, his arms hanging limp by his side.

'Yes,' he answered weakly.

'Are you William Standing?' the man asked again in a harsh shout, his face pale and hard. Billy saw the hand coming out of his pocket.

'Look, what is this ...?' Billy began, but a shot rang out and something very heavy hit him in the shoulder with enough force to spin him around and send him sprawling against the railings of the park. The pain of it was sharp and burning and seemed to knock all the strength out of his body. He tried to push himself up but he couldn't, and he slid down the railings until he was half lying on the ground. The men gathered around him, all four of them looking down at him, all four with guns in their hands. He looked around at their faces, but there was nothing there, nothing; not a shred of pity.

'William Standing, under orders from the general headquarters of the Irish Republican Army, you are hereby sentenced to death. Is there anything you want to say?'

'What are you doing?' Billy asked weakly, feeling the pain throbbing inside him now, tears welling up in his eyes. 'What are you doing? The war is over.'

'No it's not,' the man said, and he brought up his pistol again. 'Say hello to Liam Lynch.'

From the stern of the ship they could look back up the river and see the loop line bridge and the Customs House, and the two sides of Dublin crowding down to the quays. The deck was already humming under their feet and they saw the gangplank pulled in and heard the splash as the mooring ropes were let go. The ship shuddered and nosed out into the stream.

As they sailed slowly out into Dublin Bay, Stephen stared back at the city as if he was trying to imprint it on his mind. He had left home many times before, but this time was different. This time he wasn't planning to come back. He reached out and put his arm around Lillian's waist, pulling her closer to him.

'Well, Mrs Ryan, are you sorry to be leaving?'

She smiled when he called her that. They had only been married three days and she was still getting used to it. The wedding had been rushed in the end because they had both wanted to be married in Ireland. Maybe it hadn't been the ceremony she had dreamed about when she was a girl, but it had been better in other ways. After so much tragedy and so much uncertainty and fear of the future, it had felt like a fresh start for both of them. She thought they had both given something up, but had received much more in return; they were truly together now, inseparable. She didn't know where they might end up, or what might befall them in the years to come, but she wasn't afraid.

'It will always be here for us,' she said, and she looked up at him, trying to read his stony face. He had changed in these last few months. He was still the man she loved, but something had broken inside him when his brother was killed. And then to lose Billy as well – the shock had almost been the worse for the way it had happened, and yet it had seemed hardly to have registered with Stephen. It was as if Joe's death had inured him, and nothing that might happen could be any worse.

Stephen didn't answer at first. The ship slipped steadily along the Bull Wall, the green water churning brown and yellow in their wake and a lone gull following, hovering and swooping to keep his station. The city was starting to disappear, fading into the grey haze of the land. It would always be there, but would it ever be the same? But then he realized that this was an illusion. The same as what? The same as the city he grew up in? No. It would never be that. That city belonged to another world. It belonged to the world before the Great War, before the Rising, before the Auxies came and the Black and Tans, before the Treaty and the fighting that followed after. It was no more. It had changed for ever one night nearly ten years ago. He remembered it as clearly as if it was yesterday. The night of Mary D'Arcy's birthday party, when they rang the dinner gong and read out the telegram announcing war with Germany. That was the night when peace died.

'There's no place for us here any more,' he said, squeezing her a bit tighter. 'It's taken too much from both of us.'

Everything he had left was on board this ship, but he had chosen to leave a lot behind. A few medals and badges and buttons in his luggage were the only things he had left from his life as a soldier. His notebooks were more important to him now. He had leafed through one as he packed his bag and was surprised to find his curiosity piqued. The thoughts, the notions, even the handwriting had seemed slightly foreign to him, and he'd found himself settling down to read, following the logic and working out the equations in his head, feeling a faint thrill that he hadn't felt in a long time. Minutes had passed, then an hour, and by the time he had reached the end, the room had grown dark and he was hardly aware of his surroundings. He knew, as he closed the notebook, that it was good. Not only what was written on the pages, but what had stirred inside his own mind as he read. Connections had been made; ideas and insights had flashed and bloomed. He knew he had good work left in him.

When the ship cleared the Bull Wall the swell of the open sea caused it to roll heavily. The rumble of the engines grew louder and the white wake widened and streamed out behind them, hissing and bubbling audibly as the ship gathered way. The land stretched out to fill the horizon, but it also grew lower, greyer, more indistinct. Stephen tried to pick out the landmarks before they faded: the Sugarloaf, Howth Head and Lambay Island. He looked at Lillian, conscious of her pressing against him with the roll of the ship. More than the medals, more than the notebooks, she was everything. She was everything, and yet, she was all he needed. What lay ahead was uncertain. All they had between them was a letter from Professor Barrett to a friend of his at Harvard. A good recommendation and their own reputations didn't seem like much to start a new life on, but he knew they could do it so long as they stayed together. They had endured so much already that nothing could stop them now.

The ship sailed steadily eastwards and the land grew smaller and less green. Neither of them moved from the rail. They both watched and watched until their home was nothing but a smudge on the horizon. Then Stephen leaned in and kissed Lillian.

'Well, it's goodbye to all that,' he said. 'Let's see what happens next.'

AUTHOR'S NOTE

Some readers may wish to hear more about some of the historical characters encountered in the novel.

Erskine Childers, author of the acclaimed *Riddle of the Sands*, was one of seventy-seven Republican prisoners executed during the course of the war. Before his death, he shook hands with the members of his firing squad, and he insisted on giving the order to fire himself. His son, Erskine Hamilton Childers later became President of Ireland.

As is described in the novel, Michael Collins was killed in an ambush at Beal na mBláth, West Cork, on 22 August 1922. His death was profoundly shocking at the time and, to this day, the question of who fired the fatal shot remains controversial.

After resigning his commission, Emmet Dalton served briefly as clerk of the Irish Senate before moving into film production. He helped produce several notable films, including *The Blue Max* and *The Lion in Winter*, and founded Ardmore film studios in 1958. He died in Dublin in 1978.

Following the civil war, Eamon de Valera returned to constitutional politics and led the newly formed Fianna Fáil party into Dáil Eireann in

1927. Fianna Fáil later became the largest political party in the state and de Valera himself served as both *taoiseach* (Prime Minister) and President of Ireland.

Liam Lynch was killed in a running battle with Free State forces in the Knockmealdown Mountains on 10 April 1923. On 30 April, Frank Aiken, his successor as Chief of Staff of the Anti-Treaty forces, ordered a ceasefire that effectively ended the civil war.

Sir Alfred 'Andy' Cope retired into self-imposed obscurity not long after the foundation of the Irish Free State. He left no memoir and declined all requests for comment on his role in Irish affairs. When pressed for a statement by the Irish Bureau of Military History, he replied: '...I regard the period ... to be the most discreditable of your country's history – it is preferable to forget it: to let sleeping dogs lie.'

The publishers hope that this book has given you enjoyable reading. Large Print Books are especially designed to be as easy to see and hold as possible. If you wish a complete list of our books please ask at your local library or write directly to:

Magna Large Print Books
Magna House, Long Preston,
Skipton, North Yorkshire.
BD23 4ND

This Large Print Book for the partially sighted, who cannot read normal print, is published under the auspices of

THE ULVERSCROFT FOUNDATION

THE ULVERSCROFT FOUNDATION

... we hope that you have enjoyed this Large Print Book. Please think for a moment about those people who have worse eyesight problems than you ... and are unable to even read or enjoy Large Print, without great difficulty.

You can help them by sending a donation, large or small to:

The Ulverscroft Foundation, 1, The Green, Bradgate Road, Anstey, Leicestershire, LE7 7FU, England.
or request a copy of our brochure for more details.

The Foundation will use all your help to assist those people who are handicapped by various sight problems and need special attention.

Thank you very much for your help.